May 25

LETTERS
from the
DEAD

LETTERS

from the

DEAD

a novel

ISABELLA VALERI

EMILY BESTLER BOOKS

ATRIA

New York   Amsterdam/Antwerp   London
Toronto   Sydney/Melbourne   New Delhi

EMILY
BESTLER
BOOKS

ATRIA

An Imprint of Simon & Schuster, LLC
1230 Avenue of the Americas
New York, NY 10020

This book is a work of fiction. Any references to historical events, real people, or real places are used fictitiously. Other names, characters, places, and events are products of the author's imagination, and any resemblance to actual events or places or persons, living or dead, is entirely coincidental.

*for
jas
iii*

PART I

THE HAND OF THE DEAD

CHAPTER ONE

⁓

Filicide

A S MIDNIGHT APPROACHED, ONLY A FEW hours before the last winter
storm of 1992—a tremendous thunder blizzard that descended from the
High Alps and onto our lands to envelop the manor in a tempest of blinding
white—my eldest brother, Augustin, accused our parents of murder.

Our estate—a sprawling tract nestled in the forests of the Alpine foothills near the Swiss-Austrian border, property that had been in my family
for generations—was remote enough that we siblings were quite sheltered
(despite being almost twelve years old, I had to that point never set foot on
land that my family did not own) but I knew instinctively that filicide was
no light thing. Still, it says something that my first reaction wasn't shock
that my mother and father might be capable of such an act. Instead, perhaps
as a consequence of being the youngest and the only girl, I was struck with a
vague feeling of betrayal; the sting of exclusion and of shadowy conspiracies
conducted in my absence.

To an outsider those elements of the accusation might have seemed odd
things to be upset about. But, dynasties as old as ours collect dark secrets
like other families keep old photo albums; packed away in dusty corners
and ignored for years, until cracked open in the presence of others and
exposed to the light once more to accomplish some political end. On that
dark night at least, the murder of a member of the "direct line" did not seem
all that unlikely a secret for my family to harbor. Even after the import of

my brother's accusation sank in, it was not the killing itself but rather the fact that the existence of an older sister had somehow been kept from me that occupied my thoughts. I had heard nothing of this mysterious sibling prior to the indictment Augustin leveled against our parents, and something about that felt unforgivable.

Though by the next day the cold realization of what it meant to live under the rule of potentially homicidal parents would take hold, as I tried to sleep that night I was oblivious to that particular danger. Instead, I found myself trying to picture my slain older sibling and, as my visions of her solidified, it was mournful thoughts of sisterhood lost that haunted me.

She appeared in none of the family photos or portraits that I had seen and therefore, I reasoned, her existence must have been deliberately (and quite thoroughly) erased. But this made her malleable somehow and, when my mind's eye gazed in her direction, it naturally invited invention (an urge that my eleven-year-old imagination was all too happy to indulge). It was a strange thing to summon her specter that way, but the act of having, however briefly, conjured it forged in me an affinity with this lost and mysterious relation that would, as it happened, later prove quite fateful.

~⊙~

WE DIDN'T KNOW it that night, but the approaching storm was to mark the beginning of the end of a long and cold winter. Almost a month earlier, Augustin had come home from boarding school for the winter break. His roommate Yves had come along to stay with us. At sixteen, a year older than Augustin, Yves (who by some cruel twist of fate was cursed with "Gaspard" as one of his middle names) was the son and heir apparent of Klaus Böhm. I had seen him from a distance once or twice some years before when his family visited our estate, but it had been a long time and, that winter, I almost failed to recognize him at first.

He had grown older but his body had outpaced his face, which hadn't lost the soft, childlike features that I remembered from earlier encounters. There was an effete and almost feminine character to the elegant way he carried himself. He was certainly very attractive, yet with his dark hair slathered with gel in what I assumed was an effort to make it stylish (but instead came off looking overly slick), he seemed caught between ages; trying very hard indeed to counter the tendency his boyish face had of making him look fourteen. Slick or not, he was the immediate subject of my first, only, and very intense, preadolescent crush.

Yves's family had a smaller estate somewhere near Vienna but he had spent his early years in France, where his father had a diplomatic posting (and a number of business interests besides). When he spoke German, his accent, which he was at pains to conceal, was a source of endless fascination to me. My mother's family was from Vienna and, though we were expected to lurk in the background in the evenings as the adults socialized, our early, overheard conversations were predominantly in an aristocratic brand of Viennese German, an accent I still struggle to suppress. On the other hand, and despite the French taint, Yves delivered the language via a strong dose of rarefied and erudite High German. I must have been on his last nerve more than once, but he was endlessly patient with me that winter as I asked him to repeat a particular sentence or turn of phrase over and over just to hear the sound of his voice.

The tutors who were normally flown in to give my brother Bastien (who, despite being almost two years older than me, was regularly mistaken for the youngest of the siblings) and me lessons in everything from classical studies to geometry had been given their holiday by that time. I certainly did not miss them or the bland memorization by recitation that characterized their methods of instruction. My own lessons increasingly focused on protocol and etiquette, subjects I despised (though I would have been far more horrified had I seen them for the hints which they essentially were: early innuendoes of a dutiful and subservient future that was already being planned for me).

The reprieve from lessons meant that, for weeks, the four of us fell into a nearly inseparable pack. Yves's presence evened out the balance between my brothers and me, which had always been lopsided in their favor before his arrival. No matter the game, Augustin and Yves would play as opposing captains; honorable rivals; best friends who, as noble officers of adversarial armies, regretted the unfortunate political circumstances that made them, for the duration of the contest at least, enemies.

I remember resorting to any artifice to ensure that I found myself on

Yves's team for board games, hide-and-seek, and snowball fights. Outdoors he was quick and clever and, to my delight for by that year I was an avid climber, prone now and again to bear me on his shoulders or boost me up into trees, showering us both with falling snow from the disturbed branches of the Austrian pines that dominated the forests around the manor.

Once high enough, I would hide among the boughs looking for signs of the enemy but, I must admit, I spent more time watching a rosy-cheeked Yves bounding through the drifts and building snow fortifications beneath my surveillance post than keeping watch for Augustin and Bastien's inevitable sneak attack.

It was after one of these daylong forays into the snow that Augustin related his horrible tale. As the sun set and brought that enveloping dark that one only finds far from the glare of civilization, there was nothing left but to retire back into the manor.

Teeth chattering, soaked to the skin with melting snow, and desperate to avoid the attention of adults, we crept past the candlelight that flickered from the Grand Foyer, up the marble staircases, and across the long hallway to the manor's residence wing. Augustin led us into one of the unused corner suites that he and Yves had converted into their (purportedly secret) "headquarters." It was wonderfully mysterious, and that our older counterparts had revealed it to "the babies" (as Bastien and I had been branded), much less invited us in, was a special treat.

We peeled off the outer layers of our sodden winter clothes and watched impatiently as Yves lit the tapers in the candelabras and set a crackling blaze in the foyer's yawning marble fireplace. We huddled together on the floor, wrapped in blankets, giggling and still shivering, until the flames urged the chill out of our bones. I remember being afraid that someone would notice how carefully I had maneuvered to sit next to Yves.

We watched the fire for a time, listening in silence to the hiss of the not-quite-dry-enough logs. Eventually, Augustin whispered to Yves, who nodded, stood up, and extinguished the candles one by one until only the fireplace was left for illumination.

The wind started to pick up, a vague warning of the intensity of the approaching storm. It rattled the windows in the rooms beyond the suite's foyer, adding an altogether spooky atmosphere to the proceedings. Augustin looked at each of us in sequence—three ominously pregnant pauses. When he finally broke the silence, the light from the fireplace played across his face, giving him a sinister appearance.

"I want to tell you a story about our sister," Augustin said.

"What?" I choked, alarmed. "Me?"

I shuddered to imagine Augustin revealing some embarrassing secret of mine in front of Yves (and my mind eagerly called up several mortifying candidates).

"I am talking about our other sister," Augustin said.

"We don't have another sister," I objected, glancing at Bastien, but he looked just as mystified.

"What?" Augustin said, eyebrows rising. "You don't remember?"

I shook my head weakly. Augustin acted surprised.

"Wait . . ." he said, and then his voice slipped down to a whisper. "They never *told you*?" I had nothing to offer but a blank look. "About your older sister? About what happened to Sophia?"

I knew there were many secrets in our family, but the idea that Augustin, alone, had learned one so important was deeply upsetting. Moreover, telling stories was supposed to be all in good fun but, suddenly, Augustin did not sound like he was playing. He was scaring me a little, and from his expression it seemed he was relishing the effect.

"It happened a few years after you were born," he continued and, just like that, slipped into the long-hidden tale with an ease that made it seem anything but invented.

"Sophia was born in the winter months. Our mother named her despite the family legend."

"What legend?" Bastien asked.

"That girls named Sophia come to bad ends in our family," Augustin said and rolled his eyes. "Don't you know anything? The name is cursed; was cursed long ago." He grew cross. "And stop interrupting."

Cowed, Bastien pulled his blanket tighter around his shoulders.

"From the day she was delivered, Sophia cried all the time. It got better once she turned two, but by four she was crying all day and all night. Mother tried everything to quiet her. Still, Sophia would go on for hours, until she was so hoarse she could only manage an awful hissing noise."

Augustin issued a horrific rasping sound from deep in his throat to demonstrate.

On a nearby estate some of our neighbors bred spaniels. They visited us one year, bringing a few of their prized animals along after they had been debarked. It came back to me, that awful, rasping hiss those poor dogs, surgically robbed of their vocal cords, had made. My skin crawled.

"The doctors said that if she didn't stop, her voice might be damaged permanently. "Finally," he continued, "after Sophia's fifth birthday, Father had Mother take a vacation to calm her nerves, or that was the story. He sent most of the staff away with her, so the estate was almost empty. The next night, during a tremendous snowstorm, Sophia started crying. Lucas got out of bed to tend to her."

Lucas, the impossibly tall, perpetually stiff head butler of the estate, had been serving on the domestic staff since long before I was born. My mother may have led the staff with an iron fist clad in white lace, but the behind-the-scenes workings of the manor were most certainly Lucas's to command. He was as officious as he was efficient and, with a nearly mystical clairvoyance, almost nothing of importance on the estate escaped him. I should have thought him more likely to bite the neck and suck the blood of a child than to "tend to her," but, in that moment, I was too spellbound to wonder after this detail.

"As Lucas was climbing the stairs, the crying choked off and then abruptly stopped. Our father, coming from Sophia's room, met Lucas in the hall and sent him back to bed. That was the last time Sophia cried. In fact, no one ever saw her again.

"Mother was supposed to be beyond suspicion, but I know she was"— Augustin leaned forward into our half circle—"complicit."

After my brother delivered that particular detail, Yves actually looked a little alarmed.

"But what happened to Sophia?" Bastien said.

Augustin gave him a sinister smile. "They threw her body into a chest in a locked room on the third floor of the West Wing. I bet her corpse has almost totally rotted away by now. That was her bedroom, you know. That's why those rooms are off-limits."

This part about the third- and fourth-floor rooms in the West Wing on the other side of the manor being "off-limits" was sort of true, if unenforced. The official explanation (that the wings were closed to save heating the rooms) suddenly sounded like a convenient cover story.

"Lucas said that, during winter storms, he could still hear the hiss of Sophia's cry in that hallway."

Augustin turned his head to look at us and the shadows cast from the flickering fire played in his eye sockets. For a moment, his face looked like a skull. I had to look away to keep from flinching.

Just then the fire popped much louder than usual and threw a flurry of glowing embers out toward us. Bastien let out a shriek, giving us all a start, and frantically brushed a hot coal away from his blanket, but not before it had left a small scorch mark.

We all glared at him but, before Augustin could rebuke him, a powerful gust of wind rattled the outside windows again. With a loud slam, the draft that leaked through the old windows blew one of the bedroom doors shut, causing us all to jump.

After Yves got up to make sure the remaining doors were secure and returned to our circle, Augustin continued.

"You know, for a time Grandfather's dogs used to wander up to the door and whine and scratch to get in."

I remembered my Grandfather's Irish wolfhounds, two huge animals that he doted on endlessly and which roamed the manor at will when I was very young. My mother disliked them intensely. A memory struck me then: I was eight years old and happened to be in one of the salons with my mother when an aide leaned down and whispered the news that the last wolfhound had died. It wasn't yet eleven in the morning, but my mother had smiled and ordered a bottle of champagne.

"I know Lucas said you can still hear her, but I don't believe that," Augustin said.

"That's incredible," Yves breathed, and it seemed to me that there was no acting in it.

"I don't believe any of it," I exclaimed, a little too urgently; but maybe I did just a little. Maybe even more than just a little.

"Oh," Augustin said, the drama of his delivery gone. "It doesn't matter to me, dear sister. But, in light of the curse, and as the only girl left, maybe you should be on your best behavior?"

"My name isn't Sophia, Augustin."

"Well," he said, leaning back, "you better hope that is protection enough."

AFFECTED BY AUGUSTIN'S story, we had all grown quiet, but before long, Yves started getting antsy.

"What are we doing tomorrow?" he demanded of the room in general. "We could go riding in the morning."

Augustin shook his head. "My mother is holding an event this weekend. A reception, a formal dinner, then a reception again."

"So?"

"So, the entire estate will be on edge until it's over," Augustin said, and sighed to himself. "It's best if we just stay upstairs."

"The whole weekend?" Yves protested. "Who invented that rule anyhow?"

"It's not a rule," Augustin said. "It's just good practice."

Yves did not look convinced. "Says who?"

"Yves, you don't understand. One doesn't play about when my mother is entertaining."

"Come on. Isn't that a little melodramatic? Why don't we go down tomorrow evening and check it out. I mean, it's not like it is some kind of state dinner."

My brother sat up and gave Yves a grave look. "Oh, but it is."

"Who cares about downstairs?" Bastien said. "We can all play together up here."

"Sure," Augustin said, his voice laced with sarcasm. "Grand."

"I'm sure some of your formalwear would fit," Yves said, and put on his winningest smile.

"Forget it. We aren't invited. It would really be asking for trouble."

Augustin was right. My mother's entertainments were extremely elaborate and formal affairs. Dinners served in the Grand Dining Hall during such events were attended to by footmen and waitstaff attired in uniforms that, only later in life, would appear to me to be artifacts from a bygone era. On some of the grander occasions it was not unusual for the doors to the manor and the Grand Dining Hall to be flanked by pikemen in traditional dress; our own palace guard complete with halberds that were most certainly not merely ceremonial.

As if that were not enough, at least twice a year my mother would host an event that called for "White Tie with Decorations," compelling my family and our guests to deck themselves out in full regalia, including the gleaming insignias of royal or family orders, neck and breast badges, and collections of medals and ribbons that, in the case of some of our more august visitors, made me wonder how much weight the various awards added to their jackets.

In the warmer months, as much as a week before guests were due to arrive, the staffers responsible for the estate grounds could be seen hurrying about to groom the Italian Gardens to my mother's exacting standards, tending the many walking paths that wound their way around the manor, lining them with fresh torches to accommodate evening strolls, or honing the corners of the hedge maze beyond to a keen edge.

In cold weather, and though the drifts might reach fifteen feet or more, the snows were carved away along the long drive northeast from the main gate to the manor itself. On more than one occasion, looming ice sculptures nearly ten feet tall appeared virtually overnight, decorating the manor's Grand Foyer, the circle drive, the courtyard, and even lining the approach to the manor proper. As evening fell, they would refract the light cast by the headlights of approaching cars and throw dazzling, prism-bent colors across the snow-covered landscape.

For her part, as the date approached, my mother would spend her hours commanding the small army of domestic staff charged with perfecting the estate and the manor in preparation for the arrival of our distinguished guests. She seemed to evolve slowly, day by day, from an already traditional demeanor into the hyperformality and poise she demanded of herself during her entertainments.

To my way of thinking, Augustin's fear of trespassing even on the edges of my mother's psyche during her preparations was entirely justified. Years before, on the evening of my seventh birthday, a Thursday before one of my mother's grand events, Augustin tripped me while we were playing tag on the gravel driveway behind the manor. I used my hands to break my fall but only succeeded in skinning my palms badly and embedding the wounds with tiny bits of gravel and grit. Augustin had an occasional penchant for pranks, but this was an unusually mean bit of horseplay, even as between older brothers and their younger sisters. Stunned, I sat on the gravel looking at my bloody palms before the pain set in and I started to cry.

"Don't be a baby," Augustin taunted.

Annoyed, he grabbed my right wrist, quite roughly, to pull me up. It was perhaps more violent than he intended, and I felt a bolt of searing pain shoot up my arm. I cried out so loudly that he let go, dropped me right back on the ground, and then took a step back. After looking around to see if anyone had heard, he reached for me again more carefully, but, sobbing and feeling deeply betrayed by his sudden and inexplicable transformation from trusted playmate into nasty rival, I squirmed away from him and ran.

I found my mother just outside the Grand Dining Hall. She was already in formal attire and conducting members of the domestic staff here and there with curt and elegant hand motions.

In retrospect, going to her was a mistake, but what little girl does not crave from her mother a pair of kisses on her wounds; just a hint of affection to remind her that she is entitled to a bit of kindness no matter what other demands weigh in the background?

On the contrary, when I interrupted my mother to show her my tattered hands, she lowered her voice into the harsh and biting whisper that was her particular trademark when she was angry.

"I'm not sure exactly what convinced you that it was appropriate to address your elders without a proper curtsy first," she hissed. "But, unless you disabuse yourself of that notion *immediately*, there will be severe consequences."

Frozen, half a dozen members of the domestic staff fell silent and looked at me with expressions of dull horror, anxious that my mother's newly inflamed ire should not be redirected at them. Shamed that, in my distress, I had failed to offer her the expected obeisance, I tried to ignore the stinging pain from my hands and stop crying, but managed only to choke my sobs down to a series of halting whimpers. I lowered my gaze to the ground and performed the most formal curtsy I could manage under the circumstances, wincing from the effort to avoid crying out again when I moved my right wrist.

When I straightened and looked up again, my mother's expression had transformed from annoyance to cold fury. It was several seconds before I saw what she was looking at. As I had dropped the curtsy I had pulled out the sides of my damask dress and printed the lovely and flowing white garment with bright red fingerprints of blood.

"Young lady," my mother barked, the angry whisper gone. "In just a few hours the first of a number of important guests, including two heads of state I might add, will arrive on our estate for the long weekend. If you think I have time for this kind of nonsense you have another thing coming. You will go to your room *this instant* and stay there until you are summoned."

I started sobbing again, put my hands to my stomach to try to quell the knot there, and thus smeared the front of my dress with even more blood.

"*Now,*" my mother snapped, and pointed to the foyer and the marble stairway that led up to the residential wing beyond.

I fled before she had a chance to think up something more severe and spent the entire weekend alone in my room, terrified to test the limits of my confinement, and forced to call down to the kitchens for my meals.

When I was finally allowed to emerge for breakfast on Monday morning, my wrist had gotten no better. Once my grandfather finally noticed how swollen it had become, he had Dr. Ebner, the kindly old man who had by then served as our family's general practitioner for three generations, flown to the estate via helicopter. I was forced to wait on his arrival in the manor's little sick bay, a claustrophobic room filled with various medical supplies and equipment, some quite modern, and some that may well have been left over from the Second World War.

Dr. Ebner pronounced my wrist only badly sprained but, despite his coaxing, as explanation I offered only the meek half-truth that I had fallen. He put a splint on my wrist but the entire experience left a much more enduring impression.

If my mother understood the effect her fit of pique had on me that weekend, she never let on. Not knowing any better, the guilt I felt for having somehow failed her tormented me long after. In fact, it was an emotional scar that persisted well into adulthood. Even so, certainly, after that, I never forgot to curtsy to my mother again, and never dared to intrude when she was in the midst of her event preparations.

The fire in our "secret headquarters" had been burning quite hot and our clothes were almost completely dry by then, but Augustin added another log to the stack anyhow. Yves was somehow cowed by Augustin's intransigence about the weekend and a long, bored silence followed. Finally, Augustin got up and made his way to the far corner of the foyer.

There he opened a wooden cabinet and lifted out an antique gramophone with a large, ornate horn. Though probably refurbished, it must have been nearly a hundred years old. Augustin wound up the handle in the front, put on a disc, and set the needle to playing. A pinched, scratchy version of Chopin strained out of the horn.

Yves groaned. "Again? Don't you have anything else? I mean, no one here listens to *real* music?"

"Of course we do," I interjected. "Bastien plays the violin beautifully."

"That's not what I'm talking about," Yves said as Bastien began to flush bright red. "I mean like recorded music."

"We have plenty in the library," I said.

"Wait, what?" Yves said. "Augustin, you never told me that."

"We have hundreds, maybe thousands, of records there," I added, eager to please him.

"Yeah?" Yves said, squinting at me. "Like Madonna? George Michael? U2?"

In fact, I had barely heard of Madonna and had no idea at all who George Michael or U2 were.

Augustin started laughing.

"What's so funny?" Yves said, glaring at him.

Augustin rolled his eyes at Yves before turning to look at me. "Which are your favorite records in the library?"

Misunderstanding Augustin's sudden interest, I launched into the topic.

"There is the most wonderful recording of Maria Callas singing 'Vissi d'Arte,' from Puccini's *Tosca*," I said. "If you close your eyes it will just take you away."

Augustin laughed even harder. Yves looked irritated.

"What's wrong with Puccini?" Bastien said, concerned.

"Yves," Augustin managed, when he finally stopped laughing. "She's talking about our collection of *classical* records."

"Oh, brother," Yves said, and slumped back in despair.

I was mystified by the exchange. As boarding school students, Yves and Augustin likely had plenty of opportunity to be exposed to modern music and media. For Bastien and me, who had never been off the estate in our entire lives, it was all a grand mystery.

Augustin pointed at the old gramophone. "This has a steel needle too. You can only play the shellac discs. It will ruin vinyl records."

Yves squinted at Augustin. "I brought my whole CD collection, you know. Someone must have a stereo somewhere."

"We've been over this already," Augustin sighed, and jabbed a thumb at the antique gramophone again. "We're lucky to have this thing."

Before that winter, I never had cause to understand how strange the atmosphere my mother had created on the estate actually was. In fact, several years later I made something of a fool of myself when I insisted to my friends that a popular BBC period drama with a huge costume and wardrobe budget was set in the present day and not the late nineteenth century.

"I'll go get my violin," Bastien said, having missed the nature of Yves's annoyance.

"Don't bother," Augustin said, but the overeager Bastien didn't seem to hear.

He bolted up in such a hurry that he tripped over Yves and me, then crashed to the ground and into one of the table legs. In the process he knocked over the empty glass, which fell to the ground and exploded into a hundred shards.

"Okay," Augustin said, disgusted, and pointed at the door. "Babies out."

CHAPTER TWO

—

The Changing of the Guard

THOUGH I WANTED TO DISMISS IT, I was afraid that the story of my murdered sister Sophia might be true. Back in my apartments, I tried to sleep but, with the wind gusting outside, the manor was as full of all the creaks and shifting noises one would expect from such an ancient building. Before long, every one of them sounded like the rasping cry of a ghostly Sophia.

Sleep was impossible and, when the clock struck one, I put on my wool socks against the chill of cold stone floors, wrapped myself in a quilt, opened my doors, and looked both ways down the hallway before slipping out of my apartments and downstairs.

While most of the manor's domestic staff should have been asleep at that hour, it was closest to my goal (the Grand Study where my grandfather often worked into the early morning hours) that I ran the highest risk of discovery. First I had to traverse the darkened Grand Library. I felt my way around the stacks from the side entrance to get a view of the closed doors to the Grand Study beyond and was pleased to see a dim light shining beneath them.

I'm not quite sure why I didn't knock, though perhaps the fear of alerting malevolent spirits played a part. Instead, I eased one of the double doors open a crack and peered through. The man seated at my grandfather's formidable desk, however, was not my grandfather. It was my father.

His face was shrouded in the flickering edges of shadow that danced in time with flames of the candelabra on the large antique desk. The light played with the color of his dark blond hair, giving it an altogether more menacing tone. My father made a habit of reading by candlelight after darkness fell, a quirk he shared with my grandfather, but seeing him in the Grand Study, much less sitting at the oversize dark wood desk that had long been the centerpiece of the room, was a shock.

As carefully as I could, I eased the doors to the Grand Study closed and fled back into the library and the hallway beyond.

IT WAS ONLY as I made my way back down the hall to the staircase that I realized what had been wrong; what had made me too cautious to knock: the smell of my grandfather's pipe tobacco had been absent. I might not have noticed, except for catching the spicy aroma and hints of cardamom farther down the hall. I followed my nose until I was standing outside a room I would not have thought used at all but for the warm glow under the door. It took me a moment to work up the courage to knock.

"Yes?" a familiar voice sounded from within.

I opened the door and peered in. Sitting at a modest old wood desk, pipe in hand, and reading from one of a stack of oversize, green, leather-bound volumes, was my grandfather. Even at that uncommon hour, he was wearing his traditional dark three-piece suit. His eyebrows, white, bushy, and always the leading features from which his often theatrical expressions followed, rose playfully when he saw me. The wrinkles on his hairless forehead danced, and the naturally upturned corners of his mouth broadened into a wide smile. It was such a genuine and familiar expression that it put me immediately at ease.

"Well, if it isn't Madam Curie," he said, using one of his many nicknames for me, an homage to the first woman to win a Nobel Prize and, as he liked to remind me, a scientist who may have killed herself with her own curiosity.

With a haste so pronounced that it piqued my interest, he put down the green volume he had been holding and abruptly covered it (along with the stack of similar books underneath) with a lint cloth. The effort at concealment struck me as odd. My grandfather was not, so far as I knew, in the habit of keeping things from me.

Only after he had hidden the mysterious volumes did he, at a much more leisurely pace, replace the cap on his Mont Blanc fountain pen. It had an engraved silver top and, on occasion, my grandfather would let me handle it. That night, however, he tucked the pen into his breast pocket, where the silver cap and clip seemed designed to be, settled even deeper into his chair, and then addressed himself to me.

"You know, given my change of venue, I was beginning to wonder if I would be graced by your presence this evening, but how foolish of me to doubt the abilities of my favorite granddaughter-in-training. Well, now that you have uncovered the location of my new secret lair, you might as well join me."

Secret lair, I thought, and gave him an impish grin.

He gestured with his pipe to one of the chairs across from his desk. Though my grandfather would never have smoked in the library proper, being keenly aware of the damage it might do to the precious volumes that lined every available space of that hallowed athenaeum, woe to the custodian, member of the staff, or physician who tried to interpose themselves between him and his pipe elsewhere.

I sank into the leather chair but my gaze drifted to the three gray masks mounted on the wall behind and above his desk. Disembodied, monotone faces with closed lids for eyes, they had been in the Grand Study for as long as I could remember. Backlit as they were, suspended in front of the wall on their mounts, they appeared to be floating in the air of their own accord. They had always frightened me, and I disliked the fact that they had followed my grandfather into his new workspace.

"Welcome to the East Salon," my grandfather said.

"The East Salon?" I said, happy for an excuse to tear my eyes away from the masks. "Grandfather, isn't this the north side of the manor?"

"It is your mother's prerogative, and a closely guarded one at that, that she and only she should name the various rooms in our family seat. Besides, it wouldn't do for me to move into so diminutive an office as the 'Small Study,' now, would it?"

"You? No, Grandfather."

"Well, then you should be pleased to be sitting in the newly christened 'East Salon,' which I am given to understand is short for the 'Far East Salon.'"

Then I understood. My grandfather had a long-standing affinity with

Asia, having in his younger years traveled there many times, always returning with countless objects of interest.

"You are disappointed that you can no longer listen in on my secret conferences from your hiding place on the landing above my desk, is that it?"

I had no idea my grandfather had been aware of my habit. My stomach clenched. I was afraid that he was angry with me, but he only smiled.

"You imagined I did not know?"

In fact, I had convinced myself that my superior espionage abilities had masked me from detection.

"What happened to all your things?" I said, looking around in an attempt at diversion.

"Some are here, some are in storage."

The change was unnerving. The Grand Study had been my grandfather's office since before I was born, the place where he received visitors and dispatched underlings on mysterious errands, the headquarters from which he ran the far-reaching tendrils of what I would later understand as our family's global affairs.

"Speaking of the Far East," he said, reaching into the bottom drawer of his desk to produce a Japanese puzzle box. "It is a new addition to my collection from Kanagawa Prefecture, and it is quite old."

The puzzle boxes were his particular treats for me. Years before, trying to force it open, Augustin had broken one of the priceless examples kept in a glass case in the study. My brother blamed a maid for the crime and my mother dismissed the poor girl that very day. My grandfather was obviously not fooled by the ruse and the Grand Study was declared off-limits for Augustin soon thereafter. In the meantime, the puzzle boxes had become something of a tradition between us.

Whenever I managed to sneak into the Grand Study while he was working—wafts of blue-white pipe smoke twisting up to the impossibly high, vaulted ceilings—he would encourage me to handle and play with the beautiful boxes for hours on end. Any curator with experience in nineteenth-century Japanese antiques would have had a stroke upon finding a child sprawled out on an old Oriental rug of impeccable provenance trying to open several of the priceless pieces, but my grandfather was in the habit of indulging me.

That the mysterious boxes were the cause of Augustin's exile only sweetened the taste of my grandfather's liberty with me.

The new piece was a cube with beautiful inlaid designs, and it took me several minutes before I worked out the secret catch—an artfully concealed piece of sliding wood that, when properly moved, allowed the rest of the box to open. Inside was a carefully wrapped chocolate truffle that I tried (and failed) to eat with something resembling restraint.

Augustin had once told me that some of the other families we knew roped off rooms containing precious objets d'art and meted out stern punishments to the errant child careless enough to violate those frontiers, but the only area on the estate from which my brothers and I were strictly and unambiguously forbidden was beyond the red doors to the manor's Master Apartments, where my parents kept their rooms. That rule was so immutable that neither I nor my brothers had ever even seen their private space.

"I bet you don't miss the rug," my grandfather said, triggering a different memory.

Several summers before, my grandfather had spurred my interest in Japanese calligraphy. He taught me how to grind the ancient ink sticks against an ink stone in the traditional manner. I was sitting on the rug that adorned the floor of the Grand Study, playing with one of the dozens of antique calligraphy sets in his collection. My hand slipped, and I upturned a particularly lovely stone just as I had almost finished blackening the water. Ink showered everywhere—a shotgun pattern of black with a dark mass in the center.

One of the maids recoiled in horror on seeing the damage and offered to call a professional service to do their best to restore the priceless antique.

"No," my grandfather had said, waving away the hapless staffer. "My granddaughter has made her mark on this piece. Who are we to imagine we can erase it?"

I squirmed at the memory of the incident under my grandfather's amused gaze. Trying to think of something to change the subject, I surveyed his new workspace again. A little fireplace heated the modest accommodations. Unlike the daunting blaze in the Grand Study, which often competed with the drafts from the nearby lattice bow windows, in the East Salon it seemed the flames had to be kept under careful control to avoid melting the many candles about the room.

A pair of windows looked north. Moved by the wind, a branch from the sapling outside had taken to scratching and tapping on the glass panes. I was surprised the grounds crew had missed it.

"That tree will scratch your window, won't it?" I said.

My grandfather turned to look, though I was quite sure he already knew what I meant.

"I don't mind," he said after a couple of puffs on his pipe. "It reminds me that the estate is alive."

An involuntary shudder went through me.

"Listen," my grandfather said in a hushed tone, pointing the stem of his pipe at the window. "It is a hand rising from our lands. The hand of the dead beckons to us. Or begs for admittance."

I pulled my quilt around me tighter and pretended to listen to the crackling of the fire until I could shake off my grandfather's phrase "the hand of the dead," and the image of the branch as a skeletal limb reaching up from the soil, grasping for us, yearning to touch us, to claim us, or worse.

"May I ask a question?" I said.

"I do not know the man who would dare to stop you," he said, smiling again.

"Do you believe in ghosts?"

I had meant to ask why he had moved from the Grand Study and why my father was using it in his stead, but the sapling's branch and the tale of Sophia had buried their hooks deep into my psyche and my question had slipped out.

"What a strange thing to ask."

Suddenly shy, and not a little afraid that something dangerous might slip out if I spoke again, I bit my lower lip and looked at the floating masks instead.

"Well, then," my grandfather said. "Of course I do." He saw the direction of my gaze. "Is it the death masks that frighten you? But, these are not the ghosts to be afraid of. They watch over me; over all of us."

"Who are they?"

My grandfather chewed on his pipe while he composed his reply.

"Just some dead, old Romans," he said, though his expression suggested that their import was much deeper and that he had amused himself with a species of private joke. "Originally they made the masks from wax to preserve the features of a loved one, or a patrician. Later they were used to create stone versions to endure for time eternal. Sometimes with soapstone or, like these, alabaster so that when illuminated from behind by flickering candlelight, they glowed and their facial expressions seemed to move and change."

Please, no, I almost said.

My grandfather gestured behind his head at the masks without looking away from me. "Actually, some of their blood runs in your veins.

"Do you want to know another secret?" he said, with a conspiratorial whisper. I nodded enthusiastically. "It is not the death masks, but the portraits in the Hall of Ancestors that scare me."

"You, Grandfather? Really?"

"Oh my, yes. Every time I walk down that hall I see them, the patriarchs of this family, looking down at me. Pictures of men who sacrificed much, spilled a great deal of blood, some of it their own, and on the very soil beneath us.

"I am afraid of their anger, of their disappointment, of not being worthy of the sacrifices they made to build and protect this family. I feel them watching me every time I walk past. But then, that is why they are there, isn't it? It is proper that the patriarch of the family should be afraid of them."

The portraits were impressive, but I had certainly not given them as much thought as my grandfather had. With his description, their images came unbidden to my mind's eye: life-size depictions of the thirteen former heads of our family, my grandfather's predecessors, mounted high on the walls of the hall that led from the Master Apartments to the Grand Library and the Grand Study beyond.

"Why isn't your picture on the wall, too, Grandfather?"

"They are only painted posthumously, my dear girl, and I am very much alive, as you can see. That is unless . . ." My grandfather blew a cloud of pipe smoke in front of his face and wiggled the fingers of both hands at me from behind the miasma. ". . . I too am a ghost."

Just then, with remarkable timing, a candle next to his desk succumbed to a draft from the far window and flickered out. Blown in my direction by the errant breeze, paraffin from the extinguished candle mixed with the scent of his pipe smoke and hung heavily in the air.

"You see?" my grandfather said. "A ghost's breath. Now you are witness to the powers I wield from beyond the grave."

"Don't be silly," I said, trying to ignore the flutter in my chest. "Why did you move from the bigger study?"

"Well," my grandfather said, leaning back in his chair before continuing. "Your father will need the extra room now."

"Why?"

"He has more responsibilities than before."

"Why?"

"Because I have fewer responsibilities than before."

I was disappointed to think that the Grand Study was no longer my grandfather's. Though the nuances would escape me until I was older, like everyone else in my family I had heard the stories of my grandfather's early tenure as the family's patriarch; how he guided the dynasty through the horrors of the Second World War untainted by the profiteering to which many old-world families succumbed, and without so much as a modest diminution of its already vast holdings; how after the war he was responsible for the massive growth in the family's art and antique collection, and, most particularly, the collection of rare books in the towering Grand Library; and, of course, as the structures of colonialism began their rapid decay, how, in the mid-1970s, he had turned the business interests of the family away from natural resources and extraction economies and into investing and finance, with his usual perfect timing.

"Here in the East Salon, I can come and go and busy myself with my many pursuits without getting in your father's way."

"Am I allowed in the Grand Study anymore? Can I still play with the globes?"

The beautiful globes that sat next to the desk in the Grand Study were some of my favorite objects anywhere on the estate. One terrestrial and one celestial, they were eighteenth-century affairs lettered in silver wire, adorned with gold leaf, and featuring deep, cobalt blue seas or inky black skies. Each one probably weighed more than I did and I could spend hours spinning them, entranced and in awe of their beauty, but oblivious to the world beyond which they described.

"You will have to ask your father. It is his study now."

I frowned.

My grandfather sensed my displeasure, and after a pause to puff on his pipe, he continued.

"My dear, it is the responsibility of the family to heed the wishes of the patriarch, but any great leader must earn and inspire that loyalty."

"Grandfather," I ventured, "aren't you the oldest boy?"

This elicited a chuckle. "Why, yes. Yes, I am."

"Why aren't you the head of the family anymore then?"

"Aren't you clever, Madam Curie? My dear, the future; it is for the young. They alone are suited to bring a dynasty safely into their epoch. The head of the family also must recognize when it is time to start the process of stepping aside, so the next patriarch can begin to take his place."

"You mean Father," I said. My grandfather nodded. "How do you know when it is time, Grandfather?"

"A good leader always knows."

"What if he doesn't?"

"In that case," and here my grandfather leaned forward again raising his eyebrows, "the decision is . . . made for him. Perhaps even by his own heirs."

He sat back, pleased to see that I had understood the nuance.

"Has that ever been done in our family?"

"Certainly not," he said.

"Even to heirs?" I blurted out, thinking of Sophia.

I couldn't quite tell if he was feigning shock or if he had really been affronted by my outburst. Thankfully, he let the expression fade before he continued.

"The peaceful transfer of power is essential to the longevity of any trans-generational entity. In our family, Leopold I and his son solved the problem of peaceful succession between the generations long ago."

My grandfather took some thoughtful puffs from his pipe before he spoke again. "Well . . . there was one case."

His eyebrows darted up when he saw the startled curiosity light up my face, pleased to have teased me into rapt attention.

"What do you mean?" I said.

"Andres, the younger brother of Mathias, your seventh great-grandfather, wanted the position of patriarch for himself."

"What happened?"

"The Northern Ruins," my grandfather said, but did not elaborate, and puffed his pipe instead. Only my questing expression finally egged him on. "The answer to that question lies crumbling near our northern border."

"What answer?" I pressed.

"Well, if you were forced to cope with a rebellious branch of the family, might exile not be one of the less drastic options available to you? Might not you wish to keep them close enough to keep an eye on, but far enough away to prevent any trouble?"

"I guess so. But, what happened to Andres?"

"Mathias built a house and a chapel for them. Andres's children were forbidden to marry and, two generations later, his line was extinguished. Only their memory remains. Well, along with the ruins of their abode; their ghosts are a haunting reminder for future patriarchs, perhaps."

I found myself shuddering with the supernatural implications of the tale. "That's horrible," I said.

"Well," he sighed. "Let us just say what Mathias did was much kinder than the alternative."

I blinked at my grandfather, uncomprehending.

"My dear, sometimes the patriarch must embrace total amorality, even immorality, in order to grant to his family the luxury of morality."

I still didn't understand but, rather than belabor the point, I allowed my thoughts to return to the present.

"Is the event on the estate this weekend very important?" I said.

"Well, I should think so. Mind you, all of your mother's occasions are very important, though I am given to understand that one guest in particular is likely to be the focus of her, and your father's, especial interest. In fact, it would not surprise me to learn that the entire affair was crafted with this visitor in mind."

"Really?"

"Ah, but I only speculate. For once, these intrigues are not of my design."

"Augustin says we shouldn't go downstairs during Mother's events," I said.

"Does he now?"

"But his roommate says that's melodramatic."

"While his reasoning may not be perfectly sound, your brother's instincts are not far off."

My grandfather paused for a moment, considering something before he continued.

"Shall I tell you yet another secret?"

I nodded eagerly.

"Well, did you know that your mother had a twin sister?" I shook my head. "She was killed as a teenager. Poisoned in her sleep by a gas leak. The gas lines were newly installed in the family's aging castle, you see. They were almost inseparable, your mother and her sister, but, just this one evening, your mother snuck out alone to meet with her friends in the nearby forests and was thereby spared. When her sister died, your mother was inconsolable, wracked with survivor's guilt.

"In the wake of the tragedy your maternal grandmother sent your mother to live with the Wesleys, extended family of ours, as it happens, and descendants of the Duke of Wellington. She sent your mother there not least because, at that time, Wesley Manor was still essentially devoid of modern accoutrements. In particular, gas lines.

"Your mother developed a horror of all things modern, one that persists in small ways to this day. Surely you have noticed the rather archaic ambience here in the manor compared to other households?"

"But, Grandfather, I have never been anywhere else."

"What? Really?"

I nodded.

Now and again I think of that particular moment with my grandfather and remember the way he looked at me when the realization of how sheltered I was came to him. My mother and father were "hands-off" in the discharging of their parental duties, to say the least but, in my grandfather's case, I think the years just got away from him. Before he knew it, his favorite (and only) granddaughter had become a preteen who had never known anything beyond our own borders.

"Well," he said, continuing, "when your mother married your father and made our family seat her home, she converted that horror of the modern into something novel. She created a whole new persona for herself: the consummate hostess. The manor here became a forum for lavish entertainments with anachronistic themes. What might have been seen as a sign of a disturbed mind instead became a keen sense of showmanship.

"To this day invitations to your mother's events are highly sought after. Having been invited, no socialite, no master of finance, statesman, or diplomat, would dream of missing one."

My grandfather leaned forward a bit, as was his habit when he intended to dramatize the importance of what he was about to reveal.

"Do you know that for a period of almost three years your mother recreated in the most accurate and exquisite detail a Regency period gambling parlor? And later, regular 'Venetian breakfasts.'"

"Like a casino? Mother did that?"

"Indeed. It was where the Rose Salon is now. She even reproduced the authentic card games of chance of the period and trained bankers and dealers to play with the guests. I seem to remember that the Basset table was quite popular. Your mother was twice clever there. The odds of Basset are ruinious to players. Nevertheless, anyone who was anyone was at the greatest pains to be invited. There was a rumor that a certain prime minister owed her several hundred thousand Swiss francs at one point."

"Did he pay it back?"

"Alas," my grandfather said, with a wink. "If, or indeed how, his debts were finally satisfied are details lost to history.

"Your mother's events were instrumental in furthering this family's interests. I myself have managed to accomplish things I never thought possible because the right people could not bear to miss one. Likewise, your father's interests have been immeasurably advanced by your mother's adroit sense of politics and intrigue.

"What I want you to see is that we all have a part to play in securing the preservation and prosperity of this dynasty. Your mother's path, rather unprecedented for the wife of a patriarch's heir, is not for everyone. Still, you mustn't think a domestic role limited. Your mother's marriage to your father was arranged, you know. And yet, she wields quite a lot of power here on the estate."

I frowned.

"The role of dutiful wife does not appeal to you? Even if it should come with your mother's many powers? Well, in any event, you might be a little gentler with your mother now that you understand how her terrible loss shaped her and how important her role is, not just to her, but to all of us, yes?"

I nodded, and looked down at my palms.

My grandfather puffed on his pipe furiously, ruminating, but when he came out of his reverie, he only bid me kiss him good night and then shooed me off to bed.

"Now, now," he said, lifting his hand to arrest the deluge of questions I had been ready to spill to extend my time with him. "I have much work still to do and, night owl though you are, it is rather late even for you.

"You know, I could be convinced to become curious about what it is you get up to at these hours before you come to visit me."

A frightened look must have crossed my face.

"I *could* be convinced . . . but, in fact, I have not been," he said, and gave me his warmest smile. "Now, off with you before your mother feeds me hemlock as punishment for corrupting the young people of the estate."

Then, in a not-unkindly way, he ushered me out of the East Salon.

FALL HAD VANISHED under a series of almost unprecedented snowstorms that October. Though the estate was normally well prepared for the major snowfalls winter always brought to our foothills, the thunder blizzard that rolled down from the mountains after I left my grandfather was something different. Blue-white explosions of lightning turned the entirety of the snow-filled sky into a colossal strobe light and the booming thunder that followed shook the windows in my apartments. The tempest was of such magnitude that it frightened even me, a notorious lover of violent weather.

At first, I watched the storm through my bedroom windows but, after a particularly pane-rattling thunderclap, I leapt into bed and hid under my covers. As I sheltered there from the swirling tendrils of windblown snow that pressed against my windows, images of a teenaged Sophia came to me. When the blizzard's intensity grew, I was almost certain I could hear a rasping voice. Then, as the lightning became more frequent, it was as if the energy of the storm itself was calling forth Sophia's ghost.

Caught up in these visions, buried in the dark under my covers, my mind's eye worked to fill in her absent features and mannerisms. In an instant, my slain older sister had inherited my mother's self-assurance and the effortless elegance with which she carried her perpetually slender frame.

Even at eleven it was obvious that my body would eventually mimic my mother's refined physique, though her poise had not quite emerged in me that year. Still, a strong dose of her fair coloring had. Too strong, in fact. The legacy of my mother's straight, light blond hair and almost alabaster skin had combined with some ancient gene that expressed itself in me as pale eyelashes, freckle-dusted skin, and straight, strawberry blond locks kissed with a strong hint of copper. I had my mother's eyes, pale blue and encircled by dark limbal rings. They were my mother's most striking feature but, in my case, not enough to overcome the attention (and even the occasional barb about my paternity) that my red hair attracted.

On the other hand, my older sister, as I imagined her at least, had all of my mother's natural grace and hair closer to my brother Bastien's dirty blond. In my imaginings she was a vaguely older and certainly prettier image of myself—fair but unblemished by freckles, and not quite so pale; at ease ballroom dancing and never missing a step in high heels.

She would have just turned fourteen or fifteen years old that winter, at least according to the vague timeline my brother had provided for her, and that meant she would have evolved beyond the lanky frame I inhabited that season. This last detail would make her my mother's favorite, of course. And, though forced upon her by her damaged voice, the soft, whispering lilt of her speech would give her a delicate and charming presence. For a time, I almost found myself jealous of the far more feminine and graceful apparition I had momentarily brought to life.

A fatigue powerful enough to lull me to sleep despite the swirling storm that held the manor in its grip eventually overtook me. It was a slow intoxication and I lingered for some time in that ethereal space that lies between consciousness and the other side before I slipped beyond it and dreamed of my long-lost sister.

—

CHAPTER THREE

To the Manor Born

W HEN THE SUN FINALLY EMERGED AGAIN late the next morning, the estate was blanketed in white and the snow behind our manor was so high that one could open a window on the second floor of the East Wing (where our rooms were), step out, and walk on top of the accumulations.

My mother's event was to be held in honor of the 1st Duke of Chandos ("The Apollo of the Arts"), a distant relation of ours. In 1724, and at ruinous expense, the Duke completed the stately Middlesex home "Cannons," famous for the extravagance of its construction and as a haven for artists (Handel was the estate composer for a time). Just one generation later, ruined by the South Sea Bubble, the Duke's son was forced to demolish the house and sell the building materials at salvage prices. My mother found such historical ironies and scandals delicious and it was typical that such themes should find their way into her productions.

She was expecting more than fifty guests, but the storm had snowed in the estate, isolating us from the outside world even more than usual. The fact that the main access road, the only route to our manor other than by helicopter, was under several feet of snow was only one of the many problems the storm had created for my mother that morning. I suppose, had we been aware of the level of extra anxiety around us, we might have been more careful not to be caught underfoot.

Even in the absence of a planned event, we siblings rarely ventured down to the manor's ground floor for meals. It was never explicitly declared, but we all had the feeling that the ground floor was somehow "for adults," and, given the formality with which even the domestic staff carried themselves on that level, it felt somewhat alien to trespass there even in the absence of visitors.

Moreover, my mother was generally of the view that children should be neither seen *nor* heard. On those occasions when she required our attendance at dinner in the Grand Dining Hall, it was in pursuit of some political or social purpose. When we were not being displayed to outsiders as her dutiful progeny, however, we typically gathered in the second-floor dayroom and rang down to the kitchens to have the maids bring our meals up.

Kept awake by the storm, we had all slept in quite late that morning. It was nearly eleven o'clock before, still in our bedclothes, we dragged ourselves into the dayroom. When I arrived, Bastien was waiting and already impatient for food. Once Yves and Augustin finally wandered in, he made a grand fuss of calling down for eggs and breakfast meats.

When we had finished and the maids had cleared the table, a languid silence fell over us. The ghost of Sophia was still lurking in the back of my mind and, gradually, the realization that my parents might be murderers also began to encroach on my psyche. It put me on edge, but the others gave no sign of being overly concerned with the larger implications of Augustin's story. Instead, our attentions seemed to drift outside to the brilliant day that had developed after the passage of the storm.

The snow was high enough outside the dayroom to cover the lower half of the windows. I had been staring out through them for almost ten minutes, increasingly plagued by images of bodies buried under the white drifts. So, when Augustin jumped up out of his chair, he caused my heart to skip a beat.

"Paratroopers," he said.

We all looked at him, baffled.

"Meet me at the top of the stairs on the third floor dressed for outside," he said.

Then he bolted out of the dayroom without further explanation.

On the verge of sixteen, Augustin was just beginning to grow into the tall frame he had inherited from our father. His other features, however, favored my mother. His hair and complexion were both lighter than Bastien's and, when he indulged in his habit of tilting his chin downward to look up at one from under his brow, his blue eyes and sometimes severe expression could be quite intimidating. But that year he was still mostly our benevolent leader, a gallant captain whose authority stemmed not just from his status as the eldest sibling, but also from an unspoken consensus.

In the wake of his sudden departure, the three of us looked at each other, dumbfounded and unsure how to react. But his command was delivered with such a perfect combination of self-assurance, mystery, and intrigue that it was inevitable that we would follow him.

When we arrived on the third floor, Augustin had made his way into one of the unused single bedrooms that overlooked the largest snowdrift. He said nothing when we peered in from the hallway beyond and found him standing in front of the open window. Instead, he turned to look at us and gave us a crooked, wry smile. Then he stepped up on the windowsill with his heels and, in one smooth motion, fell out backward crying "Fallschirmjäger!" at the top of his lungs as he disappeared.

We ran to the window and looked down in a panic, but the deep snow below the window had perfectly cushioned his fall. After a moment, Augustin dug himself out, crawled to the far side of the drift, saluted, and beckoned us to follow.

Not to be outdone, and perhaps overcompensating for being the only girl of the pack, I made a point of jumping next, ducking in front of Yves, laughing as I play-wrestled him to mount the windowsill. I am sure he let me win, and I was the next to leap from the open window, whooping all the way down until I landed in the powdery accumulation with a muted "whump."

Prickly cold ice crystals melted on my cheeks as I dug myself out of snow that was far over my head, crawled away, and turned my attention upward to watch as Yves, with the graceful poise of an Olympic diver, fell into the snow spread-eagle on his back.

Bastien, though he had just turned thirteen (certainly old enough to have found his courage), was petrified. He tried hard not to let it show but I could see how afraid he was.

"Just close your eyes, Basti," Augustin called up to him. "And fall on your back. It's easy."

Bastien didn't look at all sure.

"Even Fuchsli can do it," Augustin said, using one of my grandfather's many nicknames for me, an affectionate moniker that roughly translated to "the little fox."

Bastien still seemed frozen.

Augustin grew impatient. "Come on, you coward," he barked.

We watched as Bastien worked himself up to the leap, clamping his eyes shut and open again four abortive times before loosening his viselike grip on the side of the window. When he finally jumped, he pinched his nose and tucked into a ball as if he were plunging into the deep end of a swimming pool.

He fell in utter silence and disappeared into the soft white mountain with the muted sound of displaced snow.

"Bravo," Yves said, and made a great show of polite applause, as if we were all at the symphony.

We all clapped in the style of Yves, and I could not suppress a giggle at the silliness of it all.

"Good show," Yves added, affecting a British accent. "Encore. Encore."

Seconds went by. There was no sign of Bastien, who, having cannonballed into the white drift, had sunk much deeper than any of us.

I felt my stomach lurch.

"Augustin," I whispered, reaching for his hand. "You don't think he hit bottom, do you?"

At first Augustin had an annoyed expression, but as the seconds passed, he gave me a stricken look. Yves seemed to go pale. An interval passed before, at the same moment, he and Augustin stumbled over and started digging frantically. I was only seconds behind them.

"He's here," Augustin called after a moment. I crawled through the drifts to him and started frantically excavating next to Yves. We found Bastien's upturned face and dusted the snow away. His eyes were closed, and he wasn't moving.

"Bastien," I pleaded. "Open your eyes."

Several seconds passed and then he finally spoke.

"Did I make it?"

Augustin, Yves, and I collapsed into relieved laughter. Pulling Bastien from the snow, Yves put him over his shoulder and hauled him through the drift to more solid footing.

Bastien looked at us, eyes shining. "Can we do it again?" he said, and we were running back into the manor then, and up to the third floor, leaving trails of melted snow on the rugs and the carpeting that adorned the marble stairwells.

This continued until Cipriana, one of the younger maids on the estate, followed the echoes of our shrieks and manic laughter up to the third floor. Having crept in behind me unnoticed, she nearly expired in fright when she peeked into the room just as I leapt from the windowsill. Terrified at first that she might have witnessed my last earthly act, her reaction (once she recovered and stopped hyperventilating) was perhaps more forceful than it should have been.

"You cannot be up here," she shouted at us when we had all climbed back up to the third floor. "This floor is off-limits." Her normally pale face was bright red and, when she turned her attention to me, I withered under her angry glare. "You could have been *killed*."

Cipriana's grandfather had worked for our family for many years and her parents had sent her to the estate that fall immediately after her fifteenth birthday, just old enough to start work as an apprentice maid. She was too young and inexperienced to fully appreciate one of the estate's unwritten rules: members of the domestic staff never confronted or verbally disciplined children in the direct line. It was a dramatic violation of the estate's archaic hierarchy.

Raising your voice to one of us could have long-reaching consequences. My mother, to whom the entirety of the domestic staff effectively reported, was content to enforce that particular stratification rather severely. Cipriana had unwittingly strayed onto dangerous ground, and my brother reacted to it rather poorly.

"What did you just say?" Augustin said, stepping in between the young maid and the rest of us.

Cipriana froze. Augustin closed the distance between them and loomed over her as he continued, menace building in his voice.

"You do not *ever* speak to us that way, do you understand?"

The young maid started to stammer.

"One word from me to my mother and you will be dismissed from service with a mark on your CV so black you'll never work again."

I doubted somehow that Augustin would actually denounce the young maid to our mother. Though he might well have gotten the young girl fired, with one of my mother's events close at hand, a scrap with even a junior member of the domestic staff was still risky. My mother could easily decide to punish all of us for the distraction as well as terminate the girl's employment. Even so, the poor girl started to tremble uncontrollably and tears welled up in her eyes as she looked at the floor.

"Hey, Augustin. Take it easy," Yves said softly and, coming up behind him, put a hand on Augustin's shoulder.

Augustin shrugged it off. "Do you understand me?" he demanded of the young maid.

"Look," Yves said, his voice soothing. "Now you've made her cry. Just look at her. It's obvious she didn't know any better."

Yves had a point. The cast of Cipriana's face, her dimples, and her high cheekbones made her look young even for her age; a frightened little blond girl—long-haired, doe-eyed, and skittish. Augustin seemed to understand, and it took some of the edge off his anger. He put his hand under her chin, lifted it, and looked into her eyes for long enough that something about it started to make me uncomfortable.

"Very well," he said, in a calmer tone. "Just get out of our sight."

Just before she turned to go, Yves gave her a cheerful little smile, which, for a moment, it almost seemed to me that she returned.

"How could you be that mean?" Yves said, watching Cipriana as she scurried away. "I mean, they are awfully cute in those uniforms."

Augustin turned to Yves, astonished at first, but then craned his neck to watch the fleeing girl as she hurried down the far stairs. Once she had vanished from view, he turned back and gave Yves a cryptic smile.

ALMOST AN HOUR after I changed out of my outdoor clothes, I found Cipriana huddled in a dark corner of the second-floor hallways. She was sitting on the cold stone floor, knees tucked into her chest, and crying softly to herself. I imagined that she must have been lonely, homesick, and scared. I felt horrible that we had frightened her so badly. I called out to her softly but, the moment she saw me, she stood up and fled.

~⊙~

WE SNUCK BACK up to the third floor a few hours later, but found all the doors in the East Wing locked. That sapped the fun out of the morning and ended the snow-diving for the day. Though we tried to resurrect the magic later that afternoon with forts and elaborate tunnels excavated in the drifts, mostly we just managed to infuriate the rest of the domestic staff, already on edge owing to the frantic preparations my mother's exacting standards demanded, by repeatedly tracking melting snow into the manor. Before long, the sun was getting low in the sky and our outdoor fun was over.

~⊙~

AUGUSTIN AND YVES slipped away as evening approached. Bastien was taken aback that we had been abandoned, and not a little hurt, but I wasn't surprised. It certainly wasn't the first time they had ditched Bastien and me to undertake their own mysterious activities.

I had planned to go to my apartments and find a book to read to pass what promised to be a dull evening, but Bastien had another idea.

"Why don't you come to my rooms?" he said.

When my reaction to his suggestion was less than enthusiastic, Bastien looked wounded.

"I don't know, Bastien."

"Please? We can play a game, or cards, or . . . something."

The expression on his face was pitiful and it tore at my heartstrings.

"Very well," I sighed.

Bastien perked up, took my hand to lead me along, and actually started skipping toward his rooms as I struggled to keep up.

I endured his glee as well as I could, but I was glad when he had settled down and we were sitting on the floor in his foyer with an ancient Monopoly board between us.

"Bastien," I said, looking at the antique. "This thing looks like it is a hundred years old."

"I found it in the cellar with a bunch of ancient artifacts. Isn't it cool?"

"It looks like it is about to fall apart. Where's the newer one?"

"I like this one better," he said, as he counted out our shares of the tattered Monopoly money.

I didn't feel like arguing with him, so I let the matter drop, but we had barely started playing when Bastien started complaining.

"I'm hungry," he whined.

"Basti, this is one reason I don't like playing board games with you. You always get distracted."

He gave me his most pitiful look. "But it is way past lunchtime."

"Fine," I said, exasperated. "Have it your way. Ring down and have something brought up."

"Excellent idea," Bastien said, brightening, and then sprang up toward the bell pull with such haste that he almost tripped and stepped on the Monopoly board.

Though he was quite slim, Bastien always seemed to have a ravenous appetite. In fact, his build was so at odds with the amount of food he regularly seemed to consume that he had to endure Augustin's frequent barbs about parasites or exotic tropical diseases.

As was often his habit when ordering, when one of the maids arrived Bastien inundated the poor girl with a list of culinary requests so extensive that, once she asked him to write it all down, he nearly covered an entire page with his oversize and crooked handwriting. I thought of reminding him that the kitchens were likely to be quite busy with preparations for the weekend. But I knew that, if I interrupted him, it might have occasioned another twenty minutes of discussion and delay.

"Do you want anything?" he called, and part of me was surprised he even remembered to ask.

"It sounds as if you have ordered quite enough for us both."

The maid hurried off and we went back to playing, but Bastien couldn't go five minutes without wondering after his order. Finally, his doorbell rang. Bastien bolted across the foyer and yanked open the double doors to reveal

Cipriana, visibly laboring under the weight of a huge silver tray laden with a half dozen covered plates. I could barely believe that the poor girl was strong enough to carry it. When she curtsied, I could see that her arms were shaking with fatigue.

Oblivious to Cipriana's distress, and without inviting the young maid in, Bastien proceeded to lift the plate covers one by one to inspect the dishes while she stood at the threshold.

"Basti, what are you doing?" I scolded. He turned around with a puzzled look on his face. "Let the poor girl in before she drops the tray."

"Oh, yes, please, come in," he stammered, and waved Cipriana past.

She set the tray down on the round table with a sigh of relief. Bastien, almost too distracted by the food to even remember her presence, attacked the plate covers and began to set out the many dishes.

I looked away and then to Cipriana, I think because I hoped she was not watching my brother's gluttonous behavior. There was a hint of perspiration above her upper lip and when she saw me looking at her she lowered her eyes and then dropped a curtsy before turning to go.

"No," I said, not quite sure what I was doing. "Wait."

She stopped and gave me a puzzled look.

"Why don't you join us?" I said.

Cipriana looked horrified and lowered her eyes again. "Oh, no, miss. I couldn't."

I glanced over at Bastien and found him plucking at a plate of steamed vegetables with his fingers, popping each piece into his mouth like he was eating popcorn.

"Bastien," I snapped. He froze. "Where are your manners? Sit down and eat properly."

"Sorry," he said.

"And invite our guest to join us," I added.

Confused at first, Bastien glanced alternately at Cipriana and me several times before he realized what I was asking.

"Of course," he managed, though he didn't sound at all sure about it. "Please sit."

Cipriana was shaking her head, about to protest again.

"There," I said, before she could respond. "You see? These are my brother's rooms so you're formally invited now."

I took her hand and led her to the table where, after a moment of panic that I tried to soothe away with my warmest smile, she finally consented to be seated. She seemed afraid we were playing some trick on her, setting her up for some prank or cruel turnabout. When Bastien set a plate with several lovely chicken cutlets in front of her, Cipriana only looked at them and wore an expression that seemed to suggest she feared she was dreaming the entire encounter.

I still did not quite understand what had prompted me to invite her to sit, a breach of protocol to be sure, but I felt guilty that she should be so ill at ease with us. I suppose because Bastien alone had never been a particularly engaging playmate, some part of me was eager that, despite the hierarchy that separated us, she should stay. After all, Cipriana being a bit young for her years, in a way we were close enough in age that, in other circumstances, we might have been friends and playmates.

I tried to make her feel more comfortable by eating in the most nonchalant way. For his part, Bastien was so intent on his food that she could not have imagined he was overly concerned with her.

"Please," I said, trying to break the ice after nearly a minute of silence. "Eat."

Reluctantly, she took up fork and knife and, with the most deliberate care, began to cut a tiny piece off the nearest cutlet. As if afraid she might wake some terrible beast if she made too much noise, she repeated the delicate gesture over and over again, without saying a word.

"It must be very busy downstairs," I suggested, and this seemed to prompt more interest from her.

"Oh, yes, miss. I've never seen so many cars and people in fancy dress."

Bastien waved his hand dismissively without looking up. "Dinner just means sitting for hours listening to the adults talk."

Cipriana gave me a tortured expression. "But don't you get to dress up too?"

"Yes," I said, and smiled. Bastien let out a little groan and I shot him a look. "It can be fun sometimes," I added.

"You must have the most wonderful dresses," she breathed, her dark blue eyes sparkling.

"Oh, yes," I said, wanting to indulge her. "I have ball gowns, and A-lines, even a mermaid dress, but that one is way too big on me. Maybe it would fit you. We could play dress-up sometime if you want to try it on?"

When Cipriana finally absorbed what I was saying she was smiling ear to ear and looked like she might actually burst.

"Oh, brother," Bastien said, rolling his eyes.

"Be polite, Basti," I said.

"Have you met many important people?" she asked me, once she had her courage back.

"I guess so."

The clock on Bastien's mantel chimed and, when Cipriana glanced at it, a frown started across her face.

"Won't you be late?" Cipriana asked.

"What do you mean?" I said.

"To dinner?"

"We aren't invited," Bastien said.

Cipriana looked shocked.

"Sometimes we are," I said. "Just not this time."

"What about miss's brother, and . . . ?"

"Yves?" I offered.

"Master Böhm, yes," she said, and her face flushed red. "Will . . . they go?"

"I don't think so," I said.

"They aren't invited either," Bastien crowed.

"Oh," Cipriana managed. "In their fancy dress the men do look so . . ." She searched for the right word.

"Gallant?" I suggested.

"Yes," she beamed.

There was a lull in the conversation, which I tried to fill by changing the subject.

"You are an apprentice maid, aren't you?" I said. Cipriana nodded. "What will you do after?"

"After, miss?"

"When you are finished being a maid, I mean."

Cipriana blinked at me. "I . . . I don't understand, miss."

She was just about to say something else when Bastien's doorbell rang. It was as if the girl had been electrocuted. She bolted up from her chair so quickly she nearly knocked it over and a terrified expression twisted her features.

"Bastien," I said in a hushed tone. "Go see who that is."

Bastien made his way to the doors and flung them both open to find one of the senior maids.

"Please forgive the interruption," the woman said, after her curtsy. "But I am looking for . . ."

Just then she caught sight of Cipriana over Bastien's shoulder. Her expression immediately darkened. She cleared her throat and gave the young maid a particularly evil look.

I winced, wishing that for once Bastien would have exercised a little discretion and only cracked his doors to see who was ringing.

"You are needed in the kitchens," the senior maid said. "*Now.*"

Cipriana looked like she might faint on the spot. She gave Bastien and me a quick curtsy and then made for the hallway outside.

At first, I made as if to defend her, but the hiss that the senior maid delivered to Cipriana ("We will discuss this *later*") was so stern that even from that distance I was cowed. Before I could intervene, Cipriana was ushered away.

AFTER CIPRIANA'S REMOVAL, I went through the motions of playing Monopoly with Bastien, but my heart wasn't really in it. Bastien detected my fading enthusiasm and, in a preemptive strike to keep me from leaving, launched into a slew of entertainment suggestions that included everything from more board games to ordering a new feast from the kitchens. None aroused in me even the remotest interest until he came up with something rather surprising.

"Why don't we go downstairs and explore?"

"Bastien, you must be kidding. Aren't you forgetting? Mother? The event?"

"I know but we could sort of . . . sneak around. You know, stay out of sight?"

"What are you talking about? The first reception is tonight. Do you have any idea how much trouble we could get in?"

"What if no one sees us? What if we were . . . like spies, I mean. It's just that, well, it sounds sort of interesting down there."

I was about to reject the idea out of hand, but then I realized what had happened. Bastien was responding to the romanticized picture Cipriana had painted of my mother's event. Something about Cipriana's idealized perspective was alluring. I caught myself chewing my lip in thought, but not before Bastien noticed.

"You know you want to," he taunted.

Even as it started to creep across my face, I knew that he would take it as encouragement if I smiled, but somehow I just couldn't help it.

"See?" he beamed.

BASTIEN AND I spent about half an hour planning our "mission," debating how best to get downstairs, where the best vantage points to watch the event preparations might be, and on the wisdom of using the staff corridors—dark little passages built behind and between rooms; their entrances concealed behind tapestries or by disguising them as wall panels, which, in the earlier years of the manor, permitted the domestic staff to move freely about and still remain invisible to guests.

We had hardly made it three-quarters across the second floor on our way to the back stairwell when I thought I heard something. I froze and Bastien looked askance at me. That section of the second floor was supposed to be unused, but I was certain there had been a noise.

"What is it?" he asked.

I was about to answer but I heard another sound in the hallway. Judging by his expression, Bastien had heard it too. Whatever it was, it was coming from one of the double doors near the end. We crept closer but, when it was clear which doorway was the source of the noise, Bastien lost his nerve and froze.

Gingerly, I drew near and listened.

Voices.

I waved Bastien over. He shook his head at first, but relented when I glared at him. The two of us knelt down and pressed our ears against the double doors.

Somehow, Bastien lost his balance and actually knocked the side of his head against the doors. The voices stopped in an instant and we found ourselves in a sort of silent standoff for what seemed like minutes, but was probably only a few seconds. I was just about to motion to Bastien that we should creep away when the double doors flew open. Bastien fell to the ground and a shrill shriek of surprise escaped him.

I looked up to find Yves glaring down at us.

"What the hell was that?" Augustin's voice called from within.

Bastien couldn't seem to form words; instead he just sat there blinking. I got up and composed myself. Augustin appeared at the doorway and ducked under Yves's arm to stand in the hallway, looming over Bastien. Oddly, Augustin and Yves were wearing similar outfits: dark pants, turtlenecks, and blazers.

"Uh . . ." Bastien stammered, trying to peer around Augustin and Yves into the rooms beyond. "Is this the new headquarters?"

"None of your business," Augustin snapped. "How did you find us? And exactly what the hell do you two think you are doing?"

Bastien stammered again.

"Perfect," Augustin sighed in exasperation. "Listen, just get lost, understand?"

"We're conducting reconnaissance," Bastien blurted out, desperate to impress Augustin.

It sounded so silly that I almost groaned aloud.

Yves peered at me over Augustin's shoulder with a frown, but then a little grin crept into his expression.

Augustin and Yves shared a look.

Yves's little grin expanded into a smirk. "Well, you know . . ."

Augustin scowled at first, but then his expression turned thoughtful.

Yves looked up and down the hallway. "Let's get inside," he said, his voice full of intrigue, "before someone comes to investigate."

CHAPTER FOUR

—

Malevolent Spirits

THIS NEW BASE OF OPERATIONS APPEARED to have been disused for years. A fine layer of dust was everywhere and it was apparent that the domestic staff had not visited the rooms for some time. Still, sheets had been taken off the furniture and at least some effort had been made to sweep and tidy up. An assortment of lamps and several candelabras that illuminated the foyer had obviously been borrowed from other rooms. Aside from the large round table in the middle of the foyer, three little tables, all of differing styles, had been pilfered from elsewhere in the manor and placed along the far wall. Mismatched chairs had been placed in front of two of them and atop the third were two crystal whisky decanters (apparently lifted from one of the salons) filled with a light brown liquid and surrounded by eight tumblers.

While Bastien and I were distracted looking around, Augustin sidled up to Bastien and cuffed him on the left bicep, hard.

Surprised, Bastien yelped loudly. He tried to put on a brave face but I could see his eyes beginning to water.

"Why did you do that?" he managed.

"Price of admission," Augustin said.

"Admission to what?" I countered.

"The club, of course," Augustin replied, as if this were entirely obvious. "The *gentlemen's* club," he added, and glared at me.

A club? I thought. *That explains the matching blazers and turtlenecks.*

"You aren't hitting me, Augustin," I said, trying not to let my voice crack.

"You're not paying the price of admission, because you aren't allowed in the club," Augustin replied.

"Why not?"

"Because this is a gentlemen's club and, quite obviously, you are no gentleman."

Despite the implicit threat, Augustin did not, I noticed, make any move to eject me. Instead, he and Yves took their places at the round table in the middle of the foyer. Yves kicked his feet up and Augustin slouched back in his chair.

"What does the club do?" Bastien asked.

"The question is," Augustin said, and cast a skeptical eye in our direction, "what have the two of you been doing?"

"Espionage," Bastien said. "We are going to sneak downstairs and watch the event preparations."

"Bastien," I hissed, and kicked him.

Augustin let out a little snort and then laughed. "You're . . . what? Spies?"

That got Yves's attention, and I could see from his expression that he was deep in thought. Several seconds of silence passed, but then he stood up and struck a dramatic pose. He turned smartly, walked to the far wall, and collected a decanter and four whisky tumblers. Their thick bases clacked together as he pinched the inside of their rims to carry them. With great flair, Yves placed one in front of each chair.

"Have a seat, miss," Yves said, indicating one of the rickety chairs by the round table.

There was something strange about his voice I could not quite put my finger on. I was so intent on it that I found myself fixed where I stood.

"Don't be a jerk," Yves said. "Sit down and have a drink. You aren't supposed to be here, but now that you are, we can all profit from this little incident."

The timbre of Yves's voice was still odd, affected. Even Augustin was giving him a puzzled look.

Being entirely sheltered from film and television on the estate, I had no exposure to the spy thriller genre. Many years later I would learn that Yves had seen essentially every spy movie ever made and had probably been impersonating Gregory Peck, or perhaps William Holden (if their English had been badly afflicted by his French accent).

Yves poured some of the brown liquid into the tumbler set for me.

"What are you doing?" Augustin said, but Yves ignored him.

"Come now," Yves said to me. "Your father keeps the very best single-malt Scotch whisky. You can hardly turn your nose up at that."

"Whisky?" I said, alarmed.

Yves didn't seem to hear my objection. Instead, he circled the table to splash the forbidden liquid into the other glasses.

"You want to know what this is all about?" Yves took a long pull from his whisky, winced a little, and continued. "Okay, miss. It's information we are after. Secrets. You got that? Is it all clear to you now?"

I looked over at Bastien, who seemed just as baffled as I was. Whatever mischief Bastien and I had planned earlier, drinking stolen whisky was certainly a major escalation.

"I'm not going to tell you again, miss," Yves said, glaring at me. "Sit. Down."

It almost seemed like he wasn't acting anymore. I sat, and then Yves turned his attention to Bastien until he sat as well.

For his part, Augustin seemed to have fallen in with Yves's act. He reclined again, watching the proceedings, rolling the dark liquid around in his glass while wearing an entertained expression.

"Cheers," Yves said. He raised his glass, and then, without taking his eyes from me, took a long pull.

Augustin followed suit. They were both looking at me as they drank and so, carefully at first, I sipped from my tumbler and, getting into the act, tried to savor it in the manner I thought an adult would (or at least not choke on the burning liquid once it passed my lips).

Somehow I managed to not react too violently to the peaty drink, and when Yves smiled and nodded his approval, the act of illicitly drinking hard alcohol felt that much more forbidden and dangerous.

"What do you think, Agent Alpha?" Yves said, looking at Augustin.

"Maybe she can be of some use to us after all," Augustin said, though he made no effort at an accent. Augustin turned his attention to Bastien. "*Drink*," he barked.

Bastien hesitated, but gave in and then fell into a fit of coughing. Yves sauntered behind him and patted him loudly on the back.

"There you go, old boy," Yves said, and his English accent seemed to be improving with practice. "There are a lot of important people coming to this estate," he continued, gesturing to the closed double doors and swirling his glass.

"We didn't expect company," Yves said, pacing. "But, now that you've seen us, you're a threat. You have two choices now. Either you join us—"

"—or we eliminate you," Augustin said.

Yves's acting made it clear that it was all just a game, but when Augustin delivered his line it gave me a little thrill and I could feel the shiver on the back of my neck.

"Welcome to . . ." Yves looked up at the ceiling for a moment and then returned his attention to me. "The Bureau of Secrets."

The Bureau of Secrets, I thought. The name itself was full of drama and mystique.

"Life here won't be easy," Yves said, sitting and leaning back in his chair. "My colleague makes a good point." He glanced at Bastien. "Him we can induct without delay, but we don't usually admit women. You'll have to prove yourself." Yves looked me in the eye. "You'll have to be properly . . . *initiated*."

"Exactly," Augustin said, catching on, his enthusiasm growing by the second. "The initiation ceremony must be completed without fail." Then his expression became a cool smile. "And I have just the thing."

BASTIEN AND I were permitted to scurry back to our apartments to compose an outfit as close to the unofficial uniform of the Bureau of Secrets as was possible. A dark blue turtleneck, black riding pants, and an old riding jacket of mine seemed imperfect but, afraid they would abandon me if I took too long, I jumped into the clothes, donned a pair of unfortunately light-colored tennis shoes, and ran back to our "headquarters."

Yves and Augustin made a show of inspecting our attire (and frowning at my sneakers) but eventually nodded their approval.

It was almost nine at night by then and, careful to evade any senior member of the domestic staff who might suggest to our mother that Bastien and I should be in bed, the four of us stole down the back stairs, slipped out one of the manor's side doors and into the winter's dark.

We were without warm clothes and our breath turned to white frost in the chill air as we hugged the side of the manor and circled around toward the main entrance. I started to shiver right away but, elated to be included once more, I wasn't about to complain.

Following Augustin, we huddled in the dark behind snow-covered hedges. It occurred to me that our black attire would be easy to spot against the blanket of white, but I held my tongue.

"Wait," Yves said, holding Augustin by the arm. "Aren't there . . . like . . . security cameras? We'll be seen."

Augustin snorted. "Are you joking? Yves, there isn't a single television on the estate."

"You're not serious."

But Augustin wasn't kidding. Televisions were nonexistent, though years later, my mother would finally permit my father to have a media room installed to pull the international news and business channels down from satellite.

"The surveillance system here consists of security guards and old peepholes," he added.

"Peepholes?" Bastien said, echoing my own curiosity.

"Never mind," Augustin said and, careful to wait for the footmen lurking in the Grand Foyer to look the other way, slipped along the near wall of the manor and to a stone in the ground near the main entrance.

Once there, he lifted the stone and took something that had been hidden underneath. He made his way back to us and then held up his prize: a ring with several skeleton keys on it.

IT WOULD BE hard to describe to someone who has not been the "little sister" exactly how large being included in their secret clique loomed in my psyche. They were older than me and to be invited to join "the club" was beyond thrilling.

Of course, the mysterious "initiation ritual" was intended to intimidate. It worked, but that night I might have submitted myself to any manner of hazing or humiliation to preserve for just a few moments that dangerously fleeting feeling of inclusion, and I am certain Augustin and Yves knew it.

Bastien and I followed them east and into the dark woods beyond the groomed grounds of the estate. Eventually, when I saw the clearing ahead of us through the trees, it began to dawn on me where we were going: our family mausoleum.

I had only been near it once or twice before, and since it was partially concealed by the forests, it was easy to forget how imposing it was up close. The edifice was the size of an unusually large carriage house; a forbidding structure—Gothic arches, tall columns, and everywhere gray stone and the oxidized green of aged copper—made all the more unnerving by the diffuse, blue-gray moonlight that filtered down from the sporadically overcast sky. Even on top of my already near-violent shivering, the mere sight of the building's age-darkened walls gave me a chill.

My feet felt heavy and my knees almost gave out when I saw the stone teeth of the slate-colored gargoyles glaring down from the roof above the looming, dark doors. Somehow Augustin was brave enough to put the correct skeleton key in the lock, turn it, and with all his weight behind him, push open the creaking metal barriers.

He and Yves stood there looking at me expectantly. Apparently just as intimidated by the structure as I had been, Bastien lingered behind.

"Now we will see if our ancestors look favorably on your initiation," Augustin said. "Or if they will use their powers to reject you. Once inside, you must select your ancestral patron and memorize his name," he added, as I tried to pretend my trembling was from the cold.

I glanced back at Bastien and, determined to make a good show of it, strode up the worn stone stairs and into the dark structure.

I had just begun to absorb my surroundings when I heard the metallic groan of the doors behind me. I was stunned to see them closing. My compatriots hadn't followed me inside as I had expected, but were instead closing me in.

"*No, wait,*" I pleaded, turning to bolt back out, but it was too late.

The doors met with an echoing slam, followed by the rasping sound of the key locking them. A scream almost escaped me, but the realization of how awful (not to mention long-lasting) the shame would be if they heard me caught it in my throat. I tried to focus on my breathing and, when I had the panic mostly under control, I began to look around.

It was musty, heavy with the earthen smells of stagnant air and ancient stone, and beneath that something faint and subtle but fouler still: a dank smell that even now my psyche recoils to recall. The ceiling above me was high enough that it was hard to see. Even so, I was fairly sure that it was painted with a fresco. I listened carefully and held my breath. But, if there were any ghosts about, if the spirits of my ancestors lingered, they did not seem overly eager to make their presence known.

The clouds slipped away for a moment and a bit more moonlight beamed in through the metal latticework over the few high windows where the walls met the ceiling. I was glad of that, as I'm not sure I could have endured had it been pitch black.

A large and intricate stone sarcophagus was positioned at the far end of the room. At first I was far too intimidated to approach it. Instead I focused on several crypts to my right, repositories marked with square plaques made of discolored stone sunk into the wall. The plaques started from the floor and extended five rows up toward the ceiling. I tried to read the inscriptions, but the moonlight was beaming to the opposite wall. It was obvious that all of them were quite old and, though I was able to make out a few dates, the names were illegible without artificial light of some kind. If I could not find a name elsewhere, that left only the sarcophagus.

I crept to the far side of the crypt. The stone coffin was set on a dais tall enough that I had to stand on my tiptoes to see the top of the lid. It was solid marble or granite and must have been enormously heavy. It featured a recumbent tomb effigy depicting a sleeping man in armor, helmed, with his shield held over his chest and his sword at his side. A beautiful high relief carving adorned the sides and seemed to depict a cavalry battle. It took some doing to find a name.

"Leopold II. Died 1773," I breathed to myself, reading from the carving by the feet.

My whispered voice echoed against the stone walls. The effigy had its head toward the far wall and his feet facing the doors. Curious as to how Leopold II was depicted, I made my way to the head. The sculpted face was bearded and seemed at once stern and deeply peaceful. I leaned closer, working up the courage to touch the frozen countenance.

I shuddered as images of his remains crept into my mind's eye. After more than two centuries I wondered if there was anything left other than dust. How long did it take for bodies to decay? Would his ghost be able to lift the stone lid and confront me?

Just as the tips of my fingers brushed Leopold's stone cheek, a cold current of air strong enough to disturb my hair caressed my face and tickled over my left ear. It was as if Leopold II had breathed on me.

I fell back in horror, nearly tripping off the dais. Even so, I managed to clamp my hand over my mouth and muffle the scream that the breath of a ghost had torn from my lungs.

Even as I watched, the expression on the white stone face of the effigy moved and darkened, as if it had come alive. My heart leapt into my throat. My mind raced to provide a rational explanation: A trick of the moonlight? Outside, as cloud began again to obscure the moon entirely, the beam streaming from the windows above abandoned Leopold II's face and painted the stone wall just behind his head with a blue-white light, and then faded to nothing.

The muffled scream that had escaped through my fingers was still echoing inside the mausoleum as the doors opened with a metallic groan. I whirled around to see Augustin and Yves leaning on them with all their weight.

It took all my willpower not to bolt out in terror. Instead, I tried to emerge with something that approximated dignity.

Apparently I had managed to stifle my scream well enough to prevent it from being heard above the creak of the metal doors. While Augustin and Yves closed them, I stood on the top stair, not quite sure what to do next.

A wide-eyed Bastien seemed to melt with relief. He gave me a big hug. I started to tremble uncontrollably and hoped no one could tell.

"Name your ancestral patron," Augustin ordered.

Still shaken from my encounter and the cold and ghostly breath, my voice cracked at first when I tried to speak.

"Leopold II," I managed, his being the only name I had seen.

Augustin frowned. "Unacceptable. He's my patron."

It had been a calm evening until then, but a gust of wind blew from the direction of the mausoleum, hard enough to make the trees groan loudly and shower snow down from the upper branches.

"Let's get out of here," Bastien said, obviously spooked. Then, without waiting for our agreement, he took off for the manor.

I had no ancestral patron, but there was little time to dwell on it. Bastien's urge to flight was contagious, and it was only a second later that we were all running through the snowy forest and back to the manor.

The Grand Foyer was empty at that hour. Augustin hid the mausoleum key under the stone near the main entrance and we ducked inside one of the side doors.

BACK IN THE corner suite headquarters, we gathered around as Yves lit the kindling in the imposing fireplace. Augustin, Yves, and Bastien listened with rapt attention while I described the inside of the mausoleum, though I held back the more "ghostly" details. Augustin and Yves seemed more than satisfied with my description of the unreadable plaques on the wall crypts, and the intricate carvings on Leopold II's sarcophagus.

"You have done well," Yves said, after I finished.

He was fully in character and we all grinned at him. I was happy to be rid of the mausoleum and everyone was getting into the spirit of a game that had essentially evolved on its own. Later that night, Augustin and Yves even invented a set of three rules for the newly formed Bureau of Secrets:

"First," Augustin said, as we huddled together under blankets, sipping whisky in front of the fireplace. "Unless given specific authorization, no member of the Bureau of Secrets may engage in a solo mission. Mission security means working together."

"Second," Yves added, "no member of the Bureau may spy on another member."

"Exactly," Augustin said. "Third, every member pledges to keep all activities of the Bureau a secret from any nonmember."

Augustin glared at us all. "Is that entirely clear?"

"Yes," we all intoned, in perfect unison.

After that Augustin and Yves even invented a series of secret hand signals. Three fingers (a nod to the three rules) pointed to the eye was code for "they are watching us," to the ear meant "they are listening to us." Three fingers in the air or a low whistle was used as the "all-clear" signal (though Bastien had trouble whistling at all).

"She must return to the mausoleum to pick a proper patron," Augustin said, once the hand signals had been developed.

"Of course," Yves said. "In the meantime, we must discuss the first assignment for our new agent. Yes? What mission should we give her?"

Augustin pondered the matter for a long time before answering. "Before the formal dinner, she must identify the highest-ranked guest visiting the estate this weekend."

Yves grinned at me. "Do you have any questions?"

I had many, and no idea how I would go about uncovering such a mystery, but, not wanting to appear immature, I nodded my assent instead.

⟋◯⟍

CLOISTERED IN THE "new headquarters," we spent hours that night just sitting by the fire, joking, teasing, and talking about nothing at all. Aside from a half glass or two of wine over the course of a four-hour dinner, I was entirely inexperienced with alcohol. The whisky was strong and, not one hour after our return, I had consumed enough to give me a serious buzz. In retrospect, perhaps my increasingly intoxicated state contributed to the carefree, romanticized ambience that, in my memory at least, surrounded that evening. Still, inebriated or not, it was one of those special nights with my brothers (and Yves) that would stay with me for a long time. It was also the last time I would feel that way with any of them.

A small part of me was annoyed that Bastien had gotten a reprieve from any initiation or hazing ritual but, in those moments, I hardly wanted to rock the boat given that our remarkable tetrarchy had been restored.

It was nearly two in the morning when, much to my disappointment, our collective, reclining bundle finally broke up and we all retired to our respective apartments.

Though I never mentioned the ghost's breath to any of them, once I was alone in my bedroom a fear began to grow within me: the certainty that I had somehow awakened malevolent spirits by trespassing in their tombs and defiling, by my touch, the face of Leopold II's effigy.

As I lay in bed, imagined images of my ancestors slowly decaying in stone vaults or sarcophagi alarmed me to no end. After a sleepless hour feeling as if my canopy bed might also be a tomb, I indulged myself in a habit I had acquired years before. I climbed up to the manor's top floor and took the spiral stairs up to the roof and the safety of what was by that time a huge, star-filled sky. After all, malevolent spirits haunted dark, enclosed spaces, not rooftops beneath the celestial dome (or so I hoped).

Astronomy and the contemplation of far-off worlds being a continuing obsession of mine, I spent some time looking at constellations, and then sought out the base of the spire with the loose stone I had found some years earlier. I took it out and there, in the space where I hid trinkets and messages to myself, used a rusty nail to carve my initials backward in a not particularly convincing effort to cast some kind of a spell of protection against whatever dark forces I might have awoken.

My foray into the mausoleum on that particular night evoked in me something that evolved into an abiding fear of (and respect for) apparitions, spirits, ghosts, and the supernatural. Had Yves and my eldest brother not picked that specific task on that specific evening, had they invented some other initiation trial for me to endure, I doubt Augustin's story of Sophia would have impacted me so. But for these moments, and the peculiar way they aligned, I might have a far different story to tell. Or none at all.

I lingered on the roof for a time, trying to work out how I might solve the mystery of the highest-ranked guest, but the wind started to come up and eventually it was too cold to stay, so I dropped back down through the trapdoor, intending to make my way back to my apartments and finally get to sleep.

But it was not to be.

⁓

CHAPTER FIVE

The Ghost of Sophia

I T WAS WELL AFTER MIDNIGHT WHEN I saw her.

I had just reached the back stairs on the fourth floor and taken them down one level when it happened. Something at the edge of my hearing, something that did not sound as if it had been caused by the wind, stopped me on the third-floor landing. Alone, in the dark, and with a healthy, if newfound, respect for the supernatural, any shuffling sound or creak might have caused me to freeze in my tracks like a ghost-hunting pointer dog, but this was something different.

There were no lights or candles in the hallway, but the moon's bluish-white light streamed down at a high angle and into the windows that lined one side of the hallway, printing window-shaped patches of moonlight between dark shadows on the hallway's stone floor and illuminating the passage just enough to see.

After standing frozen in an unnatural position for so long that my calves began to ache, and yet detecting nothing, I made to continue downstairs. Before I could, I heard a whisper just audible above the ambient creaks and fluttering of wind in the third-floor hallways. I was certain I had not imagined it a second time and, peering down the gloomy corridor, I saw, to my horror, that I was right.

About a hundred feet away at the very end of the hall was the wispy figure of a young girl, maybe fifteen or sixteen, pale against the darkness of the far shadow, and completely nude. Her little white breasts gleamed in what reflected moonlight reached her, and behind her flowed straight, long, straw-colored hair that fanned out in the air as she moved. I couldn't believe my eyes and my heart was quickly in my throat.

She glided from the stairwell on the left side of the far end of the hall and drifted in total silence across to the bedroom door opposite the stairs. If the door was locked, the apparition seemed unfazed by that physical constraint and disappeared into, I assumed, the bedroom beyond.

That is when I realized which part of the manor I was in: the third floor of the West Wing.

Sophia, a voice in my head whispered. *Your murdered sister.*

A YEAR BEFORE I had read parts of *Physica Curiosa*, an illustrated, twelve-volume, encyclopedic collection by the Jesuit Gaspar Schott printed in 1667. Our library had a magnificent set of the works, which covered a diverse set of subjects ranging from "miracles of visions (apparitions)" to "miraculous things about meteorites."

According to those texts, spirits were often made restless when not buried properly and could manifest themselves as apparitions, or reincarnate themselves in future generations of the same line. If my murdered sister Sophia had not been properly buried, her restless spirit might be doomed to forever haunt the bedroom and the halls where she had been slain. As the only relative who seemed concerned with her astral fate, didn't it fall to me to help her find a proper resting place?

Despite my fears, I vowed to try to communicate with her. Surely, I thought, she would recognize an ally, particularly a family member, and refrain from using her supernatural powers (whatever those might be) to harm me.

Drawing on some reserve of courage, I managed to tiptoe all the way down the hall toward the closed bedroom door. As I inched closer, it was obvious that noises were coming from inside. They sounded first like the tearful pleadings of a young girl, and then, with her appeals denied, heavy breathing and soft sobs of resignation.

Scarcely believing I was not in a dream, I pushed down on the door lever gently, praying that if it was unlocked, the old mechanism wouldn't squeak as I manipulated it, but the door was both unbolted and mercifully quiet, as if it had been recently oiled.

Opening the door just a crack and peering inside, I saw a small guttering candle atop a dusty table illuminating the room, which was odd. I couldn't figure out why a ghost might resort to candlelight, and the taper itself did not appear astral in nature.

In the center of the floor was a mattress. A male figure was lying on it, his eyes closed as if he was concentrating on something intently. Between his legs was a full head of long, blond hair that bobbed rhythmically to the pace of some silent metronome.

There was nothing remotely ghostly about either of these figures. The illusion was shattered and I recognized both of them: my brother Augustin and Cipriana. Nude and pale though she had been in the glare of the moonlight, it was obvious to me that she was no ghost.

~⊙~

AS GINGERLY AS I could, I closed the door and eased the latch back into place before creeping backward into the hallway. I went slowly at first before turning and almost breaking into a run. I barely made it to the halfway point again before I thought I heard a creak behind me.

Without looking back, I ducked into one of the bedroom doorway alcoves on the left side of the hallway and pressed myself into the corner, listening intently.

I waited for a full minute before peeking out and looking for my pursuer. Nothing.

I crawled as far as I could, back into the protection of the alcove, and sat down with my knees tucked into my chest and my back against the door. I stayed there to catch my breath.

Even with several minutes to consider the matter, I'm not sure I could have explained what Augustin and Cipriana had been doing. But it was clear enough to me that it was illicit, vaguely if not overtly coercive, and that there would be some kind of trouble if either of them discovered that I had seen them.

I resolved to slip back into the hallway and quick-walk to the stairway, but the door I was leaning on felt funny on my back. I turned to look in what little moonlight was seeping into the hallway and saw them: vertical scratches in the wood running down from the door handle nearly to the floor. Something about them seemed almost familiar and, almost unconsciously, I reached out to feel the grooves with the very tips of my fingers. They were deep scores, as if an animal had been trying to get in.

My encounter at the end of the hall was forgotten in an instant.

"Grandfather's dogs," I whispered, remembering what Augustin had said about their scratching.

I knew then that I was looking at the door to Sophia's tomb.

THE COMBINATION OF curiosity and terror has always been irresistible to me. That same urge that, in fiction, tempts the heroine to her doom, though she knows better. No matter what horrors I might find inside, I reasoned with myself, how could I abandon my sister's tomb?

I stood and addressed the door, fully expecting it to be locked. But when I pressed the latch down it gave easily before being wrenched out of my hand. It flew open with a loud bang. I was terrified before I understood what had happened: someone had left one of the windows partly open, and as the pressure between the long hallway and the room equalized, the door had been yanked from my hand.

Augustin and Cipriana were a long way down the hall and obviously occupied with other matters, but I listened intently for a couple of tense moments anyway. The hallway remained still, so I crept into the abandoned bedroom and closed the door behind me to keep it from blowing around again.

The air was frigid from the open window and my breath turned to frost.

A sign of the presence of ghosts, I thought, remembering a passage I'd read in *Physica Curiosa*.

A couple of dusty bedsheets covered pieces of furniture. I ignored them and opened the large closet, where I nearly tripped on some old hangers that had been left on the floor.

I found it tucked away in the very back corner of the closet: a dust-covered travel trunk with a frail-looking inset lock and worn leather handles. I had almost missed it in the dark. When I looked closer, I could see that it was filthy and covered in grime, but I worked up the courage to start fiddling with the chest's oily lock.

It was stubborn but I repurposed a hanger into a sort of pry bar and forced the hook into the tiny keyhole to manipulate the pins the best I could. A muffled "pop" sounded as something inside the lock gave way. I had broken it, and when I pulled, the old latch came away easily.

The trunk's lid was heavy and the hinges sticky, so I knelt down and pushed up on it with both hands, leaning into it with all my weight and pressing with my legs until, all of a sudden, it came unstuck. It swung up easily. Too easily. I was caught off guard and half-fell into the open trunk. There I found myself face-to-face with the contents of the dusty container.

From the gloom of the trunk, staring up at me, eyeless, was the porcelain-white, bleached-bone skull of a small child.

~⌒~

I REMEMBER HEARING MYSELF scream. Gripped with terror, I must have flown into the hallway and down two flights of stairs. The next thing I remembered clearly was the sickening cracking sound when, after tripping while descending to the ground floor, I smashed my mouth against the marble banister that led up from the manor's Grand Foyer. I saw stars for a moment and crumpled into a heap. The pain started in immediately, but it was something else entirely that overwhelmed me: the realization that I was not alone and, even well after midnight, the room I had tumbled into was rather brightly lit.

I will never forget the look of horror I saw on Lucas's face. I can only imagine what he must have thought as this awful wretch of a creature covered in oily grime from an old steamer trunk bounced off the banister and crash-landed on the cold marble floor in front of him. His impression could not have been improved by the sight of the bright red streams of crimson that started to pour from my mouth and splatter onto the front of my white nightdress. Tears and blood dribbled together onto the floor as I blubbered hysterically.

I had just managed to get out the salient points—body . . . little girl . . .

Sophia . . . murder . . . travel chest . . . third floor—when I realized that Lucas was not alone and, once I began to absorb my circumstances, I was quite glad that I had not managed to get to the part about Augustin and Cipriana.

Two couples dressed in formalwear accompanied my mother and father in the Grand Foyer, obviously about to take their leave at the tail end of their long evening. I might well have continued my frantic exposition, but the realization that I was bleeding all over myself, and the collective look of dismay my audience wore (excepting my father), were enough to shock me into silence.

Lucas was the first to recover. Though he had been rocked back on his heels by my sudden and ghoulish appearance, in a flash he was kneeling in front of me, once again the epitome of the unflappable captain of the domestic staff. He produced from somewhere, almost as if he had planned for just such an eventuality, a dark red handkerchief. He worked quickly with the makeshift dressing to stanch the flow of blood, though it had already formed a small pool—blots of darkening red atop polished white stone—on the floor beneath me.

"Well now, a bit of an injured lip, have we? No teeth unseated, it seems. No need for the doctor to make the long trip, I think," Lucas announced, more, I suspected, for the benefit of our stunned guests than anyone else. "Had a bit of a fright, did we?"

"You must forgive my daughter," my mother started, just as the maids arrived and began to clean up the splatters of my blood.

"But she is not badly hurt . . . the young woman?"

It was the most senior member of the party, a tall gentleman with a pair of miniature medals pinned to the left breast of his overcoat. He had a severe port-wine stain on his cheek. In other circumstances, I might have stared at it.

"Oh, I think not," my mother said. "Are you mending now, dear?"

I knew my mother's look well. *You will cease this foolishness and comport yourself with the decorum expected of a daughter of the line*, it hissed at me.

Unable to speak, I murmured through the handkerchief and nodded while Lucas tried to keep my trembling hands away from my mouth to avoid another bright outpouring of red.

"No need to call the doctor?" my mother wondered aloud.

Despite her tone, I knew that she wasn't actually asking. I shook my head.

"There now. She is the youngest, you know," my mother gave to her guests by way of explanation. "And, because my husband tolerates my excessive sentimentality, we indulge her far more than is prudent." Her lie delivered, she turned to Lucas again. "Have that in hand, do we now, Lucas?"

"Yes, madam. Quite settled. Just a bit of a cut. At this age they bleed a bit more than the wound itself would warrant."

With this Lucas began, not all that patiently or gently, to herd me away and out of view.

"Please," my mother singsonged to her guests in her most welcoming and persuasive voice. "A little something before you depart for the evening? I wouldn't want such a scene to be the last impression of your visit. Please, join us in the Alsatian Salon? As I recall, the chef has some Almas beluga. I'll have something prepared."

With this irresistible temptation (surely caviar was far more appealing than a bleeding guttersnipe of a little girl) the party was diverted from their impending departure and melted away in the direction of the nearby salon.

Just as they were departing, the gentleman with the port-wine stain on his cheek shed his overcoat and handed it to a waiting member of the domestic staff. By chance, the candlelight in the Grand Foyer struck the leftmost insignia on his dinner jacket just so. When it caught my eye I recognized it easily: a badge of the senior member of an archducal order.

I had found the highest-ranked guest on the estate.

PART II

THE COURSE OF EMPIRES

~

CHAPTER SIX

Sic Semper

I WAS PROMPTLY (AND QUITE STERNLY) cleaned up and sent to my rooms, where I lay trembling and tonguing the throbbing gouges on the inside of my mouth. Despite Lucas's minimizing of my wounds in front of our guests, in private there had been talk of flying Dr. Ebner to the estate to give me stitches, but no one had followed through on that particular threat.

I was still sleepless when the clock in my anteroom struck two in the morning. Just a few minutes after that, I heard footsteps inside my apartments. By the determined gait I knew it could only be Lucas. Sure enough, having let himself into my rooms and after only the most cursory of knocks on my bedroom doors, he stalked in and made the announcement official.

"Your father requires your presence in the Grand Study. Immediately."

After changing into presentable clothes and being escorted down by Lucas, I found both my parents waiting for me behind my father's desk. I curtsied formally before I dared look at them.

My mother hadn't even changed out of her evening gown, and that was not a good sign. She glared at me with such intensity that I had to focus on her pale forehead to avoid her gaze. Because I had her eyes, it was always difficult looking at her when she was angry; a bit like locking eyes with some predatory version of myself.

By contrast, my father's expression seemed passive. I tried to imagine that his gray eyes were merely intrigued, but I feared that a great temper lurked behind them.

"Well?" my mother said, and I could tell that she had already lost some modicum of the icy control she was normally famous for. A knot started to form in my abdomen.

I had no idea what to say so I just looked at my feet.

"What is all this nonsense about dead children and bodies?" she demanded.

Had I blurted that out in the foyer?

"Well?" she bellowed again. There was such a sharp snap to her voice that I jumped.

"The body, in the chest," I started to sob. "In the West Wing. On the third floor."

My mother was incredulous. "What . . . *body?*"

"Sophia's," I choked out.

"What on earth are you talking about?"

Maybe she doesn't know, I thought. *Augustin could have been wrong about her involvement. Father could have covered it up on his own.*

No one, it occurred to me then, would have asked many questions about the sudden silence of a troublesome girl who cried endlessly day and night.

My father looked at Lucas and cocked his head at the door. Lucas performed a curt bow and vanished.

I was so shaken that there was a moment when I might even have tried to explain what I had seen Augustin and Cipriana doing, but the reprimand that my mother delivered stopped me cold.

"This sort of thing simply cannot go on. *It simply cannot go on.*" My mother was only in the habit of repeating the second half of her sentences with more emphasis when she was very upset. "It seems obvious that I was wrong to assume you could be treated as an adult; that we had no need to consider sending you to boarding school. That error will now be corrected, I can assure you."

My stomach lurched. Though it obviously meant seeing some part of the world beyond the estate, just the mention of being sent away filled me with despair. Worst of all, far away at boarding school, I would be separated from my grandfather. Our late-night talks would be over for good. Silently, I hoped that it was only a bit of bluff, like Dr. Ebner and the stitches. But my mother seemed quite intent to actually follow through on this threat.

My father watched me with a detached sort of curiosity and I focused on him to keep from breaking down. I was certain he was waiting for me to reveal the secret of Sophia so that he could calmly explain away my narrative and make a fool of me. He would have planned for this moment, after all. My father planned for every moment. I had never seen him caught off guard by anything.

"I had deluded myself into thinking that, given your breeding, you didn't need the usual amount of structure for a girl your age," my mother continued. "It seems I was mistaken, as it is obvious now that, when you are afforded any degree of freedom, you take advantage of that liberty to ruin an important evening.

"You destroy your clothes, and present yourself to our guests as if you were some ghastly, Dickensian street urchin fresh from the graveyard stealing bones and corpses. Our most important guests were mortified; *mortified, do you understand?*"

Tears were running down my cheeks and onto the floor when Lucas finally returned.

"The . . . child corpse, milord," he intoned and, without much ado, placed Sophia's remains on one of the chairs across from my father's desk. I drew back, horrified that her body should be so crudely handled, but then I saw it.

What had been obscured in the grimy shadows of a dark closet was obvious in the light of the Grand Study. "Sophia" was an antique, porcelain-faced doll covered in dust. Where her glass eyes once were there was nothing but empty sockets, giving her face the appearance of a bleached skull. In an instant I was sure that there had been no Sophia, no murdered sister, no bones, no dead girl's corpse locked away in a travel trunk; only an old doll in the dark and the shame of being taken in by Augustin's well-executed, if cruel, prank.

I SPENT THE NEXT two days alone in my rooms. The door was locked from the outside with a key left in it, making it impossible for me to open it from within. I found myself hoping that Bastien might visit, but his continued absence made me wonder if he had been forbidden to see me.

I was not permitted to leave even for meals, which were instead brought to me by the domestic staff (though not, I noticed, by Cipriana). I wondered after her. I had grown up sheltered in more ways than one and, that winter, the concept of sex was not just a mystery of some sort—illuminated only by the dim and subtle light of oblique double entendres I found buried in seventeenth-century literature now and again—but, in practice, entirely alien to me. The only person I could imagine talking to about it all was my grandfather and I feared that this solace was soon to be denied me as well.

I spent most of that second evening reading old books and whiling away the hours staring out my windows until the light faded, the color leaked out of the landscape bit by bit, and darkness won over and blanketed the estate.

Cipriana was the last person I expected to see but, right around midnight, there was a timid knock and, when I answered from behind the closed doors, there was the sound of the key turning in the lock. The doors opened and she was there, eyes downcast and curtsying to me shyly. Even as I urged her inside, she hesitated, casting furtive looks down the hallway before allowing me to pull her into my foyer and close the doors.

We didn't speak a word. Instead, after she sat in one of the chairs in my foyer, it wasn't five seconds before I found myself curled up in her lap, crying softly while she stroked my hair and softly shushed me; she was returning the favor, I suppose, for the warmth I had showed her in Bastien's rooms. When I looked up at her, the yellow light from the candelabra she had lit glistened off tear streaks under her eyes. Concerned, I made as if to sit up, but she pulled me close, cradling my head and drying my tears with the back of her hand.

She was warm and the scent of her hair reminded me of lilac or perhaps jasmine. It wasn't long before I had fallen asleep and, when I woke later, curled up alone in the chair, she was gone and my doors were locked once more. I might have thought her presence a dream but for the quilt she had taken from my linen closet and covered me with before she left.

<hr />

I WAS FINALLY GIVEN my liberty the next evening, after an anonymous member of the staff had left a late dinner in my foyer. Being confined to my apartments was a rare punishment, but it was lifted in the same way it had been on past occasions. Nothing was announced or explained. Instead, there was only the sound of the key turning to unlock my doors and receding footsteps that echoed down the halls of the residential wing.

I crept up to the third-floor bedroom that I had taken for Sophia's grave and looked carefully at the door. It was locked but I could see that the scratches in the door were fresh. I had been fooled in the heat of the moment, but a more careful inspection made it obvious that the marks were made with a sharp knife, or a razor, rather than the claws of my grandfather's long-dead dogs.

Tempted at first, I didn't dare chance the headquarters of the Bureau of Secrets, or Augustin's or Bastien's doors. Instead, I went back to my apartments and sulked.

⌒

JUST BEFORE ONE in the morning, I wandered down the stairs. Thankfully, I found the Grand Library and the Grand Study beyond it empty. I crept into the hall and toward the East Salon. I was unsure of myself until I heard the distinct sound of a wooden match strike and the soft hiss of a new flame. My grandfather was awake.

I waited just outside to make sure he was alone. I looked down at the latch and saw that a lock had been installed since my last visit. That seemed unusual but, finding his door ajar, I knocked anyway. It swung open a bit when I touched it and I could smell his pipe tobacco thick in the air that I had stirred up. It made me feel warm and calm for the first time in days.

"Don't lurk about out there, my dear," he beckoned. "Come in."

I sat at his desk for a long time, trying to exorcise myself of the awful feeling of hopelessness and despair that my mother's threat had, like a filmy residue, left behind. My grandfather was used to long silences from me, but the pain must have shown because he capped his fountain pen and put his papers down to look at me.

"My dear, what on earth could be wrong?" he said.

I could not imagine he was acting, but nor could I believe that he had not been privy to the recent drama. I was already ashamed to look so weak, but he gave me the kindest expression and I knew there was no way to keep it from spilling out. And spill it did: a blur of a confession that I had no hope of stopping once it began.

Though, initially, I was vague about the Bureau of Secrets, omitted entirely our foray to the mausoleum, and managed to avoid directly mentioning Augustin's name or the scene with Cipriana—a memory that evoked some deeply confused species of shame that made me want to cry even harder—I am quite sure my grandfather had his guesses about the source of the tale of Sophia. Then, after briefly (but quite skillfully) ferreting out details about the illicit club that I had sworn to keep secret, he fell into a pensive silence, listening patiently through the entirety of my tearful explanation, and chewing on his pipe thoughtfully now and again.

"Now they want to send me to boarding school," I said. "And then I will be far away, and you will not be able to visit me because you are too busy with your many pursuits."

Though I had managed to stem the tears about midway through my exposition, they started up again in earnest.

My grandfather's eyebrows rose and he looked at me for a long time; so long that he exhausted his pipe, methodically tapped it out, and repacked it with fresh tobacco before striking another long wooden match. He watched the flame crawl down the matchstick to burn off the sulfur that doubtless would have tainted the flavor had he been hastier. After several long puffs, the smoke curled around his head and the tendrils drifted unhindered about the East Salon. His eyes followed them up to the ceiling and lingered there before he looked at me again.

"Well, one thing is for certain. You have inherited this family's affinity for intrigue." He chuckled, but then his expression grew stern, and that was unlike him. "However, it is important for you to understand something. Are you listening?"

"Yes, Grandfather."

"On this estate intrigues are everywhere, but it can be hazardous for you to pursue those you happen to uncover. Creating them anew is more dangerous still. I know that your curiosity burns, but you must begin to appreciate that some secrets are actually dangerous to learn." My grandfather paused to see that I was absorbing his meaning. He puffed on his pipe. "And there are still others that must be earned," he added, almost to himself.

"Earned?" I said, but my grandfather seemed not to hear.

"I have perhaps overindulged your sleuthing and eavesdropping."

I looked down at my hands and felt my cheeks get hot. It also occurred to me that, in telling him about it, I had broken the third rule of the Bureau of Secrets.

"There is nothing for it," he said, after a few reflective puffs on his pipe. He looked up at the ceiling through his eyebrows and spoke as if ruminating privately. "I expect it is a habit we will not be able to curb. But, perhaps we might begin to direct your curiosity a bit more productively." He looked at me once more and his eyebrows rose playfully. "Yes?"

I wasn't at all sure what he meant, but his warm expression put me at ease and so I nodded.

"I don't want to go to boarding school, Grandfather."

My grandfather puffed on his pipe furiously, reflecting. I hoped he would say something comforting, but when he came out of his reverie, he only bid me kiss him good night and then shooed me off to bed.

I CHANCED OUR "SECRET headquarters" the next day, but they were no more. The table, chairs, couches, and crystal decanters had been removed and sheets laid over the remaining furniture. Even the fireplace had been cleaned. It was as if our clandestine base had erased itself after I had betrayed my fellow agents by breaking the third rule.

I went back to my rooms and tried to sleep but woke from a half-conscious state convinced I had heard something outside my doors. Frozen in bed, I listened intently, but the sounds did not recur.

Still awake almost an hour later, and with the glow of the sun below just starting to tease the Alps on the eastern horizon, noises from outside brought me to my windows. Yves and Augustin were in the circle driveway with a contingent of the domestic staff. As I watched, their luggage was packed into one of the estate's Land Rovers, and the staff was assembled to see them off. Only then did I realize that they were going back to school.

At first I couldn't believe it. By my count they still had some weeks before classes started again. Had I had lost all track of the date? And why had no one thought (or cared) to tell me of their imminent departure so that I could go down and render my farewells? Even with the ups and downs, the four of us had all been on the estate together for more than a month, and I suppose that I had imagined (or at least silently wished) it to be permanent.

Once I understood what was happening, I had the most powerful urge to rush down the stairs, fly into their arms, and bid them goodbye. But I was too terrified of being rebuffed by Augustin (or, God forbid, Yves) to move. Instead, I just watched helplessly as the Land Rover pulled away and slowly disappeared around the first bend on its way to the main gate and the outside world beyond.

For a time I liked to remember that Yves took one last look up at my windows before climbing into the Land Rover and closing the door, but now I think that I invented that particular detail.

~⊙~

SHORTLY AFTER THE Land Rover had gone, I solved the mystery of their early departure and the strange sounds that woke me. A folded piece of paper had been tacked to the outside of my doors. Opening it, I found a note scrawled in Latin:

SIC SEMPER PRODITORIBUS

Thus always to traitors, I translated in my head.

It was a play on the words Brutus was supposed to have said after he and his coconspirators stabbed Julius Caesar to death on the Senate floor. I recognized the handwriting immediately: Augustin's. The text was written in blue, but the paper had then been splashed with a dark red ink that, at first, I took for blood. It was shocking enough that I actually dropped the note right there in the hall before recovering my wits.

Later that morning, I overheard one of the maids discussing Augustin and Yves's early departure. Unaware of my eavesdropping, she let slip that my mother had ordered their deportation. With that detail in mind, I thought I understood the note: Augustin blamed me for being sent away early, and likely for good reason.

~

CHAPTER SEVEN

Uninvited Guests

EARLY THAT AFTERNOON, LUCAS APPEARED AT my apartments bearing an engraved invitation atop a silver tray.

"Mademoiselle," he sneered, as he lowered the tray to me.

It was a subtle insult our head butler, habitually effete and notoriously intolerant of children, enjoyed delivering. Once he had served me with the document, he turned smartly on his heel and departed.

The invitation was a summons to dinner three nights later in the Grand Dining Hall. The Hall was a weapon, and woe to the guest (or member of the family) who came to this realization belatedly. The room, while stunning, was not an end unto itself, but rather a vessel to house the enormous dining room table, supposedly carved hundreds of years before from a single stone slab. It was an imposing fixture that was long enough to seat twenty-five on each side and two each at the head and the foot of the table, and wide enough to accommodate the most elaborate centerpieces in addition to full place settings. Attending an event with the table in full bloom was both memorable and intimidating.

It was just like my mother to stage dramatic announcements in this way. Somehow, I just knew dinner would go badly for me.

~⊙

WHEN MY BELL rang later that night, I realized that I had been sitting idle; staring at my empty dinner plate for an hour. I opened my doors to find

Bastien and, happy for any company at all, I swept him into my apartments and brewed tea for him in my foyer. He was oddly quiet, which was unlike him. I had to prod him to trigger even the most rudimentary small talk. Finally, after a long silence between us, he volunteered something.

"I'm leaving tomorrow," he said, and his voice was so devoid of emotion I thought he must be acting. But, when he looked into my eyes, I knew he wasn't. "They are sending me away to the music conservatory in Vienna. Mother told me this afternoon."

"Bastien, that can't be right."

"They packed my bags for me, you know. I guess they didn't think I could do that myself."

That horrible sinking feeling that I felt while my mother had been chastising me returned.

"They can't just send you away," I said.

But I knew that they could, and I remember thinking that my mother had had her fill of children that season, and that it was my performance that had pushed her over the edge.

The thoughts that followed were selfish. After Bastien, I was next. We were, all of us, to be swept far away and out of her sight.

For a moment, it seemed he might embrace me and I started to cry. But, rather than close the distance between us, he started to cry too. I reached for him but he buried his face in the crook of his elbow before fleeing into the outside hallway. I went after him but before I could stop him, he ran down the corridor and was gone.

I was losing one of my last allies on the estate and there was nothing I could do about it.

I SAW THE STRANGE little man for the first time the next day in the Grand Library.

They hadn't even waited until the sun broke the horizon to ship Bastien away. I had hoped to bid him farewell in the circle driveway, as I had wanted to do for Augustin and Yves, but he was gone well before dawn. I pretended I didn't care, but deep down I was crushed. In weak moments—and there were many of them in the hours that followed—Augustin's horrible note would flash in front of my eyes and I would wince and try to will it away.

In the absence of playmates, I turned to the Grand Library for distraction. On one of the upper floors I had found a musty tome: a five-hundred-plus-page work possessed of such histrionic and sensationalistic prose as to be an affront to serious scholars of revolutionary France everywhere. Nevertheless, the text was somehow engrossing:

> Who can read without horror the details of M. de Sombreuil, saved by the heroic devotion of his virgin daughter from the massacres of September?— and at what a cost! The ruffians extracted from her, as the price of her father's liberty, that she should drink a cup of human blood, reeking hot from the wounds of a newly murdered victim. The fate of the Princess de Lamballe was accompanied with atrocities which the mind can hardly conceive, and which the pen refuses to trace.

The boarding school threat loomed large in my imagination and I could not shake the certainty that I had some larger affinity with the Princess de Lamballe.

In midsentence, I was shocked back into the world of the living by the sound of a contemplative "hmmm" just behind me. I bolted upright in my chair and turned around. I had been certain that the library was empty.

A diminutive man of sixty or perhaps even seventy years old, crowned with a thick head of unruly white hair, peered over the tall, leather-clad back of one of the oversize chairs on the main floor of the reading room.

He was so short I hadn't seen him, slouched as he was into the depths of the chair. He wore a dramatic handlebar mustache, this being far more meticulously groomed than almost anything else about his person. From behind the high back he looked at me quizzically through a pair of round, silver, antique, wire-rimmed glasses. His eyes were barely distorted through the lenses and his gaze was unblinking; a gaze that was without even a hint of the deference I would have expected from a trespasser or, really, any guest without a title elevated enough to demand deference from me instead. On the contrary, this interloper seemed totally self-assured and at home in our library, as if he had as much right to be there as I had.

My mind raced. Who was this person and how had he gotten into the manor? Should I call out for help? But his rude stare fixed me in place until I finally blinked.

"And what exactly do you think you are doing?" I demanded.

It was an effort to mimic my mother's version of authoritative dialogue but, as soon as it came out, I realized that it sounded childish and defensive.

He only cocked his head a bit, as if homing in on something.

"You find it uninteresting?" His voice was pinched through a thick Austrian accent.

"What?"

"The text. It bores you."

"What?" I held the book up. "This?"

"You are reading more than one work?"

"Well, no. It's not boring," I said.

He squinted across the room at my upheld book. "Boring? The Revolution? The Terror? I should think not. Good. Very good."

He stood up and ambled over to me as if with great purpose.

"And what manner of . . ." he began, but he stopped after twisting his head comically to the side to read the cover more closely. "Oh no. *The Emperor wept*," he cried, with something akin to real anguish.

Having delivered this harsh indictment of my taste in reading material, he shook his head solemnly and made his way, head bowed, toward the reading room shelves.

"I had hoped for a decent text on the finances of the East India Company, but I find only a reader of nineteenth-century 'true crime' tabloids. *French* tabloids." He seemed to relish turning the word *French* into a barb, which, ever so slightly, improved my opinion of him. "It is unthinkable," he said. "*Unthinkable*."

I knew enough to be wounded by his verbal slight, but it had the effect of stoking the urge to please him. I strained to remember anything that might be helpful.

"There is a large section of works on finance here," I suggested. "I know there are some books on Italy—"

"—why it might occur to one to permit the word *finance* to linger in the same paragraph as *Italy* in the modern age is beyond me. Unthinkable. *Unthinkable.*" After a moment, his irritation softened. "History of finance, you say?"

"Well, I don't know about the history of finance, exactly, but finance, certainly."

My caution forgotten, I led him up to the second landing, where two dozen shelves on all things financial lined the walls. He followed me, walking with his hands interlaced behind his back, a posture that gave him a deliberate sort of rocking gait.

Looking at the shelves, he seemed mollified.

"Ah . . . ah," he sighed. "Yes. Thank you, indeed." With this (and a subtle wave of the back of his hand) I was dismissed.

Outside the library, suddenly at some remove from his person, I found myself freed from the spell the strange little man had apparently cast over me. I fled into the outer hallways, where I nearly collided with an already cross-looking Lucas.

"Lucas," I pled. "There is a very strange man in the library."

Lucas peered down his nose at me. "Indeed," he said, "some of us must suffer through the fact that there are many strange personages present within these walls," and, without waiting for a reply, he turned smartly on his heel and strode away toward whatever mysterious duties called for his attention.

As HARD AS I tried, I could not stem the inexorable flow of time and, before I knew it, I was getting dressed for the dinner I dreaded. Lucas announced me with great formality when I arrived at the Grand Dining Hall, but only my mother, my father, and a single guest—a woman, perhaps in her late fifties—were present.

"Frau Maddalene Fäber-Kaskel," my mother said, smiling, "this is our daughter."

My stomach fluttered as I curtsied and took my place.

Frau Fäber-Kaskel's dark eyes and stern-looking face brightened; a ravenous predator picking up the scent of fear that was surely wafting off me.

"Well," she allowed herself. She spoke with a raspy accent that might have passed for German, albeit savaged by decades of harsh, filterless European cigarettes. "Our newest pupil, I presume."

My father remained as unflappably stoic as ever. It was impossible to tell if he was one of the emerging plan's architects.

"Frau Fäber-Kaskel is the Headmistress at Academy Le Gudin," my mother beamed.

My stomach fluttered again, but from somewhere a flash of rebellion managed to flare up.

"Faber-Castell?" I said, adopting the most naïve-sounding tone I could manage. "I'm sure I just read that the Countess Faber-Castell played piano duets with Propaganda Minister Joseph Goebbels at the Berghof on D-Day. Is the countess perhaps your younger sister?"

Even as I delivered it, I was intensely proud of my insult. By my math the Countess Nina von Faber-Castell would have been seventy-two.

My mother chose that moment to inhale a large sip of wine and spent several moments recovering with as much poise as she was able. From Frau Fäber-Kaskel's reaction, I suspected she was unused to being addressed in such a fashion. My father had frozen, his glass half-lifted, watching to see what might happen next.

"Fäber-Kaskel," my mother said, emphasizing the correct pronunciation. "You must forgive our daughter. She has been out of sorts lately; not at all herself."

"I am quite . . ." I started, but my mother shot me such a look that my words caught in my throat.

The venerable headmistress recovered quickly.

"Well," she huffed. "I had certainly been aware that it has become fashionable in some less-informed circles to dispense with the mores of a traditional education and adopt a modern, that is to say a wholly unstructured, approach. I think we can all judge the wisdom of that method for ourselves."

She offered me a thin smile.

"By contrast, the approach at Academy Le Gudin has changed very little in the last 102 years. So many other administrations have found themselves unable to resist the siren song of coeducation, or the integration of *postmodernist* concepts into traditional curriculums."

The hatred that bled through the word *postmodernist* was visceral.

"How very refreshing," my mother said, and I wondered if she was referring to the Academy Le Gudin, or the hatred.

"Our girls enjoy a strictly supervised environment and are overseen by a faculty that appreciates the values of firm discipline, focused study, accountability, and surroundings untainted by the many distractions of modern life.

"We have also prepared many of our students from more prominent families for their first introduction to European society at one or more of the great coming-out balls. Some have met their future husbands for the first time, and more than one planned union between great families has been consummated in this way. We have been content to play our little part."

My mother nodded and gave the Headmistress a knowing smile. My eyes began to glaze over and much of what Frau Fäber-Kaskel said after that was lost in an anguished blur (though certain comments stood out as particularly soul-crushing).

As we drifted toward the end of the first hour, it became a constant effort to hold back the tears. One particular phrase almost broke the dam straining to contain my spiraling emotions.

"I do so look forward to working, *personally working*, with you at the Academy," the Headmistress rasped.

The third course was being taken away when Lucas appeared at the double doors and announced my grandfather and one "Herr Professor Dr. Dr. Jürgen Siegfried Lechner."

It was obvious from my parents' expressions that neither man had been expected.

"Father," my mother managed, after a halting pause.

She collected herself quickly and harnessed her surprise into a timbre that suggested that she regarded my grandfather's arrival as an unexpected pleasure.

"We hadn't planned to have you at dinner this evening," she said, and cut a sidelong glance at Lucas, who was studiously (and uncharacteristically) avoiding her gaze.

"Yes, I was out on the grounds discussing matters of philosophy with Professor Lechner for most of the day."

Distracted by my grandfather's arrival, I had somehow overlooked our new dinner guest. But once my attention drifted that way, I was surprised to recognize him: the strange little man from the library.

All eyes focused on the Professor, who, despite appearing to be a spontaneous guest, had somehow produced a perfectly tailored, black-tie evening-wear ensemble for the occasion, attire cut in a classical style that could easily have been more than a century or less than a decade old.

Frau Fäber-Kaskel fixed a bitter and suspicious gaze on the Professor. I could not have resisted that Gorgon glare, but the Professor's cheerful little smile did not waver.

"I expect I was not to be found earlier when Lucas sought to inform me of this evening's dinner schedule," my grandfather said. "How else would my invitation have been neglected? Still, I do apologize for the late arrival."

Startled members of the domestic staff hurried to arrange settings for the uninvited guests. It was a ballet that they performed with such speed and precision that, just as my grandfather was taking his place, the last of the silverware and glasses were being precisely arranged.

"And Professor . . . Lechner," my mother said. "How are you this evening? I'm sorry, but your arrival on the estate has taken me by surprise. Still, how nice to have you with us for dinner."

"I must thank you for your most generous hospitality," the Professor said, adding a subtle little bow. "Especially on short notice. It is quite wonderful to leave the bother of the city and escape to such a marvelous place. Even snow-covered, it is obvious that the landscaping, and your gardens in particular, are simply beyond compare."

This last was a clever bit of flattery. For a moment, my mother's smile had a hint of real warmth in it. It faded quickly.

My father was watching the proceedings with concealed (but to me quite palpable) interest. He signaled to Lucas, who bent down to whisper in his ear.

"We are honored to have as our dinner guest Frau Maddalene Fäber-Kaskel," my mother said.

"Madam," Professor Lechner said with another little bow, "I am charmed." Frau Fäber-Kaskel gave a decisively noncommittal smile in return.

"Professor, have you met our daughter?" my mother asked.

I froze in the midst of reaching for my water glass. I didn't quite understand why I should feel that my earlier interaction with this strange man should be some sort of secret, but it was a powerful emotion.

"Ah. Well, good evening, young lady," he beamed after turning to me and executing a slightly deeper bow than either my mother or Frau Fäber-Kaskel had warranted.

I nodded back to him as he sat and offered an inadvertently meek: "Good evening, Herr Professor."

The Professor's response had given almost nothing away. He hadn't lied about our prior meeting, exactly, but he had certainly misled. Eager for any camaraderie, I imagined that the Professor and I had formed some grand plot together.

"Well," my mother offered to the room, "we actually planned this dinner to make an announcement to our daughter but, since you are here, we are happy for you to share in the excitement. Frau Fäber-Kaskel has joined us to deliver the news that our daughter has been accepted into the Academy for the next term." My mother finished with a broad smile cast in my direction.

I felt sick. My grandfather was the first to react.

"This would be at the Academy Le Gudin?" he asked. I was crestfallen to see that his expression was bright and enthusiastic.

"Of course," my mother replied, smiling.

"That is quite an honor." My grandfather turned to me. "I understand that they are quite exclusive in their application process."

Apparently very pleased with herself, Frau Fäber-Kaskel gave the room a wolfish grin.

"Rather a structured program," Professor Lechner added. He turned to my mother. "She will be boarding at the Academy then?"

"Why, yes. The day students aren't afforded the same advantages as the boarding students. Also, living at the Academy allows a more substantial workload. She might graduate early if she applies herself."

"I see," my grandfather said. It was subtle, but a note of contemplative caution had crept into his voice. "And the educational trust will pay the tuition and fees?"

"Of course," my mother said, and turned to me. "I'm certain you will be much happier to be with girls your own age for a change."

In that moment, my mother's sanctimonious insistence that she had any idea what would make me happy was almost intolerable. I might have fallen apart then, but something in my father's expression anchored me. He was looking at my grandfather in the most curious way, as if he had seen something beneath the surface that had piqued his interest.

"So you've spoken to the trustee then?" my grandfather said.

"Sorry?" my mother said.

"You've given him a proposal?"

My mother had not expected this (or any) line of questioning, and there was hesitation before she answered. I sensed weakness there. So, it seemed, did Frau Fäber-Kaskel, whose smile had melted into the resting scowl that her face seemed to take up naturally.

"Well, surely this must be a mere formality," my mother said. "The trust's purpose is to provide funds to educate our children."

"I formed several trusts some years ago with my grandchildren as the beneficiaries," my grandfather explained to the Professor. "We are speaking of the educational trust. It is difficult, you realize, to create these structures when children are of disparate ages.

"Fairness is a difficult thing to build into the grant documents of these instruments. I believe in this case we have some language about the equality of opportunities to be afforded to each of the beneficiaries."

"Ah," the Professor said, "quite enlightened, indeed."

"You see," my grandfather said, looking thoughtful, "the trustee is likely to be rather prickly about being evenhanded. Unlike my oldest grandson, my younger grandson has not had the opportunity to live abroad and attend such a prestigious institution as Academy Le Gudin. Though I understand that he will be attending a music conservancy this year, I could imagine that the trustee will want some assurance that my granddaughter, though she has only known tutors here on the estate thus far, will not gain some advantage, financial or otherwise, by being sent off two years earlier than her older sibling."

My mother's expression darkened. Frau Fäber-Kaskel's jaw clenched repeatedly.

"Eva," my grandfather said to my mother, "I'm sure it can be worked out. After all, the trustee accepted your plan for Bastien, yes?"

My mother was at a loss for words, and it was obvious to all assembled that she had neglected this particular detail as well.

"Ah," my grandfather said. "Well, I do think the trustee will be rather annoyed at not being consulted, but I know him quite well. I will speak with him tomorrow."

"Well," my mother said, "certainly we wouldn't want to put the trustee in a difficult position as a fiduciary. There is always the possibility that we would manage the financial arrangements privately." My grandfather began to frown, but my mother pressed on. "And—"

"—hmm," my father interjected.

It was his first contribution to the exchange, but it was more than enough to silence the entire hall. All eyes darted to him, desperate to read his mood correctly.

My mother was the first to recover. "Then again," she said, "we wouldn't . . . mmm . . . want to frustrate the purpose of the very generous arrangements you've made for the children, Father. Maybe you should speak with the trustee first?"

My grandfather's pleased-looking expression returned; my father's concern seemed to evaporate, and Professor Lechner was sipping his wine with what I took to be feigned disinterest.

No one answered my mother's question. No one had to. Everyone seemed pleased with this development; everyone, that is, except for my mother and Frau Fäber-Kaskel.

"In the interim," my grandfather said, "until we make appropriate arrangements for the next evolution of her education, we would not want our youngest charge to fall behind. I recently learned that her studies here on the estate have been focused on matters of etiquette and decorum. Quite right. And yet, Eva, you are certainly correct that it is past the time that her education should be more formalized." My grandfather frowned for a moment, but then turned to the Professor. "Do you know, it occurs to me that you have had quite some experience in the education of young people, is that not so?"

Somehow, an incredulous huff escaped Frau Fäber-Kaskel. Everyone, except my mother, who looked absolutely horrified with her guest's rude outburst, ignored her.

"*Ach*," the Professor said. "Yes, it has been my privilege to oversee the studies of some very gifted students."

"The Professor is quite modest," my grandfather said. "You were, I believe, tutor to Archduke Felix of Austria during his exile, were you not?"

"Yes, indeed. Long ago. His father, the Emperor, was kind enough to grant me the appointment."

"Well, then, Professor. I should be quite relieved if you would take up the matter of my granddaughter's tutoring until we sort out the matter. I fear we have been rather negligent with her, and I would hate for her to matriculate to an institution known for academic rigor without the proper foundations.

"By a happy coincidence, we happen to have rather an extensive library right here in the manor. I should be very surprised indeed if we were not in possession of much of the material you might care to include in a curriculum appropriate for my granddaughter."

"Indeed, a most impressive collection," the Professor said. "I am afraid, however, that any course of study would be necessarily intensive, and I am far too old to return to the life of a daily commuter."

"I wouldn't hear of it. You must stay with us, of course. As you may have noticed, we have plenty of room. I would see to it you had everything you needed."

"A most generous offer," the Professor said, and turned to my mother. "And it would permit me to enjoy your superlative gardens during the approaching spring, madam. I imagine they are glorious to behold when the seasons turn."

My mother offered him only a thin smile.

"Then it is settled," my grandfather said. "Lucas?"

Our head butler appeared within moments.

"Professor Lechner has accepted appointment to the position of my granddaughter's tutor effective immediately. Please see to it that he has rooms and working space near the library suitable for his requirements."

"Certainly, milord," Lucas said, and then, almost to himself, "I believe I know just the place." With that, he vanished.

When I looked at my father again, my breath caught in my throat. His eyes were still locked on my grandfather, but across my father's mouth was the faintest, most subtle hint of a smile.

IT WOULD BE difficult to overstate the degree to which I enjoyed the remainder of our dinner. Frau Fäber-Kaskel barely said a word and seemed desperate to depart at the earliest opportunity.

After the dessert course, I was ushered to the Grand Foyer with the rest of the dinner party and made to bid the awful woman a polite farewell with a formal curtsy while the estate's helicopter pilot waited to ferry her back to her squalid lair.

As the group drifted off to pass the evening with their private pursuits, I saw my grandfather slip Professor Lechner a note with a wax seal on it. After the two of them had exchanged a quiet word, my grandfather caught my eye and cocked his head to one side. Taking the cue, I followed him.

He was waiting for me around the first corner in the hallway beyond the foyer. With the harridan vanquished, I suppose I had a self-satisfied smirk on my face, but I was surprised to see a stern look on his. He had transformed into something cold and calculating, a man I was not at all familiar with.

"Do not underestimate the seriousness of what has just happened," he scolded. "Gloating does not become you. One must never irritate one's rivals in defeat unless it is with purpose. Your mother will not be amused with me after this rather public setback.

"It was unwise of me to have done such a thing in front of outsiders. Unfortunately, there was no other way for me to prevail in that contest. Normally, I would be well overmatched by your mother in this particular theater, a theater where her strength is growing and mine weakening; and by the day, I might add. On the other hand, the outsider she selected as her pawn proved ideal for my purposes. Given the Headmistress's power over the Academy's admissions policy, I doubt they will accept you under any circumstances after the insult she suffered under our roof. But the fact that your mother's plans were thwarted by a technicality makes the insult that much more serious.

"There is a lesson in that. Do not allow the apparent elegance of a stratagem to lull you into overconfidence. The perfect strategy must still be implemented perfectly and, this being an impossible ideal to realize, imperfect implementation always has consequences that are difficult to anticipate."

His reference to consequences made me think of something else. "Grandfather," I said, "does this mean Bastien will return to the estate now too?"

My grandfather's expression darkened even more.

"You are clever enough to know that, in all likelihood, your recent antics are responsible for your mother's newfound fixation on sending the two of you away. I have expended nearly all my short-term political capital scuttling this Academy Le Gudin plan. Elsewhere, I have done as much as I can for your brother.

"Take a lesson from this: some battles must be abandoned before they are ever joined, and sometimes the sacrifices one must make strike near to home. If one lacks the stomach to make such difficult choices and to live with them thereafter, then one has no business whatsoever plotting intrigues.

"In the meantime, you must focus on yourself. You must take care that, in directing her anger at me, your mother does not also find excuse to focus any excess ire on you. Do not be overly satisfied with yourself. I have selfish reasons for intervening in this case, reasons that may not be solely in your interests. We shall forget past indiscretions, you and I, but there is a price I expect to extract for my forgiveness. It is time we directed your attentions to more dynastic concerns, and not necessarily those which your mother has designed for you.

"I know that you are too young to fully appreciate the opportunity you now have, but it is one for which I may pay rather dearly." My grandfather pointed a finger at me. "Do not squander it, do you understand?"

"Yes, Grandfather," I said.

And then he was gone, leaving me to wonder what other schemes might be at work behind the scenes and what part I was expected to play in them.

~

CHAPTER EIGHT

Academic Rivals

MY GRANDFATHER HAD NOT BEEN EXAGGERATING when he termed the Professor's appointment "effective immediately." I had barely finished my morning routine the following day when my doorbell chimed and, on answering it, I found an impatient Lucas waiting to escort me.

He led the way downstairs, to the Grand Library, and through a small door on the far side. I had never known it to be unlocked, but Lucas opened it without a key. Beyond was a narrow hallway, an area that had somehow escaped years of our immersive, daylong, hide-and-seek games.

The hall opened up into a modest reception area that played host to four doors. Lucas continued, with me in tow, to the farthest end. Obviously brand-new, a brass plaque had been affixed to the door. It read:

LECHNER HALL
PROFESSOR DR. DR. JÜRGEN SIEGFRIED LECHNER

Having delivered me, Lucas took his leave. I was so nervous that I had to take a breath and collect myself before knocking. Once I did, Professor Lechner's voice beckoned from within. I found him sitting and drinking tea, dressed in a dark suit and wearing a cravat tie with a silver pin in it.

What had apparently been an empty room quite recently was now transformed. Everywhere I looked there were elegant, dark woods. The workspace had been furnished with a large conference table and a lovely old credenza was already covered with papers and books. My eye was drawn to a writing kit on top of the desk; a self-contained box that held stately, engraved stationery and a half a dozen different writing instruments, including nib pens and two inkwells, and which folded out into a leather writing surface.

Several bookshelves that lined the far wall were still empty, but the large bar cart most certainly was not. Five engraved crystal decanters refracted the flickering, warm light from the fireplace where a flanking pair of high-back wing chairs gave the chamber the ambience of a drawing room rather than an office. The familiar scent of pipe smoke was just detectable, hinting that my grandfather had been a recent visitor.

"Do please sit," Professor Lechner said, pulling out a chair at the conference table.

Professor Lechner walked over to his desk, opened a drawer, and extracted several objects before returning to lay them before me. Two were clay pieces, both rectangular and the size and shape of a deck of playing cards. Two more looked like coins, also made of clay. The Professor also produced a clear plastic sleeve that held a certificate of some kind, and a small wood block with an intricate carving on one side in a style that looked Chinese.

"Do you recognize any of these?" Professor Lechner said, having sat down in the chair next to me.

"Is it a stock certificate?" I said, pointing to the paper.

"Just so," Professor Lechner said, and pointed. "Can you see what is printed here?"

I read aloud: "This is to certify that the bearer of this certificate is the proprietor of one hundred thousand fully paid up ordinary shares of one Pound each of the North Caucasian Oil Fields Limited."

Professor Lechner smiled, picked up the sleeve, and held it out to me. "Would you like to handle it?"

I nodded and took the certificate. The paper inside the sleeve felt heavy, the borders were ornately printed, and watermarks adorned each corner.

"Who do you think owns the shares?" Professor Lechner asked.

"There is no name. It doesn't say."

"Ach, but it does. Look closely."

"It only says 'the bearer.'"

"Just so. You are 'the bearer,' and thus owner of the shares."

A coy grin slipped across my face.

"Madam, may I see the certificate?" he said, holding his hand out with great deference.

I handed it to him.

"And now who owns one hundred thousand shares of the North Caucasian Oil Fields Limited company?"

I laughed when I understood what he was driving at.

"You do," I said, and then protested: "But you didn't pay me for them."

"Then you shouldn't have given me the certificate. Bearer shares, bearer bonds, bearer warrants, all these instruments grant rights to whoever carries them. In this case possession is not, as the saying goes, nine-tenths of the law. It is all of the law. Do you understand?"

"I think so," I said. "But isn't that dangerous? What if the certificate was lost?"

"Then woe to the holder who lost it." I gave the Professor a puzzled look. "This seems risky, yes?" When I nodded, he continued. "But then it follows that there must be some even greater benefit to using such instruments, yes?"

"But, what could that be?"

"Suppose I wanted to conceal the identity of the owner of one hundred thousand shares of the North Caucasian Oil Fields Limited company. It would hardly do for me to allow their name to be put in a ledger of shareholders, would it?"

"No," I said, beginning to catch on.

"What if the ownership of a holding company was embodied in a single bearer certificate? Do you see that all the assets of that firm could be quietly transferred to a new owner simply by handing the certificate to him? That there would be no record of the transfer?"

"Secret transfers?" I breathed, intrigued by the romance of it.

"Indeed," the Professor said, and put the certificate down.

"Do you recognize any of these other objects?"

I pointed to the block of wood. "Is it a seal of some kind?"

"Indeed," Professor Lechner said, impressed. He handed the block to me.

"This is a 'chop.' A Chinese invention. Each chop represented a bank account, or some other right or privilege. Ink was applied to the design face and the block used to stamp a draft order. The bearer might then present it for payment against the account. The carvings were intricate; made by craftsmen, and therefore difficult to forge. Some more dramatic examples, or those used by the Imperial family, were carved from jade or even opal.

"This chop might also be used to stamp an impression on written instructions to establish their authenticity. Do you see that, just as with the bearer share certificate, bearer instruments provide the bearer with a credential?"

"I think so."

"What do you make of these?" Professor Lechner said, gesturing to the clay squares and tokens. When I had no answer, he picked up the round objects and dropped them into my outstretched hands. "They are called *tesserae*, from the Latin."

My Latin was not perfect by any means, but I enjoyed the language and, even after my own lessons in it were cut short a year earlier in favor of etiquette classes, in the dead of night I would pilfer the books that Augustin's tutors assigned to him and stay up until morning reading them, always careful to return them before sunrise.

"Tiles?" I offered.

"Or tablets, yes. Very good. The Romans used them for tickets to events or receipts. These examples," Professor Lechner said as he pointed to the tokens, "were for admission to the Roman Colosseum. You can see the reserved aisle and row numbers, which would correspond to the numbers above the Colosseum doors."

"For the gladiatorial games?" I said, breathless.

"Perhaps." The Professor smiled. "Perhaps."

"Is it really true that men fought each other to the death with swords and spears in the games?"

"Now, now. To the topic at hand, yes?"

The Professor indicated the larger, rectangular clay pieces: one with a bull in bas-relief with writing in Latin around the edges, and the other with the carving of two hands clasping each other in a handshake.

"These are *tesserae hospitales*. If two great Roman families made a bond, a single clay piece twice this size was made and broken in half. Members of each family or, generations later, their descendants could present one half of the *tesserae* at the home of the other and, when it was seen that the other half fit perfectly along the broken edge, hospitality would be given to the visitor to honor the ancient pact between the families."

"It is a bearer instrument?"

"Excellent. Yes. Just so. They are all of them bearer instruments. How are they different?"

I looked at them for what felt like a long time but I had no answer. Professor Lechner pointed to the coin-shaped *tesserae*.

"What is this for?"

"Admission to the Colosseum?"

"And this?" he said, pointing to one of the *tesserae hospitales*.

"Showing that the bearer has a relationship to the family that holds the other half of the tablet?"

"And the certificate?"

"Showing that the bearer owns the shares?"

"What about this?" Professor Lechner said, and held up his right hand for me to see. On his pinky finger was a small signet ring, silver with a red stone inset. It was carved with an intricate crest. "Is this a bearer instrument?"

"Your personal seal? Well, yes."

"Quite so. Some bearer instruments can be worn, and thus always available to the bearer. The signet ring, like the chop, is also a special bearer instrument in that it can create other bearer instruments. The bearer might impress the ring into hot wax on an important document to indicate that the bearer is his agent, or has a right of passage."

Professor Lechner picked up the block with the Chinese design and set it in front of me before circling around to sit across from me.

"And this? What is it for? To whom must one go to use it?"

"I . . . I don't know."

Professor Lechner leaned back and smiled warmly. "Just so," he said. "Just so. Often there is purpose in keeping the meaning of a sigil obscure. In fact, sometimes it is beyond essential that their relevance be concealed from outsiders. Should it fall into the wrong hands, the mysteries of its proper deployment and the identity of the counterparty will guard against misuse. The secrets of such a bearer instrument can only be unlocked both by possessing the instrument and some hidden knowledge. Can you imagine how we might make such an arrangement even more secure?"

I gave the matter some thought but could come up with nothing.

"What if a sigil, a bearer instrument, were disguised as something altogether more ordinary?"

I blinked at the Professor, and smiled. "You would have to possess it, know what it is, *and* know how to use it."

"Just so," he beamed before growing serious once more. "You must commit the structure of such arrangements to memory. It may be of great importance to you someday."

Professor Lechner watched me carefully, waiting, I felt sure, to see that I had absorbed the lesson. Then he retrieved a silver pocket watch and opened the cover to look at the face.

"Ach," he said, and sipped the last from his teacup. "We have much to do."

Professor Lechner went to his desk and, extracting an exotic-looking pen and an elegant piece of stationery from his writing kit, wrote a short note, folded it twice, scratched a name on the front, and then handed it to me.

"I am quite certain this work will be in the library, but you should take this note to the curator. He will know where to find it."

I blinked and shook my head.

The Professor tutted at me. "How can it be that, living on this superlative estate, in the presence of one of the most impressive collections in private hands, you would not know the curator?"

I was beginning to feel rather chastised, but the Professor finished with a smile filled with warmth, an expression that assured me he was teasing.

"Perhaps if you explored the doors just outside," he hinted.

Professor Lechner made no move to get up, so I wandered out of his office and looked down at the note. It was addressed simply "Nigel."

The name rang a bell and, after some thought, I associated it with some functionary on my grandfather's staff, but I could not conjure up a visage to match my vague memory.

I turned my attention to the hallway instead. Two of the other doors looked unused, but the third was adorned with a slightly faded card in a brass bracket mounted to the wood. It read:

NIGEL LESLIE HAWTHORNE-PITT IV

Nigel. The same name as on the envelope.
Cautiously, I knocked.
"Yes?" a pinched voice offered from within.
I opened the door and stepped inside a surprisingly large office. It smelled, not unpleasantly, of ink, oil paint, and old paper—the scents of the Grand Library, only more so, and with a hint of rubbing alcohol beneath. Books and various objets d'art adorned the shelves that lined every available bit of wall space. A number of papers and maps, some obviously quite old, were spread out on three large tables in the middle of the room. A rack on the far wall was filled with stretched canvases and a half dozen other paintings were perched on easels to one side. Several illuminated magnifying glasses on adjustable booms were clamped to tables and desks in various places.

Presiding over the assembly of precious objects and ancient works was a singular-looking man. I had, in fact, seen him before, but had no prior cause to pay him any attention. He was tall and thin with a nose that was suggestive of a tropical bird's beak. He had silver hair, which, though perfectly coiffed, was fighting a losing battle with creeping baldness. I guessed him to be in his midfifties. He wore an impeccable three-piece suit that could only have been from a Savile Row tailor, and a bright, polka-dotted, vermilion bow tie.

He stood over a broad wood desk, ignoring the nearby office chair in a way that seemed almost to suggest he was trying to insult it. He was intent on several items, texts bound in green leather that he was studying with such an unalloyed focus that he had not even bothered to look up to greet his visitor.

"If these interruptions are to continue," the man said, without diverting his attention from the volumes, "I will be forced to renew with substantially more vigor my application for a private secretary."

His accent was that perfect form of Received Pronunciation that, though I considered myself quite proficient, only the English can truly wield. And wield it he did. Every inflection was a barb designed to snag lesser wordsmiths, and I sensed that we, the rest of humanity, were all lesser wordsmiths.

"I am to ask you for this book, Mr. Hawthorne-Pitt," I said, holding out the note Professor Lechner had written.

"You are to address me as *Sir* Nigel," he said without so much as a glance.

"Of course, Sir Nigel."

"I must say," he sighed, "the official overseeing the hiring practices employed to recruit the staff must . . ."

He finally looked up at me and stopped midsentence. His mouth hung open, revealing a set of gnarled teeth that were presumably the product of several decades of the gentle ministrations of British dentistry. Slow recognition came over him and he saw me as if for the first time. His eyes narrowed.

"What is this then?" he said.

He straightened as I handed him the note.

Once he had reviewed it, he cast the foul correspondence down onto his desk and emitted a revolted huff.

"Am I to understand that, after more than two decades as a valued employee of the foundation and curator of its collections, I am expected to be simply *thrilled* at the opportunity to drop all of my other wholly frivolous activities so that I can gracefully accept my new appointment to the elevated position of human card catalog? I suppose I should also prepare myself for my imminent appointment to the lofty title of Young Persons Tour Guide?"

I wasn't sure what to say. I avoided Sir Nigel's squinty gaze and my eyes wandered, lighting eventually on the green-bound volumes on his desk. It clicked: they were the same sort of texts I had seen my grandfather conceal under a cloth when I first came into the East Salon. My heart quickened.

"Shall we begin with the children's books?" Sir Nigel was saying. "Perhaps Miller's *Rosy Crucifixion*? Some Dante? Modern appreciations of the works of Otto Dix? Perhaps we might—"

"—I'd like to begin with those," I said, pointing at the green volumes. I had no idea where the reserve of courage had come from, but once I fixated on the books it was impossible to tear my eyes from them.

Sir Nigel shook his head, turned his chin up, and looked at the ceiling through shut eyelids. Then he began to recite in Latin:

"Hae mortuorum epistolae oculis haud initiatis non praebentur."

Near as I could tell, Sir Nigel's phrase, which I took to be a quotation from somewhere, translated roughly to "These Letters from the Dead are not for uninitiated eyes."

"Oh, I already know all about the Letters from the Dead from Grandfather, Sir Nigel," I lied.

It was the sort of stupid, bragging fib I might have delivered to my siblings to avoid admitting I didn't know something that Augustin did.

"'Grandfather'? Whose daughter are you, exactly?" he said, but seemed to come to the answer before I could reply, whereupon his squinting abated.

At first, Sir Nigel looked as if he might recoil in horror, but then formality shot through him and he stiffened as if electrocuted. He tugged his suit jacket straight and twice brushed invisible dust from his left shoulder with the back of his hand. When he finally collected himself, it took him a good five or six words for the cadence of his speech to return to the fully weaponized dialect he had first confronted me with.

"Young lady," he said, laying a reverent hand on the green volumes. His voice took on a hushed tone, as if he were about to reveal great mysteries. "I have been studying the collective diaries of the great patriarchs of your family for nearly two decades now. I hasten to make you aware that, to my knowledge, I am the only scholar, I daresay even the only non-heir, who has even been made aware of the true nature of the works, much less permitted to examine them. Two generations ago, even referring to *The Letters* in the company of an outsider would have earned the speaker a sharp rebuke, or worse. Perhaps much worse."

At first I was frightened by the sudden mania that had seized Sir Nigel. Certainly, he fit the part of the fevered and eccentric scholar. But then, to my relief, his stiff intensity slackened.

"I trust the matter is now closed? I have important tasks to finish and have no intention of permitting such a trivial errand to disrupt the flow of my work any more than is absolutely necessary. I will kindly ask you to wait for me outside until I have attained a natural pause in my present endeavors."

With that, Sir Nigel, with a posture so erect it looked almost painful, ushered me out of his office, closed his door, and locked it from within.

I FOUND MYSELF SITTING in the reception area to wait, but barely five minutes passed before Professor Lechner emerged and locked his office door behind him. He walked right past me, as if oblivious to my very existence. I expected him to continue into the Grand Library in pursuit of his own tasks but instead he stopped in front of Sir Nigel's office.

Without hesitation, he delivered three rapid-fire raps to the door. They were surprisingly loud for knocks delivered by a man of such slight stature; loud enough to make me jump. They must have been louder still from inside Sir Nigel's office because there was the sound of a loud crash as something shattered.

"*Intolerable*," Sir Nigel's voice moaned from within.

When he appeared at the door, Sir Nigel was wearing a set of eyeglasses with several adjustable magnifying lenses mounted to them with booms. I winced, imagining that he had been working on some delicate artifact when the Professor startled him.

"What is the meaning of this crass interruption?" Sir Nigel demanded.

"Ach, my dear colleague," Professor Lechner began, and issued the beginnings of a little bow.

Sir Nigel's eyes went wide. "*Colleague?*" he said.

"I have just moved into my offices next door and—"

"—preposterous," Sir Nigel breathed, horrified. "Who are you and what do you think you are you doing here?"

Sir Nigel's gaze darted from Professor Lechner to me then, and his bearing softened some.

"I have been told that you are a most excellent guide and may have some knowledge of the library," the Professor said. "I should rather enjoy a tour."

"A . . . *tour?*" Sir Nigel said, exasperated. "I think not. Now if you will excuse me, I have important work to do and . . ."

Professor Lechner produced the sealed letter my grandfather had given him the evening before and held it out. Sir Nigel made to protest, until he saw the seal. Taking the letter carefully in his hand, he scrutinized the seal before glancing at Professor Lechner again. Nimble fingers broke the wax and unfolded the paper—practiced motions familiar to hands that had handled thousands of precious documents. As he read, the slight frown that his mouth seemed to take up naturally spread into a more serious expression just before transforming his entire face into an affronted scowl.

"Dear God," he breathed; and then again louder once he was halfway through: "Dear *God.*"

His reading finished, Sir Nigel stood silently for a long time looking at the unsealed letter. Finally, his expression melted into a resigned look. He closed his eyes, put the back of his hand to his forehead, and sighed deeply.

"Come along," he announced. "We will begin with the Grand Library's Main Atrium."

Sir Nigel started for the door with Professor Lechner in tow.

"Oh, excuse me, young lady," Professor Lechner said to me, turning back at the last minute. "I did not mean to take your place in line. Did you have some business with my tour guide?"

Sir Nigel stiffened at the words "tour guide" but somehow choked down any protest. He turned back and narrowed his eyes at me in irritation, but thought better of it somehow.

"Yes, yes," he allowed, after a moment. "Do come along then."

I COULDN'T RESIST LOOKING up at the library's vaulted ceiling, but Sir Nigel was in such a hurry that, once I looked down again, I nearly found myself left behind.

To say that his efforts were halfhearted would be a dramatic under-statement. He rendered the most casual description of each of the library's sections, at one point describing nearly the entire third floor as "containing the stacks dedicated to literature."

The work the Professor had tasked me with finding turned out to be an oversize art book focused on American painters. Sir Nigel extracted it from the very top shelf and handed it down to me: a tome so large that I had to carry it in front of me with both hands like a Roman *scutum.*

"Do tell me, what is the section over here?" Professor Lechner wondered aloud, indicating a group of low tables and couches. He began to wander in that direction. "Perhaps a luncheon nook?"

"Certainly not," Sir Nigel gasped. "Consuming food in the atrium is strictly—"

"—how charming," Professor Lechner said, gesturing. "Tea service. And the finger sandwiches look delightful."

"Impossible," Sir Nigel snapped, and stalked in that direction. I scampered along, trying to keep up.

Sir Nigel looked about ready to deliver an ear-stinging rebuke to the man sitting with a full afternoon tea service in front of him but, when he saw the library's newest guest, he froze instead. There was recognition behind his expression (and something darker still behind that).

"Oh, there you are," Professor Lechner said to the sitting man. "Sir Nigel, may I present Professor William S. T. Clive, Doctor of Philosophy, Fellow of the British Academy, and—"

"—Clive," Sir Nigel scowled.

"Oh, are you already acquainted with Professor Clive, Sir Nigel?" Professor Lechner said.

"In a manner of speaking," Professor Clive growled, before Sir Nigel could reply.

Professor Clive's hair was almost as white as Professor Lechner's. He gestured with tortoiseshell glasses as he spoke, folding and unfolding them and pointing now and again with one temple tip at nothing in particular.

"Colleagues?" Professor Lechner beamed.

Quite the contrary, I thought. There was a palpable malevolence I could almost hear crackling through the air between Clive and Nigel.

"How *wonderful*," Professor Lechner continued. "What are the odds of that all this way from civilization? Earlier, Professor Clive and I were discussing the demonstrated prescience of the nineteenth-century pastoralists. I understand Professor Clive has written the definitive work on the predictive features of the period's romanticists."

"*Definitive?*" Sir Nigel sneered. "That would, I suppose, be one way of describing the material."

Professor Clive let out a disgusted snort accompanied by a subtle but dismissive wave.

I realized something significant. Sir Nigel and Professor Clive were wearing similar three-piece suit ensembles, and *exactly* the same polka-dotted, vermilion bow tie.

Professor Lechner tutted Sir Nigel. "*Ach*, but Nigel—"

"—I will thank you to remember that it is *Sir* Nigel."

"Well, Professor Lechner," Professor Clive began, "those of us without undue influence over the keepers of the honors list must rely on the long and arduous pursuit of actual scholarship to develop our reputations."

"Ah, yes. *Scholarship*," Sir Nigel spat. "Is that what we are calling it now? Unless I am mistaken, the thesis in question boils down to the claim that certain artists were imbued with the gift of future sight by . . . the muses? Some manner of divination? The examination of chicken entrails, perhaps?"

"As I was mentioning to you earlier, Professor Lechner," Professor Clive began again. "The pastoralists of the nineteenth century were before their time. Really, can anyone dispute that the central feature of the twentieth century was the collapse of Imperialism?"

"Well," Professor Lechner said, turning to Sir Nigel, "we might put this thesis to the test. Surely a collection as extensive as that possessed by your masters on this very estate must have some American romanticist pieces on hand? Perhaps some Thomas Cole?"

"*Cole?*" Professor Clive breathed. "Here? Is that possible?"

"Absolutely not," Sir Nigel said, to Professor Clive's obvious disappointment. "The artistic palette of the last four patriarchs of the estate would never permit such common fare on the property."

"Pity," Professor Lechner said. Then he looked at me. "Young lady, what is that book you have there? Give it over."

I brought the volume to Professor Lechner, whereupon he made a show of leafing through it before setting it down on the low table and settling himself into the nearest chair.

"Just so," Professor Lechner said, smiling. "A happy coincidence."

Professor Clive's eyes shot to the open book. Professor Lechner had turned to the first of a series of full-page photographs of five oil-on-canvas paintings by the artist Thomas Cole.

"These pieces are outstandingly reproduced," Professor Clive said, leaning into the book. "Where did this work come from?" Then, without waiting for an answer, and with both hands hovering over the book, he launched into an academic monologue.

"It is the first in the Course of Empire series. The most noted of Cole's allegorical works. The series depicts the same scene, a richly forested plot of land on the sea, as the touch of man transforms it from . . ."

Professor Clive indicated each work with a gesture as he turned the pages to each painting in turn.

". . . *The Savage State*, depicting man's early existence as hunter-gatherer. *The Arcadian or Pastoral State*, illustrating the beginnings of a Greco-Roman village. *The Consummation of Empire*, where the settlement has grown to an example of one of the great cities of ancient times. *Destruction*, as the peak of civilization is attacked, beset by invaders borne to its shores by ancient ships of war; the city sacked. Finally, *Desolation*, depicting the ruins of the once-great city as they slowly succumb to the relentless entropy of nature."

Professor Clive's narration on a topic he was so obviously passionate about took me by surprise. I could feel the thrill of it in my abdomen; a growing tightness tingling with anticipation.

"Notice the bridge at the center of the scene in the third painting. It is the central axis of the battle in the fourth. In the third painting, *The Consummation of Empire*, we see the trappings of celebration. A wedding? A festival?" Professor Clive asked rhetorically, as if toying with a lecture hall of students. "No. Look carefully at the procession that crosses the bridge. Do you see the figure at its center? The arch they are approaching?"

When I looked at the statues atop the arch—helmed warriors bearing spears and shields—I understood.

"A triumphal arch," Professor Clive said, pleased with himself.

"Obviously," Sir Nigel muttered.

"The scene is a triumph. For Cole, conquest is the essence of empire. The conqueror returns, crosses the bridge from far-off lands, and enters the capital bearing prisoners, spoils, fantastic beasts—"

"—*memento mori*," I said, almost to myself.

Professor Clive glared at me. "What was that?" he demanded.

"*Memento mori*," I repeated, after a moment's startled silence.

"Just so," Professor Lechner interjected. "And this means what to you?"

I could feel my cheeks going red, but Professor Lechner gave me an encouraging smile.

"During a triumph it was what a slave behind the conqueror would whisper. Remember that you must die. Remember that you are mortal. Well, supposedly."

Professor Lechner's face lit up immediately. "*Ja*. Precisely. Versnel comments on the practice in his treatise of the subject."

Professor Clive was still looking at me. "Who are you, again?" he said.

Before anyone could answer, Professor Lechner directed Professor Clive's attention back to the open book. "And here?" he said.

"Yes. The fourth painting," Professor Clive continued. "*Destruction*. Here the bridge, once the portal for the wages of conquest, the source of the empire's riches, is depicted as the center of the conflict. The artist reveals that conquest is both essential to empire and also the seed of its destruction. Yes?"

"Nonsense," Sir Nigel interjected, but Professor Clive ignored him.

"Of the last work in the series," Professor Clive said, "Cole writes . . ."

With the flourish of an actor in a play, Professor Clive stood fully erect and then, gesturing with his hands like some ancient orator, recited from memory:

"'Violence and time have crumbled the works of man, and art is again resolving into elemental nature. The gorgeous pageant has passed—the roar of battle has ceased—the multitude has sunk in the dust—the empire is extinct.'"

I felt a little chill go through me. When I looked at Professor Lechner we locked eyes and I saw that he was studying me intently.

"And now, finally, we come to it," Sir Nigel sniffed, breaking the spell. "The cycle of decay and death is inevitable. The striving of man is pointless." Sir Nigel leaned over the table and flipped the page back to the first painting in the series. "This is what we should aspire to, is that it? Hunter-gatherers teetering over the jaws of starvation with the approach each year of the snows?"

"Of course, I would expect such a trite critique from an aristocrat, *Sir Nigel*," Professor Clive said, and then turned to Professor Lechner. "There is something to be said for harmony between nature and man, don't you think?"

Sir Nigel sniffed. "Apparently, to prepare for this impending harmony I will have to make a point of familiarizing myself with the latest in loincloth fashion."

Professor Clive was quick to reply. "I really don't see how it could be disputed that empires are destined to collapse into ruin. In *The Fate of Empires*, Sir John Glubb—"

"—ah yes," Nigel singsonged. "How did I know you would resort to Glubb—"

"—Glubb," Professor Clive said, turning to Professor Lechner and raising his voice to drown out Sir Nigel, "cataloged empires from Assyria in 800 BC, to Britain, and the Russia of the Romanovs. His work suggested 250 years as the average, and very little room on either side. He characterized six stages that afflicted all empires. The ages of pioneers, conquests, commerce, affluence, intellect, and finally decadence."

"Shoddy, shoddy work," Sir Nigel insisted. "I too might make grand pronouncements about the fate of institutions if I were equally arbitrary in the examples I selected. Glubb's cherry-picking of Assyrian dates, his practice of counting as separate the Roman Republic and the Roman Empire; his refusal to consider the Byzantine Empire at all . . . Really, how his name is still mentioned in the company of serious scholars after the publication of such dross I shall never know. Another Malthusian," Sir Nigel said, addressing himself to Professor Lechner again. "Very much like the guest in our present company."

"I beg your pardon?" Professor Clive thundered.

"Sir Nigel," Professor Lechner said, "perhaps we should arrange for a visit to Professor Clive's university. Certainly, the collections there must rival any private athenaeum."

Professor Clive issued a grunt of confirmation.

"Nonsense," Sir Nigel said. "I will have you know that one of the grandest private collections is housed in this very edifice."

"I do apologize, Sir Nigel. I am quite certain that cannot be true," Professor Lechner said.

"You may see it with your own eyes," Sir Nigel said, and stalked into the library proper. "Come," he added over his shoulder, not bothering to look back to see who followed.

CHAPTER NINE

◠

Vanitas

S IR NIGEL TOOK US IN AN ascending helix, up the spiral staircase to the first landing and around the shelves there before ascending to the second and third landings in turn, exploring each against the background of his enthusiastic and expert, if nasal, narration.

It was not that I had not wandered the Grand Library before, but Sir Nigel cast everything in a new and different light. With his dialogue as voice-over, one could wander the stacks and, through the collections, see the physical manifestations of the interests of a dozen of the former patriarchs of my family ("your ancestors," as Sir Nigel took pains to remind me at various turns).

"But, Sir Nigel, what about that section?" I said, pointing to a far corner of the third-floor landing that the tour had neglected.

A locked, glass display case that contained several rather beautiful-looking astrolabes was surrounded by shelving that held a group of very old volumes. I had explored the section once or twice before (it was where I had found the *Physica Curiosa*), but Sir Nigel's rather blatant neglect of the dark corner piqued my interest.

He gave me a sour expression.

"What interest could a serious researcher possibly have in the insane scribblings of the alchemists, astrologers, and occultists that plagued the latter years of the eighteenth century? Leopold is rather lucky that the prosecution of witchcraft had fallen out of favor. Just a century earlier, any authority who saw such a collection might have ordered him burnt on the spot. I wonder if the board of the Library Foundation is even aware of the existence of such works."

"The . . . Library Foundation?" Professor Clive said. "The collection is owned by a public charity?"

"Public? Don't be ridiculous. The *private* Library Foundation was created in Switzerland by Lukas, the twelfth patriarch, to protect and manage the collection. A board of five trustees was appointed."

"What a curious notion," Professor Clive added. "Just like the aimlessly wealthy to attempt to privatize wisdom itself via an overly complex and legalistic structure. I'm sure it had nothing to do with evading taxes."

"Am I really in the position of needing to remind you," Sir Nigel said, "that two horrific world wars were sparked in regions quite near to where we stand? Are you not aware that the National Socialists thought nothing of seizing the estates of even the oldest Prussian lines when it suited their purposes? That the Gestapo was in the habit of holding relatives hostage, even torturing them, to compel the heads of families to sign their holdings over to the Reichsbank? Fortunately, and though it is not widely known, the Patriarch developed an innovative structure to cope with just such an eventuality."

"The *Patriarch*," Professor Clive sneered.

Sir Nigel looked at him with astonishment. "'The Patriarch' refers to the young woman's grandfather, the head of her family, not to mention your most gracious host while you visit within these walls. It is a title of affection and honor given him by his followers."

"You mean serfs," Professor Clive quipped.

Sir Nigel ignored the barb. "It is traditional, if perhaps a bit pedestrian, for each head of the family to be given a distinctive moniker. He acquired the unofficial, and somewhat ironic, title by virtue of being so young when he assumed power."

Sir Nigel turned to me, but I had the sense he was actually lecturing Professor Clive. "You are no doubt aware that your grandfather was merely seventeen in 1937 when he returned from his two-year tour of the world? He discovered that his father, your great-grandfather, Lukas, had been killed in an accident. Your grandfather was thrust into the role of the patriarch at a very young age on the very eve of the Second World War."

I was enthralled with the image that formed in my head: a young version of my grandfather plotting against elusive enemies.

"With the onset of the war, your grandfather felt it essential that the estate be as self-sufficient and secure as possible. The family vault, first carved out during the First World War, underwent a significant renovation, but this was only part of the infrastructure upgrade, which included generators, food stores sufficient to feed the entire staff for many months if supplies were cut off, concealed tunnels to serve as emergency escape routes—"

"—secret tunnels?" I breathed.

"Yes," Sir Nigel said, and fidgeted with his bow tie before glancing at Professor Clive. "I will have you know that, under the direct commission of the Patriarch, I am in the process of writing the definitive history of the family's involvement in *both* world wars. Of course, given the deteriorating standards of education in this horrid age, it is not surprising that you have no appreciation for the immediacy of the peril this dynasty faced in that era."

Seeing my puzzled look, Sir Nigel fixed me with a stare of such annoyance that it seemed to border on loathing.

"Surely, as a member of the immediate family, you must be aware that during the war your grandfather clandestinely aided the Allies?"

As it happened, I knew only a little of the history of either World War.

"I do not know who has been responsible for your education to this point," Sir Nigel huffed, "but they should be ignominiously, and without delay, cast from the ranks of polite society."

Professor Lechner emitted a soft hum, almost (but not quite) to himself.

Sir Nigel continued his lecture, gesturing expressively to emphasize this point or that.

"Your grandfather, at the greatest personal risk I might add, made this manor a waypoint for Allied airmen who had been shot down over Europe. In fact, below us, not far from the spot on which you are standing, are several secret rooms where aviators were concealed until they could be smuggled into Switzerland. As it happens the banker Paul Kemper once slept within these very walls as he made his escape to the United States, a plan hatched by Allen

Dulles himself, then the Swiss director of the Office of Strategic Services, the OSS. In the other direction, the estate was a path into Nazi-controlled territory for Allied agents and saboteurs.

"The Patriarch also took pains to secretly slow the production of your family's natural resource interests in South America and the Middle East when it became clear that the Nazis were interested in the tin, copper, and oil that your family controlled.

"Now," Sir Nigel said, and stalked off with us in tow, "the foundation's portrait archives contain many magnificent specimens, particularly the early portraiture works painted with allegorical elements that some insist—erroneously, I might add—alone defines them as Baroque or environmental in style."

"Ach," Professor Lechner interjected, addressing Professor Clive. "I am certain I remember that you authored a textbook on a similar topic, *nicht so?*"

Professor Clive only scowled.

Sir Nigel gave Professor Clive a knowing look over his shoulder as he led us across the Grand Study to the exit on the other end. My eyes were drawn to the far wall behind my father's desk where the great vault door was the predominant feature, one that you could easily believe had been transplanted from a Swiss bank. To my disappointment, Sir Nigel ignored it entirely as we passed.

We followed him down to the cellars and wove our way through the sprawl of passages until Sir Nigel stopped at a metallic-gray door set in the stone wall, produced a key, opened the portal, and threw a switch inside. In contrast to the other dank rooms in the manor's basements, it was brilliantly illuminated and the air pleasantly dry. The room itself was filled with racks elevated nearly two feet off the floor and filled with dozens if not hundreds of stretched paintings.

"You must forgive the condition of this storage facility," Sir Nigel said, wincing a little.

I blinked and looked around again. The room was utterly spotless. I could have eaten off the polished floor and not tasted a bit of grit for having done so.

"I have requested funds to have it improved nearly a dozen times. Do you know that three years ago the trustee had the temerity to actually have a stamp made? I assure you I am most in earnest. A rubber stamp reading

REQUEST DENIED with the date. He even uses red ink. I am certain that mine are the only requests he brands with that infernal device."

Sir Nigel had become so animated that his bow tie (normally in perfect alignment) was disturbed. The crooked accessory struck me as incredibly funny and I had to focus elsewhere to keep from laughing.

"Much effort has been expended to overcome my predecessor's laughable attempts at cataloging. The man made a mockery of the Getty Vocabularies."

Sir Nigel donned a pair of white cotton gloves and proceeded to lecture nonstop for the next ten minutes, presenting to us dozens of life-size portraits of my long-dead family members. Finally, he came to a painting dated 1689. It was a remarkable work. Even Professor Clive seemed grudgingly impressed.

Looking out through a veil of three centuries was Leopold I, founder of our dynasty, accompanied by his wife, his son, and his two daughters. Leopold was dressed in robes and, unlike his portrait in the Hall of Ancestors, appeared without a breastplate. He was seated among his family in a salon I half-expected to recognize but did not. At his right hand was a small globe on a little desk along with a bust I convinced myself must be Aristotle.

"An exceptional piece," Sir Nigel said. "Leopold had quite recently been made an Imperial Count, answerable only to the Emperor himself. His wife is flanked on either side by fifteen-year-old Leopold the younger, who would, of course, become Leopold II, and fourteen-year-old Theresia. To the far right, separate from the family, is the thirteen-year-old Sophia."

My breath caught in my throat.

Sophia. The name of cursed daughters.

Involuntarily, I stepped closer to the canvas.

After that, I barely heard Sir Nigel's oration. I was too focused on the right side of the painting. I was too focused on Sophia.

She was a pale, waifish figure standing some distance from the chair in which her mother was seated. She had attentive, dark-blue eyes, and blondish hair with perhaps a hint of red, which she wore tied up with thin light blue ribbons. Her neck was covered by an almost translucent golden headscarf. She wore a flowing dress of dark blue silk with a pattern of red roses. Next to her on a table, extending out of the picture's frame of view, the artist had included a stack of papers and books. Atop them I was surprised to see what could have been an astrolabe. That impression only grew when I realized that behind and above Sophia an open window was depicted with the stars of the night sky visible beyond.

Even I knew enough to realize that the artist's affectations were very strange for a young woman of Sophia's era. Looking closer, and though it might have been a smudge on the canvas, or a slip of the brush, I was convinced that the artist had also painted Sophia's right hand with ink stains on her fingers.

"Sir Nigel," I said, interrupting his monologue midsentence. He gave me a stricken look. "Are there any other portraits of Sophia?"

"Most certainly not."

"But, why not?"

"Happily, female children, even the children of a patriarch, were not of great import in this era. In fact—"

"—but, Sir Nigel, why would the artist include so many allegorical elements for Leopold's children if they were unimportant? In the painting Sophia seems a much richer subject than her brother."

"An excellent question," Professor Clive said.

For a moment, Sir Nigel looked stunned by the effrontery of his inquisitors.

"Remind me, if you would," he demanded of me, "where you commenced your studies in art history and critique? What respected institution of higher learning and reputation in the field granted you your advanced degree? Was it the Courtauld? Or perhaps the Warburg Institute? No? Well, then.

"In fact, the last record we have of Leopold's wife and daughters is from 1690, the year after this portrait was painted. Admittedly, it is unusual for such records, even those of younger daughters, to be discarded after they were married off and sent abroad."

"Charming family," Professor Clive sneered, and held his hands up toward the painting. "Do you know, I do believe I can feel their warmth radiating all the way through the centuries."

Professor Lechner cleared his throat and gave Professor Clive a harsh look. Clive's smirk vanished.

"I expect my predecessor's horrifically negligent practices are to blame for the deficiencies in the family records," Sir Nigel concluded.

"But was Sophia married?" I asked.

"Have I not just explained that we have no such records?" Sir Nigel said.

"She just . . . vanished?" I said, appalled. "How can that be?"

"I must say, you have quite the gift for posing the same inquiry in a half dozen ways. Still, if it is all the same to you, I would prefer to come to the end of this infernal assignment prior to the arrival of the next millennium, yes?"

Sir Nigel would brook no more argument and, therefore, our exploration of the portrait archives came to a close.

I was buried in thought as we made our way back upstairs. Given what Sir Nigel had said about the unknown fate of the daughter of our line's founder, I could not believe it a coincidence that Augustin had woven a tale from the "cursed name of Sophia." Thoughts of my long-dead ancestor and her apparent disappearance drove me to distraction.

It was ironic then that our "official" tour ended in the Hall of Ancestors. We traveled down the hall in reverse chronological order, stopping in turn at each patriarch's portrait, whereupon Sir Nigel expounded on its history and the style of portraiture. When we finally arrived in front of the visage of Leopold I, Sir Nigel was entirely absorbed in his narrative.

The portrait of my thirteenth great-grandfather was a dark and faded affair in which Leopold—black breastplate and flowing red robes; white scarves and furs about his neck—struck a deeply statesmanlike pose. He was surrounded by dark scarlet drapes. His right hand rested casually on the hilt of an elegant sword, with only an inch or so of bright steel showing above the scabbard. Merciless, dark blue eyes peered out of the canvas directly at the viewer.

"The partially unsheathed sword is a symbol of Leopold's readiness to defend the interests of the Emperor and a reminder of his valor in the Battle of Vienna in 1683, the Siege of Érsekújvár, and the Battle of Kassa. The portrait has been dated to 1689, the same year as the family portrait you have already seen. No doubt in this work, a more official depiction in contrast to the personal tenor of the family portrait, the artist sought to capture the recent violence Leopold had inflicted upon the enemies of the Emperor."

"Barbarous, and entirely expected," Professor Clive said with a disgusted grunt. "The blood-soaked legacy of power-mad sociopaths cloaked in the deceitful guise of 'civilization.'"

Sir Nigel was not to be sidetracked. "Affixed to his breast is the Order of . . ."

But something else had caught my eye.

"What is in Leopold's other hand?" I whispered to myself.

Standing behind me, Professor Lechner spoke up. "Did you have a question, young lady?"

"It's just . . ." I pointed at the canvas, and this elicited an affronted look from Sir Nigel. "It looks like Leopold is holding something, just there."

"Apparently, impertinence is no longer considered a vice in young children," Sir Nigel sighed, and then turned his eyes upward. "*O tempora, o mores,*" he moaned before returning his attention to me. "That is merely part of his pose; his hand is resting on a piece of furniture, obviously inconsequential enough that the artist was not inclined to keep it in frame."

"But, Sir Nigel, can that be right?" I leaned closer and Sir Nigel stiffened, as if terrified I might pollute the canvas by proximity alone. "His fingers look curled around it, as if he is holding it up."

I stepped even closer, squinting at the lower left part of the canvas. Then, all at once, it was obvious to me.

"*Sir Nigel,*" I shouted, unable to contain my excitement.

It was loud enough to upset him and, as my voice echoed off the stone floor and down the long hall, he squeezed his eyes closed as if in pain.

"Dear God," he protested, and the back of his hand went to his forehead.

"Look, Sir Nigel. It's a book. He is holding a book."

"It does look quite like a volume of some sort," Professor Clive said, and looked rather pleased with himself.

"That is preposterous. Young lady, I have examined this piece hundreds of times."

Yet, even as he turned away from the canvas, Sir Nigel seemed unsure, and I caught him looking at it out of the corner of his eye.

"Is it one of the green volumes?"

Sir Nigel's eyes darted back and forth, and I knew I had made a mistake in mentioning, even obliquely, the Letters from the Dead.

"The object in question is blue, not green," Sir Nigel said, giving Professor Clive a glance to see if he had picked up on anything sensitive.

"But couldn't the paint have faded?" I suggested.

"I see. An expert on the ageing of sixteenth-century oils and pigments now, are you? As it happens, green pigments from the time were formulated almost exclusively by the *vendecolori* of Venice, specialists in the field of paints and oils."

Sir Nigel slipped into a trancelike monologue again.

"The most popular green of the day would have been the mineral pigment Verde Azzuro, though it was considered pedestrian by many of the more accomplished painters of the time. As it happens, these more particular portrait artists typically mixed their own colors and used blue that was normally tinted with the horrifically expensive ultramarine, one of the most durable pigments. The yellows mixed with blue to make green would have been formulated from Gamboge, made from Southeast Asian tree resin. Unfortunately, resin pigments often faded when exposed to sunlight. In this case, the faster leaching of the yellow from a green coloring would cause . . ."

Sir Nigel trailed off and all the color drained from his face. He blinked as if to clear his vision and then leaned close to Leopold's painting, scrutinizing with great intensity the blue object that had attracted my attention. Long moments passed in silence.

"Sir Nigel?" I said.

But Sir Nigel did not answer. Instead, unable to tear his eyes away from the portrait, he dismissed us with a wave of the back of his hand.

IF IT HAD been Professor Lechner's intention to instill in me a sense of wonder and a nearly unquenchable thirst for more, he had succeeded beyond his wildest hopes. I bounded up to my apartments giddy and devoured my lunch so as to speed my return to the Professor's office.

On my way back, I heard a commotion from behind Sir Nigel's closed door: Sir Nigel and Professor Clive bickering. I hurried along to the Professor's office, where I found him sitting behind his desk, flipping through a book so old that dust flew every time he turned a page. He gestured for me to take the chair opposite him.

"Professor Lechner?" I ventured. My mind had drifted back to the Cole paintings and the mere thought of them ran a shiver through me. I found myself unable to wait for his attention.

He looked up from the book. "A question? Yes?"

"Two hundred and fifty years does seem a very long time." There was a kind of despair in my voice.

Professor Lechner's eyes widened. Some small cunning crept into his expression at first, and then a broad smile crossed his face.

"For the life of an empire? Indeed not. It was the final painting, *Desolation*, that moved you, no? Which part?"

"The remains of the bridge."

"And well it should. We should recoil from scenes of ruin; from the recognition that civilization has yielded to chaos. The bridge, the source of the empire's wealth and power, is shattered. Horrible.

"With me it is the ruins of the Doric temple in the distance on the hilltop. They served also as repositories for knowledge; learning. The Great Library of Alexandria was a religious research institute first."

"It was burned, wasn't it?"

"Ach. But this is less certain than is generally supposed. Julius Caesar did set fire to the docks when besieged at Alexandria. Titus Livius, quoted by Seneca the Younger, claims the fire destroyed the Library, but Livius's original work? Long since lost. This claim seems much exaggerated, *ja*?

"But one cannot know for sure. It is as with Cole's work. The destruction of knowledge, once lost, is absolute. It is what saddens me most."

I shuddered. He saw it at once.

"Yes. *Yes*," he said, with an urgency that almost frightened me. Our eyes met. "It is terrible, *nicht so*?"

"Yes," I managed.

From his desk drawer, Professor Lechner produced a sheet of paper and bade me read from it out loud.

Ozymandias
I met a traveller from an antique land
Who said: Two vast and trunkless legs of stone
Stand in the desert. Near them, on the sand,

Half sunk, a shattered visage lies, whose frown,
And wrinkled lip, and sneer of cold command,
Tell that its sculptor well those passions read
Which yet survive, stamped on these lifeless things,
The hand that mocked them and the heart that fed:
And on the pedestal these words appear:
"My name is Ozymandias, king of kings:
Look on my works, ye Mighty, and despair!"
Nothing beside remains. Round the decay
Of that colossal wreck, boundless and bare
The lone and level sands stretch far away.

"An empire in ruins," I said.

"'. . . art again resolves into elemental nature . . .'" Professor Lechner said, quoting Cole. "'. . . the empire is extinct.' All but washed away by the sands. Its secrets, and riches, material or otherwise, lost forever.

"The poem . . . it is by Shelley, inspired by the works of Diodorus Siculus, who recounts a passage on the base of a statue of Ramesses II."

The Professor closed his eyes. He transformed into an orator, far weightier somehow than Professor Clive had been.

"King of Kings Ozymandias am I. If any want to know how great I am and where I lie, let him outdo me in my work.

"All around us are the ruins of empires, *ja*? Greece. Italy. Egypt. Though they may leave signs, how much knowledge and wisdom do we lose as each one falls and slips beneath the waves of time? At what cost to mankind?

"The cure for scurvy, devastating to sailors, was discovered and lost again nearly a dozen times. Thinis was the capital city of the first Egyptian dynasties, home of the first pharaoh. Yet we find no physical sign of it or its famed riches."

My head was swimming with visions of buried capitals, secret library chambers in forgotten tombs, lost stone tablets inscribed with ancient knowledge; the secrets of priests long turned to dust. I nearly jumped out of my skin when there was a knock at the office door.

It was Cipriana bearing our tea. I was glad to see her, but when I smiled she only curtsied and put the tray down in front of me. I looked down at the teacups, but something else caught my eye: an ugly bruise—yellow and dark purple—surrounding her left wrist. Concerned, I tried to make eye contact, but Professor Lechner, oblivious to what I had seen, thanked her and shooed her away.

The Professor served us both and then sat across from me with a very contented expression on his face.

"Ozymandias expects the mighty to despair of ever matching his greatness," he said. "In fact, it is the inevitable ruin in the face of his hubris that occasions the despair of 'ye Mighty.' Yes? *Sic transit gloria mundi*. It is a reminder that all glory is fleeting."

"*Memento mori*," I breathed.

"Just so. For Cole empires are doomed to ruin."

"But are they?" I said, disturbed by the notion.

"How can we know? They always have been."

"Professor Clive thinks they are."

"He was quite vocal in his opinions, no?"

"So was Sir Nigel."

"Indeed, in normal circumstances one might expect your grandfather's man to be more discreet among outsiders. Hmmm?"

I wondered if his comment was a barb at my mention of the "green volumes," but he smiled at me, closed the dusty old book, stood, and began to pace slowly back and forth behind his desk.

"In the midst of the Battle of the Three Emperors, a certain Frenchman of great renown . . ." He stopped and gave me a pregnant look. "The Emperor, you understand? The Emperor was urged by his generals to attack a strategically important plateau, the Pratzen Heights. These generals had noticed, you see, that the enemy armies led by Tsar Alexander I and the Holy Roman Emperor, Francis II, were in the process of vacating the plateau.

"The French Emperor asked his general how long it would take to march his troops up to the top of Pratzen Heights. Twenty minutes, the general responded. The Emperor told his general to wait for fifteen, and then to attack. When the general expressed puzzlement at the delay, the French Emperor uttered a phrase that became as famous as it is misquoted.

"*Quand l'ennemi fait un faux mouvement, il faut se garder de l'interrompre.*"

The Professor paused, regarding me.

"When the enemy makes a false move, you must be careful not to interrupt him," I translated. "You mean that you allowed Sir Nigel to . . . make a false move? To keep speaking?"

The Professor smiled.

"As with many such historical vignettes, so much of its true lesson is lost in favor of crafting a clever quote to be delivered during an irrelevant social event by some junior diplomat of no distinction. You see, in fact, the French Emperor had himself abandoned the Pratzen Heights long before and ordered a dramatic, but entirely staged, retreat of his cavalry to draw back his right flank and make it appear weak and unreliable. It was intended to lure the enemy down from the heights and to the French Emperor's right.

"The mists and fogs that settled in front of the Heights had concealed the forces he would thrust through the enemy's center to retake the Pratzen Heights and, from high ground, encircle to the rear the troops lured to assault his right flank. This accomplished, the French army was later free to encircle the enemy's left flank as well, and thus achieved a decisive victory. A costly mistake for the allied emperors who opposed him. Indeed, eventually it resulted in the dissolution of the Holy Roman Empire."

The Professor stopped pacing and resumed the chair behind his desk.

"What lesson might we draw from this?" he asked, and waited patiently for my answer.

Finally, I admitted I could not come up with anything.

"Perhaps that is quite enough for your first day," the Professor offered, and I was surprised to find how disappointed I was that it should end.

The Professor led me out of his office. Behind Sir Nigel's closed door, the verbal conflict seemed to have escalated. That is when the epiphany came to me. Professor Lechner had quite cunningly identified and manipulated Sir Nigel's mortal weakness: vanity.

"You already knew Professor Clive, didn't you? Was it you who invited him to the estate?"

"What makes you think so?"

"But it must have been you. You didn't just let Sir Nigel make mistakes. You goaded him into talking more than he should have."

"Even the most adroit men have a weakness," he admitted. "Some have half a dozen."

"And, then, like Napoleon, you were careful not to interrupt them," I declared.

Slowly, the Professor's expression melted into an even broader smile. He stood that way, assessing me for some time, before he nodded, as much to himself as to me.

"Just so," he whispered. "Just so."

PROFESSOR LECHNER LED me out of his office and, bound for the Italian Gardens for what had become his ritual stroll, walked with me through the Grand Library into the Hall of Ancestors.

"Professor Lechner," I said, stopping to turn and look at him. "You've been on the estate before, haven't you?"

The Professor gave me a broad smile, his eyes blazing, and stroked his handlebar mustache delicately, but said nothing.

"Are there really secret passages under us?"

"*Ach*, you wish me to betray the long-held mysteries of the manor . . ." He turned and looked up at the oversize portrait of Leopold I, and an expression something like reverence washed across his face.

"It is dangerous, the temptation to romanticize danger or war. *Ja*, the thrill; the rush of hazards almost appeals through the foggy lens of history. But it is the curse of the historian that she drapes her subject in unwarranted glory. The terror of chaos is less romantic in person, eh?

"You must believe me when I tell you that wisdom washes away this appeal. I must admit that I, too, was once intoxicated by it." The Professor produced a little silver pillbox from an inside pocket and shook it with a rattle. "But I am not a young man anymore and my heart is too weak for such folly."

Professor Lechner gestured to the portrait again. "Dare we treat so lightly the secrets he and his descendants so jealously guarded? These must be earned, not yielded to misguided, romantic notions of battle."

It was a concept my grandfather had also articulated: that certain secrets must be earned.

"Would you have me betray the secrets they gave their lives to protect?"

Betrayer of secrets. Traitor.

The Professor's idle comment was a casual reminder of Augustin's accusations. My expression must have darkened, and the Professor saw it.

"Yes. Just so," he said, and gestured to Leopold. "He is dust now." He pointed down the long hallway at the other portraits. "All of them. Dust. You must study them. Look into their eyes. See just some hint of the dangers they faced. It is no light thing to be a member of your family.

"A secret, *ja?*" he said, breaking the moment. "This is what you want?"

I tried to suppress a grin. The Professor knelt down and reached up under the half-moon wall table beneath Leopold's portrait and retrieved something hidden there. When I recognized it as a large knife with a blade nearly eight inches long I almost took a step back.

"To cut the canvas from the frame in case of fire. To save Leopold. This is the patriarch's responsibility."

Professor Lechner slipped the knife back into its concealed sheath under the table and stood before he spoke again.

"This is *ethos*. The portrait is as a Roman legion's standard. Sacred. Do you understand?"

I nodded my head, and his talk of fire and the image of the manor ablaze terrified me.

"Is Professor Clive right, that empires only last 250 years?"

Professor Lechner smiled. "You have jumped ahead in our lessons, young lady. Shall I give you the secret to outlasting empires?"

I nodded eagerly.

Professor Lechner pointed to Leopold's portrait again.

"Begin with him," he said, and swept his hand toward the rest of the Hall of Ancestors. "And study them in turn. There you will find your answer."

~

CHAPTER TEN

The Fate of Empires

T HOUGH IT KEPT ME UP ALL night, the answer to Professor Lechner's puzzle about empires eluded me. The next morning, after breaking my fast, I dressed and hurried downstairs. But, on my way to "Lechner Hall," voices floating out from the half-open door to Sir Nigel's office stopped me. I crept closer, careful to hug the wall so as not to be seen through the cracked door.

"The *Examiner*?" Professor Clive was saying.

"I assure you," Sir Nigel answered. "He sent one of the staff to ask for it specifically."

For men who had been locked in vicious verbal conflict only the day before, their tone seemed awfully collegial in comparison.

"I must say," Sir Nigel continued, "that I was rather shocked that someone actually wished to *read* the overwrought scribblings of a long-extinct circle of radical progressives."

"What do you mean, exactly?" Professor Clive said, a note of caution slipping into his voice.

"Whigs," Sir Nigel breathed, as if it pained him even to name these demons from the past.

"Come now. You can hardly critique the movement away from raw aristocracy into constitutional monarchy as some sort of—"

"—yes, yes. But this is exactly my point. What interest could such an absolutist have in the *Examiner*, the propaganda outlet of the Hunt Circle?"

"An . . . absolutist?"

"But, it is not possible that you did not know this," Sir Nigel breathed. "Though I admit that I too was quite surprised to find assigned as the young woman's educator an unrepentant monarchist."

Professor Clive took a moment to digest this. "Really?"

"My dear man, and I know we have had our differences, but I must point out, with the best of intentions of course, that continuing to wallow in social ignorance in these circles can rise to the level of actual danger. The man's *Who's Who* entry makes for horrifying reading. See for yourself." There was the sound of a thick volume being dropped on Sir Nigel's desk. "Did you not know he was tutor to the Archduke Felix?"

"How on earth would I know that?" Professor Clive objected.

"Of course, the monarchy and the Hapsburg family itself were dissolved after the Great War. The Archduke's father, Charles, was exiled to Switzerland and not long after the entire family was even expelled from there, when, if you can imagine, he attempted to seize the Hungarian throne and restore himself as king.

"The Archduke and his brother had never renounced their claims, you see, preferring to flee rather than have pulled from their shoulders the purple robes of aristocracy. This new 'tutor,' such as he is, was responsible for preparing the young Archduke to overthrow the Austrian government."

"*Overthrow?*" Professor Clive breathed, horrified.

"And then to install the young pupil upon the Austro-Hungarian throne, and restore the monarchy to power. I must tell you that, from other independent research I have conducted, it seems clear that this same Lechner was also an advisor to the Egyptian president Anwar Sadat."

"Surely not."

"He was resident in Egypt at least until Sadat was assassinated by his own military in 1981. I expect this 'tutor' was forced to flee the country in fear for his life. I am astounded he is permitted *near* children, much less to instruct them."

"I must say, Nigel, all this is quite fascinating, I'm sure, but I find your supposed pretensions to liberal thought a bit late to the party and, I think I can be forgiven for saying so, rather affected."

Sir Nigel sounded increasingly nervous. "Now just a minute. One cannot rise to such heights of professional scholarship as I have managed to achieve without having at least a passing affinity for the concepts of the Enlightenment."

He paused, as if waiting for Professor Clive to acknowledge his disclaimer.

"Well," Sir Nigel continued. "Some of them. Truly, one can be a royalist without believing in the divine right of kings, after all." Another pause. "I am certain you take my meaning."

"Of course, *Sir* Nigel," Professor Clive said, emphasizing the honorific.

I slipped away and toward Professor Lechner's office, but something caught my eye first: a brass plaque had replaced the old, faded business card on Sir Nigel's door. It was conspicuously larger and more ornate than Professor Lechner's and had obviously been recently (and vigorously) polished. It read:

SIR NIGEL LESLIE HAWTHORNE-PITT IV KBE, DLITT, FBA

BY THAT SECOND day, Professor Lechner had developed a rather unconventional academic routine for us. The Professor and I would meet in the library or his office in the late morning and simply discuss, and discuss, and discuss. Often the Professor would have lunch served on his conference table to avoid interrupting the flow of his lessons. We would converse together for hours on end, hours that melted away until it was so late that I might miss dinner.

It could not have been a greater contrast to lessons delivered by my previous tutors: mindless recitation of rules of etiquette, the proper order for the use of silverware, or styles of address for various noble and common ranks and titles. Professor Lechner required my active participation, insisted on a real dialogue, and never hesitated to engage me in deep, wide-ranging conversations. And, when the discussion extended into territory where my knowledge was inadequate to continue, the Professor would assign relevant study material to me. We might be in the middle of discussing the limits of democracy, or constructing solutions for failures in market systems, when the Professor would end our session abruptly.

"I am just not sure how we can continue a discussion on the ethics of rulers when you haven't even a passing acquaintance with the *Secretum Secretorum*," he might say. "I understand that the Copland translation is on the shelves somewhere."

Then he would carefully pack up his little writing kit and depart, leaving me to hunt for the certain-to-be-obscure volume and pore over it by the next morning.

Much later, I realized that what appeared to be free-flowing conversations were actually very intense, interactive lectures with carefully defined (if unrevealed to me) goals.

Our library's rare deficiencies did not always close the books on a scholarly project. In these cases, the Professor adopted the habit of sending researchers from my grandfather's staff to London by private plane to visit the Public Record Office or the Royal Commission on Historical Manuscripts, and to return with copies or briefings summarizing the relevant material.

Later, there followed a long progression of "guest lecturers" that Professor Lechner would produce without warning. I would come downstairs in the morning to find him engaged in energetic debate with, for example, the foremost expert on *kleroteria* (the random tabulating devices used to select citizens to state offices in ancient Greece), or a scholar who had spent decades studying the poisons used by assassins of the ancient world.

I wrote Bastien often in those days, trying in vain to articulate how my world was changing, the experience of having my intellect tickled and challenged, rather than being treated like a Dictaphone. Often I wondered in print how the conservatory was, if Bastien was making friends, or what sort of music he was playing.

More than once I started a letter to Augustin, but those I could never manage to finish. I toyed with the idea of writing to Yves as well, but, terrified that Augustin would read them, too, never got any further than the salutation.

Soon enough, I barely had time for letter writing. Still, I was so entertained that it seemed a mere side effect that I found myself becoming an expert on topics that ranged from the diplomacy of the Papal States, the history of the East India Company and the Opium Wars, and the rise of London banking in the mid-1600s, to the impact of the Boer Wars on colonial commerce. Without even knowing it, I was being given a princely education in everything from classical economics to international relations.

I was too young—and far too engrossed—to wonder why.

When I expressed greater interest in my family's activities during the Second World War, Professor Lechner began to notice.

"Can it be," the Professor taunted me in a not unkindly way, "that we have found a student with such romantic notions that she must side ever with the underdog?"

"But I want to learn about Grandfather. During the war, I mean."

The Professor smiled at me, but changed the subject.

Two days later he found me waiting outside his office, nearly an hour before our lesson time, reading several works by the North Vietnamese general Giáp I had found in the library. On seeing the books, he seemed concerned.

"Now, my dear," he scolded me. "Again this fascination with irregular warfare? The foibles of youth, I suppose? You must leave these with me," he said, collecting the books. "Warriors are but pawns to statesmen. Which would you prefer to be, do you think?"

That evening, when I caught sight of the Professor carrying the confiscated books toward the East Salon, I fell in behind him. When he was safely ensconced inside, I crept close and pressed my ear against the door to listen.

"What strange subject matter," my grandfather was saying. "You haven't created a Marxist revolutionary under my roof, have you?"

"I don't think it is the politics she is interested in," the Professor said. "It is your history that attracts her."

"I was only jesting, my old friend. You cannot imagine I would be worried about your instruction. Also, she could do far worse than Giáp, you know."

"Yes, certainly his success against the Americans was noteworthy. But, I must also venture an opinion."

"Yes?"

"She has only ever known this estate. If we have any cause to be worried about her politics, how long can this be healthy? She has the romantic tendencies of youth, but it is naïveté mixed with romanticism that breeds revolutionaries. The revolution eats its own in the end, certainly, but it always seems to be the idealists that serve as the appetizers."

"You did always have a way with words," my grandfather said, with a wry laugh. "I have already taken note of this particular deficiency in her experience. Leave it with me."

～⌒～

AS SPRING APPROACHED, for the first time since he had arrived, Professor Lechner left the estate on a mysterious errand. Strangely, my grandfather also seemed to be missing, and for two days in a row my late-night knocks on his door went unanswered. I had no one to talk to.

I think it was this idleness that attracted me to that dark corner of the Grand Library that had so annoyed Sir Nigel. Or perhaps Sir Nigel's obvious distaste for those shelves made a certain appeal to youthful rebellion.

After trying the lock on a display case with the astrolabes and finding it disappointingly secure, I pulled several books on spiritualism and the occult and sat on the floor to peruse them.

What started as an exploration into eighteenth-century notions of ghosts and spirits quickly shifted back to astronomy once I began to browse those pages of *Physica Curiosa* that dealt with meteorites. Before long, I had unshelved a dozen old texts on the topic and was absorbed in those instead. When later I looked down into the library proper, I saw that the sun had long since set.

I was too lazy to get the stepladder from the other side of the floor. Instead, I stood on my tiptoes to urge the last of the books (two large volumes I had not had time to examine) back onto the higher shelves. I was in the process of tilting the larger of the two, a weighty book in Latin, when I lost my grip. It fell, striking me on the forehead before crashing to the floor, kicking up a small cloud of ancient dust, and falling open in the process.

When I recovered and went to pick up the fallen volume, I saw that a second, smaller book that had been closed inside the larger work had slipped out and onto the floor. Flipping through it, I found the pages covered in handwriting, though the last dozen were blank. The text had been written in an elegant, enthusiastic hand, though in places the cursive was conspicuously ornate, difficult to read, and the archaic use of language difficult to understand.

The ink varied from page to page and in places there were notes scrawled in the margins, or snatches of verse covering the whole page but written sideways. Near the end, I was thrilled to find hand-drawn, annotated illustrations of constellations in the night sky. Apparently I was holding the seventeenth-century scratchbook of an astronomy-obsessed author, perhaps one who had once peered at the stars from the same roof I often did. But it was when I skipped to the last entry that my heart really started to pound.

I leave in haste and must abandon these pages so as not to be discovered with them. Yet, though I dare not commit my darker revelations to paper, I fear my words shall be read by eyes from which I would conceal my discoveries. What clues I may have unwittingly left in these pages I cannot with confidence say. I know now that I must hide these words just as I saw Father hide his, and hope they remain just as secret still, and that I shall find that they await me should ever I return home. Should instead misfortune befall me, should this entry be my last, perhaps it would be some small comfort that, though I be gone, you, dear reader, should know and remember me as,

—Sophia Marie, October, 1691

"Sophia, the daughter of Leopold I," I breathed. "A year after she 'disappeared.'"

I SCOOPED UP THE diary and the larger volume, flew down the stairs and through the main reading floor of the Grand Library. I was in such haste that I nearly plowed headlong into one of the maids before barging into the narrow hallway. Despite the darkened skies outside, I found Sir Nigel in his office looking over an oversize and very old-looking book and taking notes in longhand.

"Ah," he sighed when he saw me. "If it isn't the young lady of the many questions, arrived here, no doubt, with a new pack of scintillating queries. It seems far too long ago, the era in which children were sacrificed in exchange for a few weeks of good weather, don't you think?"

"Sir Nigel," I said, trying to catch my breath, "do you know when Professor Lechner is to return?"

"As it seems clear you are laboring under the misapprehension that I am some sort of personal assistant to trespassing academics, let me disabuse you of that notion immediately."

Sir Nigel's eyes drifted to the books I was carrying.

"And, what exactly are you doing running about with those? Perhaps this begins to explain the recent and precipitous climb of our restoration budget. I must tell you that I am inclined to petition the foundation to limit all access to those over the age of majority. Who gave you those works?"

"No one. I found this book mislaid inside—"

"Mislaid? Mislaid?" Sir Nigel shook his head, as if my very presence was more than he could endure. "No, I don't think so. In over twenty years of curation, including, I might add, a review of nearly every single volume in the library, I have only once found a mislaid text. My predecessor, in his infinite wisdom, elected to shelve a horrific work on Soviet architecture under the larger category of 'public structures,' if you can imagine. And so there it sat, corrupting by its mere proximity, a brilliant work by Dmitri Shvidkovsky. In fact, some years before my tenure here . . ."

I laid the large book I had found on his desk in front of him.

"It was inside this," I said.

Sir Nigel trailed off as he began to register the details of the find. He opened it gently and, once his gaze fell upon the title page, his entire body was gripped by a sharp intake of breath. He pulled his hands away from the book as if it had burned his fingers. Only after donning white gloves did he begin turning the pages. Then he reached absently for the nearest boom-mounted magnifying glass and switched on the light.

"It cannot be," he offered to no one in particular. His hands began to tremble. "A . . . first edition? Impossible."

I held out the diary for him to see. "I found this inside it," I said, but Sir Nigel ignored me.

"Who gave you this piece?" he demanded, after a long interlude.

"I found it."

"You *found* what may be an authentic first edition of *Astronomia Nova*? Abandoned in the kitchens? On a walk in the gardens? Preposterous. I have cataloged every volume here." A pause. "Essentially every volume."

"It was with the occult books."

"Do you mean to tell me . . ." Sir Nigel was incredulous at first, but grew silent before he finished his sentence.

"What sort of book is it?" I said.

"What sort of . . . ? Young lady, this is Johannes Kepler's masterwork. It is the first publication in which he describes the laws of planetary motion. It is—"

"I know who Kepler is," I said, realizing that, in my haste to look at the diary, I had missed the name on the larger book.

Sir Nigel closed his eyes and put the back of his hand to his head. "The insolence of modern youth knows no bounds," he whispered to himself.

"I am to believe this book, a central piece of the history of natural sciences, was shelved next to some fool's sulfur-encrusted laboratory notes composed during his quest for the philosopher's stone? If you do not start telling me the truth, I shall be forced to—"

"Sir Nigel, I think it was purposefully hidden there long ago. I think it was meant to conceal this."

I held out the diary again. Sir Nigel ignored my offering and went back to Kepler's work, turning the pages delicately, scarcely daring to touch it.

"It fell out when I dropped the Kepler book."

Sir Nigel paled.

"You . . . *dropped it?*" he breathed.

"I think this is the diary of Leopold I's daughter. She signed her name here, see?"

Slowly, Sir Nigel began to regain his color. I opened the smaller book to the last entry and pressed it into his hands.

I thought he might be about to fly into a blind rage, but once he caught sight of the handwriting in the smaller book, the curator in him returned. He turned a few pages and then seemed to forget the Kepler volume.

"A diary? Well, after a fashion. It is a commonplace book. A diary, scrapbook, and a notepad in a single bound volume. They were popular with young women beginning in the fifteenth and lasting into the seventeenth centuries."

Gingerly, Sir Nigel moved the Kepler work to the side, placed the new text on his desk, and then leaned close and peered at it through the illuminated magnifying glass.

"This one is quite old. Late 1600s I should think from the paper."

"Look where I showed you. It says 1691."

"Young lady, it is axiomatic, perhaps even the very first axiom of curation, that one never, ever accepts as definitive any date written on a document." He hesitated. "Where did you see this date?"

"It's right there on the last page, where Sophia signed it."

"Preposterous," Sir Nigel said as he meticulously turned to the last pages. "October . . . sixteen . . . ninety . . . one . . . Sophia Marie." Sir Nigel bolted upright. "But . . . this cannot be."

"Sophia must have been studying the Kepler volume and used it for a hiding place."

Even as I said it, I could feel myself getting excited, picturing Sophia sitting at her desk, a copy of *Astronomia Nova* open next to her, drawing constellations and the paths of the planets in her commonplace book as she looked out her window into the cold, night sky.

"Dear *God*," Sir Nigel gasped, leaning so close that his breath fogged the magnifying glass.

"What is it?"

He shook his head. "It is quite impossible to say for sure this early in the evaluation process," Sir Nigel said, and then muttered to himself. "There is certainly a rather distinguished history in the practice of forging diaries. Then again, who would bother to forge a commonplace book? And to what end?"

"Is it Sophia's? The daughter of Leopold I, I mean."

"Young lady, you must leave these volumes with me."

My heart fell. "But I wasn't done looking at the diary," I said. "May I finish reading it first?"

"I'm afraid that is quite impossible."

"Well, may I read it when you reshelve it? I mean, reshelve it in the proper place, of course."

"That's out of the question."

Sir Nigel held his hand out, hovering it over the Kepler book.

"There are perhaps a dozen copies of this volume left in good condition in the entire world. If it is authentic, it might well fetch over a hundred thousand pounds sterling at auction, though the foundation would never dream of selling it.

"But this . . ." he said of the diary, "*this* work may be the only example in existence of a diary from the rule of Leopold I, the founding patriarch of your family. Unless this is a very clever forgery, it is a truly singular historical document, containing the contemporaneous musings and thoughts of the daughter of the founder of the dynasty, not just a contemporary of Leopold, but a member of the direct line and, I might add, a personage about whom almost no record exists after her coming of age. I couldn't begin to assign a value to this piece. It is literally priceless.

"Reshelve it? Certainly not. My first duty is to preserve and stabilize it, to consider developing a restoration protocol, and most of all to protect it. In the meantime, it will be stored in the vault. I cannot believe it was left out of a carefully controlled climate for so long. The entire section in which it was found will have to be reviewed volume by volume and recataloged. If indeed he can be found, my predecessor should be thoroughly flogged for criminal negligence. These finds must be attended to. The schedule of my entire research program will be disrupted now. I must ask you to leave at once."

After a spate of fruitless protest, Sir Nigel ushered me out of his office. Silently, I chided myself for not reading the whole diary through before showing it to anyone. There was some consolation in the knowledge that I had made a great discovery (two great discoveries, if the Kepler book was included) but I moped around the library for half an hour feeling sorry for myself regardless.

PROFESSOR LECHNER RETURNED the morning after. He had settled into the estate by that time and had moved many of his scholarly effects—a seemingly endless collection of volumes, notes, articles, and even the occasional historical object—into his office.

I wanted to tell him about my discoveries but wondered if I should keep the diary secret. In any event, the Professor barely gave me the chance. Our last "conversation" had started with the Wars of the Roses and progressed steadily into the particulars of lines and treaties of succession and various mechanisms of inheritance and, as if he had never departed, the Professor picked up right where we left off. We had just begun discussing modern trusts and foundations when I was called off to dinner. For the entire meal my head was filled with notions of entities with ancient and mysterious purposes, giving sway to what Professor Lechner had termed "the hand of the dead" and the constant efforts of governments to frustrate or even destroy those same forces. It was a term my grandfather had also used to describe the branch that scratched at his window, though his example had been much more visceral. Those visions followed me back to my room and occupied my thoughts well into the late hours.

THOUGH I THOUGHT it unwise to discuss the commonplace book with Professor Lechner, I could certainly talk about it with my grandfather. Normally I would have waited longer, but I was excited enough that it was barely midnight when I crept downstairs.

The scent of his pipe smoke in the hallway outside the East Salon had its usual calming effect on me, but when I reached the door it was ajar. A sliver of light—a warning beacon—beamed into the hallway. I stopped short of inviting myself in and instead lingered to listen to the voices inside.

"I am not exaggerating to say that it had been under our noses the entire time," Sir Nigel was saying.

"Under *your* nose you mean," my grandfather said.

"Ah . . . yes. Quite. I must beg your forgive—"

"I am jesting with you. Nigel, you really must work on your sense of humor."

"It has been of little use to me in life. If I might continue, it was the oil paint, you see, and the more rapid leaching of the yellow that aged the pigment from green to the dull blue one sees today. Quite remarkable, actually. And then, when it was unhung, the balance of the frame was so obviously off. All these years the missing first volume was hidden inside the portrait itself."

I heard the familiar sound of old paper, the aged pages of a book being turned.

"Do be careful, sir," Sir Nigel said.

"Do you think it authentic?"

"One must always resist the temptation to allow excitement to color the skeptical appraisal of authenticity," Sir Nigel said sagely, and then with much less restraint: "And yet how could it not be? His was the only portrait not made posthumously. But why conceal the volume that way? Who did he fear would read it? His contemporaries? His heirs?"

"That last is a very dangerous question," my grandfather said.

Sir Nigel laughed.

"That, my friend, was not a jest. It was a much more violent time, the formative years of this dynasty. There is no telling what we may uncover."

"Sir, it is in this spirit that I brought you the volume. If you would care to look at the text here."

"It looks like gibberish in German."

"Precisely. It is, in fact, Classical Latin, but written with German phonetics. Easy to write and read, but only if one knows both languages and the transposition method. Quite cleverly designed and intended, I believe, to conceal."

"To conceal what, precisely?"

"I have prepared a preliminary translation here."

I heard the shuffling of papers.

"He would have it," my grandfather's voice read, "and lacks for patience. Should I perceive the approach of foulest knavery I shall carve the bloodred heart from it and it shall forever bear witness to treachery."

"You think he writes this of his own heir?"

"I am most certain of it. And this language, 'the bloodred heart.' You think it means something?"

"I did not, until I found this document." There was another shuffling of paper. "An invoice, of sorts. Dated months after Leopold's death. Repair of an 'insignia.' Replacement of a ruby gemstone. Fifteen carats to be cut from the common stone."

"The 'common stone'?"

"Yes, milord. I have, as yet, been unable to decipher the meaning of that phrase, but it seems clear that Leopold removed the ruby, the 'bloodred heart' of the insignia of his newly founded order, to deny it to his heir. Don't you see? It is Uther Pendragon burying the sword Excalibur in the stone to deny it to pretenders. A denial and a sign. A warning that he—"

"Enough," my grandfather interrupted.

"You must permit me to examine the insignia of the order. What if—"

"I said enough."

There was a long silence before my grandfather spoke again.

"You are to discuss this discovery with no one."

"But, shouldn't your son be—"

"I said *no one*," my grandfather snapped. Then, recovering his composure, he sighed. "Forgive me, but I want to make sure that order is abundantly clear."

"Of course."

"And this?"

"A commonplace book. She found it in the stacks. I believe it might actually be from Leopold's daughter. Absolutely remarkable. A crass oversight by my predecessor, and on that note I must say—"

"Two such discoveries in the same week? It would seem my granddaughter has a greater affinity with her ancestors, and Leopold I in particular, than anyone might have guessed."

My ancestral patron, I thought. *It should be Leopold I.*

"She is a remark—"

In my excitement, I had leaned too close to the door, just brushing it with my sleeve. It shifted slightly and the old hinge on the top emitted a low, creaking groan. All conversation stopped. My heart seemed inclined to do the same. I could feel them looking at the door; through it. I held my breath.

"You left the door unlatched, Nigel."

I heard footsteps approach and then, gently, the door was closed from the inside.

After my narrow escape, it was all I could do not to run back to my apartments. But, on the way, something in the Hall of Ancestors stopped me cold. Even in the gloom of night it was obvious: Leopold I's portrait was gone.

—

CHAPTER ELEVEN

One Small Step

MY GRANDFATHER'S CONVERSATION WITH SIR NIGEL bled into my dreams that night and, more than once, threatened to transform into the beginnings of a nightmare—faceless portraits, hidden meanings, inscrutable mysteries. But, before those dark phantasms could coalesce into something coherent enough to spawn a night terror, a dim flickering of red through my closed eyelids woke me: candlelight.

I opened my eyes to find a dark figure leaning across the side of my bed and looming over me. Frightened, I drew in a sharp breath, but the figure pressed a finger to its lips for silence. I blinked until my eyes began to adjust and the figure resolved into the shadowy outline of a man holding a candelabra. It was a man I recognized from the estate, but could not name.

I was still battling the sleep away when my brain finally registered his presence as wholly material. In that moment, I knew him for one of my grandfather's aides, and with that came the understanding that, like many members of my grandfather's entourage, he had been lingering just outside the edge of my vision for as long as I could remember. It was not that he was invisible but rather that, in passing, the eye never seemed quite drawn to him, like a soft background sound one hears for a long time before it finally (and all at once) rises up to the level of perception.

He held his position—dark brown eyes peering down from a tall, broad-shouldered frame topped with dark, short-cropped hair, and a shadow of a salt-and-pepper beard—until he was sure I understood his pantomime. Then he led me—barefoot and still in my nightdress—out of my rooms in complete silence.

The clock in my foyer showed twelve minutes after two in the morning. For light we had only the candles he held as I followed him through the long hallway and downstairs. It never occurred to me to question him. The entire encounter had a dreamlike quality, and I assumed that anyone permitted to work closely with my grandfather was by definition absolutely trustworthy. I followed along rather innocently and with no thought of danger or betrayal.

When we reached one of the side doors he laid the candelabra on a table and methodically pinched out each of the burning wicks. He was much better dressed for the occasion, wearing a black overcoat atop a dark blazer, and a white dress shirt with the collar open and no tie (an outfit I would eventually find so typical of him I would regard it as a uniform).

At the motor pool the aide opened the door to one of the estate's Land Rovers and took out a coat that he held for me to put on. I noticed something strange before I climbed into the passenger seat. Despite the fact that the cold morning air had turned my breath into a hint of frost, it hadn't seemed to me that the dark figure had emitted any. For a moment, my imagination convinced me that he was somehow inhuman.

MY EXCITEMENT GREW when I saw the aide was driving us to the helipad. Some years before, my mother had insisted that the landing surface, once only a few hundred yards from the manor, was an undue intrusion on the aesthetic ambience of the estate (and her Italian Gardens in particular). I think she hoped that my grandfather would abandon his admittedly self-indulgent habit of taking one of the helicopters for the three-mile trip from our private airstrip to the manor, but instead he had the pad moved to the other side of a wooded ridge about five hundred yards farther down. He ordered a dirt road cut through the forest between the new pad and the manor's main driveway, which meant a solid week inundated with the harsh buzzing of chain saws. My mother let the matter drop after that.

The Land Rover emerged from the tree-lined road to find one of the helicopters—rotors still; sheathed in black; as spotless as if it were in a showroom—waiting silently. I had flown in them with my grandfather before, though only on those short hops from the manor to our airstrip, where I would bid him farewell before he boarded one of the jets and flew off on another of his mysterious missions.

But that night, as we pulled up to the helicopter and the aide got out of the Land Rover, opened my door, and motioned for me to follow, my grandfather was nowhere to be found. I could see the pilot alone in the helicopter, illuminated in the soft, amber glow of the instrument lights. As the aide led me toward the craft, the low whine of the turbine spinning up began and the rotors started to churn the cold air. He held the door for me and I was thrilled to find that I would be sitting next to the pilot in the cockpit. As we lifted off and made for the airstrip, I watched the many dials on the instrument panels. My grandfather had once described all of their functions to me and, as we flew, I mentally cycled through them to remember what they were for.

Our private airstrip had been laid down before I was born, a paved affair at the far southwestern extreme of the estate that was just large enough to accommodate all but the most runway-hungry private planes. As the helicopter approached it, I could see that only one of our jets sat on the tarmac. We landed about five hundred feet from it and the helicopter pilot shut off the landing lights as soon as the skids had settled so that the rotorcraft was enveloped by the night once more.

Not five seconds after we stepped out of the helicopter and closed the doors, the pilot lifted his hand to my grandfather's aide, a gesture the aide returned formally. The pilot put on the power and the helicopter pulled away and out of view, angry red lights blinking, bathing the terrain around us in a dark ruby hue as it climbed up and off into the dark sky. As the sounds of the turbine and the blades faded into the distance, we were lowered into a cold pool of nighttime silence.

The departure of the helicopter startled me. Would we be expected to walk all the way back to the manor? I had no time to wonder. Instead, I hurried along behind my escort, wincing when I stepped on the occasional pebble with my bare feet, struggling to keep up with his long strides as we approached the darkened jet. I thought the craft abandoned until the repeating red flash of its beacon light started up.

When we were within 150 feet, the jet's door opened and a set of folding stairs presented themselves under an inviting curtain of light from the cabin. My guide waited at the bottom while I climbed up. Inside, the cockpit was already closed off and the pilots were, I assumed, busying themselves with the mysterious rituals of preparation.

It wasn't the first time I had been aboard one of our jets. Once, when my grandfather's departure had been delayed, he had let me join him in the cabin as the sleek craft waited on our tarmac for the weather to clear up enough for the plane's air traffic control release to come through. I remember crying when conditions improved and I had to debark and watch as it took off without me.

The plane I had just boarded, however, was newer. The interior was wood and leather wherever I looked. The little galley smelled of fresh coffee. In the first row, two sets of chairs on either side of the middle aisle faced each other. Farther toward the rear was a doorway to the aft private compartment. The door was half-open and I could see my father sitting in a swivel chair. He was concentrating on some papers and did not look up.

It only dawned on me that I was going somewhere when the aide closed the cabin door and the jet's three engines began to wind up. I was going on a trip. With my father. It took a long moment to sink in.

The aide got me settled into the front row. Though I had grown since my last visit aboard one of our jets, my chair was still just a bit too big. I had to scoot forward to the very edge to touch the soft carpet below, and sitting there with my dirty bare feet felt somehow sacrilegious.

The quiet game everyone was playing was unnerving but I reminded myself that my father's default disposition was silence. I resolved not to be the first one to break the unwritten "no talking" rule. It took a great deal of effort to resist the urge to play with the chairs, try the buttons that turned the lights on and off, or open and close the folding tables, but I managed.

I distracted myself by gazing out the window as the plane started to taxi, turned into a takeoff roll, and I felt it in my stomach as we jumped into the sky. I wondered if my father had taken Augustin on similarly mysterious journeys. I thought of my older brother's many unexplained absences from the estate and speculated (jealously) which of them might have encompassed an exotic trip to parts unknown.

Even when climbing, the jet was much quieter than the helicopter and, about five minutes after takeoff, I was watching the flashes of the red beacon light up the soupy clouds we were flying through. There were soft footsteps behind me. I turned, expecting to see the aide, but it was my father.

He turned to my escort and said, "Karl, I'd like to speak to my daughter for a moment."

Karl.

Had I ever known his name?

I tried to remember the last time my father had called me his "daughter" in front of others. Karl nodded curtly and shifted to an aft seat.

My father sat down across from me. I wanted to ask him a million questions, but his expression did not invite inquiry. I remember thinking that it was as if I were seeing him for the first time as a person, rather than some mysterious and intimidating entity; an opaque protagonist in someone else's play. In my memory there was a consistent perfection about him. Always immaculately groomed. Always wearing cuff links. Never, apparently, surprised by anything. Always possessed of a stoic strength that was at once impenetrable and yet somehow comforting.

"We are going to South Africa," he said, and then paused a beat. "However, this trip is '*unter vier Augen*,' absolutely private. You will not discuss it with anyone on our return. Is that clear?"

I was having a hard time absorbing what my father was saying, but I nodded.

My thoughts shifted to Augustin. I wanted to be bitter over his Sophia prank, but hadn't the strange confluence of events that followed worked somehow to put me on a jet with my father? To instill in me the interest in the imaginary Sophia that would lead me to the daughter of Leopold I? I couldn't help but smile. Having done so I recoiled, thinking I had made a mistake, but my father smiled too.

"So this will be our trip. Agreed?"

Our trip. I nodded and then bit my lip to keep from grinning again.

"You will meet many outsiders. We will be watched carefully. You must betray nothing to them."

"Yes, Father," I said.

Conversations with my father were rare. I savored the timbre of his voice—soft, almost lyric stanzas delivered with a calculated meter and tone. I had never heard him raise his voice. To the contrary, to hear him lower it (or to whisper) was what raised alarm among his aides, and his enemies. The influence my father wielded did not require volume.

"What has Professor Lechner taught you about power?"

I was eager to impress him and my mind raced to think of something relevant. *Clausewitz? Machiavelli?*

"There are only three sources of it? Accretion, grant, or conquest?" I offered.

My father smiled. "No. That's sovereignty, but very good. Historically, what were transfers of power like?"

I wasn't sure I understood what he was asking.

"Messy," he said. "What innovation provides for the smooth transfer of power?"

Again I didn't know.

"Institutions. Trusted, effective institutions. At the moment it is not at all clear that South Africa has any. That makes people very nervous. Watch and listen with that in mind. Whatever happens, remember who you are. Do you understand?"

I was afraid that I didn't, but I nodded.

My father stood up and produced a small black roller bag from the space behind my seat and put it on the floor in front of me.

"We will have to make a fuel stop, but that isn't for almost seven hours. There is a change of clothes in there for the flight. After you get dressed, come to the back and we will have an early breakfast together."

IT WAS STILL dark outside three hours after we ate. I was far too excited to sleep. My father stood up then and gestured for me to follow him forward. He knocked on the cockpit door and our copilot opened it and peered out. When he saw my father, a moment passed between the two men and the copilot smiled at me.

"Well, look who it is," the man said, turning to our pilot. He opened the door wider. "Our flight engineer decided to report for duty. Come in. I was just hoping for a break."

I obliged him and, before I knew it, I had taken the copilot's place and he was sitting in the cockpit's jump seat behind us. I had to struggle to see over the console and out the front windshields, but it was a clear night and the view was breathtaking. Ahead of us in the distance and just to the left of the nose, the dark gray silhouettes of a cluster of puffy clouds close to the surface crept over the ground near a large body of water. The moon—just starting to wane from full—gave the clouds a silver-gray look. Below us the telltale glow of human activity was dim, and its spotty clusters few and far between.

Unlike the copilot, our pilot sat stoically, wordlessly scanning the deep black before us.

"What's that over there?" I asked, pointing to the body of water.

"That's Lake Chad," our copilot said, without a second glance.

"It looks so quiet down there."

"It is not the place you would want to land," he said.

"Why not?"

He paused before he answered.

"There isn't much in the way of civilization down there. Wouldn't you rather go somewhere else?"

"Like where?"

"Well, what if we wanted to go see the Great Pyramids in Egypt?"

My smile gave me away. The copilot pointed to a panel.

"This is the Global Positioning System. Turn the big dial until it says destination, then punch in 'HECA' on the keyboard. That's the airport code for Cairo International Airport. There. You can see that if we wanted to change our destination and head there we'd just have to come left to 039 degrees and fly not quite 1,500 nautical miles, that's less than three hours."

"What if we ran out of fuel?" I asked, suddenly a little anxious.

"We wouldn't." He leaned forward and pointed to a bank of three dials on the panel in front of us. "We have three sets of tanks. They are all more than half full."

"Can you find any place with the GPS?" I said, remembering something Professor Lechner had mentioned.

"Just about."

"Can I try Thinis?"

"Where is that?"

"Egypt."

"Does it have an airport code?"

"I don't think so."

"Well, put the city name in then."

I punched in the letters but nothing showed up.

"Are you sure it has an airport?" the copilot said, frowning.

"I don't think so. It was the capital of the first Egyptian Dynasty, but the city was lost. I thought maybe we could find it again."

The captain laughed. It was the first sound he had made.

"She's got you outclassed, Tommy," he said to the copilot.

We flew for a time in silence. I gazed in wonder at the pinpricks in the dark blanket of night. Now and again a particularly bright twinkle far off in the sky would catch my eye. Invariably, it would turn out to be the blinking anticollision lights of another aircraft.

"I far prefer it at night," our copilot said, noticing my interest. "You can see all the other traffic and it is more peaceful and serene up here. What about you? Do you prefer flying at night, or during the day?"

"Night," I blurted out.

The copilot smiled, and the cockpit drifted back into silence.

I felt as if I were at the cusp of a grand journey. The dim amber glow of a hundred dials and gauges, tirelessly feeding us information on every aspect of the plane's performance; the slow crawl as the nose hungrily consumed mile after mile of the barren terrain below us; and the soft hiss of the air flowing over the aluminum skin at five hundred knots collectively filled me with delight. Though we plunged ever southward it would only take a gentle tilt of the yoke to turn us in the direction of any one of a million exotic places scattered about the globe. It was a particular feeling of freedom I would associate with flying for the rest of my life.

NOT THAT I appreciated it at the time, but my first step on ground that was not owned by my family was onto the oil-smudged concrete tarmac at the Jan Smuts International Airport in Johannesburg. I didn't feel any different stepping off the bottom of the jet's stairs onto South African soil—both feet together like a little girl jumping in rain puddles—but there was more concrete, more modernity than I had ever seen in the same place before. Age, by contrast, was everywhere on the estate. Carved into the very stones of the manor were masonry signs worn away by the centuries, left by builders who had long since turned to dust. I was thousands of miles away from home, and it felt like it.

It was unseasonably hot in Johannesburg that year. The afternoon sun was brilliant, and the sporadic gusts of parching air were harsh and alien to the pale and freckled skin on my face. We began making our way from the plane to the buildings beyond; buildings like I had never seen before, built entirely of concrete, gleaming metal, and reflective glass.

Customs and immigration was a trivial exercise, handled privately at the executive terminal. With that ritual performed, a driver in a new-model Land Rover was waiting for us in the lot outside. After I climbed in the back with my father, Karl took the front seat and we were off.

OUR DESTINATION WAS in the suburbs north of Johannesburg. A villa, almost a colonial affair, dominated by white columns and rooms opened to the outside air. The grounds were less dramatic than our own, perhaps, but immaculately groomed. A large wading pool dominated the front lawn, a reflective mirror that brought down to earth the deep blue of an expansive sky above us.

We were ushered inside by a man I took to be a butler and shown into a large, dim office, surrounded by shutters closed to the outside world. Behind a desk at the far end of the room sat a diminutive gentleman. He was clean-shaven with a bald head and what looked like an old burn scar, a pale and irregular ripple of skin that marred his left cheek and ran up to what was left of his eyebrow. Though he reminded me of my grandfather, he was noticeably older, perhaps in his eighties.

He looked up from his papers when we came in. His eyes were dark, a raptor's—a hawk, perhaps. There was something predatory in his look, but it evaporated completely when he saw us and a broad smile spread across his face.

Standing behind him and to his right was a young woman of perhaps twenty. She was beautiful and quite tall, with an oval face highlighted by dark red lipstick and a touch of sunburn on her cheeks, marked contrasts to her otherwise pale skin. She wore her almost black hair pulled back and in a tight bun skewered by two long hair sticks. Something about her bearing fascinated me. Though she seemed surprised at the arrival of outsiders, her poise projected an uninterrupted dignity and grace. There was an immense confidence in her and I was jealous of it the moment I recognized how much it affected me.

"Ah, of course," the man said.

His accent was what I would later learn was Afrikaans, and there seemed to be genuine warmth and pleasure in his greeting.

"Do come in," he beckoned, and then stood, perhaps with some difficulty, though he hid it well, and rounded the desk to offer my father his hand.

"Mr. Ackermann," my father said. "It is a pleasure to meet you."

"But we have already met, you see. You were still quite young."

My father smiled. "Ah, yes. I think I must have been fifteen."

"Please call me Rynold. 'Mr. Ackermann' is far too formal for old friends of our family."

My father gestured to us. "This is Karl Schellenberg, and my daughter."

"My daughter Viona," Ackermann said, indicating the woman behind him, and I remember being taken aback by the great age difference between them. "And where," Ackermann said, turning to Viona, "is Ruben?"

Viona gave him a blank look. "I'm sorry, Father," she said. "I do not know."

Her voice was light and had a lyrical quality to it, some combination of formal British English and her father's Afrikaans.

A flash of anger threatened his expression, but he managed to bury it. "You must forgive my son," he said. "Apparently he has other priorities today."

"Please, sit," Mr. Ackermann said, gesturing to the chairs in front of his desk. "Hendrik," he called to the butler, "would you bring tea and ask Reinier to join us?"

Ackermann gestured to his daughter, indicating the second of two chairs next to him and behind his desk. With perfect posture—ankles crossed, hands in her lap as if at a formal function—Viona sat, leaving the chair immediately next to her father empty.

"How is your father?" Mr. Ackermann asked.

"Quite well," my father said. "He insisted that I take the time to meet with you."

"Ah, Phillip. The formalities have always been a passion of his. Unnecessary though it may be, I appreciate the courtesy. You mustn't take seriously the banter about our families being adversaries. I'm afraid that bit of gossip began with Phillip. He did so enjoy taunting the press in those days. But, despite what might have ended up in print, Phillip and I were never enemies or even competitors. In fact, it might be stretching the point to suggest we were even business rivals."

A pair of double doors at the far end of the room opened and a very tall man came in. His fair skin was badly sunburned and the pinkish hue clashed with his washed-out blue eyes. I took him to be about my father's age.

"Reinier Van Zyl is the managing director of Ackermann et Cie," Mr. Ackermann said.

He seemed on the verge of saying something else when two giant dogs exploded into the room from the open doors, almost knocking the managing director over in the process.

Mr. Ackermann held up a staying hand. "Don't be alarmed," he said. "They are quite friendly, though they have no sense of their own size."

The animals were magnificent, with bright, intelligent eyes that peered out from the wrinkled skin on their heads. Despite their bulk, they covered the distance from the double doors to us in a fraction of a second. Ackermann affected a cross look and scolded them playfully.

"Argon, Xenon, shame on you. Lie down," he commanded.

They ignored him completely and proceeded to make a circuit of the room to sniff loudly at each of us.

Ackermann looked to be at the verge of growing truly angry with the animals when Viona spoke three short commands in Afrikaans. Without a hint of protest the two beasts froze in place, went to her, fell completely silent, and slumped to the floor at her feet. Once settled, they gazed up at her longingly.

Ackermann turned to us. "I do apologize. Normally they are not permitted in the house when we have guests."

"Mastiffs?" my father said.

"Boerboels, though they are often incorrectly called 'South African mastiffs.' They are supposedly descended from the bulldogs brought over by Van Riebeeck himself and then mixed with local breeds with an eye toward guarding homesteads."

The commotion over, Van Zyl circled around until he hovered behind Viona's right shoulder and, as Ackermann began speaking again, Van Zyl leaned down to whisper in her ear. After a few seconds, Viona stood and sat in the chair immediately next to her father. Slowly, the dogs crept across the floor until they were once again at her feet.

With so much of my attention occupied by Viona Ackermann, who seemed to be looking at me whenever I glanced in her direction, I had trouble following the conversation. Before I knew it, our little meeting was drawing to a close. When I was finally undistracted enough to really look at him, Rynold Ackermann seemed tired to me, as if even our short meeting had drained him.

"I have very much enjoyed seeing you again and meeting your lovely daughter," Ackermann was saying as we made our way to the front door. "I hope your commercial venture here meets with success. This way you will have an excuse to visit with us again." He must have seen something in my father's expression then because Ackermann smiled. "Oh, don't be alarmed. I am hardly a mafia don of whom you must ask permission or to whom you must pay tribute when operating in my territory. What has your father been telling you about me?"

Ackermann turned to Van Zyl. "Is everyone of your generation so serious?"

Van Zyl offered only a thin smile in answer.

As we drove away and off the estate, I caught a last glimpse of Viona. She was standing motionless on a little hill, under the shade of a tree, with Argon and Xenon flanking her on either side, watching our Land Rover depart.

MY FATHER AND Karl were completely silent during the drive back to the airport and I realized that our driver was the reason for the lack of conversation.

"Is he as you remembered?" my father asked Karl, once we had gotten out of the Land Rover.

"No," Karl said.

It was the first I heard him speak. His voice was an unexpectedly deep baritone and it startled me.

"Older? Frail?" my father asked.

"The man controls nothing. The animals. His heir. Nothing. Nature abhors a vacuum; will endeavor to fill it."

My father mulled this over, but kept whatever he was thinking to himself.

—

CHAPTER TWELVE

Weight and Balance

WE ARRIVED AT THE CONCIERGE DESK of the executive aviation terminal and for a time I thought we were getting back on the jet to fly home. It seemed an extravagance to make such a long trip for a single meeting that barely took two hours. Instead, we passed into the hangar, the floor of which shone with a brilliance that made it look like polished stone. A single-engine plane sat waiting on the far side. It was white with sand-colored highlights. The propeller had three imposing-looking blades emanating from a shiny silver nose cone that capped a long nose. The entire craft sat on oversize tricycle wheels—fat, rubber donuts affixed to the bottom of comically long Popsicle sticks—that gave it an almost cartoonish appearance. Our luggage had been set down next to the craft.

My father opened the left cockpit door, climbed inside, and busied himself with the flight controls. Done with those tasks, he circled the plane, tugging on this part, inspecting that piece, until he seemed grudgingly satisfied.

I supposed it was like my father to want to know the condition of any small craft he was about to board, but then he did something that surprised me greatly: he stepped up on the left-hand wing strut and slipped into the front-left seat with a knowing agility that made it obvious it was not his first time.

Karl motioned for me to board the little plane. I scampered to the door on the left side behind the wings. I left my roller bag at the side of the plane for Karl to manage, struggled to pull myself up, and climbed into the back, where my view would encompass the bank of dials, knobs, gauges, and levers on the front panel.

My father went through a strange and involved ritual, reciting chants to himself from a spiral-bound booklet and running his hands in preordained patterns over the controls. It was a litany memorized from common use, and a bit of ceremony that I found quite beautiful.

I heard the familiar whine of a turbine spooling up and the prop began to turn until it was difficult to hear in the cabin. There was a hand on my shoulder. When I turned it was Karl pointing out of the open door and trying to tell me something. I strained to hear over the growing noise from the prop.

"Your bag," he was saying. I looked outside the plane and saw my black roller bag sitting by itself on the tarmac.

"This is Africa," he added. "Carry your own weight."

AN HOUR INTO the flight I was still reeling and, perhaps for the first time in my life, feeling sheepish for having treated someone (Karl, no less) like a servant. By some mechanism I did not understand our respective social rankings had changed, but this shift paled in comparison with the transformation my father underwent.

On the estate, power was measured by those you could command and the degree to which tasks were managed for you without ever having to ask. My father rarely spoke, and rarely had to, but watching him fly I wondered: To what extent could a passenger on a plane, subject to the whim of the person manning the controls, ever call herself "mistress"? To what extent could the pilot, upon whose good graces the passenger depended, ever be called "servant"?

I knew when we were getting close. The change in my father's flying was palpable. He had been barely touching the controls, instead almost letting our small craft fly itself; then, in a beat, he was all focus, adjusting levers, looking about the cockpit and down at the ground.

He pulled out the throttle and, in my stomach first and then my head and my ears, I felt the plane begin to sink. Before long the ground had come up to meet us, and I was alarmed to see that our intended landing strip was not much more than a dirt road.

My father landed the plane with great skill, coaxing the forward velocity from it gradually until it barely hung in the air, allowing it then to sink gently onto the big tires with the rumble of gravel and the odd irregularities of the runway's surface.

The facilities were spartan, to say the least. In place of a terminal there was only a makeshift shed, barely adequate to protect the three beat-up, olive-drab Land Rovers parked under it. There was no hangar at all. Instead we taxied to the shady side of a strange tree (I had never seen its like before) before my father shut the engine down and we deplaned. Slowly, the high, ambient sound of insects—cicadas or the like, a prehistoric orchestra that had obviously fallen silent when we landed—grew and surrounded us.

The Land Rover was unlocked and my father started it up and pulled it out of the shed. Karl and I put our bags in the back and got inside.

We headed west for about fifteen minutes before the terrain turned rugged, highlighted by small hills and a number of daunting, uphill gradients. In places the foliage slapped against the front and sides of the Land Rover as we plunged forward.

Eventually we broke into a small clearing. A gateway of sorts arched over the road, bearing the legend "Eva Game Lodge."

"It is named for Mother," I whispered to myself.

⌒◦

THE "GAME LODGE" proved to be seven distinct buildings made of poured concrete with a dark brown sandstone coating. From a distance it was easy to mistake the structures as part of the landscape and I sensed that this was by design.

Inside, the ceilings were high and the windows fortified with stout-looking beams, which I assumed were intended to deter the larger of the local inhabitants from snacking on those within. Still, with the floor-to-ceiling sliding windows retracted, you could close your eyes and almost imagine yourself standing outside.

At dinner, I thought about the change in my father that had started on board the jet. I quite liked the idea that formed then: that his "true self" found me worthy of his notice, and that it was only the formal strictures of the estate that otherwise oppressed this expression.

"Is this place named for Mother?" I said.

My father looked up from his after-dinner reading.

"Yes, it is. It was a gift to her from your grandfather."

"She didn't like it, did she?"

"Indeed not."

"Was it an earnest gift?"

My father directed his full attention to me. "That is an interesting question. Why would you ask that?"

"They don't like each other very much, do they? Mother and Grandfather."

"You are full of surprises this year. I wouldn't say they dislike each other. They are just from different worlds. Your mother's family is very unlike mine. Actually, this preserve has been in the family for a long time. Your grandfather carved a piece of it out and built this lodge as a wedding present for your mother. And yes, I think it was intended in earnest."

"Does she come here often?"

"Never. Sleeping outside . . . does not exactly agree with your mother."

"It wouldn't bother me," I said.

Karl, who had shown no interest in the conversation before that, looked up at me, and then to my father.

"Of that, I am certain," my father said.

AS I LAY in bed that night, the African night was filled with strange noises, wild calls and replies that wafted right through the mosquito netting that surrounded my bed. The ambient sounds served as harsh background music for the dreams that followed. At one point, I woke thinking I had perhaps heard the roar of a lion, but when I came to and listened intently to the darkness beyond, there was nothing.

THE MORNING WAS quieter and, with no clock to chime the hours for me, when I woke I was afraid that I had overslept. I found my father and Karl dressed in khaki and drinking coffee on the terrace.

"Our guests will arrive in a couple of hours," my father said. "Remember what I said."

I nodded.

A "couple of hours" drifted into "four." "African time," my father had quipped. Finally, the arrival of our guests was telegraphed first by the drone of a low-flying airplane.

"Taking a peek at us before landing?" my father said.

"Likely," Karl answered.

"He's a careful one."

The slow crunch of tires up the driveway finally followed nearly half an hour later. I followed Karl and my father as we walked to the open area just inside the archway.

A group of three men had arrived in one of the Land Rovers. One of the men—very tall, very blond, perhaps forty years old with very short hair—climbed out and walked forward.

Karl stepped forward and offered his hand. "Karl," he said.

"Mike," the man said.

Mike's accent sounded vaguely German to me, but not Afrikaans. Just German enough to be German. After he surveyed the immediate surroundings the other two men stepped out of the Land Rover. The taller looked a great deal like Mike and for a moment I thought they might be twins. The third man, however, was much shorter, at least seventy years old, and almost completely bald, a fact he hid by donning a floppy hat. To my delight his headwear looked very much like my own. Two intelligent eyes peered out over a hawklike nose, and his mouth seemed to naturally hint at a crooked smile.

He stalked forward as if his legs were stiff from the trip and stopped in front of my father for a long moment before, with great formality, presenting his hand. My father clasped it. Both men locked eyes and the moment seemed filled with some hidden meaning. Finally, after our guest offered a cautious smile, they shook their clasped hands.

"It is nice to see you again, Mr. Kriel," my father said.

"Please, call me Alfred. Forgive me, but I was hoping to see your father again."

"He prefers to stay on the Continent now."

"Pity. And no one to welcome us at the airstrip?" Alfred chided, but there was no anger in his voice.

"Would you have gotten into a strange car without having a good look at it first?" my father asked.

"Probably not," Alfred said.

"Then my instincts were correct."

"They certainly were." Alfred seemed to relax. "So, perhaps some hunting?"

Karl seemed about to interject but my father beat him to it.

"Though it was traditional with my father, I thought this time, in view of his absence, something with fewer firearms would be . . . more prudent. Though, perhaps my daughter and I will take up some stalking in the next few days."

Alfred gave me a curious look before turning back to my father. "You have spent a lot of time thinking about this."

"I have."

"Well, then we are in your hands."

Karl drove us off the lodge grounds with our guests following behind us in the second Land Rover as we wound farther and farther up into the increasingly wild terrain. Finally, we broke through the vegetation and emerged on the top of a large overlook above a light amber sea of rolling hills. At the highest point, a few solitary trees threw shade onto a bed of wild grass and provided some measure of protection from the African sun.

Karl produced several bundles from the back of our Land Rover. He left three about halfway between the vehicles and the trees and deposited the remaining three in the shade before falling back to where the Land Rovers were.

When my father unpacked them, the bundles turned out to be elegant-looking folding chairs with matching tables. He offered the leftmost chair to Alfred and then, to my surprise (and to Alfred's), presented me with the chair on the right. Once I was seated, I looked back to see that Karl and the "blond brothers" were sitting in similar chairs about fifty feet behind us, just out of earshot, I supposed.

The view over the hill hit me like a crashing wave. Laid out beneath us on the African plain were dozens upon dozens of animals milling about in herds. A slight breeze from our right washed across the landscape and left undulating patterns in the sea of grass.

While I was intent on maintaining the facade of a mature adult for whom all this was old hat, Alfred was intent on me.

"Is this the conversation to be having in front of a young woman?" he asked.

My father poured himself some white wine from a sweating bottle. "Ah, but Alfred, this is not a young woman. This is my daughter."

It was all I could do not to inflate several sizes on the spot.

"Your eldest, did he not want to be here?"

"This is my eldest," my father said. "My eldest daughter."

"I meant your son, does he not hunt?"

"Of late, only the female of the species."

For a moment I thought Alfred had taken offense, but then he laughed loudly, breaking the tension.

"The game is better back home, I suspect," Alfred said.

"Perhaps, but as a hunter yourself, you will know that the female of the species is often far deadlier than the male."

"Are we talking about your daughter now, or your son's conquests?" Alfred asked.

"Yes," my father said.

This tickled Alfred even more. For the moment disarmed, he took a deep breath and picked up the wineglass my father had poured for him.

"I must admit I had my doubts," Alfred said to my father, "but Phillip was right about you."

I was so intent on the scenery, I barely noticed the glass my father had left for me. My father took a deep draw from his and I followed. Only then did Alfred drink as well.

My father and Alfred made small talk for a while, remarking over the zebras or the wildebeest, which they spotted with binoculars while editorializing on the subject of their various behaviors and habits. The wine was almost gone before Alfred shifted the tenor of the discussion.

"We should discuss the matter at hand," he said, dabbing at his forehead with a white handkerchief.

I fixated on it and on the embroidered emblem stitched into it: a shield with lions over a castle. It was an intricate design and when it was turned in Alfred's hand I cocked my head almost ninety degrees sideways and squinted to scrutinize it. To my alarm, Alfred caught the movement and turned to look at me with a puzzled expression.

"Alfred," my father said, and I was happy for the distraction. "We are in no rush. My daughter and I are on retreat." My father gestured to the plains below. "We have this breathtaking landscape for company. We can stay more or less indefinitely, and we are happy to have you as our guest whenever you like until you feel we have arrived at the perfect moment to undertake a serious discussion."

"Young man, in Africa there is no perfect moment. Though, truly, you are your father's son. That is enough to content me in a pinch and, at the moment, time is a luxury and in short supply."

"We've worked with you for a long time, Alfred. Just tell us what you need."

"There are about to be some serious upheavals in South Africa," Alfred said.

"We have heard rumblings."

"Whatever you've heard is likely understated. What's more, your press is in the middle of a misguided love affair with the African National Congress and by extension the South African Communist Party. Only in Europe could hypocrisy run so deep that the intelligentsia would ignore the history of the ANC, its propensity for violence, and celebrate the prospect of communist rule."

"They aren't particularly 'my press,' Alfred, and the politics to me are academic."

"You finance people are annoyingly neutral," Alfred snapped, but then recovered himself. "I don't care one whit for the racial policies. None of that matters to me—"

"Alfred, you know that we have no moral interest in any of these issues."

"We want to move assets out of the country."

"I'm not sure you need us for that."

"*Physical* . . . assets," Alfred added.

My father looked at Alfred. Alfred held his gaze for a long time.

"Physical assets," my father repeated.

"Quite a lot of them."

"Alfred, that isn't exactly what we do."

"Come now. I know for a fact that Phillip was involved in very similar projects in Rhodesia before the end, and that he assisted the government in evading sanctions."

My father made as if to speak, but Alfred held up a hand to stay him.

"Yes, yes. I know you must deny it, but I also know it for truth. It is a pity more families didn't heed his warnings. True, this has been our home for generations, but that is the sort of blind sentiment that destroyed any number of Rhodesian families. I do not intend to make the same mistake."

"Alfred, there are a number of trustworthy international shipping agents in Cape Town. And then there is Ackermann et Cie. I would think you would want to use a local bank and the Ackermanns are—"

"—too entrenched. Too close to the ANC. Ackermann thinks that if they suck up to the communists properly they will be the last to be eaten. I am very fond of Rynold, but his family and their bank are too entangled and the old man, and I say it with all affection, is fading. They are slow to sense danger. Moreover, his son Ruben, his only heir, and this is certainly no secret, is a disappointment. We need absolute discretion. Johannesburg has too many ears and eyes, and what we are planning will make a lot of people . . . unhappy."

"I begin to understand, I think, why you wanted to meet all the way out here."

"You, my dear boy, are discreet. I don't need ships. I need planes, and you have planes. Like your father, you are a pilot yourself. You will understand the ins and outs of customs, immigration, and airspace. I may be wrong about what is facing the older families of South Africa, but I don't think so. Even if I am, I now believe that diversifying out of a single geography is the smart move. And I'm not the only one. Before you leave there are other families I want you to meet, in total secrecy of course."

"And where would you like these assets deposited, exactly?"

Alfred blinked, as if surprised by the question. "Quite obviously we would like you to manage them."

"Alfred, I just want to make sure I understand you. You want us to smuggle large amounts of physical assets out of the country and then take over from Ackermann et Cie., a firm you've entrusted for generations, the management of the bulk of your family's wealth?"

Alfred only smiled, and turned his attention back to the view below us.

"They have safety in numbers, you know," he said, referring to the milling herds. "It is an advantage the great families in South Africa do not possess."

We all sat in silence for a long while before my father reached over to the basket under his folding table and produced three silver cups. He poured a brown liquid into them from a leather-covered flask. One he gave to Alfred and the other to me.

My father lifted his cup first to Alfred and then to me, meeting our eyes solemnly with each toast. I imitated my father when Alfred raised his cup to me. When my father drank, Alfred followed. I was last.

"Single malt," Alfred said, with evident pleasure, and I was amused to find that I already knew the taste.

ALFRED POLITELY DECLINED my father's invitations to dinner.

"No," he said, before he climbed into the Land Rover, "I have been gone too long already. It is not in either of our interests for me to attract any more attention than I already have."

We stood in silence watching them go. When the dust had cleared my father turned to Karl.

"Could it be done?"

"Dangerous," Karl grunted, "but possible."

We flew back to the airport the next afternoon and climbed into a chauffeured Land Rover to drive into the northern suburbs to meet with the Bikkers, one of the "old families" that Alfred had spoken of.

Travel fatigue was beginning to wear at me. Not wanting to fall asleep in my father's presence, I concentrated on the view outside my window and the walled-in estates that flanked both sides of the tree-lined road.

I felt it before I saw it: Karl stiffened in the front passenger seat, intent on something he saw as we approached a curve.

"Stop the vehicle," Karl said. Our driver looked at him, confused. "Stop the vehicle now," Karl ordered loud enough to hurt my ears, but our befuddled driver merely took his foot off the gas.

It happened quickly after that. Karl lifted his right leg and slammed it into the driver's footwell, smashing the brake pedal so hard that my shoulder belt bit painfully into my chest as the Land Rover jolted to a halt with a piercing screech of tires.

Our driver, obviously offended by Karl's brusque behavior, made to object, but never got a word out. The driver's side window exploded into fragments which hung for a moment in the frame before, deprived of the tensile strength of intact glass, they collapsed straight down into a rain of greenish-white shards that showered the interior. Something hot and wet struck my face. I remember thinking of the warm water in my eyes from a well-placed burst out of Augustin's squirt gun the summer before. I squinted and blinked.

"Down!" Karl was shouting, and I felt my father's arm pulling at me.

Our driver was slumped over and, through what was by then the spidered glass of the front windshield, I had a horrifying glimpse of the scene outside just before my father popped my seat belt open and hauled me down into the floor wells: men with rifles pointed at us were running toward the Land Rover.

The rest was a blur. Karl sitting in the right seat, squeezed in on top of our unresponsive driver, throwing the Land Rover into reverse; the world outside spinning around a half-turn before he slammed it back into gear; glass flying and the *plunk, plunk, thunk, tink* sounds of metal piercing sheet metal; the rear window shattering and collapsing, showering us with even more fragments of tempered glass.

After about two minutes of furious driving, Karl pulled into a random driveway and leapt out. He was leaning into the back of the Land Rover to tend to us in an instant. There was blood on his face, trickling down from his forehead and off his chin onto his white collared shirt, which soaked it up into large inkblots of dark red.

"Are you hurt?" Karl asked my father.

"No," my father said, sitting up. "I don't think so. My daughter?"

Karl's hands were on me then, sliding over my arms, and legs, and then, quite rudely, inside my shirt. When he wiped my face with the back of his sleeve it came away red.

My father stiffened.

"It is not hers," Karl said, and with one hand lifted me out of the back of the Land Rover as if I were made of paper.

Then he was attending to our wounded vehicle, using something from the road kit to knock out what remained of the auto glass in the window frames. My hands started to shake.

"Could it have been random?" my father asked.

"We will not go to the first airport" was Karl's only reply.

He pulled a cell phone from a pocket and stabbed at the keypad.

"Leave Jan Smuts immediately for Rand Airport," he barked into the phone when the other party answered. "No questions. I am with the Chairman. Depart at once. Call immediately on your arrival."

He hung up without waiting for an answer.

"The driver?" my father asked.

Karl just shook his head. My father leaned into the driver's-side window to see for himself.

"We can't go on with him like that."

"No," Karl said, opened the driver's-side door, and pulled out the lifeless body.

I turned away when I saw the driver's grievous head wound—a twisted mass of pink, white, gray, and red. My father helped carry the body and the two of them unceremoniously dumped it into the back of the Land Rover. Karl ripped off a bit of the dead man's shirt, wiped a blood smear from the exterior of the Land Rover, and slammed the rear hatch closed.

Five bullet holes in the front windshield were impossible to miss but, with the glass cleaned out of the others, from a distance our wounded vehicle might just look like the windows were rolled down (from the sides at least).

Even as I watched him, I could see a dark red stain growing on the left side of Karl's white shirt. I must have made a little noise, because Karl looked at me to see what might be amiss. I pointed at the bloodstain.

Carefully, he took off his blazer, examined a long cut on the top half of the left sleeve, one that was mirrored on his shirt sleeve underneath. I could see that the entire left side of his shirt from shoulder to abdomen was soaked in blood. Karl pulled at the driver's-side door and examined the frame. In one spot two rounds had penetrated the sheet metal close together, near the edge of the door. They had carved out a vicious-looking piece of triangular metal that protruded from the door like a scalpel. Karl must have caught himself on it when he jumped out.

He peeled off his shirt and used the unsaturated half to mop dark blood off his left arm and chest, exposing a gaping slash that ran all the way from the inside of his left elbow almost up to his shoulder. Blood leaked out in pulses from at least two places, faster than Karl seemed able to mop it up.

I let out an involuntary gasp.

"We need to see to that," my father said, his voice even, despite the obvious urgency.

Wordlessly, Karl tore two long strips from his bloody shirt and fashioned a double tourniquet just below his left shoulder before putting his blazer back on and buttoning it all the way up to conceal the blood.

The sounds of sirens approached. Karl froze, but they peaked in volume and then faded away in the direction of the attack.

"Time is up," he said, and climbed back into the gore-soaked driver's seat.

⤳○

KARL PARKED US on an out-of-the-way street close to Rand Airport.

"Remain here," he ordered.

As he left us with the Rover, I could see that his pants and blazer were still bloody and hoped that, since they were dark, no one else would notice. He returned in a few minutes.

"Security is light," he said, and then knelt down and focused on me. "Do not stop," he said, looking directly into my eyes.

I wanted to flinch away but I could not.

"Walk fast. Straight to the plane. Look only at the plane no matter what you see or hear. Do not attract notice. Do not run. Is this clear?"

I nodded.

A few minutes later we slipped around the side of the general aviation building, through an unlocked pedestrian gate, and onto the tarmac without being challenged. We boarded the plane and took off. It was only much later that I remembered that we had left our driver's broken body stuffed in the back of the Land Rover.

⤳○

ON THE PLANE, I stripped my bloodied clothes off and, as I stood in the aisle in just my underwear, Karl produced the plane's medical kit and swabbed me down with alcohol anywhere the driver's blood had touched me. It stung where I had picked up little nicks and scratches from the flying glass.

That finished, I changed into fresh clothes and, when I turned back, I found Karl kneeling in the aisle with the medical kit opened and towels spread beneath him, apparently to keep his blood off the carpeting. He had just taken the tourniquets off and dark red began to flow again.

"Will you need stitches?" I said, thinking back to my wounded mouth, worried (and not a little embarrassed) by my morbid fascination.

Karl just grunted at first, but then thought better of it. My father was in the back of the plane and Karl gave him a glance. Something passed between them, and Karl turned toward me to show me what he was doing. When I saw the deep laceration again I began to feel faint. I wanted to seem mature, so I fought off the lightheadedness and tried to focus on his voice.

"In austere conditions stitches are not immediately needed and may introduce infection," he said. "In such wounds, bleeding is the first concern. Elevation and direct pressure are applied for several minutes."

Using his right hand, Karl pressed a gauze pad against his left bicep and then leaned against the chair next to him, putting even more pressure on the top of his right hand and, through it, the wound below.

"Skin glue is superior to sutures in smaller wounds," he said. He sounded like someone reading from a textbook. I tried to suppress a fit of involuntary squirming. "But, even in the most serious wounds and without a closure agent, once the bleeding is controlled with direct pressure, packing the wound with gauze and applying a pressure bandage is normally sufficient."

I watched as Karl finished dressing the wound, packed it with gauze, and wrapped the dressing tightly with a roll of elastic bandage.

Karl closed the medical kit, picked up the towels, settled into his seat, and closed his eyes.

Whatever form of post-traumatic stress I was supposed to encounter did not take hold right away. Certainly, I had been frightened. The immediate aftereffects of what must have been an adrenaline dump showed themselves in the trembling of my hands. Still, though I kept waiting for some genus of hysteria to dig in her claws, nothing happened. On the contrary, I felt safe. Karl and my father had known what to do, had acted decisively, and this had made the difference. I passed the time thinking, and watching the land below us crawl by as we headed back north.

Sometime later, Karl knelt in front of my seat, pulling me away from my distractions.

"You are well?" he asked.

"Yes," I said.

He gave me a curt nod then, and for a moment I thought I saw some small hint of pride in his expression.

—

CHAPTER THIRTEEN

Ciphers and Locks

WE LANDED SOMETIME AROUND TWO IN the morning. I was so exhausted that I barely remember how I got to bed. I must have slept close to twenty-four hours because, when I heard the soft chimes of my clock striking one, it was pitch black outside. I spent nearly an hour in my bathtub. The ritual did nothing to quiet my mind, so I dressed and crept downstairs. Sneaking around in the dark during the wee hours should have been familiar and comforting, but something was different; something elusive.

Outside the East Salon, I relished the smell of pipe tobacco and the light under the door seemed a clear invitation. But, as I approached, I heard voices inside.

Even after my grandfather's comments about eavesdropping and dangerous secrets, I just couldn't help myself. I knelt down by the door frame to listen. It was my grandfather's voice, but different somehow. The pleasant and comforting old man I knew was suddenly composed of altogether sterner stuff. The tenor of his voice was harsher; his sentences curt and efficient, devoid of the rich, flowery vocabulary and meter I was so used to hearing from him.

"A planned attack," my grandfather said. It was not a question.

"Yes," my father's voice replied.

"They knew you were coming."

"Yes."

"Or they mistook you for someone else."

"Unlikely," my father said. "An 'L' ambush."

"Oh? Professionals. Former military, perhaps."

"Perhaps."

"In daylight. In an affluent suburb of Johannesburg."

"Yes."

A hum escaped my grandfather. "They do not fear the authorities."

"No."

"They tell us more than they mean to. Your car was armored?"

"No," my father said.

"No? And yet only the driver was killed?"

"Karl saw it early. The support element was careless. Their concealment was poor."

"They didn't expect you to be looking," my grandfather said.

"Who would have cause? Kriel?"

"What cause could that be? Alfred has enough mercenary types on his payroll that the attack profile fits. But, after so many years, why invite us to Johannesburg only to shoot at us?"

"Ackermann?" my father offered.

"A squad of riflemen shooting up one of the wealthiest suburbs in the country in broad daylight? Inelegant. Not his style at all. He is too subtle for that. He would make it look like an accident and look so well that everyone would accept it, even us. He probably wouldn't have missed either. Even so, I could never believe it of him. There is great affection between us. Years ago, before Ackermann et Cie. opened the little branch office they still maintain in Luzern, he tried to ask me for permission to do business there. I had to laugh."

"This is different," my father said. "We are stealing a material portion of his asset management business. Their family bank will necessarily suffer. We cannot believe that old feelings of sentiment will be enough to—"

"*Stealing* is a crass and inappropriate term." My grandfather sounded cross. "Ackermann et Cie. is one of the most established private banks in South Africa. They have no interest in fighting over a few fickle asset management clients. If Ackermann is concerned about our activities in his backyard he will say so. One does not shoot at business rivals in our circles. Remember that."

"It was not always so."

"Enough," my grandfather said, clearly upset.

"Forgive me."

"It is right that you are taking the reins," my grandfather said, calmer. "I have no regrets, but in this I beg you to listen to my counsel. The solution is plain. Transparency."

"Tell them Alfred's plan? What of Alfred's concerns about the ANC?"

"He thinks the Ackermanns indiscreet. I do not. Neither do I believe it was the Ackermanns or the Kriels who attacked us. Ergo, they are potential allies. We must find a way to include the Ackermann clan in our project with Alfred. Perhaps eventually they will see the danger well enough to move their own assets to safety here."

"Very clever."

"Never let others set the terms and pace of an engagement. My affection for the man notwithstanding, I have no intention of permitting Alfred Kriel's biases to dictate who we do business with. You must always seek to turn resistance into alliance. To align interests."

"We need a lever then?"

"Yes, quite," my grandfather said. "You mentioned the indolent Ackermann heir. The eldest."

"Ruben?"

"It is difficult to be the firstborn in such a family, as you well know, and yet his loyalty is critical to Rynold. Imagine the service we would render to that dynasty by bringing the heir apparent back into the fold. We will apprentice him, give him responsibility. Let him prove his worth to his father. I owe that to Rynold. That way the younger Ackermann can see the services we provide firsthand and, if we manage him correctly, become the one to sell our vision to his father."

"Co-opt the heir?"

My grandfather tutted. "You must resist your temptation to view things always through the lens of competition. It is only sometimes so. We have long-standing and deep ties with these families. Deeper than you know. Never forget that the best long-term allies often take the most early convincing.

"The Ackermann heir can work on the air operations perhaps. It's a sexy project suitable for a young rebel. And on that note, you should put Jäger in charge."

"Jäger? He is just a mercenary, and very young."

"You underestimate him, and his age means nothing. He saved my life in Chile. Truly. I wish I had put him in charge of things down there two years ago. Even Karl seems impressed with him."

"High praise, that," my father admitted.

"They are more alike than either of them realizes, I think. Have Jäger brought to the estate so we can meet with him. If you have second thoughts after that, fine. Otherwise, he runs things in South Africa and we have Ruben Ackermann report to him."

"Will the Ackermann heir agree?"

"Oh, I think so. Like I said, it's a sexy project, and who doesn't want Jäger for a peer?"

"Well then," my father said. "If the attack was not Ackermann's doing, who does that leave? The Bikkers? One of the other old families Alfred mentioned?"

"I think not."

"The ANC? Perhaps they got wind of what Alfred is planning."

"That old fox? I would be surprised if the ANC knows as much as Alfred's middle name. No. There is something else afoot. Something . . ."

Just then there was a hand on my upper arm and I was lifted into the air as if I weighed nothing. I yelped and looked up, feet kicking, wincing against the load on my shoulder. Looking down at me with an inscrutable expression was Karl. He had come up the hall behind me so silently I had not noticed his approach.

KARL PUSHED THE door to the East Salon open and deposited me back on my feet in the middle of the room. My father snapped around in his chair to look at me. The expression that came over him was cryptic but he was obviously not amused.

"Listening at the door," Karl announced.

A chill ran through me and I looked down at my feet.

My grandfather squinted at me for a moment as if trying to be sure of what he was seeing and then leaned back in his chair. The hard edge evaporated and when he spoke it was once again in the kindly voice I had always known.

"Well, gentlemen. It appears we have captured"—my grandfather leaned forward and raised his eyebrows for effect—"a spy."

It was my father who spoke next. "Father," he said, "I apologize for her behavior. She . . ."

He trailed off as my grandfather raised a staying hand. "It is my fault. I should have expected her to come visiting. We should have met elsewhere if we had not wanted to be overheard."

My grandfather took a deep breath and sighed before addressing himself to Karl.

"Thank you for joining us at such a late hour. Once again, I am reminded how much this family owes you, my old friend. We now add the lives of my son and granddaughter to the list." Karl made as if to speak. "No, no. Modesty does not become you." He turned to me. "Had a bit of excitement on your trip, I am given to understand."

I was about to answer, but then remembered my father's admonition not to discuss our trip with "anyone." Did that include my grandfather?

"Sorry?" I said, and hated the thought of keeping anything from my grandfather.

Confused, his eyebrows knotted closer together, but then he seemed to understand.

"Ah, yes. Of course." He puffed on his pipe and nodded slowly. "Quite right," he said, and turned to my father. "See how she keeps your secrets?"

Karl made an indistinct noise.

"Yes, yes," my grandfather said, waving a dismissive hand. He and Karl seemed to understand each other without resorting to words. "But my granddaughter was a target as well. She has as much right to this conversation as anyone, no?"

"She is young," Karl said.

"Not too young to be shot at, apparently," my grandfather said. He smiled at me. "I was fourteen the first time I was shot at."

"You, Grandfather?" I said, amazed.

"Mmmm, indeed. Also in Africa, as it happens. In northern Africa. We tried to land in what was then French Morocco. Whoever was on the ground apparently took great exception to it."

"Who was it, Grandfather?"

"I'm pretty sure it was the French, actually. Likely it didn't help that we were flying a German BFW M.23." My grandfather lowered his voice for effect. "The M.23s were a very hot aircraft in their day, you know. Won all sorts of races in 1930." He sat back again. "I think it was the French anyway. We didn't remain long enough to inspect their passports. So you see, you have beat my record as the youngest to be shot at by nearly . . . what is it . . . two years?

"As for the topic at hand . . ."

Karl shifted in his chair.

"Yes, yes," my grandfather said again. "I know, Karl. You do not approve of her presence. Your objection is noted."

My grandfather chewed on the stem of his pipe for a long time and looked at Karl when he was ready to speak again. "You think it was Ackermann," he said.

Karl shook his head. "He is weak."

"Oh? Years have not been kind to him? Well, likely it is a mystery we will not solve tonight. In the meantime, it appears that I might need to have a conversation with my granddaughter."

Without a word of argument, my father and Karl departed.

"Madam Curie," my grandfather said, and then made a show of looking at his wristwatch. "It is well after two. That's a bit of a late arrival even for you, isn't it? I suppose you'd better have a seat."

We sat in silence for what seemed like a long while. Then, all of a sudden, he stood, circled around his desk, and knelt next to my chair. I was so taken aback I almost flinched. He took my hand and looked into my eyes. When he spoke it was in the softest voice, but still, somehow it startled me.

"I intended for you to experience more of the world. It seems that, without warning, the world has become quite a bit more dangerous for us. I'm afraid that in the process of sending you out into it, I unwittingly delivered you to knavery.

"Displays of overt sentimentality are not well tolerated in patriarchs, but here I cannot help myself." My grandfather kissed my hand, and then my cheek. "I don't know what I would have done if you had been hurt. I hope you will forgive me."

I wasn't sure what to say, and so I was glad when my grandfather returned to his desk, collected himself, and changed the subject.

"As for the eavesdropping . . . well, it is impolite."

"I'm sorry, Grandfather. I really am."

"It is a rare gift to make one's self invisible. I wish I could do it. Still, from now on I would like you to do me a favor."

"Anything, Grandfather."

"Don't get caught," he said with a wide grin.

I had to try not to laugh or smile. We fell quiet again.

The death masks seemed to be looking down on me from their mounts above my grandfather's head and the longer the silence went on the more desperate I was to say something.

"What do you think happens when you die?" I said, surprising myself.

My grandfather's eyebrows shot up. "Well, now. To the deepest questions without delay, is it? I suppose it depends on whom you ask, my dear." My grandfather leaned back in his chair and looked up, watching the smoke puffs he sent toward the ceiling as he spoke. "The Egyptians believed that at the end of the journey to the underworld the soul was judged by weighing the deceased's heart against Maat, the goddess of truth, or sometimes the feather from her headdress, on a huge balance. The right spells, however, would prevent the heart from bearing witness against the dead. It's a rare example, I think, of a religion providing an explicit way to lie and cheat the gods."

"With spells?" I said.

"Yes. They are quite elaborately listed in the Book of the Dead. One wonders after the potency of Egyptian gods if they were so easily deceived. Apparently, even the ancients viewed deceit as a necessary tool and, after all, no price is too high to pay when eternity is at stake.

"Death and deception seem to be the topics of the evening, but there is no shame in it if you would rather not discuss these things. Or shall I go on?"

He caught me off guard, but I knew right away I didn't want to be babied. I wanted to be strong and resolute; stoic and worldly like my grandfather; like my father. A member of the direct line, I thought, would not go to custard so easily. Feeling courage building from some deep reserve, I looked my grandfather in the eye.

"They were trying to hurt Father?"

It must have been the right thing because my grandfather leaned back, puffed on his pipe, and smiled.

"It would appear so."

"Who?"

"I expect we shall find out presently."

"But why?"

"That is a much more complicated question. A dynasty like ours is a living thing. It has needs, lusts, potentials, and limitations. As patriarch, meeting one's responsibilities to such an entity, to one's predecessors and heirs, even in a sense to the established traditions, is an enormous undertaking. Moreover, the position of patriarch is not chosen by its officeholder. It is foisted upon him, and men like my father, like your father, men who are born to it, must thereafter be crafted into figures of awesome presence and potency in order to be worthy of it. Now and again, someone might get the idea that they can hurt or change the course of a dynasty by removing its leader."

"Like stabbing Julius Caesar on the Senate floor?"

My grandfather chuckled and lifted his eyebrows in my direction. His calm demeanor made it easier somehow to talk of murder; of assassination and conspiracy.

"One of the more dramatic historical examples," he said. "Though Caesar's mistakes were rather larger than most. The margins for error afforded to the patriarch of this family are quite a bit slimmer. Worse, a modern dynasty has institutional enemies: multinational corporations, governments, even other dynastic families.

The natural enemies of our dynasty are some of the most well-resourced and cunning enterprises on the planet. Some of these consider the contest between their peers as a zero-sum game. For those infected with this worldview there is little incentive for cooperation. To them, for every win someone else must lose. It is a primitive perspective, but the predominant one among our enemies.

"Most of our rivals measure their time horizons in decades, generations, or even centuries. They are ever watchful for the merest sign of weakness:

a craven or overly ambitious cousin to the patriarch, a temporary liquidity crisis, a disgruntled aide, an indolent heir apparent—"

"Like Ruben Ackermann?" I offered, excitement bleeding into my voice.

"Perhaps even"—he raised his eyebrows—"an errant granddaughter."

I squirmed in my chair, but my grandfather only winked at me and continued.

"It is the paradox of family that a patriarch must face. They are both the only ones the patriarch can really trust, and also the most dangerous to him in betrayal. However loyal your vassals, so to speak, they are not blood. Often blood is the only thing you can count on, but also the most daunting threat from within. That is, when blood denies itself; when it loses its way. Do you understand?"

I nodded my head, but I wasn't really so sure.

"Because they may know the family's darkest secrets and may split the loyalty of a dynasty if recruited into a coup, heirs are particularly attractive targets for intrigue. But everyone in a dynastic family is vulnerable. Careless decision making, a slip of the tongue at a social event, the merest hint of a sliver of disloyalty or betrayal in the ranks, even an innocent mistake or oversight, might easily cost tens or hundreds of millions in losses, or worse.

"Sometimes it is important to protect heirs by keeping the secrets they know to a minimum. Sometimes it is important that they know everything. Either way, in such a hostile environment any form of carelessness, indiscretion, infidelity, or simple error must be relentlessly hunted down and eliminated. In this connection I must ask you to promise that, from now on, you must never speak to anyone about the nature of your lessons with Professor Lechner. There are some who would misunderstand their purpose. Still others would understand all too well.

"I will not apologize for my methods. Do you remember what I told you before? Amorality, perhaps even total *immorality*, is almost by definition necessary of a patriarch to give others in his family the luxury of morality."

"What will we do, Grandfather?"

"This is precisely the wrong question. Action without design is folly. We must first understand what has happened. Our enemies can be most cunning. When attacks come they are not necessarily obvious. When they are obvious, usually they are obvious for a purpose. How do we know this is the first, or the only prong we are being probed with? Perhaps it is watching our reaction that is the purpose. Then again, what may look like an attack may just be coincidence. Perhaps your vehicle resembled someone else's. Worse, what may look innocent or the result of random chance could be the most existential threat imaginable. It follows that one must first know for certain that one is being deliberately attacked, do you see this?"

I nodded, enthralled.

"Then, the nature of the attack must be divined. Our adversaries are rarely impulsive. They calculate. One must ask after the design behind the action, to know the truth of it. Only then may we design action to respond properly. To act according to design. Do you see this?"

"Yes, Grandfather," I said.

"'The man of action is always unprincipled; none but the contemplative has a conscience.' Thus contemplation must be disposed of first; must precede action. *Veritatem cognoscere*," he added, in Latin.

"Learn knowledge?" I said, trying to translate the phrase on the fly.

Real surprise and pleasure showed itself on my grandfather's face.

"Know the truth," he corrected me gently.

PART OF ME could not believe that my grandfather had been so forthright in our conversation. But the sense of being a part of something larger, and something that involved the outside world—still so alien to me—was impossible to ignore.

I had darker feelings too. The image of our driver's body, abandoned at the airport, stuck with me. And, though my grandfather had tried to make light of the danger, the thought of powerful and hidden enemies stalking our family frightened me. It was only that he had seemed so calm and analytical about it all that gave me some measure of comfort that he had matters in hand.

I WOKE TO THE bell at my door early the next morning to find a member of the staff bearing a handwritten note from Professor Lechner indicating that I was expected in his offices that morning at the usual time.

If he was aware of my excursion, and it seemed difficult to think he had not noticed my absence, the Professor did not let on.

"We were discussing the fall of empires, I believe?" he said, as soon as I opened his door, and launched right into his lesson.

"You will have noticed that Glubb's supposed 250-year life span for empires is some ten generations, yes?"

I nodded but, in fact, I hadn't thought about Glubb at all since our last lesson.

"And Glubb adds that, in the later stages of empire, the ages of affluence, intellect, and decadence, several dynamics conspire to sow the seeds of destruction and desolation. Yes?"

I was trying to compose a delicate way to admit that I had completed no further study of substance, but instead the Professor paced back and forth with his hands behind his back and forged on without pressing any of his questions.

"As the empire approaches the limits of its expansion and exploits the gains secured by the age of conquests, the great wealth accumulated during the age of commerce is turned inward. The merchant classes become incredibly rich. Art and architecture become dominant pursuits. This, Glubb says, is the age of affluence. The greed for money quashes concepts of duty and virtue. In education, militancy, and with it the discipline of honor, is abandoned for commercialism. The military parade grounds give way to the lecture hall and the development of the empire's most promising young men becomes dominated by the university. This phase, for Glubb, is when the empire seeks knowledge above all else. An influx of foreigners dilutes the traditions and ethos of the empire. Their assimilation is difficult, if it is attempted at all. Decadence, the loss of any sense of duty or tradition, naturally follows."

I had closed my eyes to picture the rise and fall of invented empires—all too real to me—that waxed and waned as I imagined them. When I opened my eyes again, I found the Professor looking at me fondly, apparently pleased that he had affected me so.

"Do you think Glubb is correct?" he whispered.

"I don't know."

"Let us presume that he is. Or at least that empires are not as long-lived as we might prefer. Should we ever trust great knowledge to empires alone?

How might we prevent the loss of knowledge that the fall of an empire necessarily precipitates?"

"Create an empire that does not fall?"

Professor Lechner let out a good-natured chuckle.

"An eternal empire. An ambitious project," he said. "Ambitious indeed. Worthy of Ozymandias."

I understood the rebuke immediately. Professor Lechner saw how crestfallen I was and put a comforting hand on my shoulder.

"And other more odious figures of more recent history," he mumbled, before beginning to pace once again.

"There is a great hall in this manor," he said with a renewed brightness in his voice. "It is lined with grand portraits."

"The Hall of Ancestors," I exclaimed.

"Just so. And how many portraits appear there?"

"Thirteen," I answered.

Professor Lechner stopped pacing and gave me an expectant look.

"I invite you to consider their import."

"Thirteen generations," I whispered, when it came to me.

"Indeed. More even. You are issue of the fifteenth generation of your line. You, yourself, are a member of the sixteenth generation."

"But, that's longer than 250 years."

"Just so. But your family is not an empire. It is a dynasty. Perhaps for our purposes Glubb was looking in the wrong places, *ja*? Might we posit that a properly organized dynasty may outlive empires?"

"But how?"

Professor Lechner's eyes went wide with pleasure.

"Precisely," he said. "Precisely."

TRADITIONALLY, BIRTHDAYS WERE nonevents in our family and, in the early part of April 1993, my twelfth came and went without the least fanfare. I barely noticed either. Though in reality it was some species of stress disorder, my self-isolation—ten- to twelve-hour stints spent alone at study in a far corner of the library—was treated as cause for praise.

"I am quite sure I have never had a pupil so committed to advancement as your granddaughter," Professor Lechner beamed to my grandfather on one of his rare visits to our sessions in "Lechner Hall."

"Good," my grandfather said, softly. "Very good indeed."

But then my grandfather gave me a look of concern—knitted skin pinched between his eyebrows; just a hint of a frown. At first it seemed that he had seen through some grand facade that I didn't even know I had erected, but a moment later he smiled again, though it was tainted with a twinge of sadness. He looked tired. Though he had not been there, it was as if the South Africa trip had changed him as well. Thereafter, I could find him in the East Salon at all hours, poring over books and papers, searching for answers to mysterious questions. So absorbing were his efforts that, now and again, with a shake of the head, he would actually deny me admittance to his private sanctuary, a completely novel experience for me.

"No," he would say, and I couldn't tell who was more disappointed, him or me. "I'm sorry. Not tonight."

Other times I would actually find his door locked and, though I knew him to be inside, I never dared knock more than once if he did not answer.

That day he visited Professor Lechner's office, however, I had the impression that he was silently bearing some great and unseen weight. He reflected on something in the interlude that followed; contemplating a dilemma of some gravity. Then, and I could see precisely when it happened, the answer came to him, and he addressed himself to Professor Lechner.

"It is essential," he said, "that you proceed as we have discussed, and with all discretion."

Then, without waiting for a reply, he departed, leaving a cloud of pipe smoke in his wake.

Professor Lechner's curriculum intensified after that. He began to carry a leather-bound diary. It was a lovely and elegant book of several hundred pages with a locking cover. He was in the habit of consulting it or scrawling notes before and after each lesson. When I managed a glance at its contents, I saw that it contained detailed lesson plans for every session. Though the diary was full to the last page, I was surprised to see that we had barely worked through a quarter of the material it contained.

My course of study had already been strange for a girl not yet in her teens. By that time we had exhausted the cliché texts on strategy by Machiavelli, Sun Tzu, and Clausewitz and were well into an immensely dense tome on Sir Francis Walsingham and a detailed work on the Marian military reforms during the later years of the Roman Republic.

Around that time, Professor Lechner presented me with a pile of books that included the works by General Giáp he had taken from me before my trip to South Africa.

"Giáp presents interesting perspectives," he said, "but you may wish to focus on the work of Major Hans von Dach, a Swiss officer. I have left you the first of his seven-volume treatise on guerrilla warfare written in 1957. You can find the remainder of the collection in the library.

"His work is brilliant, but was frowned upon by his contemporaries as it advocated tactics that were arguably against the laws of war at the time. One wonders if the Soviets would have followed such rules had they invaded Switzerland, but this is another matter."

This reversal seemed odd enough but, early that summer, Professor Lechner's instruction branched into even more obscure topics like white-collar crime, game theory, and abnormal psychology.

For years my grandfather had been my only source of that particular, unconditional warmth that a daughter expects from her parents. There was a profound sadness that came over me as I grew to understand that, though he was still playful with me on occasion, he would no longer treat me to the sort of affection one directs to a child. Gone forever were the nicknames and the puzzle boxes.

At times I took it badly, but I was oblivious to the forces at work in the background and the larger motivations that hovered above and guided my studies. Other times I was blinded by the dark brilliance of the unorthodox attentions of my tutor and his master: the patriarch of my family.

Even though I would later come to appreciate the necessities that forced my grandfather to abandon me in that way, part of me still mourns for the childhood I lost when he did. In retrospect, my grandfather and Professor Lechner had crafted a rather dark course of study for a young girl. But, though I had no way of knowing it at the time, neither of them could afford to regard me as a child any longer.

CHAPTER FOURTEEN

—

Ruins

AFTER AN EARLY PERIOD OF CONSTANT storms and rain, the weather that summer turned glorious. Cloistered away in the library, I had barely appreciated it at all until a surprise visit managed to divert my attention away from Professor Lechner's curriculum.

I had woken up before dawn and finished the last of the readings the professor had assigned me from Callwell's *Small Wars: Their Principles and Practice*. It was rare to catch up with the Professor's reading list and it says something about my mental state at the time that, as respite, I found myself cracking open the Grand Library's ancient copy of Herodotus's *Histories*.

I was so absorbed that I barely noticed the violin music outside my rooms, much less the brightening dawn. Instead the melody wormed its way into my subconscious, setting to floating music a number of Herodotus's passages on Gyges, the founder of the Mermnad dynasty of Lydian kings who, after murdering Candaules and stealing his crown and his queen, bribed the Oracle of Delphi to publicly confirm the legitimacy of his rule.

I was too engrossed in the notion that bribing the Oracle was a fascinating route to power to overtly notice the melodic background until Bastien, who had been playing in the hallway outside my apartments for nearly a quarter hour, finally gave up his ineffectual serenade, ignored my doorbell, and knocked.

He was in the middle of a musician's bow when I squinted out from between my doors. With a cautious smile, he looked up from under the bangs that fell into his eyes. I was stunned to see him and too dazed to give him the warm welcome he had every reason to feel entitled to.

"Bastien," I managed. "What are you doing here?"

His expression fell and that little hint of mischief that was so often in his features evaporated.

It pulled at my heartstrings to have hurt his feelings and, after a moment's recovery, I admitted him and gave him an awkward hug. He laid his violin on a side table in my foyer and sank into the nearest chair while I retrieved my book and came back to join him.

"I must have written you ten letters," I said, after sitting down.

"I know."

"You never wrote me back."

He shifted in his chair. "I know."

I wasn't sure what to make of his nonanswers other than to assume that he was embarrassed by his neglected correspondence with me.

"Gosh," he said. "Everything here looks so big now. The ceilings are so tall. My dormitory room is tiny."

"Do you like the conservatory? Vienna must be beautiful. At least it is in the pictures I've seen."

Bastien looked around the foyer, obviously desperate to change the subject. At first I wanted to probe him more about his time away; to revel in his stories of the city, his new friends, and his lessons, but I could tell the topic was upsetting him for some reason. I let the matter drop instead.

"I suppose I should say hello to Augustin," Bastien sighed.

"He's not here, Basti."

"But it's summer break."

"I haven't seen him."

"Oh." He fidgeted, and I took the nervous energy as awkwardness; as if he was somehow unprepared for our reunion and unsure how to react when it had turned out differently than he had imagined. "What are you reading?" he asked, tilting his head to see my book.

I sighed with a great deal more melodrama than the occasion called for before turning the cover in his direction.

"Something long and boring," he mocked. "What a surprise."

"It is not boring," I said.

Irritated, I turned my attention to the new instrument he had been playing.

Two years before, my grandfather had given him a magnificent (and likely priceless) instrument named "Castor," one of a matched pair ("Castor" and "Pollux") made by the famous Italian luthier Bartolomeo Giuseppe Antonio Guarneri. The instrument my brother had been playing looked plain by comparison.

"Where is the violin Grandfather gave you?" I asked. "You didn't break it, did you?"

He gave me a shocked look. "The Guarneri? Of course not. It's just that it is still a little too big for my hands." He wiggled his fingers at me. "I can't play it well yet."

"Oh. That's too bad."

"I brought you something," he said, recovering from a frown. "I found it buried outside in the gardens near the driveway; nearly tripped over it coming into the manor."

He produced an object from his pocket but lost his grip and fumbled it such that it landed on the low table in the foyer with a loud thump. It was caked in dirt that scattered everywhere across the table and the volume I had been reading.

"Bastien," I moaned. I shot him a deadly look while I tried to brush away the clods of muck without smearing them on the cover. "This book is nearly 150 years old."

"That's older," Bastien said, pointing at the grime-encrusted object, an old compass. "Augustin had one just like it once. He said his was from Roman times."

"The Empire? The Republic? And how would he know?"

"Stop being a smart aleck. He meant old Rome. Like Caesar's time, I guess." I just shook my head at him.

Examining it, it was quickly apparent that the object was modern and, with printing in English etched on the sides, it was about the least likely artifact to have seen one of Caesar's battles with the Gauls.

"Bastien, this isn't even a hundred years old."

"Sure it is," he insisted.

I sighed and put the filthy thing down.

"Anyway," he said, "I bet there are other Roman artifacts. We should do an archaeological dig. Have you even looked outside?"

The view from my desk started with the estate gardens and panned down over the hills and into our valley below. Peering out, I had to admit that the sun and clear sky were temptations.

"You promised we could have an adventure again when the weather got nice," Bastien said.

"That was a long time ago. And," I added, "digging around in Mother's gardens was not what I had in mind."

"We don't have to do an excavation. C'mon. It's so boring here."

"Basti, you've barely been home, what, an hour?"

He gave me a piteous look. "Please?"

At first I didn't like the idea, but I had been at study almost continuously for as long as I could remember. The notion of a bit of sunshine started to grow on me.

"Why don't I get the safari tents?" he volunteered.

Bastien and I had found the tents the summer before while exploring the manor's depths. For two seasons we used them as forts, erecting them in the far reaches of the estate and playing in them until the sun fell. They had been tucked away in a dark corner along with the rest of our grandfather's safari gear, a slew of steamer chests, and several wardrobes of dusty khaki that still smelled like exotic deserts (or how I imagined exotic deserts must smell).

Visions of far-off adventures prompted us to try the clothes on. They were much too large, of course, but the mystique of it all only grew when we discovered that there was still sand caught in the seams of the pockets. There was nothing like desert sand on the estate and, there in the basements, we ran it through our fingers until it was lost in the cracks and seams of the ancient stone floors.

Something made me shudder. Perhaps a twinge of embarrassment that I had once been so childish, or maybe that the memories highlighted how far from Bastien I had drifted in only a few months.

"Aren't you a bit old to be playing at forts, Basti?" I said.

"Yeah," he said. "I guess so." But I could tell he didn't mean it.

"We can go exploring," I offered him as consolation.

"A trek? A quest? Really?"

"But, I have to take a bath first."

"Aww. Your baths can go on for hours," Bastien whined.

"You should have thought of that before you dropped that filthy thing on my desk," I said, pointing at the compass.

He looked hurt. It reminded me that, beneath my posturing, a sibling's affection burned brightly, and I felt guilty for being difficult with him.

"Why don't you ring down for Cipriana while I'm in my bath?" I said. "We can have breakfast brought up."

That caught Bastien off guard. "I can stay here?" he said, and looked around. "In your rooms?"

"I guess so, as long as you clean up the dirt. And don't touch anything."

I GOT DRESSED AFTER our breakfast, but when I emerged from my closets wearing my riding apparel, Bastien looked alarmed.

Though he was at great pains to hide it, somewhere along the way Bastien had become petrified of horseback riding and would invent any excuse to avoid being invited to vault into a saddle. I had kept it a strict secret between us. After all, it would never do for a son of the direct line to be afraid of equestrian pursuits.

That morning I caught on quickly. "Bastien, you don't have to ride if you don't want to," I said.

And so, that pressure relieved, and as he had so many times before, Bastien packed up his violin case, concealed it in my bag, and ran ahead to meet me in the gardens while I finished brushing my hair.

I followed presently, and then we made our way down the path to the stables. Normally, I, who had been riding since I was seven, would have the groom saddle Vim, my favorite black and white Appaloosa. But the groom was absent, and so I put Vim's bridle on and, as her saddle was too heavy for me, climbed up on the side of the stable wall to mount her bareback.

Vim had been a gift of sorts from my grandfather. Though she was one of many horses in the stables (my grandfather had been breeding Appaloosas for some time), the arrow-shaped spot above her right eye caught my attention when first I saw her. Later, noting how the spotted animal favored me, a product of my habit of secretly feeding her apples on a regular basis, my grandfather announced to the groom one afternoon that Vim had "obviously chosen to be my granddaughter's horse."

The previous summer I had been thrilled to find that Vim had given birth. The foal was gorgeous and I delighted in seeing her skipping around and dancing back and forth, careful not to get caught underfoot when playing with her mother.

My grandfather insisted that I name her and, after I had thought about it for a while, I picked "Verve."

"Vim and Verve," the groom had said, trying the names on. "Very good, miss."

Among the horses, Vim was gentle enough. In prior years, I could even talk Bastien (just) into climbing up behind me if she was saddled, but eventually Bastien would refuse even that, preferring instead to walk alongside us for the duration.

With Bastien in tow, we set off. The sun was higher in the sky and a light breeze flirted with the grass in the meadows that surrounded the stables. I leaned back on Vim and closed my eyes to feel the warmth on my face. For a long moment I was lost in the red eyelid movies that the sun played into my brain.

We siblings always felt closed in by the weather during the winter, and for good reason. Though we were happy to frolic in the forests that surrounded the manor, the hills to the north were quite dangerous. More than one of the estate's many ghost stories featured hapless relatives doomed to a slow, crippled death at the bottom of a crevasse that had been concealed by solid-looking snowdrifts.

Spring and fall presented their own barriers. In those seasons, a milky-gray plasma often settled into the valley, furiously resisting the sun's daily battle with the low clouds. During that time of year, the estate's fog gods could be unrelenting. On those few days when the winds drove the mists downhill, wisps of torn cloud pulled from their bases by the ridges would part now and again around the structures of the estate.

My brothers seemed content to be confined by the fickle mores of the

weather, but even at an early age I had discovered ways to cheat those con-
straints. By the time I was seven, I had found the courage to climb up to the
manor's rooftop. Nestled alone among the battlements and the crows' nests
in the upper spires, huddling under two or three quilts when it was cold, I
would spend hours imagining the puffs of torn cloud as living creatures, and
on days they were low enough, it seemed almost as if I could reach up and
touch them before they slipped into the valley below.

Though Bastien and Augustin professed to hate the cold and the wet of
fall, I looked forward to Octobers on the estate and employed every ruse to
walk through the mists, feel the cold prickle of the dew on my closed eyelids,
and dream that I was a character in one of my favorite books. One day I was
lost in the fogs of a foreign land and desperately searching for a patch of sun
so that I might find a recognizable landmark and recover my way. On another,
banished to a prison of fog for eternity, immortal, but gripped by steely pangs
of loneliness. My head filled with the giddy gloom of such fantasies, I would
wander the grounds randomly, or perhaps seek out my favorite tree to climb.

Summer, on the other hand, was the one season where all the curtains
were lifted and the limits of the estate itself were our only restriction.

"What do you want to do?" Bastien said, bringing me back to the moment.

"It is your adventure, Basti," I said.

He grinned. "It's not an adventure. It's a campaign. Let us conquer the
valley to the south," he said, striking a statuesque pose and pointing.

"What on earth will we do down there?" I said.

Bastien considered this and squinted.

"Once we have occupied the lands we will survey sites to construct our
fortifications to hold off . . ."

". . . the barbarian tribes?" I offered.

"Exactly."

"With our World War I compass?" I teased, pointing at the filthy thing
Bastien had since lashed to his belt. He scowled.

It was one of those times when Bastien's dislike of horses was more than
just inconvenient. Our estate was shaped like an inverted teardrop falling
upward to the northeast, where it encompassed the beginnings of the Alpine
foothills. The land flattened as one went south until, opposite the hills, the

narrow point of our borders was directed threateningly southwest at nothing in particular. The manor stood where the rolling hills overlooked the valley below, almost three-quarters of the way to our northernmost property line. To walk the farthest extent of the estate (from the south-southwest border to the northern frontier) was nearly four miles, most of it uphill. Getting down to the valley from the manor meant nearly a three-mile hike.

The trek down would be hard enough, but I did not relish the way back. I was sure that Bastien, having bitten off more than he could chew, would spend most of the return journey whining about how much his feet hurt. If we started uphill instead, I reasoned, he would tire soon enough and pick a nearby spot to take a break. Our walk would be shorter and the return trip would be downhill instead of up.

"Bastien, would any Roman general worth his salt place a fortification on low ground?"

Bastien squinted into the valley. "What do you mean?"

I cut my gaze to the north, beyond and above the manor to the hills. Bastien's eyes grew wide.

"Of course," he said, catching my meaning. "The hills and the cliffs. And the Vista is on the way. Perfect," he said, and clapped his hands.

THE "VISTA" WAS a clearing at the peak of one of the foothills from which one could see the manor and nearly all of the estate arrayed below. The building itself was an Elizabethan affair of 21,000 square feet, construction of which had begun in the sixteenth century atop the ruins of other fortifications. The off-white structure was full of blocky squares and cubes punctuated on the top with jutting spires.

It was an unusual style for its time and place and easily stood out against the Italian Gardens, an ordered expanse of light and dark vegetation. The southern side of the gardens and the meadow beyond served as my mother's private sanctuary. Farther beyond and to our left, just visible through the trees, was the gray stone of the mausoleum, and beyond that the beginnings of the sprawling forests where my grandfather used to hunt stag, wild boar, and sometimes even alpine ibex and chamois.

I dismounted and let Vim wander and graze where she wanted. As was his habit, Bastien settled himself in the short grass, sitting cross-legged, and started to play his violin.

As always, Vim was fascinated by the sound and she looked up and at Bastien from the first note, cocked her ears his direction, and, but for her swishing tail, stood completely still listening to him. I knew that if I tried to urge her away too soon she would tug for rein until I relented. Eventually I might coax her away to explore the far reaches of the estate alone, sometimes for hours. But no matter how long I took, Bastien never complained and was often right where we had left him (and still playing) when we returned.

That morning we only stayed for a couple of pieces but, while the impromptu concert lasted, I lay on my back looking at the sky and listening to my talented brother play. When he finished, Bastien drew out the last note for a long time. Only when it finally ended did I realize that my eyes were closed.

I COLLECTED VIM, BASTIEN boosted me up, and we found the path that led north and up into the foothills. After only a mile, Bastien began to look winded.

"We could survey just over there," I said, pointing to a small landing.

To my surprise, Bastien shook his head. "A fort would be vulnerable here. We have to find higher ground."

We continued up toward the cliffs, eventually coming to the gorge that marked the border between the rolling hills below and the rockier terrain to the north. Normally I would have slipped west toward a path that Vim and I had traversed many times, but Bastien had already skirted the gorge and squirmed under a fallen tree ahead of us. In the process, he had found another path, disused and choked with undergrowth.

I called for him to wait but he didn't seem to hear and we only caught up with him after Vim had vaulted the fallen tree and wormed another hundred yards through the overgrown path. Bastien had stopped at the edge of a wide clearing. When we reached him, what I saw caused me to pull up on Vim's reins and freeze.

The stone skeletons of several old structures rose from the grounds like the petrified bones of long-dead beasts, half-buried, slowly succumbing to a tangle of moss and creepers that, fingerlike, seemed to be pulling them down into the soil beneath.

"What is it?" Bastien said.

"I don't know. I've never been here before."

"I thought you had ridden every inch of the estate."

"Not here, obviously," I said.

"Why are you whispering?"

"I don't know."

I dismounted Vim and led her farther from the forest's edge. On the ridge of the hill just beyond I could see the low-slung, mortarless stone wall that marked the edge of our property. That meant that the ruins were on the far northern edge of the estate and isolated on three sides by the narrow gorge.

The remnants sketched a sad picture of what might once have been a beautiful (if small) country house, but the remains of the chapel about two hundred yards farther on were breathtaking. The Gothic-arched entryway looked almost preserved, though thick tendrils of ivy had taken over the rear of the edifice.

We crept farther into the clearing. A dark cloud slipped in front of the sun, giving everything a spooky hue of shadow and casting eerie shades across the ancient stones. Somewhere in the distance some species of insect or fauna marked time with a low, repeating croak.

Suddenly I was sure I knew what we had found but, before I could say anything, Bastien called out.

"Hellooooo?" he bellowed, cupping his hands on either side of his mouth.

My hand shot out and grabbed his arm.

"Shhhh," I hissed.

Bastien's voice echoed from the still far-off northern cliffs. The mysterious species of croaking fauna went silent. We stood frozen until the reverberations faded.

"We are in the Northern Ruins," I breathed.

Bastien blinked at me. "The . . . what?"

"It is where our uncle from long ago was exiled after plotting against our seventh great-grandfather. The family was forbidden to marry and their line was extinguished."

"*Extinguished*," Bastien gasped. "How do you know that?"

"Grandfather told me."

"Is that why we are whispering? Do you think there's someone here?" Bastien asked.

I shook my head. "They've been dead for more than 150 years. Be quiet anyway."

Bastien's suggestion had been enough to run chills up my spine. I had omitted the part my grandfather had said about the memory held within the ruins ("ghosts," he had said) and their former occupants haunting future patriarchs. From there my imagination threatened to slip to visions of lost civilizations, crumbling empires, fallen kingdoms, and other horrors.

We snuck closer to the chapel and just about leapt out of our skins when a mute of hares exploded from the underbrush. Bastien let out a shriek, but once the moment had passed, we sank to the ground together laughing nervously.

The sun emerged from the other side of the cloud. That brightened our spirits and sapped something of the sinister aspect of the decaying structures away.

"This place is cool," Bastien said, surprising me.

I had been sure that the ruins would spook him more, but the sun seemed to have cheered my brother, and whatever apprehension he felt had leaked away. Vim had found a patch of vegetation to her liking and was grazing languidly. Bastien joined me on the ground and we lay there enjoying the sun until the clouds returned and it began to drizzle.

"Quick," Bastien said, playing up the drama. "We must find shelter."

"Climb up there," I said, pointing to one of the crumbling walls. "It should be a good vantage point to see a fallen tree or something."

Bastien looked at me with an expression of dull horror.

"Okay, Basti," I said, catching the hint. "I'll do it."

I vaulted myself onto a low ledge and pulled myself up on the rusty iron prongs that were sunk into the masonry until I was atop the broken wall.

"I don't see any trees to huddle under, but part of the chapel's roof is still intact. We can shelter there until the squall passes."

I jumped down from the wall but when Bastien saw me, he started, and all the color drained out of his face.

"What is it?" I said, taking a step toward him, but he mirrored it with a step back. "Bastien, what is the matter?"

Bastien pointed at my midsection. When I looked down I saw what he was upset about: there was blood all over the fly of my riding pants.

I had snagged my left hand on something sharp and my pinky was bleeding rather profusely. In the process of climbing down I must have brushed it across my pants and bloodied them nicely. Once I noticed it, my hand began to throb with my heartbeat.

"Bastien," I said in my most soothing voice, "it's just a cut." I held up my hand for him.

He watched in mute horror as the blood dripped down my arm and onto the ground before soaking into the dirt.

"It will be fine. I promise," I said. Bastien stiffened, bit his lower lip, and nodded at me, but then sank to a sitting position.

Thinking it was best to just ignore his distress and stem the flow of blood before he fainted, I poured some bottled water on the cut, elevated it above my heart, and applied direct pressure, just as Karl had taught me. After a couple of minutes I bound my hand with a handkerchief from our makeshift kit. Once I had as much of the blood cleaned up as I could manage, I sat down and put my arm around him.

"Hey," I said. "I'm fine." Bastien nodded unconvincingly. "It's like the estate bit me." That elicited a smile.

"You won't tell anyone?" Bastien said. "That I was afraid, I mean?"

"Of course I won't."

It started to rain harder, and that finally roused my brother. We made our way to the far corner of the chapel.

"Make haste, milady," Bastien said, sweeping his arm toward the large hole in the wall. "In here."

I dropped as elegant a curtsy as I could muster while being rained upon.

I tugged at Vim's reins and, after a snort or two of hesitation, she consented to be led into the chapel.

I let Vim's reins fall and, shivering from the cold rain, Bastien and I huddled together giggling.

Before long we were drawing diagrams of defense lines in the dirt and organizing military campaigns from our "field headquarters," planning that continued well after the rain had stopped.

The sound was in the back of my awareness for some time, but it was finally obvious enough for me to take notice when I heard the crunch of footsteps on vegetation.

I could already see by Bastien's expression that he had heard it as well.

"It's coming from downhill," I said. "Why would anyone else be out this far?"

We both froze in terror, staring at each other in the diffuse light that filtered through the tree leaves above the chapel. As we fell silent, the steps stopped as well. Bastien and I slipped into a soundless standoff with our unknown stalker. This went on until I almost caved in to the temptation to peek out and around the chapel wall, but our faceless pursuer struck first and, with alarming speed, hurdled through a nearby hole in the closest wall and bellowed at us with a horrible cry.

Bastien and I fell over each other and collapsed into a tangled heap in the moss and dirt that made up the decaying chapel's floor.

Looming over us, and laughing with an uncharacteristically nasal cackle, was Augustin.

CHAPTER FIFTEEN

⌒

Borders

VIM DID NOT TAKE AUGUSTIN'S PRANK well. She started, reared, and snorted twice before I took her reins, patting her gently on the neck and cooing in her ear until she seemed calm once more.

I was about to snap at Augustin for spooking her, but even as I opened my mouth, something about his appearance stopped me cold: there was a long, thin, but shallow cut running along the right side of his jaw. His once fair blond hair seemed to have darkened considerably. Moreover, he seemed to have grown in just a few months. It was all more than imposing enough to intimidate Bastien and me. Suddenly I wasn't at all sure that I was relieved to find that our nameless pursuer was in fact Augustin rather than some trespassing villain from beyond the estate.

"So this is what you two have gotten up to," he said. "Had I come a bit earlier I bet I would have found the two of you naked in here."

Bastien turned an alarming shade of scarlet.

"Oh my god," Augustin mocked, pointing to the still-drying blood on my riding pants. "She was a virgin too? Well, it probably wasn't incest. No one else in the family has her flaming red hair, you know. Still, she's only eleven, you little pervert."

"I'm twelve," I countered.

"Augustin, you scared us," Bastien said.

Augustin ignored him. Instead, having crept close enough to reach them, he snatched Vim's reins right out of my hands.

"Augustin, don't," I shouted, clutching after them, but Augustin warded me off easily, keeping me at arm's length with his free hand.

"Why are you being so mean all of a sudden?" Bastien said.

"Don't be a baby," Augustin said, and that cowed Bastien.

"Give me back her reins," I said.

"I don't think so," he chided, yanking her bridle this way and that so he could examine both sides of her head.

"You'll hurt her," I said, reaching around the other side of him. But he was too quick for me and just pushed me away again, hard enough that I almost tripped and fell to the mossy flagstones of the chapel's floor.

"I don't take orders from you," he said.

"We don't have to take orders from you either," Bastien replied.

Augustin held his left hand up. "Actually, you do. Because I wear this."

On his middle finger was an antique, silver signet ring with a crest inlaid in red stone. Even on his largest finger, the ring was so big that he had wound the base of the shank with twine so it wouldn't fall off.

"That's Father's," Bastien insisted.

"Not anymore."

Though I tried not to show it, I was shocked. The ring was many generations old, large enough to be unwieldy, and had been designed to be pressed into wax. Neither our grandfather nor our father wore signet rings, but for us siblings they had tremendous symbolic power. I recalled Professor Lechner's lessons on the importance of such seals. That our father would have given one to Augustin was frightening.

"That still doesn't make you the boss of us," Bastien said. I cringed at how childish he sounded. "You're only the second in line. Father is in front of you."

"Oh, you think so?" Augustin said.

"You are being a real jerk," I said, finding my courage from somewhere. "Did you learn that at your stupid *boarding school?*"

It was all I could come up with, but it sounded weak and immature.

Augustin gave me an angry look. "Yes, in fact. That . . . and other things. Come to think of it, why are you even speaking? You are the youngest and you aren't even a boy. You are nothing."

He made a show of appraising Vim again, tugging at her reins even more aggressively than before.

"She doesn't like that, Augustin," I said.

"How would you know?"

"She's got her ears all the way back. Please be careful, she might . . ."

I could see it develop even as the warning began to slip past my lips: Vim rolled her eye at Augustin after the third time he pulled her head around. She leaned toward him and then, as horses sometimes do, bit him hard on the arm.

Augustin yelped and dropped the reins, whereupon Vim deftly bolted out the gaping hole in the chapel wall and into the clearing beyond.

The pain seemed to set in then and Augustin sank to his knees, holding his forearm.

"Are you okay?" Bastien asked, horrified.

I walked over to Augustin and leaned down to look at the wound. Augustin pulled his shirt sleeve up, exposing his left forearm where Vim had caught him. The skin was broken in a couple of places. It didn't look too bad, but even as I watched, it started to swell and darken.

"That horse is a fucking menace," Augustin hissed.

"Augustin," I said, reaching for his arm, trying to use my most soothing voice. "Let me see."

"Get the hell away from me," he yelled, so loudly that I flinched.

It was still echoing against the chapel's interior when Augustin pulled himself up and staggered through the hole in the wall. At first I thought he would go after Vim, but when Bastien and I followed, I could see that she was nearly on the other side of the clearing, watching closely to keep her distance from him.

"Augustin," Bastien called. "Come back."

"Go to hell," he said, without turning around. "Both of you."

With that, he headed uphill to the north. We looked on as, quite nonchalantly, he walked up to the border wall and then, to our utter amazement, vaulted over it.

"Augustin," Bastien called after him. "We're not allowed to go past that. Not ever!"

But Augustin kept on and crested the next hill before vanishing behind a bluff.

WITH AUGUSTIN GONE, I collected Vim from the little patch of grass she had retreated to. Bastien and I lingered in the ruins, trying to shake off the encounter, but the day was more or less scuttled and our surroundings a bit too spooky besides. Dejected, we started back down to the manor. In deference to Bastien, I dismounted to lead Vim downhill and walk next to him.

"What is wrong with Augustin?" Bastien said when we were about halfway home.

Certainly, as siblings are prone to do, we'd had our little scraps with Augustin before, but the smug and aggressive Augustin on display in the Northern Ruins that day was something new.

"Did you hear me?" Bastien said, clutching at my sleeve. I had been lost in thought.

"What do you mean, exactly?" I said, stalling.

"He looks different."

"I guess so," I allowed. "Maybe because he was dressed in Father's shirt?"

"It wasn't Father's. They are from Father's tailor. Augustin has had them for a while. The sleeves are monogrammed with his initials."

"Oh. Well, he had a cut on his jaw. Has he been fighting or something?"

"That's probably from shaving. Father gave him a straight razor and he doesn't know how to use it yet."

"Really?" I said, and it was earnest fascination, a younger sister's fearful interest in the mysterious rituals of masculine grooming that begin to appear in her preadolescent brothers. The thought of running a sharp blade across one's face, particularly one as sinister looking as a straight razor, was both fascinating and horrible to me. Horrible enough to give me a little chill that I tried to conceal.

"I don't have special shirts," Bastien said, and looked off toward the manor. "Or a special razor."

"Bastien—"

"Or a signet ring."

"It's just that you are not old enough yet," I suggested.

"No, it's because I'm not firstborn."

I made a vaguely dismissive noise, but it smacked of truth. I wondered if what Augustin had said about my being "nothing" was also true.

"What's wrong with him?" Bastien asked, breaking my reverie.

"Something changed him."

This answer did not agree with Bastien. He looked on the verge of tears. I stopped walking, dropped Vim's reins, took him by the shoulders, and turned him to face me.

"What is it?" I said.

Bastien wavered for a moment. Though his voice cracked, he managed to regain his composure.

"Are you going to change too?"

"No, Basti," I said.

"I won't either. I promise."

He fiddled with his belt, then came away with the old compass and held it out to me.

"What's this for?" I asked.

"I am constant as the northern star," he said, and there were tears in his eyes.

I took the compass and smiled at him as warmly as I could. He buried his face in my chest when I hugged him close. We stood like that for a moment. But my thoughts drifted as I watched over his shoulder, gazing into the woods beyond as a gust of wind filtered through the trees, causing their branches to moan and whisper.

⟋◯⟍

BACK IN MY apartments, I almost dropped the filthy compass again. Though certainly a well-intentioned gift, it was also an irritant, so I tucked it away in the center drawer of my desk.

Late that night, I found my way to the East Salon and was relieved to discover my grandfather alone. He looked uncharacteristically tired, as if he had aged years in just a few months, but when he raised his eyebrows at me and smiled, some of the fatigue seemed to melt away.

He had been poring over a collection of papers and old documents and, for a moment, I was afraid he would shoo me away, but instead he put them aside and waved me in.

We made small talk as I worked myself up to the topic I wanted to address. He knew that I was holding something back but entertained the polite fiction for my sake.

"Augustin showed us one of Father's signet rings," I said, finally.

"Did he now?"

"He says wearing it makes him the heir."

"Does he now?" My grandfather frowned and chewed on the stem of his pipe. "Well," he murmured, mostly to himself. "That was rather rash."

"The signet rings are for sealing messages from the leader of the family, aren't they?" I asked, breaking him out of a brooding pensiveness.

"They have been used this way, though more commonly long ago. Tell me, do you believe in magic rings that bestow mystical powers on the wearer?"

"No."

"Well, apparently Augustin does, hmmm? Shall I tell you a secret?"

I nodded.

"Your brother Augustin doesn't know quite so much as he thinks. The signet rings of the family are not what is important. True, they can be used to mark messages, and jeweled accessories may sometimes have hidden purposes, but do you think a true leader needs to advertise his power with something so vulgar as a gaudy bit of jewelry?"

"I don't know."

"That your brother thinks this way shows us that he is not ready for the responsibility. It is true that a ring may mark a man; may identify him—"

"A bearer instrument."

"Precisely. But men do not follow a ring, and a leader who depends on such crass displays will not remain a leader for very long. Instead, over the long term, a true leader must derive power from leadership. Do you understand the difference?"

I shook my head.

"The unrestrained wielding of naked power is sometimes necessary but, over time, it breeds resentment in men. Men value and respect power, but it must be tempered with justice, which men appeal to against the exercise of raw power."

My grandfather sent pipe smoke toward the ceiling.

"When you returned from your trip, we spoke of Julius Caesar. Do you remember?"

"Yes, Grandfather."

"What was his title when he died?"

"*Dictator in perpetuum*," I said, excited that I knew the answer by heart.

"Yes. Dictator for life. Was that why he was killed, do you think?"

"I'm not sure."

"Well, what was Brutus supposed to have said after Caesar was assassinated?"

"*Sic semper tyrannis.*"

"Always thus to tyrants," my grandfather said, nodding.

I shuddered, remembering the play on those words in the note that Augustin had left me after my betrayal of the Bureau of Secrets.

"But it is not certain he said that, Grandfather," I blurted out, not least because I wanted Augustin's reference to be flawed. "Plutarch says that Brutus made as if to speak but the senators ran from the Senate in terror and confusion before he could be heard."

"Why am I not surprised that you would be able to correct the historical record for me? But the title of Dictator, if not perhaps Dictator for Life, was a legitimate Roman office, essentially the 'first magistrate.' The tyrant, from the Ancient Greek *tyrannos*, on the other hand, has somehow usurped legitimate authority, or has reached power in an unconventional way. In its early use there was no moral judgment in the term. Only later did the word *tyrant* come to have the modern, negative connotation, and to mean a leader who was unrestrained by law. The missing element is—"

"Justice," I said.

"Indeed. One might sound silly saying 'always thus to legitimately appointed dictators,' eh?"

I smiled a little.

"Leopold understood these nuances, and built structures to assure that his aides, heirs, and counselors all felt their views respected if not always followed. Obviously, this is a lesson your brother has not yet learned."

"What kind of structures?"

"Well," my grandfather began, but then trailed off. He worried at his pipe with one hand, and fiddled with something under his vest with the other.

"Grandfather?" I said, after a few moments.

"He created the Council of Leopold," my grandfather said, and I had the impression that it had taken him some effort. "So that his heir and his three most trusted advisors could meet and consult with him on the matters most important to the family. So that they could feel themselves heard. Later, he expanded the structures to include allies; other nobles and their families."

I had never heard such a thing. It sounded mysterious, exotic, and wonderful.

"Can I join?"

My grandfather hesitated.

"I want to be one of your advisors. I mean a trusted one. Like a member of the Council of Leopold."

"Ah. That is a bit more complicated."

"Is it because of my red hair?" I said.

"What on earth do you mean?"

"Augustin says I'm not Father's daughter and everyone can tell because I'm the only one with red hair."

"Well, it just so happens that your hair is red like that because you got an extra dose of the blood of Leopold I, notorious killer of Turks. He had a full head of fiery red hair. There is more of our founder in you than in Augustin, I dare say."

"But, Grandfather," I said, remembering Leopold's portraits, "his hair is black in his portrayals."

"Like many nobles in that age he wore a luxurious black wig. You know, now that I think of it, perhaps we should see that they come back into style. I think a good wig would complement me nicely." My grandfather shook his balding head and pantomimed a long mane of hair.

I wasn't in a laughing mood but did my best to give him a polite smile.

"Well, is it because I am a girl then?"

"What's this now?"

"Am I forbidden from joining the Council because I'm a girl? Augustin says because I'm a girl and the youngest that I'm nothing."

"Again with Augustin?"

"There aren't any paintings of girls in the Hall of Ancestors," I pointed out.

"Our family has never had a matriarch."

"Why?"

"Well, female leaders were rare. Are rare."

"What about Queen Elizabeth?"

"Well, yes, but—"

"And Queen Mary."

"Now, now—"

"Queen Victoria. Elizabeth II—"

"England was a very peculiar historical—"

"What about Cleopatra?" I said.

"You must understand—"

"Catherine the Great. Empress Suiko."

"All right, enough," my grandfather said, holding up a hand. "Do you spend all your time reading about such obscure subjects?"

"And Fulvia Flacca."

My grandfather looked puzzled. "Fulvia?"

"Flacca. The third wife of Mark Antony?" I prompted.

My grandfather pondered the matter, tapping out, and then packing his pipe before lighting it again.

"She was influential, was she?"

"She was the only woman to have her face on Roman coins."

"Was she now?"

"Well, the only nongoddess. Nike was on lots of coins commemorating Roman victories."

"And what became of Fulvia after her mintings?"

"She died in exile in Greece," I said after the long moment it took me to remember. "And Octavian and Antony blamed her for their fighting to save face."

"Well, that doesn't sound all that appealing, does it?"

"No," I agreed.

"What did she do wrong?"

I wasn't sure I had an answer for this. After a moment my grandfather prodded me.

"Where did her political power come from? I'll give you a hint. If you marry into it, it was never yours in the first place. Did she die suddenly and mysteriously?"

"I don't know."

"I bet she did at that; but, my dear, it was rare that girls should have had to worry about that sort of thing. The struggles of power? That was for the boys, hmmm?"

I wasn't sure I liked his answer. "How did you learn how to be a leader, Grandfather?" I said.

"Well, my father, your great-grandfather, insisted that I have the requisite experience. I traveled the world at a very young age."

"Is that why Augustin can cross the walls of the estate? For experience?"

His expression darkened. "You know very well that is not permitted. Where was this?"

For a moment I felt a pang of guilt, the belated regret of a tattletale, but in response to my silence my grandfather narrowed his eyes at me and began to look crosser still.

"By the Northern Ruins," I admitted.

"Ah. I see," my grandfather said, and his expression softened. "You found them then, the ruins?"

I nodded, worried that I hadn't been supposed to.

"Augustin has, I suspect, discovered the existence of the girls' finishing school that lies about six miles beyond the Austrian border."

The confusion must have shown on my face.

"Never mind, my dear," my grandfather said. "Suffice it to say that Augustin will soon have rather a lot of new responsibilities. Between now and then there are other, baser forces at work within him. Be understanding with him for a time. In any event, I should not gossip about your brother, and neither should you. This will be our secret, all right?"

"Is it because of South Africa that I cannot leave the estate?"

"Don't be silly. The walls around the estate are there for good reason and for now I expect you to respect them. On this side of them we make our own rules, despite what the authorities may think. Beyond those walls our power wanes considerably. Remember that. There will be plenty of opportunities to gain experience here on the estate, and off it, in the coming months."

"Off it?"

"Oh, no. You won't lure me that easily. You will just have to wait and see."

"But—"

"Enough, enough. I am far too liberal with you already," he said, though there was little edge to his rebuke. "And do remember, the things you and I discuss in here are family confidences, and not to be taken lightly."

This gentle scolding delivered, he sent me off to bed.

⁓☉

THE NEXT MORNING there was a palpable tension in the air. After breakfast, I caught sight of several members of the domestic staff scurrying about. Then I understood: my mother was beginning to prepare for another grand event.

After my shameful performance in front of the Archduke, I thought it best to recede into the background; to linger in my apartments and focus on Professor Lechner's assignments. I was surprised, therefore, when I was summoned to one of the salons to attend my mother. When I arrived, she was talking to Lucas in an annoyed tone.

"I cannot possibly be expected to keep track of all the domestics," she said. "If she does not present herself for work today then she is dismissed."

"Yes, ma'am," Lucas said, bowing himself out of the room.

My mother's perpetually Armani-clad aide, Hannah, was lurking nearby. I was afraid of Hannah. Like Karl, whom I took to be her counterpart on my grandfather's staff, Hannah spoke very little and had a distant, almost rude presence about her. Like Karl, it seemed to me that she owned only one outfit, an ensemble consisting of a black skirt and jacket she wore open, a collared, white, silk shirt, and dark, tortoiseshell sunglasses, which she donned even in failing light.

I had once, and entirely by accident, found Hannah's quarters while snooping about in the manor. Her room was bare of personal items excepting a framed picture on an otherwise clean desk. At first I thought the picture—a professional-looking shot featuring a pleasant-looking, well-adjusted couple in casual clothes with a nearly perfect sunset scene in the background—must be of Hannah's brother and sister, or sister and spouse. When I looked closer, however, I could detect no family resemblance.

Hannah's ash-blond hair might have been dyed, but her severe lips and square jaw were not reflected in the facial features of either of the picture's subjects. Hannah looked to be from far deeper in the Eastern Bloc than the vaguely Dutch-looking couple that was depicted smiling tritely in front of the setting sun. I picked up the picture frame for a closer look and found the answer: it was a stock photograph that had come with the frame. The price tag was still on the back.

That was enough to blunt my curiosity but on my way out, I saw the toy white rabbit under a table in one corner. It had the look of a once-beloved stuffed animal marooned in an earlier time as its owner matured past the point of bedtime hugs and cuddles. Its eyes had long ago fallen off or been removed, I didn't care to know which. Startled, I fled.

There in the salon, memories of my intrusion into Hannah's abode made me shudder. I gave my mother a proper curtsy, mostly for the long moment of looking at the floor it afforded me.

"Hannah," my mother said, "my husband will be traveling abroad this coming Sunday. My daughter will be accompanying him. I want you to take her to select some appropriate business attire. I have prearranged a private session with a delightful boutique in Zürich this evening."

"Yes, ma'am," Hannah said, and we were dismissed.

I had not expected that my grandfather's promise that I might continue to explore the world beyond the estate would be fulfilled so quickly. I was excited, apprehensive, and baffled, all at once. Still, the idea of clothes shopping with Hannah was less than appealing.

THE HELICOPTER FLIGHT to Zürich was much longer than the short jaunts between the helipad and our airstrip. Hannah spent her time looking out her window in silence. Finally, I tried to spur her into conversation.

"Do you like to fly?" I said.

It was a weak offering, but nothing else came to mind.

"I have no opinion on the matter," she said.

"I mean, when you and my mother travel."

"I will not discuss your mother's affairs," she said, and, for the remainder of the flight, that was that.

We were ushered into a Mercedes sedan after landing. It was after nine thirty in the evening and by that time the shops had closed, but I sat plastered to my window the entire way, looking out in awe at the denizens of Zürich, my first "big city" after Johannesburg.

Our hostess at the boutique was a woman of perhaps fifty who wasted no time before looking me over in a way I found almost obscene. After half a minute of silence she furrowed her brow, squinted at me, and pursed her lips before tapping them with her pointer finger.

"Something classic for the young executive, I think." She spoke with a thick French accent. She shot a cross glance at Hannah, who had taken a seat at the far end of the boutique facing the windows. "Though not Armani. Too mercenary. Too . . . slick, no?"

If Hannah took offense, or even noticed, she gave no sign.

Apparently disappointed at having elicited no response from Hannah, the boutique's proprietrix turned her attentions back to me.

Before I knew it, with a "No," "No," "Never, never," "Another," "Better," and a few examples of "Well then," I had pulled onto and then stripped from my body nearly two dozen outfits, finally arriving at a collection of five jackets, four pencil skirts, five silk shirts, and three sheath dresses that complemented my new jackets. Then came the scarves. Beautiful, soft silk scarves in dozens of patterns, with a slew of textures and shapes.

Finally, in a moment of what I took to be maternal weakness, my dresser slipped a brilliant, deep red and silver Hermès scarf around my neck. It was so wonderful and the red so rich, I nearly cried to look at it.

"This," she whispered in my ear so closely I could feel her hot breath, "is too much for a young woman I think. And yet . . . I know you will find the right . . . no, the most singularly special occasion to wear it. But you must promise me that you will use it sparingly . . . are we agreed?"

I nodded.

"I will see that the clothes are altered. You should have them tomorrow, I think," the woman said.

"Thank you, Hannah," I offered after nearly twenty minutes of silence during the flight back. She looked at me as if no one had ever thanked her before.

"What did you think of the red scarf?" I added, trying to break her silence.

"I don't prefer colors," she managed.

That was the last time I tried to make small talk with Hannah.

EARLY ON FRIDAY morning, Bastien came by my apartments to present me with a carefully handwritten invitation to his room to listen to a recital that evening. I was charmed by the offer, so I gave him a deep curtsy as I accepted. That brought a wide smile to his face. He beamed and gave me a warm hug.

"Do you know where Augustin is?" Bastien asked after our embrace.

I shrugged, puzzled that he would even ask after the last encounter with our brother. "He's not in his rooms?"

"He didn't answer the door."

"Maybe he's sleeping in," I suggested. "Just leave the invitation for him." Bastien frowned.

"Do you want me to dress up for the recital?" By way of an answer, Bastien proffered another huge grin and darted off without another word.

A few minutes later, as I was getting ready for my morning bath, my bell rang again. I opened my doors with a sigh, expecting to find Bastien again, but instead was confronted by one of the underbutlers bearing a folded piece of paper closed with a wax seal.

When I sat down at my desk I was surprised to find that the dark wax had been impressed with my grandfather's personal seal. I broke it and unfolded the paper to read my second invitation of the day, this one to late lunch with my grandfather in the East Salon.

I had feared I might be forced to spend the duration of my mother's event in my apartments listening to the sounds of her entertainments waxing and waning downstairs. Instead, it appeared that I had rather a busy social calendar ahead of me.

MY GRANDFATHER WAS waiting for me in the East Salon. A spread of food—three different soups and several kinds of finger sandwiches—was already laid out, and with the windows open, I could hear snatches of birdsong outside.

After I curtsied and our traditional pleasantries had been exchanged, he gestured for me to sit. Once we had eaten, he leaned back in his chair and lit up his pipe. He passed an engraved invitation across the table.

"As you can see, tomorrow marks the two-hundredth anniversary of the completion of the manor's construction. Your mother has arranged for a series of events over the next three days, events she started planning over a year ago.

"There will be some very important people arriving before the rest of the guests and this evening there will be a private reception for them. By tomorrow evening, the estate is expecting more than fifty visitors for dinner."

My grandfather looked at me, puffing on his pipe thoughtfully.

"Would you like me to tell you a secret? It is . . ."

I nodded before he could continue.

"No," he tutted me. "Don't answer yet. Hear it all first. Knowing this secret has risks. You must be certain that what I tell you will not change how you behave in front of others. In fact, it would be safer not to know at all. Do you understand?"

My grandfather's expression was very serious. I could feel a tightening in my throat and I had the urge to swallow.

"I think so," I said.

"Do you still want me to tell you?"

I tried to take his warning seriously, to give his concern its due, but my curiosity was silently screaming at me to just say "yes." With my heart pounding, but after what I thought was a respectful pause, I nodded.

"Very well," he said, and lowered his voice. "It is entirely possible, in fact it is quite likely, that whoever was behind the attack on you and your father will be a guest of this estate this weekend."

My grandfather paused, allowing what he had said to sink in. I put my hands in my lap, desperate that my grandfather should not see them tremble.

"You know who it was?" I managed. "Mother invited them? Why?"

"In point of fact, we still do not know exactly who was responsible. But what we do know makes it far more likely than not that they are on the guest list. As for your mother's invitations, she knows nothing of your trip or our suspicions and it is quite essential that she remain in the dark. Do you understand?"

I nodded.

"As for why, well, really it does not matter one bit if you invite them or not. The enemy is always there. Always watching. Always waiting. That is what it is to be a member of a family like ours. And we hardly want to alert our enemies to our suspicions by excluding them from an event they would naturally expect to be invited to.

"In bringing them out of the shadows, or even providing shadows for them, there is always the possibility that we might induce them to make some mistake, allow us to see some misplaced gesture, or let through some slip of the tongue that will unveil them. Yes? Perhaps we might even engineer some temptation to draw them out. At the same time, the likelihood that, having already failed in their attempt on their own ground, they would undertake some malfeasance here on our own lands, is remote indeed.

"I doubt that anyone on the estate would agree with my decision to bring you into my confidence, but I do not feel that these matters should be kept from you. Our mysterious adversaries tried to harm you as well, did they not? I feel you have a right to know. Moreover, our family can ill afford for your father's heirs to be naïve."

"Does Bastien know? Does Augustin?"

"I have not told them, nor do I believe your father will. I have my reasons for favoring you in this, but I must ask you to leave me with them."

My grandfather gave me a cross look and made a show of looking me over.

"It is getting late. Why aren't you dressed yet?"

Confused, I just shook my head.

"Your date to tonight's reception will be rather perturbed if you make him late."

"My date?"

"Well, of course. It would be entirely inappropriate for a young lady of your stature to attend such an event alone. What would people say?"

"But, I don't understand. Who is my date?"

My grandfather took a deep puff from his pipe. As he spoke again it was with tendrils of smoke suspended about his face.

"Why, *me*, of course," he said.

CHAPTER SIXTEEN

⁓

Overtaken by Events

T HE PRIVATE RECEPTION WAS SCHEDULED TO begin at eight o'clock that very evening, the Friday before Saturday's main entertainments. I ran up to my rooms, intending to follow my grandfather's instructions to the letter and present myself dressed and ready at the East Salon no later than seven forty-five. Though we siblings did not use them often, my mother took pains to make sure that we all had a selection of appropriate formalwear for black- or white-tie events, a task that could not have been easy to keep up with in those years when we hit our respective growth spurts. I rang for Cipriana and dove into my closets.

I had my windows open and, by that time, I could make out the turbine whine—the high, throbbing call of some mechanical bird of prey—of the helicopter in the distance now and again, ferrying, I supposed, arriving guests from our private airstrip up to the helipad. What, I wondered, if the masters of my would-be assassins were on it; minutes away from setting foot in our ancestral home where they would be doted upon by our staff, plied with our wine, and lavishly fed? It was a hideous thing to imagine the visage of Leopold I, powerless to intervene, as the knave who tried to have his twelfth grandson murdered wandered the Hall of Ancestors at perfect liberty.

I jumped when my bell rang. It was Emma, one of the younger maids. After a nervous curtsy, she was able to tell me nothing about why Cipriana was unavailable, only that she had been sent as a replacement.

The reception called for black-tie attire, and I remembered advice about formal events my grandfather once gave in another context to the effect that the younger the person, the more subdued should be their clothing. After I tried on four options, Emma helped me decide on a simple, full-length, long-sleeved black gown.

After a brief scare that I had lost it, I found the silk-lined box with my family order in one of my desk drawers. The bow made of black and silver ribbon had come undone somehow. I had to sit down and tie it again before Emma pinned the order insignia through the ribbon and to the left side of my gown so that it hung pendant from the bow. When I looked in the mirror, I couldn't help but beam at myself. Even Emma managed a nervous little grin.

Dusk turned to evening, so I crept down the far stairs and darted through the back hallway to the East Salon. Proud of my careful timing, I knocked at the door just as the clock down the hall began to sound the third quarter hour's chime.

I had seen him in black tie before, but for some reason it affected me more than usual when my grandfather opened the door. The gemstones in the neck badge hanging under his bow tie caught the light in a particular way, and the breast star and bar of miniature medals on his jacket looked as if someone had spent hours polishing them (and likely someone had).

His eyes went wide when he saw me and it seemed as if he was as taken with my appearance as I was with his.

"Well," he said, recovering his formality, "I will be the envy of all the men in attendance this evening."

⌒

WE WERE IN the hallway just a few yards from the open double doors to the Rose Salon when my grandfather leaned down to whisper in my ear.

"Remember what I told you," he cautioned. "Spend more time listening and watching than speaking. This is not advice to a child, my dear, but the practice of great diplomats, and leaders." My grandfather gave me a sidelong look. "And even *spies*."

"Spies?" I said. "Here?"

"You might be surprised. I am jesting with you, but only a little. There is much to be learned at events like these, but one must be attuned to the opportunity. For the next two days, you must regard as artifice every interaction, every turn of phrase, every gesture, and every outburst that seems occasioned by careless intoxication. In suspecting deception, more often than not, you will be correct. Remember that it is a statement even for you to be at an event of this stratum. Children are not normally invited."

"Mother invited me?"

My grandfather ignored this question.

"Since you *are* invited, and children are not, therefore, you must be quite something else, mustn't you?"

The compliment was not lost on me.

"Many of our guests will not yet have met the daughter of the line. Many curious eyes will be upon you. They will probe for idiosyncrasies; seek to unearth weaknesses. Stay within yourself and your capabilities. Don't be lured into interactions that others control."

"Ask after the design behind the action," I quoted my grandfather from memory. "Know the truth of it. Only then may we act according to design."

Something unsettling happened then as my grandfather looked down at me: tears welled up in his eyes.

"Grandfather," I breathed, alarmed. "What is wrong?"

But he only produced a handkerchief and dabbed at his eyes before shaking his head.

"Nothing. Only that I am very proud of you."

He straightened his jacket, fiddled with the bar on his left lapel that held his miniature medals, and took my hand. Holding it formally aloft, he led me to the double doors.

IT WAS RARE for my mother to arrange for the estate's halberd-bearing guards to be in attendance, but there they were, flanking the double doors in all their finery. They saluted silently by snapping their pikes to the vertical in perfect unison, just as my grandfather and I passed the threshold.

The Rose Salon was the largest of the manor's many parlor rooms and one my mother paid particular attention to even when the estate was bereft of guests. It was full of dark red, brilliant whites, and even the occasional trim of gold, a color my mother normally abhorred but had, in the Rose Salon, used to great effect. Two imposing chandeliers hung from the ceiling and cast a warm light that brought out the crimson accents in the rugs and the curtains. The floor-to-ceiling windows looked out into the section of the Italian Gardens dominated by my mother's personal rosebushes.

Vases filled with hundreds of fresh-cut roses, some varieties the result of my mother's own interbreeding efforts, adorned almost every table surface. The high, vaulted ceiling was painted with a beautiful fresco of rose gardens, the central element of which was a wonderfully crafted trompe l'oeil of a faux dome.

Though I had idly played in the grand room many times before and taken only casual notice of the decor, it had a particular effect on me that evening. The color was so vibrant and the three-dimensional effect of the artificial dome so realistic that, now and again, pairs of our guests would gaze upward and point.

It was still a few minutes until eight, but members of the domestic staff already milled about bearing silver trays with wine, champagne, and hors d'oeuvres, all to the evident delight of perhaps a dozen guests who had arrived early and congregated into a few groups of twos and threes. My grandfather led me first to an out-of-the-way spot. At once I understood that he was using the space and the time to read the room and decide how he wanted to work it. It was artful and deliberate, and I marveled in the fact that I had recognized his tactic.

I caught sight of Professor Lechner sipping from a champagne flute and talking with an older woman I did not recognize. I put my hand on my grandfather's forearm and inclined my chin in the direction of the Professor, proud of myself for mastering that particular gesture, a subtle signal that I had occasionally seen my mother and my father use with each other.

Without moving his head, my grandfather cut his eyes that way, and then gave me a hint of a nod. We had fallen into a kind of wordless communication that felt so natural that it was as if we had been silently speaking to each other in that way my entire life.

"Ah," my grandfather declared. "Is that Professor Lechner over there, do you think?"

His indulging our little conspiracy was the perfect note to sound and I found myself unable to suppress a huge grin.

"Ah," I said, with greatly exaggerated formality. "Now that you mention it, I do think so. Shall we saunter that way?"

"Certainly," my grandfather said, and took my hand.

In contrast to the wild head of white hair I was used to, Professor Lechner was impeccably groomed. For a moment I entertained the fantasy that I was seeing an impostor. He gave my grandfather a warm smile and then gracefully diverted the attention of the woman in his company away from a man who had more than a dozen miniature medals pinned to his jacket.

When I saw her up close, I could tell that she was older than I had first thought; certainly in her midseventies, though she was so slim, well dressed, and made up that she could have easily passed for ten years younger. She had dark, almost black eyes of a severe and intelligent intensity that contrasted with the softer features of a round and wrinkled, but rather beautiful, face. Her jet-black hair was shot through here and there with silver-white strands that, for a brief moment, caused me to imagine her a sorceress of some sort. It was an impression only bolstered by the great poise and dignity with which she held herself. She was wearing a full-length, long-sleeved, black gown to which two medals I did not recognize were pinned. Both ribbons were adorned with rosettes. The senior decoration was a five-armed Maltese Cross of white and green that hung from a bloodred ribbon. The second was a much plainer bronze medallion bearing a Cross of Lorraine under a black ribbon with red trim.

My grandfather stopped dead in his tracks when he saw her. There was an interval of a few seconds before his hand gripped mine, tightly enough that I almost protested before he let it go.

"Bernadette," he breathed, and the ardor that welled up just under the surface of his voice was almost palpable. Accompanying it was a singular effect: the fatigue and worry that he had carried in his expression since my South African trip appeared to melt away.

A sly smile came to her, one that transformed in stages to an expression of pure joy. When she spoke it was in an English thickly accented with what I knew immediately to be a very erudite Parisian affectation.

"Imagine finding here such a rascal," she said, turning to Professor Lechner briefly before embracing my grandfather.

After his comments about observers, I was surprised to see such emotive behavior from my grandfather. Was it a ruse? I chanced a glance at Professor Lechner and found him wearing some version of the woman's sly grin, only deeper and more self-satisfied. I knew then that Professor Lechner, master of the set-piece social interaction, had taken pains to engineer the reunion I was witnessing.

When I looked back at my grandfather and the woman, I could see there was something awkward about their embrace. It took me a few moments to understand: the woman kept her right arm tucked in against her abdomen, just as it had been when I first saw her.

"Now, Bernadette," my grandfather said, finding his poise again and extracting himself from her long embrace, "you must be careful. My date is prone to bouts of vicious, even violent, jealousy."

Bernadette collected herself and then looked at me.

"But of course," she said. "Her hair . . . it is the red of passion." Her voice sank into a conspiratorial tone. "And of course you always did prefer your women younger, Phillip."

I began to curtsy, but my grandfather gave a little tug on my elbow.

"No, my dear," he said. "We are beyond such formalities with each other."

I could feel the blood going to my earlobes and when I looked down, my eyes shifted to Bernadette's right arm. I was horrified to see that she was missing the last three fingers on her right hand, all apparently severed at the base knuckles.

She reached under to take my right hand, somewhat awkwardly, in her left. Her skin was cool and soft to the touch.

"Do not worry, my dear. As for jealousy, it is misplaced. Phillip and I have already had our torrid love affair."

Out of the corner of my eye I might have caught my grandfather blushing just a little.

"It was during the war," he said, an aside to me and almost apologetic. "Before I married your grandmother."

Bernadette clicked her tongue at him. "Have you become so prudish in your dotage, Phillip?"

My grandfather laughed, taking her ribbing in perfect stride as if, though decades had intervened, they had resumed a tête-à-tête both ancient and intimately familiar.

Familiar or no, there was still tension between the two of them. I thought perhaps I understood: much as they might want to, my grandfather had already exceeded the bounds of etiquette, and it would be improper for either of them to show any more of the emotion that their reunion seemed to demand.

Bernadette looked at me again. "But you *must* forgive me. He was so handsome. I was powerless to resist his seduction." Her expression took on some faux species of offense when she saw my reaction. "Do not look so shocked. We women of a certain age have no shame about sex. Especially those of us who lived through the war."

"And happen to be French," my grandfather interjected.

Bernadette smiled. "Naturally, that."

"I don't think I've ever seen you in such formal attire, Bernadette," my grandfather said, changing the subject.

Bernadette looked embarrassed. Absently, her left hand went to the medals pinned to her gown and, seamlessly, she shifted into French.

"*C'est avec les babioles que les hommes sont menés.*"

"And women, too," my grandfather said. They looked sad then, as if some shared sorrow had taken both of them together.

"Lechner, you old dog," my grandfather said. "Why didn't you tell me she was coming? I would have worn a better jacket.

"Bernadette, where is Jean Paul?"

Bernadette looked away, and shook her head.

"Phillip," Professor Lechner said, and put his hand on my grandfather's arm. "Jean Paul was killed during a robbery some months ago."

My grandfather looked horrified. "But, that simply cannot be."

Professor Lechner deposited his not-quite-empty flute on the tray borne by a passing member of the waitstaff and turned to me.

"My dear," he said, "would you do an old man the kindness of joining in his quest for a proper drink? Intolerably, all this champagne seems to be French."

Bernadette let out a playfully offended huff, obviously happy for the change of subject. "All champagne is French, you old fool."

He gave her a knowing smirk.

"But, Professor Lechner," I said, and looked for a member of staff to flag down, "you need only ask—"

"I am certain," he said, "that I saw a rather intriguing bar over there on the far side of the salon."

He took my hand in his and started to lead me away. Belatedly, I understood: Professor Lechner was arranging for my grandfather and Bernadette to have a private conversation. When the Professor saw that I had made the connection, he gave me a satisfied look.

As we made our way, he peered right through me and down to the burning curiosity I was desperately trying to hide.

"You may ask your questions now," he said, after ordering a vodka martini at the bar.

"Who is—"

"Jean Paul was Bernadette's only son," Professor Lechner said.

"Bernadette's medals . . . ?"

"It is not the medals you want to ask about."

"No," I admitted.

"It is her fingers."

Reluctantly, I nodded.

"As it happens they are related, the fingers and the medals. You see, Bernadette knew several very important secrets; secrets the Nazis also wanted quite badly to know. Bernadette would not tell them these secrets. And so they tried to change her mind."

It was so horrible that I refused to accept it, but the Professor's expression was grave and tainted with pain.

"As an Officer of the Order, she wears the medal of the French Légion d'honneur with rosette. The other decoration marks her as an Officer of the Resistance. I imagine that, together with other awards, they make her one of the most highly decorated women in France."

"What was the French phrase she said about baubles?"

"'It is with baubles that men are led.' It was uttered by the founder of the Légion d'honneur. This Bonaparte fellow. Perhaps you've heard of him?"

I smiled, and it was just the diversion I needed.

"Men do not follow a ring," I said, remembering my grandfather's comment.

"Ah," Professor Lechner breathed, obviously recognizing the turn of phrase. "Indeed not. Leaders must be much more than bearers of a ring, or the decorations they wear. But many things inspire men. It is in the other part of Napoleon's quote that he asks, 'Do you think that you would be able to make men fight by reasoning? Never. The soldier needs glory, distinctions, rewards.'

"But, perhaps you might think, as I do, that Napoleon understood these matters less well than he supposed. She didn't want them, you know, the baubles. But she was not asked if she wanted them. Perhaps Napoleon was right in one small way. I expect many men were led by Bernadette's baubles, shamed that a woman should have earned them when they had not. Perhaps they were led by that shame more than the desire to wear medals. Yes? Clever of someone, then, to award them to a woman. Eh?"

"But it seems so cynical to think this way," I said.

"You know, I do believe Bernadette agrees with you. But she is past her days as a 'woman of action.' She has the luxury of romantic reminiscence. You do not. In fact, soon you must begin to think in this 'cynical way' as a matter of habit."

Before I could ask him what he meant, Professor Lechner looked around the salon, surveying the guests, a group that had grown to about two dozen.

"In this room are some of your grandfather's closest and most loyal friends. The 'old guard,' one might say. Even now, I see two who are alive today only because Bernadette decided that their lives were worth more than three fingers and the use of her arm. Would we ever really suppose it was Bonaparte's ridiculously colored bauble that inspired her?

"It is your grandfather's particular gift that he sees in others more than what they see in themselves. That he inspires them to realize greater destinies than they imagined they might ever fulfill. Perhaps you have taken note of one particular individual who has, of late, become the focus of his attentions in this vein?"

His eyes were ablaze and I was taken aback to understand that he meant me. I was struggling to organize a dozen questions into words when the chime on the salon's grandfather clock began to ring eight. As it did, the side doors to the Rose Salon opened and four musicians, two women and two men, filed in and sat on chairs placed just in time for them by the domestic staff. At the very moment that the clock's last chime sounded the string quartet struck their first notes and slipped into a wonderful piece by Brahms.

Our conversation (and, indeed, all sound or movement in the salon) came to an abrupt halt as we all took in the first measures. I looked around, wondering if I could guess which guests owed Bernadette their very lives. There were perhaps ten in attendance old enough to have been of the age of majority during the Second World War. With my grandfather's warning about our enemies still ringing in my ears, I was startled to see three of the men I had first met in South Africa in attendance. Rynold Ackermann and Alfred Kriel were standing together, drinks in hand, near the windows. Reinier Van Zyl stood a little ways apart from the older men. He was hardly old enough to have been alive in the Second World War, but he caught my eye for another reason: he was apparently oblivious to the quartet playing and instead surveyed the crowd as if he was looking for someone in particular.

On the other side of my grandfather and Bernadette were two men both well into their eighties, and whom I took for twins. Shorter, balding in a comically similar pattern, and wearing exactly the same formalwear, they might have switched places as I blinked and I wouldn't have noticed. With them, but seated at one of the low tables and smoking a short, fat cigar, was a portly man in his midseventies who was almost certainly German. He was leaning forward to scrutinize the label of a bottle held patiently by one of our underbutlers. A much younger woman (whom I nevertheless took to be his wife) stood beside him to his left, her perfectly manicured hand resting languidly on his shoulder.

My mother and father stepped through the double doors with another dozen guests in tow. In years past, during the most formal events on the estate, one of the four pairs of uniformed, pike-carrying escorts would flank my grandfather as he moved between rooms. That night, however, they were taking up the rear behind my father. Once inside the Rose Salon, they settled in, facing the guests on either side of the main doors; flamboyant bodyguards; mirror images of the pair outside the room. I thought I understood the significance, and it prompted a twinge of sadness. It was a message to all assembled that the torch had been passed to my father.

With the arrival of my parents, all eyes turned from the quartet toward those doors.

That timing was not an accident, I thought. *We were all made to look to the far end of the room toward the quartet and then turn back to the main doors for their entrance. Mother's deft touch at work.*

My mother and father started the first of their rounds. I recognized the tactic: together they would greet the little knots of guests, following in a rough orbit around the room. Then they would split up and make a slow circle in opposite directions to speak to their guests individually.

Professor Lechner led me back to my grandfather and Bernadette. When we returned, they were all smiles. Her laughter, light and lovely, floated across the salon like the soft tittering of a fountain or a burbling spring.

"This was not originally the 'Rose Salon,'" my grandfather was saying to Bernadette. "When Eva first redecorated this room, in a rare slip of judgment I doubt she will repeat, she solicited my opinion."

Bernadette and Professor Lechner chuckled.

"'It looks very . . . French,' I said to her. I meant it with all affection but, and I should have known, her own family tradition includes an intense animosity toward all things French."

"Heavens," Bernadette said. "I shall have to make myself scarce. Sneaking off the estate in the middle of the night? Phillip, you have managed to perfectly re-create the circumstances of my last visit."

Professor Lechner seemed surprised. "Can it be possible that this is your first time returning here since the war?"

"It is not simply possible," Bernadette said. "It is the truth. It was 1942 when I departed last." She turned back to my grandfather, and spoke in an anxious whisper. "I hardly wish to cause offense to our gracious hostess." She clutched at my grandfather's sleeve with her undamaged hand. "Phillip, you don't think she will recognize my accent, do you?"

We all laughed, and Bernadette, pleased to have entertained us so well, was grinning ear to ear.

"Well," my grandfather continued, "Eva took my offhand remark about the decor having a French appearance as a grievous insult. Within a week she had the original rugs torn out and replaced with the most beautiful cobalt blue and white carpets I had ever seen. Most strikingly, they were adorned with amazingly intricate gold fleurs-de-lis."

Bernadette began to laugh again. "With the fleurs-de-lis design she could not have made it more overtly French. This she did only to see the expression on your face when you saw it, Phillip. You know, I begin to like this Eva."

"Mmm, yes," my grandfather replied. "And we held my reception for the consul general of Austria in here not long after, I seem to remember."

"How can this be?" Professor Lechner said. "I have it on good authority that Eva despised the consul general and, more particularly, his wife."

"Of course she did," my grandfather said. "And after the reception they were quite sure the extreme French tone of the decor was a deliberate insult to Austria. They correctly assumed the woman of the house had made all such arrangements and, thereafter, the hatred was well returned."

Bernadette gave a wry smile.

"That woman could weaponize cucumber sandwiches," my grandfather added, and more chuckles followed. But then he seemed to remember that I was present. "You do understand that this is a tremendous compliment to your mother?"

"If your opponent is of choleric temper, irritate him," I said, remembering my Sun Tzu.

All three of them turned to look at me.

"This is the pupil you spoke of?" Bernadette said, turning to Professor Lechner with something like astonishment.

The Professor only smiled.

It wasn't long before my parents had worked their way around to us. Strangely, and in something of a breach in etiquette, my mother addressed me first. Reflexively, after my heart skipped a beat, I gave her a deep curtsy. This time my grandfather did not intervene to stop me.

"I hadn't expected to see you here, my dear," she said.

There was a hint of irritation in her expression, but I thought it too subtle for anyone else, other than my grandfather, perhaps, to see.

"Professor Lechner," my mother said, turning to him.

I expected a confrontation. Instead, as my father watched with apparent interest, she embraced the Professor warmly, kissing his cheeks three times in succession before standing back to make a show of looking him over.

"Now, Professor, I am quite certain that you would be entitled to wear any number of decorations in a formal setting. And yet, your breast is bare."

"Madam," he said, bowing elegantly, "you must forgive me, but my appointment was quite rushed and I never anticipated that I would have need of those old and tarnished trinkets here on this beautiful estate. I rather thought that I had left all need of regalia behind when I departed Vienna."

"Well," my mother said, "the dinner tomorrow is 'White Tie with Decorations,' you understand."

I began to see what my mother was getting at. It would not do to have a guest attend without the appropriate decorations. How could other guests on the estate be expected to know how to act or how to address Professor Lechner if he refused to wear his insignia?

"Shall I task Lucas with finding replacements? He is quite resourceful, you know. Just this morning we found ourselves in need of . . ." My mother turned to my father. "What was it, Valentin? 'Hero of the Soviet Union'?"

"The Gold Star Medal of the Hero of the Soviet Union, yes," my father said.

"Exactly. I'm sure we could accommodate you."

"I would be most grateful, madam," Professor Lechner said, and smiled.

My mother was about to say something else, but she was interrupted by a lull in the music. It was apparently her cue because, along with my father, she turned to face the room, took three steps toward the middle, and addressed herself to the crowd.

"Most distinguished guests," she said, and though her voice was not harsh or loud, all conversation stopped.

"Normally I would not dream of interrupting your entertainment, but our musicians this evening are of such a caliber that I find I cannot help but acquaint you with them."

Across the room, the members of the string quartet stood in turn as my mother introduced them, but my attention was drawn back to the whispering in our little knot.

"You are impossible, Jürgen," Bernadette hissed under her breath, batting at the Professor playfully with her hand. "As I am a lady of some refinement, I have refrained from comment. Now I must protest. For days you insisted that I must wear these egotistical accessories and yet your own awards . . . you cannot bother to display?"

"I hope you are not planning on fabricating some obscure order of merit merely to frustrate and embarrass our head butler," my grandfather added.

Professor Lechner looked thoughtful. "I was thinking perhaps 'Fleet Admiral of the Swiss Navy'?"

"That is an old and tired joke."

"Maybe," the Professor said, "'Sky Marshal, Second Class, of the Most Illustrious Royal Air Force of Cape Horn'?"

Even my father, who by all outward appearances had been lending his full attention to my mother's introductions, could not suppress a smile.

"My old friend," the Professor said, "you must know that, now that I have been scolded, I would never dream of omitting decorations I am entitled to display."

"That is precisely what worries me," my grandfather said.

"However, your daughter-in-law has put me in a difficult position. No matter how efficient he is, I cannot imagine your Lucas will be able to accommodate my more obscure insignia. And then where will I be, having marred the reputation of the most renowned head butler on the Continent? Do not think I am not keenly aware of his reputation, Phillip. Not to mention the implied insult to the hostess it would be to show him up."

"She has cornered you, hasn't she? Perhaps those rarest of your awards are junior enough to omit?"

"Omit? At a white-tie event put on by your daughter-in-law? Be serious, Phillip."

"How bad can it . . . oh . . . I seem to remember a certain Egyptian—"

"Yes, yes," the Professor said with a wave of his hand. "We need not discuss such things in mixed company after all."

At this, Bernadette almost broke into laughter, even as my mother was finishing her speech.

I marveled at the three of them, leaning close, together in a semicircle. For a moment, I saw them as I imagined they might have been fifty years before: a trio of twentysomething pranksters driven by whim to adolescent forays— sneaking out of the manor into the forests beyond so the domestic staff would not catch them smoking cigarettes—while all around them the danger of the war and the risk of denunciation, arrest, incarceration (and worse) loomed.

"Hush now," my grandfather urged the group, breaking the spell. "Eva has gone through quite some trouble to arrange all this. I understand she seriously disrupted the Philharmonic's schedule to bring their stars here."

Bernadette looked shocked.

"Oh, I wouldn't be too concerned," my grandfather said. "I believe Eva might be the Philharmonic's most generous individual donor by quite some margin."

"Is this true? One thinks one might hear of such things."

"Not at all. You must remember that my daughter-in-law's family is as old as my own."

"Sclerotic, you mean?" Bernadette said.

"Yes, well . . . quite. Still, Eva is adamant that her gifts remain anonymous. I quite admire her for her soft touch in such matters."

My mother's speech delivered, the musicians began to play again, and she gravitated back to us as my father drifted off to socialize.

"Professor Lechner," my mother said. "I must apologize for the interruption. The duties of a hostess, you understand."

She turned to Bernadette, and Professor Lechner picked up the cue.

"Madam," he said, "please allow me to present Madam Bernadette Chapuis."

Bernadette began to curtsy but my mother stepped forward and put a hand under her left elbow to prevent her.

"Certainly not, madam," my mother said. "I do believe you must be the first female Officer of the Légion d'honneur who has set foot in this manor. It is I who should curtsy to you."

My mother had obviously recognized the award but, despite what she said, I noticed that she did not, in fact, curtsy to Bernadette.

"Trinkets," Bernadette said dismissively. And then gave Phillip a quick look. "Baubles."

"I am quite sure the Fourth Republic would not think so," my mother said with an expectant look. "Nor grant such an award for trivialities."

I could tell what my mother was doing and I expected Bernadette to bend to her will and volunteer something about her deeds, but her answer surprised me.

"It was only that I was much prettier back then," she said.

My mother seemed about to press her line of inquiry but, from across the room, one of the underbutlers, who appeared to be fielding a difficult request from a guest, managed to catch her eye.

"Oh, dear," my mother sighed. "You must excuse me." And she was off.

Bernadette stopped a member of the waitstaff and, with amazing dexterity, cupped her left hand under the stems of two flutes filled with streaming rosé champagne and lifted them together from the silver tray. Then, surprising me so much that I nearly dropped it, she pressed one into my hands.

A small glass of wine at dinner was hardly taboo for my siblings and me (and there was of course the Scotch that had been snuck into the Bureau of Secrets) but I was certain that something as frivolous as a glass of champagne at a reception would be inappropriate at my age. Bernadette saw my expression but only smiled.

"Do not be stupid," she said. "Life is short and cruel. You must believe me when I tell you there is no excuse not to drink good champagne."

～⚬

AFTER THEIR SET, the four musicians also made their rounds. My grandfather introduced me formally to the beautiful young woman in her midtwenties—long, dark hair and perfect skin—who was the quartet's cellist. My mother had presented her to the room as Claudia Böhm, but as I only discovered when he waddled up to us, she was the daughter of Klaus, the rotund, ruddy-faced, cigar-smoking German I had seen earlier. The rest of our party seemed to know him well already and my grandfather introduced him to me as one of his oldest and dearest friends. I should have connected the names but only much later did I realize that Klaus was Yves's father (which suggested that Yves got his dashing good looks from his mother's side of the family).

As the hour grew late and the reception began to wane, my father formed the vanguard of a group of men who made their way to the billiard room for cigars and brandy. His ceremonial guards followed and took their places flanking the doors inside before they were closed.

Throughout the event I had been trying to keep tabs on the older guests Professor Lechner's comments had brought to my attention. I would catch glimpses of them now and again, but the balding twins had vanished at some point. Then I realized that I had lost track of Rynold Ackermann and Alfred Kriel as well.

Bearing another pair of champagne glasses, Bernadette fell in beside me with a conspiratorial look in her eye.

"They will go on this way for some time," she said, in response to a snatch of laughter from the billiard room.

"I am too old now for cigars. It is the outdoors that appeals to me. And yet, one might easily get lost in all these hallways. Perhaps you will take the air with me so I should not lose my bearings?"

When I nodded, she handed me one of the flutes and took my elbow.

We wandered the torchlit paths around the manor and through my mother's rose gardens. A little bonfire near the far gazebo had attracted a small group—faces cast in yellow and orange by the flickering flames. I started that way, but slowly discovered that, while I thought I had been leading Bernadette, she had actually been leading me.

Before long we were sitting on one of the stone benches in the middle of the gardens. The golden light from the manor's windows bathed the surrounding landscape in color, brilliant enough that I had to turn and look the other way toward the valley below for the sky to be dark enough that the stars were visible.

After I had enjoyed her intoxicating laughter and quick wit most of the evening, Bernadette seemed unduly quiet to me.

"Madam Chapuis . . . ?"

"No, no, no," she chided me. "For you it must be 'Bernadette.'"

"Bernadette," I said, gathering my courage, "were you and my grandfather in love?"

"Well," she answered, "how could I not be? He was dashing. Heroic. So very clever. What woman could resist him? And I"—she waved her champagne flute, gesturing about—"trapped for months in so romantic a setting? We used to stargaze, Phillip and I." She turned toward the darkened sky and pointed. "There she is. It was Cassiopeia he made me memorize."

I knew the constellation well, and picked it up easily.

"'For your beauty,' he said to me. When I reminded him that Cassiopeia may have been a famous beauty but was also famously vain and arrogant, he only laughed. 'Exactly,' he said. When parted we should look at it at the same time every night and know the other was doing the same, he said. It was hopelessly cliché.

"In love? Oh, yes. And all the while hiding from the Germans; prowling about in secret passages."

"It's true?" I gasped. "About the secret passages?"

I thought perhaps I could see her smile in the dark, but then her tone grew serious.

"You must not be taken in by overly romantic notions, my darling. Love you cannot depend on. Love does not conquer all. On the contrary. Your foes will use love, and those you love, to harm you."

Thinking of our enemies, shadowy opponents, I wrapped my arms around my body.

"You endanger them, those you may love, particularly outsiders, those who do not enjoy the protection of your family. Do you understand?"

I must have given her a blank look because she continued.

"There is always temptation to confide in a lover, to tell them something more than you ought. If you succumb to this temptation you make your lover a useful tool to your enemies, to the rivals of your family. It is thus that you endanger them. This is especially true in war. Phillip had confided too much in me. Had they found me again, they would have used me against Phillip, the Nazis. I would have lost far more than a few fingers. Phillip could not bring himself to send me away. But, knowing what I knew, it was not impossible that those around him, even his allies, might have taken matters into their own hands to deal with me. Fortunately, I came to my senses first. In the end it was love that compelled me to leave him."

As the horrible implications sank in, I could hardly believe what Bernadette had said. But I had no time to reflect on her words.

Bernadette set down her glass, took my hand, and looked at me in the faint light. "Do not be saddened by the impracticality of love for women such as us. It is silly to mourn the loss of a fantasy. These ideas you have of love are fairy tales. Disguised, yes, but fairy tales. Repeated to little girls by weak parents to keep daughters just a little longer from the colder parts of the world. But I am told that, young as you are, you have left these behind now, no?"

I nodded, but I wasn't so sure. I sensed she knew this and she gripped my hand harder.

"It is plain that you are beyond your years. But you must promise never to be taken in by fairy tales. Only when they abandon these can promising girls grow into formidable women; women who do not need men to guide them. To enjoy men? But of course. But never to *require* them. We women have our own wiles, you understand. One need not compete with men. I drove race cars, shot rifles in anger, flew planes, even killed Germans with my own hands."

"You did?" I said, shocked.

"But, of course. Just the same as the men of my generation. I learned how to do what was required of me and then I did it. But first, I abandoned fairy tales. Shall I tell you the secret? To recognize them? Fairy tales, I mean."

I nodded again, afraid my voice might crack if I tried to speak.

"In fairy tales, happy endings, even merely contented endings, have no cost. In life, happy endings are rare. And they always cost. Often dearly."

"You weren't afraid?"

"But of course I was afraid. You must take leave of your senses not to be afraid, and then you are of no use to anyone. But it is what you do with fear, no? Should it paralyze you, or drive you harder to meet your goal?"

"But, what they did to you. How could you go on?"

Bernadette held up her mangled hand. I squeezed my eyes shut. "This? This is but a cruelty. There will be many. And in the face of life's many cruelties there is nothing but to go on. Therefore, one must embrace life's occasional joys without question when she offers them."

Bernadette smiled at me in the dim light and took a sip from her flute.

"Champagne, for instance," she said, and then her tone grew serious.

"But when one accepts a duty, matters are different. This is the essence of duty. To forgo life's frivolous joys and, indeed, to embrace her many cruelties to achieve larger ends. For yourself, your acquaintances, your family. Or"— Bernadette gestured toward the manor and then locked eyes with me—"for something even larger still.

"Once you accept this duty, you betray these things if you are not prepared to sacrifice for them. And then, what else is there to do but to 'go on'?" Bernadette took my hand again and pulled me closer to her. "To retire to *La Grave*?"

It was a strange turn of phrase for her to use, as if she could not bring herself to use the English word *tomb*.

"We all like to think that we will bravely stand up to tyranny when it comes," she continued, "but when it looks us in the face, not everyone is able to 'sacrifice for the greater good.' This too is a fairy tale. That anyone can summon the strength to serve a higher purpose. That most people will give their lives for such causes. Indeed not. The numbers of the *turpificatus*, even among great families, swelled in the early years of the war. And there is a lesson here too.

"If you have not the stomach for it, you must not pretend at loyalty. To do so is to betray everything. Do you understand?"

I nodded as confidently as I could and tried to bury deep down the cold knot of fear that threatened to rise up from my abdomen.

BERNADETTE EXCUSED HERSELF after I directed her to the powder rooms, leaving me in the midst of one of the last little throngs of guests in the Rose Salon. It was nearly empty, but I spotted Professor Lechner at the bar taking possession of a martini. I made my way in his direction. Along the way, I caught a fragment of the conversation between my mother and Mila, the Ukrainian girl who, despite looking rather young, my mother had introduced as "First Violin" of the Vienna Philharmonic Orchestra. Voices low, they were talking at one of the round, standing tables that lined the walls of the Rose Salon.

". . . certainly, he is a very handsome man," my mother was saying. She put her hand on Mila's. "And a very powerful man."

My mother gave me a glance as I walked by. Not wanting to appear the eavesdropper, I looked straight ahead. Before I had passed them, and just out of the corner of my eye, I caught Mila sneak a peek across the salon at a much older man. I recognized the port-wine stain on his cheek. It was the Archduke, who had witnessed my unfortunate display in the Grand Foyer so many months before.

PROFESSOR LECHNER WAS obviously pleased with himself about something. When I joined him at the bar, he gave me a wolfish grin after sipping from his martini.

"Bernadette is wonderful," I said.

"Just so," he said, then reached into his inside jacket pocket, retrieved a piece of folded paper, and handed it to me.

"What is this?"

"Tomorrow morning you shall open it and then you shall see."

It was another of his intrigues, and I couldn't help but smile.

"I am very happy for my grandfather. That you brought her to see him, I mean."

"Oh, but you are so very wrong, my dear," the Professor said. "I did not bring her to see him. I brought her to see you."

ASIDE FROM THE muffled noise leaking through the closed doors to the drawing room, the evening was winding down. I was reluctant to let it end, but even Professor Lechner had faded away, and I found myself one of the last to leave the Rose Salon along with my mother, the Archduke, and a few final stragglers.

On my way into the hallway, I nearly collided with Hannah, who had been lurking just outside the doorway. I made my apologies, but she was intent on my mother, who, in the moment I looked, gave Hannah a particular glance. It caught my eye because I thought perhaps my mother was silently scolding Hannah for nearly colliding with me, but (and though I was a little tipsy from the champagne) their soundless exchange had a different feel to it. It was over in an instant, but I suspected that I had seen something that I wasn't supposed to. Intimidated, I drifted away from the Rose Salon and toward the foyer.

As I went, there was a commotion behind me. I turned back to see Hannah dusting herself off, having apparently collided with the Archduke with enough force to nearly knock her over. For his part, the Archduke was a million apologies, entreaties that, after giving him a cross look that actually gave me a shiver, Hannah accepted with only mildly annoyed grace. Before parting, the much taller Archduke put a hand on Hannah's shoulder. It seemed meant as a friendly gesture, but Hannah stiffened, and her entire bearing settled into an intense and malevolent quiet that, while obvious to me even at some distance, seemed to escape the Archduke's notice entirely.

His apologies duly rendered, and Hannah forgotten, the Archduke made his way to the stairs and up to the portion of the residential wing reserved for our overnight guests.

Hannah walked to my mother and a whispered exchange passed between them. My mother caught me looking and I hurried away.

WORRIED I MIGHT be in trouble, I slipped into the hallway beyond the foyer and waited for the last stragglers from the Rose Salon to ascend the stairs. Some followed instead a siren song of light conversation and the occasional peal of soft laughter emanating from a group that had congregated outside on the stone benches around one of the firepits in the gardens. I waited in the shadows for the foot traffic to pass.

The sound of soft footsteps down the hallway in the other direction made me peek out from my hiding place. I spied Professor Lechner, hands laced behind his back, walking in his familiar, pacing gait; deliberate but languid.

My first instinct was to go to him, but he seemed content with his solitude. It was rude to follow him, I knew; to act the spy; but I was curious and, in that particular moment, whatever Professor Lechner was doing seemed far more interesting than going to bed. I waited for him to reach the edge of the Hall of Ancestors. The overhead lights had been extinguished for the evening, leaving the dark hallway illuminated only by the spots directed on the portraits. Long spans of shadow between each painting gave the length of the hall a spooky cast.

Once the Professor crossed the threshold to the Hall of Ancestors, I slipped out of the doorway and followed, hugging the wall of the long corridor and keeping at least sixty feet behind him.

He gave me a start when he stopped at the first portrait on that end of the hall, the depiction of my great-grandfather Lukas, and turned to look up at the visage. Worried he might peer back, I slipped into the closest doorway and shrank as far into the shadow as I could and still peek around into the hallway beyond. It was the right instinct as, after a long contemplation of the portrait, and not before giving my long-dead ancestor a sage nod, Professor Lechner turned back in my direction.

I searched for an excuse to explain what I was doing lurking in dark doorways, but when he was only thirty feet or so away, he stopped in front of another doorway, straightened his decorations, dusted off the shoulders of his jacket, and gave four soft knocks.

After a brief pause, the door opened and the warm light of incandescents and a fireplace streamed out into the dim environs of the hallway, bathing him for a moment in a brilliance that made me want to squint and blink. It was Karl who had answered, and he nodded at the Professor before opening the door wider, stepping aside, and allowing him to pass. With the door open to its widest extent, I just managed to peer inside. It was enough to catch sight of my grandfather talking to Rynold Ackermann and Alfred Kriel. The familiar sound of Bernadette's laugh was easily discernible above the murmur of informal discussion and, before Karl closed the door again, I caught a glimpse of one of the twins and a slice of conversation slipped out.

"And so," said a voice I knew for my grandfather's. He was in high form: the orator commanding attention. "After so many years, we are all here but one; and he cannot be among us. So let us begin."

The door closed and the corridor was silent and dark once more. They had all made separate excuses and slipped away from the reception. Their departures had been almost overtly random. Random by design. I was sure that if I had a better look inside the salon I would have found all of the "old guard" in attendance. And then there was Karl, guarding the door.

A secret meeting.

Could I have been witnessing a ritual that extended back five decades or more? With that thought came something like fear, and guilt. Not so much that I had been spying and eavesdropping, but that the target of my illicit surveillance had been Professor Lechner.

Unnerved, I darted out of my hiding place and into the hallway to head for the stairs and my apartments. I managed only two steps before I bumped into a tall man. It was Reinier Van Zyl.

"Excuse me," he said, and his voice was soft enough that it barely echoed even in the stone hallway. "I didn't see you there."

My first instinct was to wonder how he had gotten so close to my hiding place without my hearing him, but I had been so intent on the door to the salon and who was behind it that it was possible I had not perceived his footsteps.

The dim lights above the hallway cast shadows across his face and gave the impression that his blue eyes peered out at me from dark pools in his eye sockets. I knew it was silly, but it scared me.

"Are you all right?" he was asking me.

"Yes, quite well."

"I didn't mean to startle you."

"No apologies necessary," I said. I gave a quick curtsy and then took my leave, resisting, barely, the urge to break into a run for the stairway beyond.

⌒〜

WHEN I GOT inside my rooms, I almost stepped on a note that had been slipped under my doors. I picked it up, walked to my sitting room, dropped it on the table, and collapsed into one of the sofas. I took out the paper that Professor Lechner had given me. The seal on it was red wax that had been impressed with a signet ring. The heraldic achievement of the seal was small and difficult to see, but I could make out an owl in the coat of arms with what looked like sleeping lions as supporters. The shield device was charged with the heraldic crown of a barony, which, though the detail was tiny, appeared almost to be early Austrian or Hungarian in design.

I almost broke the seal open, but remembered Professor Lechner's admonition to wait until morning.

Opening the other, more pedestrian note that had been slipped under my doors, I found an angry scrawl written inside: "Where are you?"

The note was unsigned, but I knew right away it was from Bastien. I had forgotten entirely about his recital.

CHAPTER SEVENTEEN

⌒

Beyond the Frontier

IT TOOK THE SUN STREAMING THROUGH my windows to wake me up the next morning. I crawled out of bed and, intent on breakfast, almost forgot about Professor Lechner's sealed document. On finding it again, I broke the wax and opened it. Inside was nothing but a hand-drawn diagram.

Eventually, I recognized it for a minimalistically sketched map. The manor was featured in the center and a winding line running from north to south was familiar to me as the stream that ran across the estate from the foothills down into the valley. Far south at what must have been the pointy border of our lands, a prominent X had been drawn, along with a time: "10:00."

I had less than two and a half hours to travel nearly three miles to the marked spot in the valley below.

⌒

IT WAS A welcome excuse to ride Vim, so I grabbed my leather shoulder bag, dressed in riding clothes, and hurried to the stables. I put her bridle on and mounted her bareback, but not before she, excited to see me, almost knocked me over twice with enthusiastic nudges of her nose.

There was a chill in the air as we departed, but the rising sun promised warmth, and what clouds were in the sky were far off and drifting away from the valley.

As one worked south and downhill from the manor, the estate's terrain shifted from flat grass and rolling meadows by the stables, to the lightly forested ground threaded through here and there with hunting paths or two-track dirt roads. As the valley loomed closer, one encountered areas thick with trees. Once there, I often had to pull my legs up or kneel on Vim's back so that she could squeeze through narrow spaces without scraping my legs. By the time I was near the southern border wall, I had repeatedly doubled back from impassable patches of vegetation and clusters of deadfall in order to find a way through.

The X on the map was drawn upon the southernmost border of the estate, just east of where the stream left our property. A victim of a centuries-long assault by the elements, the wall that marked the edge of the estate had vanished or been overgrown in many places along that frontier. Remembering my grandfather's warnings as I approached the point where I imagined our lands must end, I found myself slowing Vim and looking for remnants of the dry stone wall that would mark the edge of our influence. It was an area I had spent very little time exploring, and I hesitated in those spots where I thought the line of demarcation might be concealed by the detritus of the forest but, hard as I looked, I could find nothing. With no navigational references at all, the farther I went the more anxious I became that I had guided Vim onto land that was not our own.

It was the Land Rover that I saw first; one of the old, olive-green workhorses of the estate, just visible parked on the edge of a long and narrow clearing in the trees. Wary, not least because I had never imagined there would be a clearing in that area, I dismounted and held Vim well back, patting her neck and whispering softly in her ear to keep her quiet. After a few minutes I hadn't heard or seen anything, so, almost holding my breath, I led Vim the remaining sixty feet or so to the overgrown glade as silently as the two of us could manage.

Though the clearing was obviously artificial (trees had been cut down in a rectangular strip nearly one thousand feet long and eighty feet wide) it had not been tended to in many years. What looked as if it had once been a flat patch of grass was marred by shrubbery, creepers and vines, and the occasional solitary sapling. Vim twitched her ears, pivoting them around, feeling the strangeness of the place the same way I did.

We crept closer to the Land Rover. Behind it, a large folding table was obviously out of place. A rather extensive picnic spread, including a lovely tea set, had been laid out. There, reclining in one of two folding chairs, was Professor Lechner.

⌒

VIM GAVE A little snort and Professor Lechner looked up at me and then checked his pocket watch before his expression broke into a wide smile.

"*Ach*, just so," he said, and stood up. "My pupil honors her tutor by solving the mystery and arriving just on time."

I led Vim over to the table and the Professor cooed over her for a bit, offering his hand in a way that told me that he had more than a passing familiarity with horses.

"She was a gift from my grandfather."

"A lovely mount," he said, and stroked Vim's muzzle to her evident satisfaction.

"Come, sit for tea."

I took off Vim's bridle and retrieved an apple from my shoulder bag. I palmed it for Vim and, after she took it, she wandered farther into the clearing to graze.

"She will not run off?" Professor Lechner asked, once we were seated.

"No," I said.

"Truly, a remarkable creature."

I was burning with questions but tea had been served. Spring had given way to summer's full bloom and the occasional flurry of birdsong made for an idyllic setting. Only after tea did the Professor address me.

"With all the fuss on the estate, I thought it might be useful to have today's lesson somewhere away from prying eyes and eavesdropping ears, yes?"

He gestured for me to follow him as he stood and sauntered into the clearing.

"The reception?" he said, as we walked together. "You found it . . . engaging? What did you learn?"

"That there is more under the surface than above it?"

Professor Lechner laughed. "Just so. Secrets, yes? And so we have come to the motif of today."

Professor Lechner stopped and looked at me expectantly. We had arrived at the end of the long clearing and something out of place caught my eye: just beyond the trees was some kind of wreckage in the vegetation. Almost forgetting the Professor, I took a few steps forward.

It was an old airplane, a single-engine high-wing with badly faded black paint and the skeletal remains of a long canopy from which all the glass had long since broken and fallen away.

"Westland Lysander," Professor Lechner said. I had been so enthralled, and he so stealthy, that I hadn't noticed him by my side again and I jumped when he spoke. "Mark III."

"But, how long has it been here?"

Fascinated, I tried to navigate the undergrowth beyond the tree line to get closer. Professor Lechner followed behind me.

"She crashed in 1942."

"Was anyone hurt?" I said, suddenly fearful of finding a body.

"*Ach*, no. Not seriously."

"But, why was it here?"

"The British. To pick men up. Or to put them down." After a pause he spoke again. "And women, of course."

"*Agents?*" I asked, excited. "OSS agents?"

"And from the SOE. *Natürlich*."

"SOE?"

"The Special Operations Executive," Professor Lechner said, in imitation of a British officer's accent. I was reminded of Yves, and it was an effort for me not to giggle.

"It was your grandfather's plan. An airstrip for the estate; for his own plane. But then the war . . . and then the British were here to meet with your grandfather. To meet with us. To recruit him, you understand. And your grandfather had reason to build his airstrip again. For the Royal Air Force Squadron 161. To fly from Suffolk, into France, here, and elsewhere."

"Here?"

"Just so." Professor Lechner pointed off to the right. "The fuel was kept there." He gestured to the sky above the clearing. "And there, nets across the trees."

"Camouflage? They must have been huge."

Professor Lechner smiled.

"What was it like? What was my grandfather like?"

"It is not proper to speak of such times lightly."

By placing himself so firmly in a moment within my family's history, the Professor seemed to invite some sort of conversation into a mysterious past. It was a past that I knew almost nothing about, aside from my grandfather's brief introduction during dinner all those nights ago, and Sir Nigel's arch narration on my family's history. My eyes shifted to his hand for some reason, and there I saw his signet ring.

"Your seal," I said, and knew I was being more than presumptuous. "It bears the coronet of a barony." The Professor's eyes widened a bit. As I spoke, pieces fell into place. "You were the tutor of Archduke Felix. Just after the Hapsburg law. After the Great War the monarchy was dissolved. They took your family lands? Exiled you?"

The Professor's sad smile returned, and he sighed.

"Come," he said. "Let us go back to the table."

Once we were seated, he collected himself and started in.

"There are times when the small difference between secrets concealed and secrets exposed can mean life and death. It is entirely possible that we are in the midst of one of these times.

"Can you imagine what acts might be resorted to by those threatened with more concrete dangers? The flight of billions in capital? A loss of power in an environment where weakness means certain death?"

"You are talking about South Africa."

The Professor squeezed his eyes shut and then shook his head. "You misunderstand. What is happening in South Africa and your family's part in it is only a small fraction of the changes that are afoot. The Iron Curtain is no more. Raised only last year. Governments may fall, others may rise, only to fall again. The various powers that threaten to clash will shake the continent, and be felt here as well.

"This is the start of a new era, and such times are beyond dangerous. Do you understand?"

"Yes. Well, no. I mean, tell me what I am to do."

"Ah, but this is not my place to say. This is for your grandfather to decide."

He squeezed my hands tight in his. "Soon now, a door will be opened for you. Only you can decide if you wish to pass through it and be thrust into what lies beyond. As with all such doors, once you use them, there is no going back."

I must have had a shocked look on my face, because the Professor released my hands, leaned back, and gave me a soothing smile. Then he became the affable tutor once more, gently prodding me with leading questions.

"Why is there more under the surface than above?" he said, recalling my observation about the reception.

"Because the things that are hidden might be unwound if they were exposed?"

"Should this strip have been set closer to the manor?"

"No," I said, alarmed.

"Squadron 161 was not public. Should the British instead have advertised it? Their *secret* squadron?"

"No."

"Indeed not. There are moments, even eras, when it is best to be quiet and inscrutable. You must understand the importance of, and the difference between, opacity and faux transparency. Opacity can attract even more scrutiny from those searching for answers. The appearance of transparency—to allow the gaze of others, persons or institutions alike, to pass through you and yet reveal nothing—this is the more valuable deception. One stops looking only when one believes there is nothing to be found. Do you understand?"

"No," I admitted.

"There is no better camouflage for you than to be thought irrelevant."

"For me? Do you mean because I am a girl?"

The Professor smiled. "The enemy of this effort is the ego. Do not be quick to show knowledge unless it serves a goal; in particular to surprise an adversary, or even an ally, but then only if you have purpose in giving the impression of omniscience.

"This," the Professor said, holding up his signet ring for me to see, "this is a reminder of failure."

"But your family didn't fail. Did it? I mean, weren't your lands taken from you?"

Professor Lechner tutted me and then shook his head sadly.

"In this you are mistaken. And this is a mistake you cannot afford. Forced errors are still errors. There is darkness to face in the world. Even more so for a family such as yours. And, you are a daughter '*of the line*.'"

The way he intoned it gave me a chill.

"This you must not forget. There are those who wish you and your family ill. They are close. Perhaps even among our own. It does not serve us to let you pretend otherwise.

"What have you learned of asymmetric warfare? What does Sun Tzu tell us?" I had no ready answer, but Professor Lechner prompted me. "When we are weak and the enemy is strong?"

"'Though the enemy be stronger in numbers, we may prevent him from fighting. Scheme so as to discover his plans and the likelihood of their success,'" I recited.

"And to discover these plans?"

"'Knowledge of the enemy's dispositions can only be obtained from other men,'" I recited again, and then, though I had long before memorized it, I felt I really understood the passage for the first time. "Spies," I breathed.

Professor Lechner gave me another sad smile and then gestured to the end of the strip and the wreckage beyond.

"Even with others as allies, your grandfather was surrounded; outnumbered. And yet he fought back. There are times for dynasties to be open and to wield power openly." Professor Lechner held up his signet ring again. "But there are times when they must hide from their enemies, from larger institutions, from empires, lest they be destroyed by outside forces. Outside forces, when powerful and adroit, or just nimble and clever, will seek to divide, to atomize their enemies. My father did not learn this lesson in time. Now I am the last of my line and it will die with me."

Professor Lechner must have seen the expression of horror on my face because he reached forward and cupped my cheek with his hand.

"No, no. Do not be sad. Family is not the only institution to avail us. Men may resist atomization to bind together. They may unite in other societies to further a common purpose. Though these are not always popular aims, or in tune with the fickle mores of any particular generation. Do you understand what this means?"

"They must know when not to fight," I said. "As Sun Tzu says, and as Major Hans von Dach wrote, they must know when to deceive; to stay hidden; to watch for an opening."

"Yes," Professor Lechner said, pleased, and then prompted me. "These societies must stay . . . ?"

"Secret. *Secret societies?*" I exclaimed, excited once more.

"Just so. And these, their ethos, their pathos, their rules, and the *tesserae hospitales* given to members to recognize one another, the heirs of their members must eventually learn. *You* must learn. Do you understand?"

"Me?"

"Just so."

"*Tesserae hospitales?* For a secret society?"

"*Ach,* but patience. This shall be Monday's lesson. That knowledge and the *tesserae* to unlock it must come from your grandfather."

"But, have they been given to Augustin? To Bastien?"

"And how do you imagine I should know this? The Patriarch has not appointed me as their tutor. He has appointed me as yours."

I made to ask him another question but he held up a staying hand.

"Hush now. This is for Monday. We shall end early today."

I pled with my eyes for him to continue, but Professor Lechner was having none of it. Instead we passed the better part of an hour drinking tea and indulging (unironically) in light conversations about the Weimar Republic.

When we had finished, I walked over to Vim and put her bridle on. I was about to bid the Professor farewell, but when I turned to address him I found that he was already starting up the Land Rover.

In a flash and with the furious splattering of mud as he stabbed at the accelerator, he tore the Land Rover into a thin patch of vegetation. Only after he broke through it could I see what had been hidden behind: an overgrown, two-track road that seemed to carry on for two hundred yards or so before looping around back in the direction of our property line.

CHAPTER EIGHTEEN

Event Horizon

LATE THAT AFTERNOON, I WAS ROUSED from my studies by a pounding on my doors. I found one of the young maids in the hallway with a panicked look on her face.

"You must come at once, miss," she said, and pulled me out of my rooms by the hand.

Without a hint of explanation she whisked me out one of the manor's side entrances and to a waiting Land Rover. The driver closed the door and took off immediately.

"Where are we going?" I asked. "What is it?"

"I am not sure, ma'am," he said. "I have instructions to drive you to the stables. That is all I know."

I don't think I can find the words to express the feeling of horror that came over me after I got out of the Land Rover and heard the first screams. I took off for the stable door at a dead run. Inside, the groom was directing two stable hands on either side of Vim. The taller one was talking to her in a soothing voice and patting her neck to calm her.

"What happened?" I said, rushing forward, but the groom stuck an arm out and blocked my way.

"No, miss," he said. "She is not herself."

Just then Vim screamed again and bucked, trying to bolt away from the men and thrashing against her bridle.

"What are you doing?" I shouted. "Let her go."

I saw her stagger, and it froze me. When she put weight on her right rear leg it nearly collapsed. My mouth still open, I took a half step forward and looked closer. The back of Vim's leg was covered in blood. More oozed out even as I watched. I tried to get closer but then the groom was holding me back by the shoulders.

"What happened?" I demanded, turning to him, but when I looked into the groom's eyes I saw that he was crying.

"I don't know, miss," he said, choking back a sob. "I heard something and found her here. Her back leg was bleeding." He pointed to three long spans of rusty barbed wire that had been discarded in a pool of blood on the far side of the stables. "I had to cut it away from her leg. It must be that she was tangled in it and cut herself even worse struggling to get free. I told Dorian to fetch you first thing."

"Where is Verve?" I demanded.

"The lower stable," the groom said. "Better she not see her mother like this."

Vim was calmer for a moment. Ignoring his protests, I pulled away from the groom and went to her slowly. She cast a big brown eye at me, pointing the arrow-shaped spot in my direction. I put my hand on the side of her neck. Two great breaths escaped from her flaring nostrils. She nudged me with her nose and her breathing slowed.

I looked at the groom, a question poised on my lips, but his expression was answer enough. He shook his head slowly and I knew what he meant. I started to cry.

"The tendon was cut and she must have panicked and tried to run on it," he said. "With such a wound if they get tangled and thrash to get free . . ." He took a deep breath. "There is nothing for it if they aggravate it like that."

I turned to the nearest stable hand, but he shook his head, and then looked down at the cement floor.

"I don't understand how she could have gotten out," I sobbed. "I put her in the fenced-off pasture when I came back this morning."

"You mustn't blame yourself, miss. She's always been a wily one. She can vault the near fence, you know. Quick as you please." He tried to smile at me, but somehow it only upset me more. "Sure it was the old barbed wire in the far pasture. We should have pulled that out years ago. I will see to it today. I'm so sorry, miss."

There was little else to say. I held the side of her bridle and sobbed softly for a quarter hour, trying desperately (and with little success) to maintain some measure of composure in front of the groom and the stable hands. They indulged me, stood silent vigil making sure Vim didn't try to put weight on her damaged leg again.

Finally, though gently, the groom took my elbow and started to pull me away.

"No," I cried. "You have to fetch my grandfather."

The groom knelt in front of me, held my shoulders, and looked into my eyes.

"Miss, you must understand. There's nothing he can do for her, and your grandfather will have his own matters to attend to today. Weighty matters, yes? Best wait for the guests to depart before delivering such news. We do not serve him by giving him such awful tidings just now. You must leave that with me. Agreed?"

I stared at him, uncomprehending.

"She's in pain, miss."

"Another minute," I begged through tears.

"We waited for you because I knew you would want to say goodbye, but now we must think of her rather than ourselves. It's time, miss. I'm sorry."

Speechless, all I could do was nod. I took a deep breath, pressed my cheek one last time to Vim's, and then turned to go.

I had just climbed into the Land Rover when the shot went off, but I pretended not to hear.

～⌒

LOCKED IN MY bedroom, I bawled as hard as I had ever cried about anything. I cried until my diaphragm hurt from my relentless sobbing. But then something happened. It wasn't a catharsis, exactly. Rather, I think something the groom had said: there were weightier matters to attend to and, like my grandfather, I was expected to attend to them as well.

After that, it wasn't that the pain of losing Vim was gone. That was still a cold knot of loss at the very core of my being. Somehow, though, something in me had been hardened against it. Bernadette's words from the night before about life's many cruelties came back to me, too, and I was ashamed of crying so hard. I took a long bath, and did my best to focus on the future.

As early evening approached, the pace of arrivals on the estate had picked up considerably and the whine of the helicopter in the distance, ferrying passengers up from the airstrip, seemed ever-present. Vehicles arrived every quarter hour and I marveled at the staff's ability to carry out an intense greeting ritual for each one with unflagging enthusiasm, even after more than a dozen identical performances.

In the past, such events as we siblings were invited to never seemed particularly intriguing. They promised half an hour of novelty followed inevitably by hours and hours of crushing boredom. But something had changed for me since then. I found myself eager to engage in conversation; to observe the interactions between the guests; to feel the little thrill of catching the meaning of an offhanded comment that was laced with intent "between the lines."

The itinerary called for a cocktail reception at 7:00 followed by dinner at 8:00 and an event in the Italian Gardens at 10:30. I started getting ready nearly three hours early. It was Emma who appeared again when I rang down and, though I wondered after Cipriana, I was preoccupied enough that the substitution was quickly forgotten.

I decided on a long-sleeved gown in my closets that was appropriate to the occasion. In the end it was the fact that I did not have to bother with long gloves that commended the piece. After three abortive attempts at an updo, including a French twist that I could barely unknot, I finally combed my hair out and left it down. Emma and I spent nearly twenty minutes fiddling with my order badge and the ribbon before it seemed properly placed.

Nervous, I gathered myself up and hurried to the East Salon in order to present myself at 6:45. I was standing in front of the door before I realized my grandfather had not specifically extended me an invitation. A lump formed in my throat as it came to me that perhaps he did not intend to escort me that evening. I had to take a deep breath to collect myself before knocking. It seemed an eternity, but then he was there, wearing a pleasant smile and adorned with the many gleaming accoutrements of rank and status.

"Ah, yes," he said, and his eyebrows rose with evident pleasure. "My date has arrived. And she is a vision to behold. But you are rather early, my dear."

Just then the clock down the hall chimed the quarter hour.

"But Grandfather, doesn't the reception start at seven?"

"Indeed, but how might we be expected to make our dramatic entrance to the Grand Dining Hall if we have already been seen wandering around the salons during a reception? No, no. Neither will your father and mother show themselves before dinner this time. But don't fret. I had precious little chance to speak with you last night. Come inside."

WITH A JINGLING of medals, my grandfather took off his coat and hung it up on the silent valet behind his desk. I sat down across from him and, as always, my gaze drifted up to the hanging death masks. I averted my eyes to find my grandfather lighting his pipe.

"Are you all right?" he asked.

"Yes."

"A lot has been asked of you in these last days and weeks, yes? Is it too much?"

"I don't know."

"Very well. Tell me what you learned from Bernadette."

"Duty? That once accepted it must be done?"

My grandfather smiled and leaned back farther in his chair.

"Then I shall ask you again. Is it too much? Or do you wish to go on?"

It was the phrase Bernadette had used. Involuntarily, I found myself sitting up perfectly straight and then, almost as if I was animated by some remote force, nodding my assent.

My grandfather leaned back and puffed on his pipe, watching the drifting smoke tendrils in silence. I had the sense that some decision had been made, some line crossed before he spoke again.

"Skepticism and doubt are essential tools to a leader. He must always question himself, what he thinks he knows, what he assumes, what he does not know. But, to show this doubt to others is poison. Uncertainty on the face of a leader can sap the confidence of followers. And so I should not speak to you of my doubts, but then I see that dark light behind your eyes that flashed just now. I recognize it perfectly, and I know that I have been right all along.

That my doubts; that you were too young; that you were not ready; that you are a daughter and not a son—all of them were misplaced."

His expression turned grave.

"I had a little speech prepared about the young overthrowing the old," he said. "But perhaps it is enough to say that young leaders must look to the past to act in the present, but for old leaders to secure the present, they can look only to the future."

My grandfather sighed to himself. "But never mind the sentiments of an old fool."

"You, Grandfather? But you aren't—"

"Now, enough of that. I am self-aware enough to know better. Shall we discuss the evening?"

I nodded.

"Last night's private reception was limited to a certain circle. Tonight the circle is much wider and, in some cases, your encounters will be less friendly. It is not an accident that the greatest formality is required when the guest list is largest. Your mother is quite aware that formality has the effect of limiting the capacity of our guests to make mischief. Remember that by virtue of your status as a daughter of the line, you outrank almost everyone you will meet. Wield this power, though carefully, gingerly at first. You might find it much more potent than you realize.

"This evening is really a series of scenes and dramatic encounters with your mother as the director. There is a rhythm to them. They build, wax, climax, and then wane to their denouements. Once you learn these cycles, you can easily predict what is about to happen next; even what has happened behind closed doors in a scene to which you were not invited. Whether they know it or not, each of our guests has a role to play. Each was invited with a purpose. Some purposes were designed by your mother, but some"—my grandfather winked—"were not entirely of her own making."

He paused before leaning forward to have a closer look at me. Then he frowned, his eyebrows furrowed together. His expression was so stern I feared I had offended him.

"You are aware," my grandfather said, his voice low and almost scolding, "that tonight's attire is 'White Tie with Decorations,' yes?"

"Of course, Grandfather."

"You cannot be ignorant of the fact that white tie calls for all major decorations to be worn and worn in the order of the insignia's seniority from your right to your left."

"No, Grandfather."

"Well, then it is inexcusable that you are missing insignia."

My grandfather stood, opened the top drawer of his desk, and produced a flat case about the size of a large book. He rounded his desk and placed it in front of me.

"Well," he said after a moment. "Open it."

I opened the clasp on the front and lifted the hinged lid of the case. Inside was a platinum insignia in the form of an eight-pointed star with a ruby in the middle. The insignia was pinned to a violet and black ribbon and next to it in the box was the miniature medal version intended to be worn at less formal occasions.

My grandfather bid me stand and, with great ceremony, pinned the ribbon and the order insignia just above my left breast on my gown and senior to the insignia of my family order.

"But, Grandfather, what is it?"

"Now, now. Soon we will be more than fashionably late. We shall discuss the particulars, privileges, traditions, and duties that are involved when we have the luxury of time, yes? For now it should suffice that more is expected of you in exchange for the right to display it."

"Duty?"

My grandfather took me by the shoulders at arm's length, looked at me, and then gave me an uncharacteristically long hug.

NOW, IN DARK moments, I often wonder after the causal chain, hidden from me, that triggered the events that followed and the order in which they played out. Was it my grandfather's machinations that doomed me to those future paths in the first place? Or was it my doing; something in my choices, or my responses to the more tragic events of that year that hardened me to "life's many cruelties," as Bernadette had put it? Had the paths I had taken prompted my grandfather to see something in me that allowed him to act in the way that he later did?

Sometimes I dream the events of that weekend so vividly that it is as if I have been transported back to those places and that time. Often in such dreams, I find myself sitting with my grandfather in the East Salon again, watching the tendrils of his pipe smoke drift up and among the death masks until I realize that he is looking at me, expectantly; waiting for me to ask the questions that have haunted me so for all the years that have passed since that night. But, before I can give such questions voice, the door behind me bursts open. I whirl around to see who is there but instead I find myself awake, the dream ended, and the questions themselves lost and forgotten.

WHEN WE ARRIVED in the Grand Dining Hall, I was seated near the head of the table and to my grandfather's right. I was flanked on the other side by Klaus Böhm. His wife, who I had since learned was named Felicia and was more than thirty years his junior, was a pretty, if precariously thin, platinum blonde, whose fluency with the local gossip marked her clearly as an accomplished socialite.

My father was at the head of the table with my mother to his left. She was wearing an intricate necklace: laced platinum ablaze with deep blue sapphires surrounded by diamonds, colors that played off the sheen of her dark blue gown perfectly.

Bastien was not present, but I was surprised to find Augustin seated across the table from me. It was the first time I had seen him since the Northern Ruins, and I suppose I had hoped he would not attend. His companion for the evening was a shy-looking girl of about sixteen with dark hair who, despite her introverted demeanor, nevertheless managed to look rather irritated with her circumstances. She wore an insignia I did not recognize and so I took her for the daughter of someone of note and then imagined, knowing my mother, that there was design behind her selection; that the choice of seat mate for my brother would be an important enough statement that it could not possibly have been casual.

An uncomfortable thought came to me: How long would it be before I was seated at the very same table, forced to attend next to some vapid lordling my mother had selected to secure an obscure political purpose known only to her and my father?

That awful image receded only when I realized that Augustin was not seated in the place of honor at my father's right hand. Once I saw that, I found myself deeply interested in the young man who was. I guessed he was in his early twenties. He was dark-haired, with just a hint of olive in his complexion. At first I thought he was sitting stiffly as a matter of habit, but when he shifted in his chair, I could see that his right arm was in a sling. He wore three miniature medals on his left lapel and, while I could not quite make them out from across the table, I thought they must be military decorations.

I was certain that the girl next to him was a model of some sort: blond, conspicuously tall, and with a disarmingly attractive oval face. My opinion was clearly not an isolated one since, near as I could tell, there was not a single male guest on our side of the table who did not sneak looks at her at regular intervals.

"You are not listening to me," my grandfather whispered.

"Who is that man next to Father?"

"Ah. Jäger. He has been responsible for the Africa project. One of my most promising protégés." My grandfather leaned closer. "But not *the most promising*."

"How did he get hurt?"

"It is impolite to gossip about battle wounds."

"*Battle* wounds?" I said, startled.

"Our rivals think nothing of resorting to black deeds to accomplish their ends. There are times when we must mirror, or even surpass them, to frustrate our enemies, or to meet our objectives. It follows that we must surround ourselves with men, or even women, able and willing to do such deeds, yes?"

I had no idea what to say to that.

"Don't look so worried," he said, and put a hand on my arm to calm me. "Jäger has put in his time. He has performed exceptionally and he is, in any event, wasted in the field. He has as brilliant a mind for finance as anyone who has worked for me, and I fully intend to develop and cultivate it. The asset who has mastery of both intellect and action is the rarest of all. Once you discover them, you must always keep such men close to you.

"I think his thirst for, shall we say, 'adventure' might not be quenched quite yet. Still, I cannot afford to lose him to some damn fool randomly spraying bullets around in some backwater third-world village, so I have invited him to live here on the estate." My grandfather's expression turned thoughtful. "Now that I consider the matter, Professor Lechner's lessons are a bit light on modern finance, aren't they? I should think Jäger might supplement them rather well."

I was about to spit out a dozen questions, but my grandfather gave me the little smile that I knew meant he would not discuss the matter any further.

Dinner proceeded more or less uneventfully for five courses. I worked hard to remain observant, reminding myself that one or more of our family's enemies might well be at the table with us, but my attention began to wander, helped into distraction by the two glasses of red wine I had consumed by the time the sixth course was served.

"Try not to look so bored, my dear," my grandfather whispered. "Though I do sympathize. As it happens there is some place I should much rather be."

"Where?"

"The hunting lodge."

The hunting lodge was up in the hills, a mile or so hike up a narrow and winding trail through the woods. I turned to squint at my grandfather, trying to discern if he was teasing me.

"Why would you want to go there?"

"Can you find Alfred?"

"He's at the far end of the table," I said, remembering not to point or otherwise give away my interest to anyone who might be watching me.

"And when you met him in South Africa, was he alone?"

"No," I said.

"Indeed not. Alfred would never travel without his bodyguards. Tell me, where do you think they have gotten off to?"

"The hunting lodge?" I said, picking up on my grandfather's meaning.

"Precisely."

"But, why?"

"They are not permitted in the manor. We should take it as an insult if our guests intimated that they did not feel safe with our own security staff, but the more high-profile guests who visit the estate would not travel without their own. So, during events like this they make their way up to the hunting lodge. That, my dear, is where the real party usually is."

I could not help but grin thinking of a dozen or more bodyguards all playing cards and smoking cigars at the hunting lodge.

FOLLOWING THE DESSERT course, our guests were invited to the gardens. The domestic staff had been busy during dinner and a substantial segment of the Italian Gardens had been transformed in the interim. The large clearing between the manor and the hedge maze beyond had been surrounded by torches, and their flickering gave what had already been a balmy evening an even warmer feeling. As the guests filtered out, the manor's lights behind us were dimmed.

Five displays had been set up in a semicircle. Each was about ten feet square and when I stepped closer, I could see that they depicted scale-models of a building on a topographical model of the landscape beneath, all intricately crafted down to the finest detail. I realized what we were looking at: the evolution of the manor through the centuries.

My mother walked into the center of the semicircle. A member of the domestic staff held a torch near her, lighting up her face as if she were telling ghost stories around a campfire. The orange-yellow light and the shadows played across her profile in a dark but very beautiful way.

"As most of you know," she began. Her voice was clear and light, and the murmuring of the crowd ceased immediately before she was on her third syllable. "Today is the two-hundredth anniversary of the completion of the manor behind us, the ancestral home of our family. To celebrate the occasion, we are very excited to have so many of our friends and colleagues. And rivals."

The coy smile she gave everyone triggered the perfect amount of chuckling among our guests. She was in her element. She floated over to the first display and the torch was held closer to the model to illuminate it.

"The original castle that stood on this spot was completed in 1621, and was the main seat of power for the county, though for reasons best left unuttered, it is no longer considered polite to mention the name of the count who resided here and held these lands.

"In 1681, at the age of twenty, Leopold I, the founder of our family, was invested by the count as a baron of some importance, and given lands to the south of here. The Great Turkish War was only two years away, and plots and intrigues, even here, far to the west of the frontier with the Ottoman Empire, flourished, fueled by the great riches the Turks secretly showered on Hapsburg nobles or anyone in the West who would support their ambitions of conquest.

"Ever loyal, our Leopold fought for the Emperor during the Battle of Vienna in 1683, the Siege of Érsekújvár, and the Battle of Kassa in 1685. The Emperor was so pleased with Leopold that in 1687 he made him an Imperial Count, answerable directly to the Emperor so that he no longer had any liege save the Imperial person. He also granted him the Count's lands, and the many fortifications that served to control access to Lake Constance from the south."

My mother drifted to the second display, where the beginnings of the manor's construction were depicted.

"Having grown quite rich during the wars and from the Emperor's rewards, Leopold set to rebuilding. With the Ottoman Empire nearly defeated, he commissioned a strangely Elizabethan edifice instead of a proper castle. It took nearly a century before the finishing touches were put on the structure by his great-great-great-grandson, but before he died, Leopold took pains to form an enlightened court, filled with scholars and artists, and even the occasional alchemist."

The collected guests laughed again.

"Truly," my mother said, raising her eyebrows. "For almost a year Robert Boyle had a laboratory in what is now the East Salon. Only an explosion in the dead of night finally ended Leopold's patience with the fumes and foul odors."

"Now I know why she gave me that room," my grandfather murmured under his breath.

Bernadette was standing on the other side of him and I thought I saw her elbow him in the ribs. She looked at me then, and her amused expression melted into deep concern.

"What is it, my dear?" she whispered. "Come now. Perhaps not everyone can see the pain you are in, but I can."

I didn't want to answer, afraid that if I were even to call up the memory of Vim's demise, I might not be able to maintain my composure.

"Only one of life's many cruelties," I said, finally, and gave her a thin smile.

Bernadette's look of concern darkened even more, but then she sighed deeply, gave me a knowing nod, and kissed the top of my head.

As my mother breezed by the death of Leopold I and focused on the continued and enlightened management of the court by his son, Leopold II, my mind wandered. I found myself thinking of Leopold I's daughter Sophia, her disappearance, the conversation between Sir Nigel and my grandfather that I had overheard. By the time I had recovered from my reverie, my mother had moved to the last display, a scale model of the completed manor, faithfully reproduced in every detail.

The light from the torch borne by the member of the staff still flirted with my mother's features, but something else caught my eye besides. From where I was standing, the flickering torchlight was also reflected in the model's windows. I grew fascinated with the trick of light, and realized that they must have been made from real glass. The longer I looked, the more it appeared as if the red-orange flames from the torch flickered from inside the model; as if the manor's interior was on fire.

⤳

MY MOTHER'S LECTURE delivered, our guests were encouraged to roam the grounds in the open air and enjoy refreshments borne on silver trays. With the starlit evening, the flickering torches, and landscaping around the manor, dark corners and wavering shadows were thrown everywhere. Combined with the formal attire of the guests, it seemed a perfect environment for conspiracies, intrigues, and illicit encounters. And, of course, that was no accident.

. . . *by bringing them out of the shadows, or even providing shadows for them,* my grandfather had said, *there is always the possibility that they will make some mistake . . .*

"Rather surprising to have such an extensive exegesis on the events of

1792 and neglect even brief mention of the French Revolution," an older man was saying.

"My daughter-in-law is nothing if not careful about the political circumstances she inflicts on her guests," my grandfather replied. "I do believe some manner of French official is on the guest list this evening, after all."

"It might be quite difficult to address the execution of Louis XVI in a tasteful way," another guest quipped.

"But that was a year later, in 1793," I said, unable to contain myself.

"Ah yes," my grandfather said. "The after party."

The group fell into laughter, and that attracted the attention of my mother from across the grounds. I looked for an excuse to slip away and spied Bastien among the group she had just abandoned. I circled behind her path, slipped around some rosebushes and toward Bastien, thinking that I owed him an apology for missing his concert.

I was still thirty feet away when our eyes met. Bastien looked away, and raised three fingers of his right hand to his eye, as if sweeping away a speck from his cheekbone, and then put his hand over his heart. At first it was hard to see in the dim light, but I was convinced that I hadn't imagined it. It was an awkward-looking gesture, but I thought I recognized it: the Bureau of Secrets hand signal for "they are watching."

I froze. Had Bastien seen something? Did he know that our family's enemies might be present? Who would have told him that?

I glanced around, trying not to be too obvious. Whatever or whomever it was that Bastien might be trying to warn me about, I couldn't see anything out of the ordinary, but he had spooked me and I drifted back toward my grandfather as nonchalantly as I could. Distracted, I nearly collided with Augustin, who was lurking in a bit of shadow, watching a knot of guests I had circled to avoid.

"Well, hello, sister mine," he said, and a wide smile crossed his face.

"Augustin," I said. I was about to try to slip away but he stepped closer and then, to my alarm, leaned in, held my shoulders, and kissed my cheeks three times.

"What was that for?"

"In case you had not noticed, it is a formal event. And anyway, how else am I to greet my favorite sister in public?"

"You are acting strange, Augustin; *have been* acting strange."

"Have I? Well, these are strange circumstances."

Augustin's comment was incongruous, and I had the sudden urge not to be left out of any secrets he might have been privy to.

"'Strange circumstances'?" I said.

"Events of great moment are taking place on our estate tonight."

"And how exactly would you know?"

"Look over there," he said, and nodded his chin in the direction of the people collected around my grandfather. My mother and father had joined the group, along with Professor Lechner.

"Do you know who the short man talking to Father is?" He meant Alfred Kriel. "That," he said, pausing for effect, "is probably the most important man to our family right now."

Before I could say anything, Augustin seized my wrist and guided my hand to his elbow.

"Come," he said, pulling me along with a gleam in his eye. "I'll introduce you."

I tried to think of some excuse to beg off, remembering that I had been sworn to secrecy about South Africa, but Augustin was already delivering me to the periphery of the group and I did not want to make a scene.

"I did tell you that he is very resourceful, Professor Lechner," my mother was saying.

Professor Lechner patted the dazzling breast star on his jacket. "I am well and truly amazed, madam. It is hardly a common insignia. And yet I should have expected nothing less."

The group's attention turned to us as we approached.

"Mr. Kriel," my brother started. "May I present—"

"Well, my dear," Alfred exclaimed, and his expression was pure, and apparently genuine, joy.

He appeared tipsy, and I thought it the source of his augmented affection, but I remembered my grandfather's comments about artifice and they made me suspicious of his enthusiasm. He took hold of me, gently pulled me from Augustin's possessive grasp, and embraced me warmly.

"Now I am the one far from home," he said. "And so it is very lovely to see a familiar face."

Though he was stone silent behind me, I could feel Augustin's eyes boring into my back.

Alfred turned to my mother. "Your daughter is the picture of loveliness," he said.

"We are very proud of her," my mother allowed, and put on her warmest smile.

I still wasn't sure about Alfred, but my mother's expression I knew for a facade. Alfred had drawn her gaze to me, and she seemed ready to speak again, but something stopped her. She was glaring at me, her attention fixed on my left breast.

My greeting ritual with Alfred over, I did something I would later regret.

"Alfred," I said, and turned to Augustin, "have you met my brother Augustin?"

It was impulsive and petty, and doubly insulting because, as Augustin had done with me, I had presented Augustin to Alfred, rather than the other way around, implying that Alfred outranked my brother, which wasn't strictly true. And, as if that was not enough, Alfred managed to twist the knife a bit himself.

"Yes, of course," he said with a dismissive air, and then returned to conversation with my father.

Augustin fumed in silence. I slipped away and toward my grandfather, but my mother's glare never left me. Eventually she worked her way over to us, her eyes blazing.

Finally, as the ebb and flow of conversation gave our little cluster a hint of privacy, my mother addressed my grandfather.

"*What on earth* do you think you are doing, Phillip?" she said.

My grandfather looked confused. "I don't know what you mean, Eva."

Subtly, my mother gestured to the new insignia on my gown.

"What exactly is the meaning of this?" she demanded as forcefully as she could without attracting attention. It wasn't subtle enough to escape my brother's notice. He followed her gaze and then focused on the decoration as well.

My grandfather gave her a thin smile. "Why, Eva," he cooed. "You must be one of the people most versed in protocol and heraldry that I know. I find it hard to believe that you would not appreciate the significance of the insignia of a Dame Commander of the Order of Leopold I."

I was stunned. My mother was speechless. I have no idea why I had not thought to do it earlier, but I scanned my grandfather's decorations more carefully. The most senior of them was a platinum star with inlaid diamonds and a dark red ruby at its center: the insignia of the Grand Commander of the Order of Leopold I.

As Augustin absorbed what my grandfather had said, he turned to the other side of the collected guests where my father was standing. Though there was no love lost between us just then, the look on my brother's face—twisted with shock and bitter betrayal—was still heart-wrenching to me.

My father's expression was as inscrutable as ever. Even from that distance in the torchlit gloom his gray eyes were impenetrable granite orbs.

Before I looked away, something else worked its way into my perception: though there were several insignias on my father's jacket, the Order of Leopold I was not among them.

CHAPTER NINETEEN

The Vault

I WAS SHAKEN BY MY MOTHER'S reaction to the insignia of the Order of Leopold I, not to mention the rising rage I saw burning behind the barely maintained facade of calm that Augustin wore. Perhaps I should have heeded my first instinct, that I was a pawn in a larger game of someone else's making, but I had let vanity get the better of me. Though I relished having something to hold over Augustin, I felt out of my depth and thus glued myself to my grandfather. Lurking in his shadow, I tried to shift back into the observant, quiet mode that he had advocated earlier.

As things finally began to wind down—shrinking knots of guests, couples here and there sitting by firepits or wandering along the darker fringes of the outdoor reception's borders—I began looking for any chance to slip away.

Augustin had vanished and, with my parents distracted elsewhere, my opportunity came when my grandfather and Bernadette descended into whispered conversation. I crept off, wormed my way along the torchlit paths, and slipped past the odd collection of guests on my way back to the manor. It was well after midnight and, here and there, those visitors not staying the night were taking their leave. More than once, I found myself stuck bidding farewells to people I wasn't sure I had actually been introduced to. Finally I made my way to a side entrance to avoid the guest traffic that was sure to clog the Grand Foyer, intending to take the back stairs up to my rooms.

Just before the bend in the darkened hallway that led to the foot of the stairs, voices stopped me in my tracks. I crept up and peered around. Cipriana was backed into a corner and Augustin loomed over her, his hands on the wall on either side of her, boxing her in.

"Don't you think I know that you've been hiding from me? Eventually you're going to come upstairs with me again," Augustin was saying. Slowly, his right hand went to her throat, gripping around it and pinning her head against the stone wall behind her. "Why be so coy about it?"

Cipriana emitted a sob and that's when I realized that she was crying. Augustin leaned closer to her until his lips were almost touching the side of her face, his shadow obscuring her expression. He lowered his voice and whispered something to her. I had to lean around the corner farther and strain to hear him.

"Don't act so innocent," he said.

Cipriana must have caught the movement because she looked at me from over Augustin's shoulder. I saw the recognition sweep over her along with an expression of abject shame and terror.

Augustin saw her reaction and twisted his neck around to see what she was looking at. His hand came off her throat for just a moment but, when it did, Cipriana darted under his left arm. In a flash, she had mounted the stairs and was scurrying up them to escape.

Augustin gave me an angry glare that melted into a sort of contempt.

"Don't think I've forgotten about you, dear sister," he breathed. "I'll settle accounts with the traitor of the family soon enough."

Then he looked up the stairs after Cipriana, and his expression was overcome by something I thought much more sinister and ravenous. He glanced back at me once with that hunger still written on his face and then casually walked upstairs after her.

I CAN'T EXPLAIN WHY I did nothing, or why what I had seen was so easily forgotten. Surely I was supposed to tell someone, or to do something about what I had witnessed, but I had no idea what that might be. I think that part of me just shut down, or that I convinced myself that I had misunderstood the situation.

In a daze, I turned and made my way toward the Grand Foyer. I was still in that state when I found myself in the library. I suppose I must have been looking for a book to read; for any distraction to while away the hours until the merciful cleansing of sleep could wash away the evening. Candles were burning in the Grand Study beyond and, dazed or not, I was drawn to them. Maybe I hoped to find my father or my grandfather there. Instead I found the study curiously empty. Several books and papers were on my father's desk. I crept closer, stood next to the desk chair, and—careful not to disturb anything—discovered them for rather drab materials on copper mining. I was just beginning to wonder if I should feel guilty for snooping when a strange feeling came over me.

Over a long enough time, one becomes used to the acoustics of a familiar space; the way even the softest sounds reflect or are absorbed by it. It was this familiarity that convinced me that the ambient sound in the Grand Study was somehow off. The awareness that something significant was missing—an unexpected emptiness—came on slowly. It clicked when I turned around.

The vault door was wide open.

A flurry of thoughts came to me in the same moment. The lights in the vault were off, so it was unlikely that anyone was inside. Still, it would be very strange indeed for it to be left open and unattended for any length of time. With so many guests milling about, it should have been closed in the late afternoon, before the aide who normally sat at the nearby desk was dismissed for the day.

Visions of dark conspiracies and plots crept into my thoughts. Would a daughter of the line permit the open vault to remain unguarded, or linger to assure it was protected? And if someone, one of my family's enemies, perhaps, emerged from it and then tried to force their way past me? What could I do but scream for help?

Then, another thread of possibilities that I should have dismissed out of hand but somehow did not: Sophia's commonplace book was inside. And what could be better nighttime reading than that? With the study and library empty, I could be in and out before anyone noticed.

I spent several moments weighing my decision, but deep down I knew the second I thought of the commonplace book that I would end up darting inside. Sure enough only a few seconds later I had overcome all resistance and slipped past the imposing steel door.

I knelt down just inside the threshold and realized that I had not thought my plan out particularly well. Inside, the only source of light was what leaked through the doorway from the candles and desk lamp in the Grand Study. Further, the interior of the vault was almost pitch black and, if I turned on the lights, it would be obvious to anyone who happened along that someone was inside.

I was just considering this dilemma when I heard voices in the Grand Library. My heart quickened and I could feel my pulse in my temples. Silently, I pled for whoever it was to go away. It was not to be.

I recognized my mother's voice. Feeling around in the dim light, I crawled deeper into the gloom and pressed myself against one of the walls. Kneeling in the shadows, I could just see out the open vault door and into the Grand Study as my mother came in with Hannah and the man with the port-wine stain on his cheek: the Archduke.

". . . but I must insist," the Archduke was saying, "that this is one of the most delightful events I have attended in some years. It was beyond generous of you to open your home to all of us."

"Not at all," my mother beamed. The trio stopped in front of my father's desk. "We were honored that you accepted the invitation. Still, a pity your wife was unable to join us."

"Ah, yes," he sighed. "I am afraid she is not feeling well."

"Oh, nothing serious, I hope?"

There was a silence while my mother waited for him to elaborate, but he changed the subject instead. "What was it you had for me?"

"Ah, yes."

My mother stepped around my father's desk and I cringed, thinking for a moment that she might come into the vault. Instead she opened one of the desk drawers and took something out.

"This," my mother said, holding a dark red passport aloft, "was found in one of the guest rooms. You know, I do believe it is a diplomatic credential. Haven't you also an ambassadorial appointment? I am certain I remember that. I haven't bothered to open it yet, and it is not as if you are the only diplomat on the estate this weekend, but I thought it might be yours."

Even in the dim light I could see the Archduke's face fall. His hand went to his jacket, padding the breast pockets like a restaurant patron who had just realized that his wallet was missing.

"Ah," he stammered, "I—"

"It was found . . . where again, Hannah?"

"In the quarters of one of the musicians, ma'am," Hannah said.

"Ah, yes," my mother said, her voice drawn out as if in deep contemplation. "The young violinist. Mila, wasn't it?"

"Yes, milady," Hannah said.

The Archduke had stopped fidgeting. He stood completely still.

"Lovely girl. Rather young though. She is the daughter of the Russian foreign minister, I believe, is she not, Hannah?"

"The deputy minister of foreign affairs, yes," Hannah replied.

"Well, that is a bit of bother. I am certain I read somewhere that active members of the foreign service are supposed to report . . . *contacts* with foreign nationals."

"*Spies*," I thought.

My mother paused for effect before rounding the desk, standing in front of the speechless Archduke and inspecting the cover of the passport.

"I must admit, I'm rather curious to have a look inside," my mother said, and turned it over to glance at the back cover. "Then again, I'm not sure the . . . *affairs* of my guests are any business of some drab little counterintelligence clerk. What sort of hosts would we be if we occasioned such trouble for our esteemed visitors?"

My mother reached out and took the Archduke's hand gently, turned it palm up, and delicately laid the passport in it.

"Much less our *closest friends*," she said, and closed his hand over the booklet with hers. She held his hand for a moment before letting go. "On reflection, I think it best if you handled the return of this . . . lost item to its rightful owner."

With as much dignity as he could muster, the Archduke tucked the passport into his inside breast pocket.

There was a cautious tone in his voice when he spoke again. "It is important to have close friends," he said.

"Exactly, Your Highness," my mother beamed. "Exactly."

The Archduke and my mother stood regarding each other for a brief moment. Then he gave her a little bow of the head, turned, and strode out of the Grand Study.

"Well done," my mother said to Hannah.

"Thank you, milady."

"And the girl?"

"She bears some watching. She may think she is in love."

My mother looked alarmed. "That will certainly not do. It is the sort of thing that can flare up at the most inconvenient time." My mother folded her hands together in front of her and succumbed to a thoughtful expression. "I will speak with her."

"Yes, milady."

There was movement in the library beyond, and for a moment I thought the Archduke might be returning, but the figure who came into the study was my father.

"Ah," my mother said when she saw him, and turned to Hannah. "Leave us."

Hannah gave a curt little curtsy and departed. My mother stood waiting as my father sat at his desk.

"I saw our esteemed guest leaving the library," my father said. "This is why you wanted the study to yourself?"

"It was."

I realized then that I had wandered into a bit of conspiracy; that I had arrived just as my father had vacated the room to allow my mother to lure the Archduke in.

"Well, then," my father said. "I depart for Moscow rather soon. Your intrigue with him . . . ?"

"Not only will he offer you no opposition, but in fact you may arrive in Moscow with an extra arrow in your quiver."

"Excellent. Though I must ask how, precisely, you were able to keep his wife away."

"She's been sick for quite some time."

"Oh?"

"It is not common knowledge. Cancer. As I understand it, he'll be a widower before the year is out."

"Ah. Pity."

"Convenient for our purposes, though." My mother circled around the desk to stand behind my father and laid her hand on his shoulder. "I am sorry, Valentin, but I have to ask. Exactly what does your father think he is doing?"

"I am not certain."

"I wish you would become certain. It would not do to have a conflict between—"

"There are more pressing matters," my father said, interrupting. "You must leave it to me for the moment."

"Do you really think it a good idea to bring our daughter with you?"

"If you are so worried about my father's behavior, you would rather she stay here?"

My mother considered this before answering. "Perhaps not."

"It is decided then."

My father took her hand and kissed it formally, and then stood up.

"It has been a very long few days," he said, and gestured to her necklace.

She turned around and my father undid the clasp before, with great and deliberate tenderness, he kissed the back of her neck.

As long as I could remember, my mother and father had never overtly displayed affection for each other. Later I would come to understand this attitude, that such expressions telegraphed weakness and that this motivated a defensive penchant to conceal them. I would find it to be a rather common affectation among dynastic and aristocratic families. But back then, the kiss was almost shocking. I was touched enough by their interaction—I think my heart actually quickened for a few beats—that it broke the spell of icy stoicism they normally cast around themselves. For just a moment, I saw them almost as a loving pair, though, given what I had witnessed and overheard, that image quickly transformed into visions of the two of them conducting grand conspiracies and deceptions together.

I was lost in thought for some time, remembering what Bernadette had said about the dangers of love, what my grandfather had mentioned about intrigues, and my mother's role supporting our family, and that distracted me from recognizing my father's approach. When I finally understood his intention, a creeping horror began to crawl up my back. He was going to put the necklace in the vault for safekeeping.

As quietly as I could, and feeling in front of me with my hand to keep from running into something, I quick-crawled deeper into the blackness of the vault, navigated by touch to a corner, and curled into it, making myself as small as I could.

The lights flicked on and I had to pinch my eyelids closed against the sudden brightness. Luckily, the hiding place I had found—wedged into a corner of the first room in the vault with a file cabinet partially concealing me—wasn't bad at all.

My father carried the necklace past my hiding spot and then, a moment or so later, passed me again on his way out and turned off the lights.

I heard a low rumble from the direction of the vault door, followed by a metallic thud and then silence. I knew instantly that it was the sound of the bolts driving home and locking me in.

THE PROSPECT OF being locked in the vault overnight stirred up any number of disturbing questions. Was the vault airtight? If so, how many hours until I was killed by carbon dioxide buildup? Suddenly I wished I had paid more attention to Professor Lechner's basic biology discussions. What if the vault door wasn't opened the next morning? Would there be a search? Would my father leave for Moscow without me?

I had no food or water and there was no bathroom either. I had a sudden vision of my father returning to the vault after his business trip only to have the desiccated skeleton of his only daughter tumble out of the door and into a heap at his feet when he opened it. Further examination by the forensic team called in to investigate would reveal bloody, desperate-looking nail scratches on the inside surface of the vault door.

I shuddered.

Surviving overnight in the vault wasn't the only problem. I would have to find some way to sneak back out unseen when (or if) the vault was opened in the morning. Because of the position of my father's desk and the station of the nearby aide, this was bound to be difficult.

Given all my nocturnal experience up to that point, one would think I would know better than to expect waiting in the dark to take the edge off fear. Instead, it turned every imagined sound into visions of rodents, another hidden intruder stalking me, or some malevolent spirit (perhaps the dark shade of the last patriarch's daughter to be locked behind the massive vault door).

I finally worked up the courage to move and felt around for a light switch. The overheads winked on and hummed loudly, or so it seemed in the vault's close quarters. No hidden intruder revealed himself, and whatever ghostly force may have thrived in the dark had been vanquished by the light (or I had just been alone the entire time).

Some of the fear melted away when I recognized that I was unchaperoned and in the presence of my family's most valuable treasures and secrets. What else might I find, aside from Sophia's commonplace book? Despite the risk of a long and unplanned stay inside, I was intrigued.

The vault itself was essentially a multiroomed suite with steel-lined walls and ceilings. The first room inside the vault door was about fifteen by twenty feet. Some paintings hung on the wall across from a couch positioned for viewing. Along with a series of file cabinets holding binders that I assumed were filled with corporate records and the like, racks and shelves took up the remaining space on the walls.

It was the shelves that drew my attention at first. A collection of neatly stacked gold bars gleamed from the bottom shelf behind locked steel-mesh cages. There must have been over a hundred in total. Imprinted on the bars was the stamp:

1 KG

GOLD

995,0

On the second shelf was a collection of smaller gold and silver bars, and ingots of all shapes and sizes. Some looked like thick dinner mints and others as if they had been crudely stamped from melted square candles and emblazoned with Chinese characters. Farther up there were a number of sacks closed with drawstrings, which I assumed were filled with coins or the like, and then a set of thin drawers about the dimensions of a center desk drawer with labels like "Rounds 1.00 – 1.49 CT." I counted fifty of the drawers and marveled at the vast numbers of gemstones that must have been contained within.

In all there were twenty-two locked shelves in the first vault room, stacked with a blur of coins, banknotes, and locked drawers with mysterious labels like "Padparadscha" and "Misc. Loose."

Deeper in the vault, a second room, larger than the first, was behind an unlocked door. The shelves there held books and binders. A number of file cabinets lined the far wall on either side of a door that I assumed led to another chamber beyond. More than a dozen paintings were hung and another two dozen were covered with protective cloth and stacked in storage units next to a display case with many antique watches and clocks.

The file cabinets were locked, so I looked at the books on the open shelving. A substantial collection of texts seemed to be corporate records, bound up together in volumes marked by year going back to the 1920s. They were unexciting to me and so I tried the door at the far end of the room. On my first try I thought it was locked, but once I leaned into it, it came open suddenly enough that I almost fell in.

The air was slightly different there. Racks mounted on the far wall held dozens of military rifles; part of my grandfather's plan that the estate should be self-sufficient even in times of chaos or conflict, I assumed. I was far more interested in the shelves. They were locked, cagelike bookshelves with books of all types and sizes. Three volumes were on a nearby reading desk, remnants, I imagined, of someone's late-night study session.

A little overwhelmed, I sat at the little desk. I pulled the chain on the banker's lamp and began to wonder where Sophia's commonplace book might be stored. But then I noticed something: the books on the desk looked very much like the volumes my grandfather had been perusing in the East Salon—the very same texts he had so quickly covered up.

I jumped up and went back to the shelves. Nearly thirty of the same green leather-bound volumes were tucked away there. They were locked up, but the three works on the desk had been left out. I could not believe my good fortune.

The volume on the bottom was much thinner than the others and the cover was different. The binding was modern, but, leafing through it, the pages appeared to be a collection of various papers of different sizes, weights, and textures. All of them were very old.

The spine was inscribed simply with "*epistolae mortuorum i.*"

"The Letters from the Dead, volume one," I breathed to myself.

Deep down I knew very well that the texts were forbidden to me, not to mention the fact that I had no business being in the vault in the first place. All caution, however, melted away while in proximity to the burning radiance of my curiosity. Carefully, I opened the topmost tome somewhere near the middle. The pages were fragile and yellowed. Both the flowing cursive and the language itself were so archaic that it was difficult for me to follow, but after turning a few pages I found a header with a date: 9 June 1792. And then another: 11 June 1792. And another: 12 June 1792.

"Leopold I," I whispered.

It was the long-lost diary Sir Nigel had mentioned. I set it aside and opened the next book. Though it had no inscription on its spine, it didn't take me long to identify it. The entries were from my grandfather and addressed to my father. I turned to the first of them and began to read:

My Dear Son:

> *Every man has demons and inspirations that drive him, and it serves us not at all to seek to indict the authors of this larger corpus of work (your ancestors) without the benefit of this perspective. It is the topic of "perspective" that I should like to write of to you in this, my first of what I hope are many entries to come.*
>
> *It will be essential that you seek to understand how our family appears to outside eyes. Perhaps it is obvious to note that from the inside, things appear much, much different. Perhaps not.*
>
> *Even our most prominent symbol, the family seat, sprawling and beautiful as it is to us, must look dauntingly and darkly intimidating to modern eyes. Likewise, outsiders might be overly taken with what it says about our longevity as a dynasty. Who of them can match the number of generations over which our imposing stone edifices have glared down onto our valley below? Despite this, our family is young as the standards of such things go.*
>
> *The descendants of Leo de Maximis, who now style themselves*

"Massimo-Brancaccio" or simply "Massimo," are enjoying their family's 1,000th birthday even as I write these words, though I often suspect them of double-counting several generations.

Whatever the true age of that clan, for all their celebrated history and self-congratulatory glee, the Roman palaces of the Massimo family did not survive the rampaging troops of Charles V in 1527. The Palazzo Massimo alle Colonne that today stands atop those charred ruins has all the architectural authority of a failed bank in the Manhattan of the 1930s.

Consider the fate of the descendants of Leo de Maximis as a cautionary tale. Always remember that, on the scales which are important to us, a dynasty's longevity is tied to its financial and political, rather than military, resilience. Of course, in the decades to come, I will see to it that your tutors neglect none of the great strategic thinkers of ancient and modern history.

Is it possible, I thought, that I am given the same education my father received when he was young?

Last summer, I made the long hike up to the Vista and looked down onto nearly the whole of our lands at once. It is an annual pilgrimage of sorts; a practice I am careful not to neglect, and one I invite you to adopt.

Standing there looking down into the vast swaths of green I was reminded of lines from William Cowper's "The Solitude of Alexander Selkirk":

I am monarch of all I survey,
My right there is none to dispute;
From the center all round to the sea,
I am lord of the fowl and the brute.

These words are a warning to me that such regency is illusory, for, as you must know, Selkirk's supposed verse refers to his complete dominion over a section of the archipelago of Juan Fernández, where

*he was stranded alone for four long, and lonely years. Prisons, you see,
have all manner of outward appearances.*

*Thousands of "castles" litter the near and far reaches of Europe,
each increasingly dilapidated, and each prone in a different and highly
unique way to exsanguinate from family treasuries nearly limitless
quantities of cash in maintenance and repair.*

A shiver gripped me, and I was reminded of a story my grandfather had
told at dinner one night. An estate quite close to our own sank millions and
millions into thrice restoring the family crypt so that runoff from heavy
rains draining through it would not continue to leak into the drinking wells.

"There is poetry in that somewhere, don't you think?" my grandfather had
asked me. "Our ancestors sustain us, do they not?" My mother had frowned at him.

I continued reading.

*Our own properties share this propensity but I think you will find
that, with their completion, the renovations I have, at painful expense,
commissioned have now dramatically reduced the capital required to
maintain the estate. It is my small gift to future generations that I hope
will provide outsized returns.*

*Our own lands remained relatively, and mercifully, isolated from
the many arteries and veins that carried the red and fevered blood
of "the modern" through blue, oxygen-starved aristocratic tissue. The
current age is unforgiving to aristocrats and there is no shame in using
isolation and camouflage as survival tactics, to the extent our lands
could ever be subtle.*

*In that connection, take care that our family does not sacrifice
discretion for status. We can ill-afford the pomp and notice from outside
our circles that an attention-craving, public figure in our ranks would
bring. Historically, time is not kind to old estates, or old families unused
to the practice of trade.*

*You will find that it has been the dynasties that resisted the
siren song of new money, and the traffic in new world brides from
wealthy families, that endured. In our case, you will recognize that*

*our predecessors very shrewdly used their capital to finance the cash
thirsty ventures of the emergent merchant classes without granting
them equity (so to speak) in the family proper. Instead, the former
heads of our family established themselves as the old-world bankers
and financiers that were among the only aristocracy that survived the
empire-shattering Great War, and endured, such as they could, into
more current eras.*

*Always remember, my son, that this is the blood that flows through
your veins, and that it and it alone can claim that legacy. Dilution is death.*

*You Have All My Faith,
Your Loving Father*

My audacity in reading words intended for my father quickened my pulse,
and some sentiment from my grandfather's prose, a feeling that I imagined
came from the very blood within my veins, put a lump in my throat.

I turned the pages to the most recent entry in my grandfather's volume,
dated just five days earlier.

My Dear Son,

*It will come as no surprise to you that I abhor deception. Even
more, I abhor the fact that it is often a necessary tool that a patriarch
must use. Given these facts I hope you will come to understand why I
have not shared the entirety of my thoughts with you in recent days.
Even (or perhaps especially) to his heir, a patriarch must never openly
show indecision, uncertainty, or distraction.*

*If my suspicions about the attack in South Africa are correct, then
the danger we face is very serious indeed and it is a threat that has been
developing for some time.*

*In isolation it is nonsensical for one of the great families to attack
another patriarch or the line of succession of another great family.
There exists a fragile balance among many of the dynastic families that
enables something like peaceful coexistence, even where their interests*

diverge (or actually conflict). Many pillars support this balance, but to my mind the most important is deliberate cooperation between them.

Overt cooperation of this kind is not as simple as it may seem. Society at large is already suspicious of dynastic families (old or new). Should they be seen to be colluding, no matter how noble the purpose, it will be assumed that the intent of such a coalition is to do violence (political, economic, or even literal) to the lower classes.

Leopold I also had to contend with the fact that the Emperor might well misunderstand and misinterpret an extra-Imperial cabal of his vassals. He reasoned that concealment was the only defense from such threats.

Though his writings on the topic are wisely vague, I believe Leopold I responded to these concerns, and the threat of the Ottoman Empire, by establishing a second, covert order. This is the secret order alluded to in other epistolae mortuorum volumes. A clandestine cabal to complement the very public royal order allowed him by the Emperor: the Order of Leopold I. Though it has been an important part of our family's history, the origin of the more secret order was a mystery before the recent discovery of Leopold I's original work.

Thinking the matter of less import before now, I have not addressed in my prior writings to you the fact that, though the order faded over time as the Ottoman threat waned and, over the centuries that followed, populist movements directed their attentions away from our family and her neighbors, I revived the second, secret order on the eve of the Second World War. I will write a more definitive exegesis on the order and its resurrection (in fact the second reconstitution of the order after its founding and restoration in 1799 by your Sixth Great-Grandfather Mathias).

Turning back to present events, in the face of an attack on our family so deliberate and so clearly planned, there can be no conclusion other than that something has disrupted the delicate balance that has, for decades, kept the peace between the older European dynastic families. The forces once held in check are very powerful and, with their equilibrium disrupted, their collision could be devastating.

All of the Members of the Line in this family must be prepared for the worst and, until we know more, there is no telling from which direction, or against which of us the next blow might fall.

I have so much more I must write, but I find my time is no longer my own. Still, I cannot hesitate to admit that I have, of my own accord, revived the order and taken such other measures as I believe necessary to prepare us for conflict. In this, I will certainly and clandestinely have usurped some of your authority and violated the spirit of succession I set in motion last year. I do not beg your pardon, only your understanding.

With All My Affection,
Your Loving Father

My mind raced back to Professor Lechner's lecture on the secret airfield. *A clandestine cabal to complement the Order of Leopold I? Could this be the secret society Professor Lechner had hinted at?*

Involuntarily, my hand went to the insignia of the Order of Leopold I that was still pinned to my chest. It seemed very heavy.

Almost forgetting to treat the old pages with the care and reverence they deserved, I turned back to Leopold I's volume and hunted through it, struggling with the long-disused dialect to decipher the writing the best that I could.

Finally, barely a third of the way from the first pages in the volume, I found an intriguing entry. It was dated the 13th of June 1678. It caught my eye because there was little writing on the page. Instead, four hand-drawn coat-of-arms diagrams were sketched. The year 1678 was written under the first three. The fourth seemed to have been penned with different ink, as if it had been added later. Under that last sketch was the year 1679. I recognized the first coat of arms as ours, but the other three were mysterious. The first of them depicted a wild boar with stag supporters, the second a tightly bundled set of twelve arrows with lion supporters, the third an eagle with vicious-looking talons flanked by griffins.

The word *Nyx* was printed below the coats of arms and beneath that a motto: "*In tenebris, salus.*"

"In the darkness, safety," I whispered to myself.

Eager to find more, I turned back to my grandfather's letters and began flipping the pages looking for hints. I found the entry I wanted about three-quarters of the way into his letters. Though it was dated in 1956, after a short preamble the following pages were of a different paper stock and ink and bore dates from 1937 until 1944. The timing began to make sense to me. In 1937 my grandfather had returned to the estate from his long adventures abroad. With global chaos impending, he and my grandmother had decided to abstain from having children, a decision they reversed only after the Second World War was safely over.

My father had been born in 1951. It stood to reason that my grandfather would not begin to write his entries until my father was born but, once he began, it must have been natural for him to take the pages of his wartime diaries and add them to the volume.

Having put the chronology together, I might have skipped forward, but for what I found on the seventh page of the wartime entries: several sketches of coats of arms.

Ours was depicted first with the same 1678 written underneath. My grandfather had reproduced the following three, though the fourth coat of arms, the one with the eagle and griffin supporters and the year 1679 written beneath, was carefully crossed out and the words "line extinguished" were written under the year.

Unbidden, an image jolted into my mind's eye: a vision of the last patriarch of that line, aged and alone in a drafty castle, perhaps on his deathbed without children to attend him, finally slipping away, and his name with him. I shuddered before turning back to the volume.

The year had a question mark written next to it, which I took to mean that the year the mysterious family had ceased to be was unknown to my grandfather when he had penned the entry.

More than two dozen other coats of arms had been sketched, each with a year I took to mark the induction into the order of the family represented. Many had been carefully crossed out with a second year and short explanations like "lost to history," "issued only daughters," "destroyed during the Austro-Prussian War," or "expelled from the Order."

With the world on the brink of war it seemed my grandfather had started researching the Order with thoughts of reviving it. Viewed together, the sketches, dates, and commentary presented a running history of the secret society and its members. By 1750 the Order had expanded to seven families, then waned again until there were only three members in 1866: ours, the coats of arms depicting the bundle of twelve arrows, and a new sketch with an owl as the shield element and the inauguration year 1798. Then the Order seemed to go idle. No families were added or removed again until 1937, but by the end of the Second World War the Order's members were represented by seven coats of arms in total.

Beyond ours, their elements were the twelve bundled arrows, the owl, a smiling wolf, a square-rigged frigate under sail, a device split between five lions in an upside-down pyramid and a castle keep, an obelisk occulting a crescent moon against the background of a starry sky, and a dragon clutching the blade of a sword in its talons.

Beneath the sketches were lines of verse:

When trade and traffic and all the noise of town
Is dimmed, and on the streets and squares
The filmy curtain of the night sinks down
With sleep, the recompense of cares,
To me the darkness brings not sleep nor rest.

I was trying to understand the relevance of the verse when something occurred to me: the last seven sketches hadn't been crossed out. Was that because they were still members of the Order, or because my grandfather had not updated his sketches since the end of the war? I could not know.

In an entry dated 1949 I found a list of more than a dozen family names under the heading *turpificatus*. Next to one of the names ("von Pfilen"), "action taken to guide succession" was written.

I was studying the list closely, trying to remember if I recognized any of the names, and so my thoughts were far away when the noise started. It began softly, and I was slow to react even when I recognized it: the low rumble of the vault bolts opening.

It was a particular kind of panic; a panic so gripping that I could not move. I was helpless to do anything more than watch it, a foaming wave that inexorably rolled up to the shore where it would surely crash over me. I sat there, stuck with the most recent volume of the *epistolae mortuorum* open in front of me, as my father, doubtless attracted by the light and the open door, walked into the third room.

His gaze shifted from me to the volumes in front of me and back to me again. His gray eyes narrowed and, for a moment, I imagined that his notoriously inscrutable expression let pass a flash of anger (and that might even have been some solace) but, in fact, there was nothing.

—

CHAPTER TWENTY

See Not the Wound

I T WOULD BE EASY TO IMAGINE a dramatic confrontation between us. Though I expected it (and part of me even preferred it to the cold and distant sort of distaste he expressed instead), my father did not scold me. In fact, he did not speak to me at all.

I had managed to close the green volume to conceal exactly what I had been reading, but I could feel myself shrinking under his gaze as he walked behind me, reached over my shoulder, opened the cover, and turned a few pages to examine the book. He stood there for a long time. I started shaking. Finally, he stepped back out into the doorway of the third room and called out beyond the vault door to the Grand Study.

"Karl, will you step in here for a moment please?"

Karl understood the moment he set eyes on the scene. He took two long steps, clamped a firm hand around my arm, and led me away in silence.

It was still before dawn but the evening's events had drawn mostly to a close. The halls were empty and I was grateful for that. I would have been beside myself to be seen led away from the scene by the arm; a naughty child in formalwear. I managed to hold back the tears while Karl led me to my apartments, but when I heard him lock my doors from the outside I could not restrain myself anymore.

I was alone for hours. Eventually I pulled my bell cord, but the summons was ignored. About halfway through my detention, and well after dawn, someone opened my door and left a silver tray from the kitchens before locking me in again.

Even by late afternoon, no one else had come to my room. Had word leaked out? Did everyone know?

I fell asleep in my clothes and, when the distant whine of the helicopter's turbine woke me, it was early evening. I rushed to my windows in time to make out the blinking anticollision lights when the craft turned and picked up speed as it angled for our airstrip. It was my father departing for Moscow without me.

Finally, well after the dinner hour, Lucas appeared at my door and announced that I was to be escorted to the Grand Dining Hall. I had been so despondent that I didn't even think to change out of my formalwear. Lucas ushered me downstairs with the watchfulness of a security guard, as if I were some errant guest caught out of bounds.

My mother was already seated but the guest chairs across from her had been removed, leaving me standing. After I curtsied, she started in on me.

"Well, you've had quite a busy couple of days, haven't you? I must say that it is not often, particularly on the eve of the most important event this family has hosted in over *two centuries*, that a mother has the pleasure of learning that her own daughter, who has had every advantage and opportunity a young girl could ask for, has devolved into a filthy little quidnunc."

"Where's Grandfather?" I asked.

It was ill-advised.

"You will *stand silently* until we are finished here," my mother erupted.

There was an explosion of shattering glass from behind the door to the kitchens. My mother's outburst was so forceful that she had startled some nameless eavesdropper among the domestic staff who had been lurking behind the door. I had never seen my mother lose control in that way.

"And *when* we are finished, you will go back to your rooms until you are summoned," she continued, ignoring the noise.

Professor Lechner was shown in at that moment, and I remember thinking that the timing had been deliberately choreographed.

"Well, and here's the enabling party now," my mother said. "Professor Lechner, I have never thought highly of your ideas about my daughter's curriculum—if in fact we can torture the definition of that word so hideously—or, to be entirely frank, your person. I can see now that my instincts were absolutely correct and, to my shame, I erred by not acting on them more forcefully in the first place."

"Madam, I must protest," he began, but my mother was having none of it.

"Not this time. Professor Lechner, I've asked you here to inform you that you are dismissed from service effective *immediately*. Your last official duty will be to compose proper reference letters for my daughter, addressed to the Academy Le Gudin."

I couldn't help it anymore and I began, as quietly as I could, to cry.

"The Academy Le Gudin? Unthinkable. Absolutely not," the Professor said.

"Excuse me?" My mother was incredulous.

"I cannot in good conscience commit a young woman as gifted as your daughter to an academic oubliette, or, indeed, to the custody of Academy Le Gudin's abysmal administrators. No, madam. Most certainly not."

"Professor Lechner." I recognized the measured timbre of my mother's voice and knew instinctively that Professor Lechner was in actual danger. I hoped against hope that he would pick up on the same cues. "I will only suggest to you once that this family is not an enemy you wish to make."

Professor Lechner straightened and seemed by will alone determined to overcome his diminutive height and present as imposing a figure as he was able.

"I believe I will first consult with your father-in-law, madam," he said.

"Actually, Professor Lechner, you will not find him available to you. I represent the entire family in this matter."

It hit Professor Lechner like a blow and what had been steely resolve melted into a formal and very dignified plea.

"Madam, I implore you. You cannot ask this of me."

But my mother would brook no argument.

Professor Lechner looked at me and then looked to one of the chairs farther down the table, as if he intended to sink into it.

"You," my mother bellowed, "have not been invited to sit at this table. I have outlined for you the closing duties required of you. I expect them to be completed without delay. Good night, Professor."

Professor Lechner gave me an inscrutable expression. I searched it for some measure of hope or encouragement, but I could neither divine anything of the sort nor decode it further. Then, without uttering a word, the Professor turned on his heel and took his leave.

My mother's frigid gaze bored into the Professor's receding back as he left and then she directed her attention back to me.

"I believe we've seen quite enough of you this evening, young lady. You will wait for me in your rooms until I have decided upon appropriate punishments, corporal or otherwise, for your transgressions."

⌒◎

NOT WANTING TO chance an encounter with anyone in the Grand Foyer, I ran into the Hall of Ancestors and toward the back stairs with my head down to hide my face. I was barely looking where I was going when I ran smack into Augustin. I bounced off him and fell back onto the hard floor.

Something was amiss with my older brother. His hair was disheveled, a pair of red scratches showed on his cheek, and he glared down at me with bloodshot eyes.

"I heard about what you did," he said. "You think you are special somehow? Is that it? Well, you're not. Just another conniving bitch."

"Augustin, please, just leave me alone," I said, struggling to get up.

He reached down and grabbed my elbow, pulling me to my feet. I turned to go but his grip tightened and he yanked me around until I was facing him, wrenching my shoulder in the process.

"Augustin, you're hurting me. Let go."

"You are going to do something for me first," he said.

I saw something deeper in his expression. Something dark and desperate. It had a predatory edge; the sickly smell of sour sweat and vomit. He started to pull me toward the far stairwell and it dawned on me then where those stairs led: the abandoned bedrooms on the third floor.

The image of a nude Cipriana in a third-floor bedroom came to me. And then a crying Cipriana cornered by Augustin, not far from where we were standing. I thought I knew what Augustin wanted then; that his desire was base, violent, even sexual. I tore at my brother's grip on my elbow, twisting and squirming to get away, but he was much stronger than I expected and I only managed to lose my footing so that he ended up dragging me by the arm.

"Augustin, stop it," I begged. "*Let me go.*"

"Stop squirming. Do you want to be in even more trouble? I'm the heir. Mother will believe whatever I tell her. Walk or I will haul you up the stairs by your hair."

"I'll scream," I said, and there was an increasingly panicked timbre to my voice.

"No, you won't," Augustin said.

So I did.

Augustin's response was immediate and brutal. He wrenched me back to my feet by my elbow and clamped his free hand over my mouth. Once I started screaming, I couldn't stop, but I only got out half a full-lunged cry before his hand muffled the rest.

"Quiet," he ordered in a hoarse whisper. His grip on my face tightened. "You *have to be quiet.*"

I tried to bite him, but his hand was cupped over my mouth and I couldn't close my teeth on the skin of his palm.

He shook me. Hard. I felt a sharp pain in my neck, clamped my eyes shut, and saw stars. I must have stopped screaming because his grip on my elbow had loosened and his other hand had come away from my mouth. When I opened my eyes again, he was holding the gleaming blade of his straight razor right in front of my face. My legs gave out and I was afraid my bladder might let go as well. I sank down to my knees on the cold stone floor.

"You are being a selfish bitch. A fucking menace."

It was Augustin's use of the phrase *fucking menace.* The same phrase he had used to describe Vim in the Northern Ruins. I thought I knew something then, and it was so horrible it was impossible for me to prevent the accusation from slipping out.

"It was you," I said, and it was almost as if it were someone else's voice. "You cut my horse, or tangled her in the wire. You killed her."

He looked stunned for a moment, but then recovered, and the manic grimace returned.

"And I can do worse too. You are going to help me with something. You owe me your loyalty, do you understand? Instead you are acting like a traitor."

He glared at me as he said it, and I remember thinking that his expression was almost pained, tormented.

"Do you know what they did to female traitors after the war?" he said, and that's when his grimace turned into a smile; a smile that crept across his face slowly, as if he had resolved what he would do and was just realizing how much the notion pleased him.

"They shaved their heads," he sneered.

I looked around desperately for someone to help me, but the Hall of Ancestors was empty and we were far from the Grand Dining Hall, where anyone might be. I wanted to call out for help again, but all I could manage was a whisper.

"Augustin . . . *don't.*"

Everything was moving in slow motion. My next thought was that Augustin was wrong. It was collaborators, and the women who slept with the Germans, who had their heads shaved. Traitors they shot, or hung. But before I could point this out, Augustin had let go of my elbow and was reaching for my hair.

I don't know why I looked past him exactly, but the light in the hallway played across the portrait behind Augustin just so: Leopold I.

Leopold's eyes, those two dark eyes, were almost a rebuke. What would he have thought to see the heirs to his legacy grappling in that sacred hall? I imagined he was looking at me, on the verge of some utterance.

Leopold I, my ancestral patron.

It felt a childish thought at first, but the relevance of the portrait came to me in a flash and, somehow just after Augustin let go of my arm but before he grabbed my hair, I scrambled away from him on my hands and knees. In a flash, I was under the table beneath the portrait and, after a quick bit of fumbling, came out with the hidden knife.

I was just turning when he was upon me again. He was too fast for me and I found myself prone with Augustin standing on my wrist. When he understood what I had in my hand he scowled and put more and more weight on my wrist, until I thought it would break. I cried out in pain and then let go of the knife. Augustin kicked it away and it clattered across the floor and back under the table.

"You'll pay for that," he sneered.

He took his foot off my wrist, grabbed a fistful of my hair in his left hand, and hauled me up by it. The pain was blinding and my hands involuntarily went up to grab his left wrist and try to take the weight off my scalp. I felt some hair give way and I opened my eyes in horror. Long locks of my hair drifted to the floor. Augustin had cut them off with the straight razor.

I was too stunned to cry anymore, and finally, as Augustin began to saw at another fistful of my hair, despair turned into the desperate, aggressive panic of a cornered animal. I planted my feet and awkwardly rabbit-punched upward on the closest thing on Augustin I could reach: his right elbow.

I must have caught him by surprise because his arm kicked back and his right hand (and with it the razor) nicked my left wrist and then cut into the ribbon of the Order of Leopold I. The blade went on to slice open a long gash in the fabric of my gown over my left breast before flashing by Augustin's face.

He let go of me instantly. I fell to the floor. He stopped then, and just stood there with his mouth agape. After a few seconds his hand lost its muscle tone and went slack. The razor slipped from his fingers and struck the floor right next to something, an object it took me some time to recognize: a sizable and bloody chunk of Augustin's right ear.

When the realization of what had happened came to him, Augustin's hand shot up to the side of his head. Blood was pouring out from between his fingers so fast I couldn't see exactly what was left of his ear. Not a second later the right side of his face was slick with it. I was on my feet and I started to run, but I stepped on the severed part. I could feel (and hear) a sickening squishing under my shoe as the fleshy piece—a pale slice of tissue larger than a schilling coin—slipped and rolled under my foot. I almost lost my balance. Recovering, I bolted up the stairs for my rooms but not before I heard him scream after me.

"You fucking bitch! You bloody fucking menace! I will fucking kill you!"

I SLAMMED MY APARTMENT doors closed, locked them, and wedged a chair under the latches. When I caught my breath I saw a stack of boxes wrapped in ribbons and neatly set on the floor in my little foyer. They were the clothes from the boutique in Zürich. I wanted to tear them open and throw them out of my windows, but I tried to calm down and went to my bathroom instead.

When I looked at myself in the mirror, I could barely see the places where Augustin had cut my hair. That, at least, was a relief, but my face was splattered and smeared with large, dark drops of his blood. I was shaking, and I gawked at myself for a long time until I heard a sound on the floor. I looked down to find blood dripping from my left wrist onto the white marble in big, ugly splashes.

I was just going to let it bleed, but something else didn't feel right. There was blood on my chest, and on the ribbon of the Order of Leopold I where it had been cut (though the insignia itself was intact). Even as I watched, the dark stain on my chest grew. The blood that was dripping to the floor was not just from my wrist, but also a long wound across my left breast peeking out from the slash in the fabric of my gown. Augustin's razor had scored me deeply there and I was bleeding so profusely it was running down my rib cage, my left arm, and onto the floor.

I peeled off my dress in a panic. No longer constrained by the tight top of my gown, the blood began to flow even more liberally. Before I knew it, the white marble underneath me was slick with red.

Augustin had drawn a deep scarlet line diagonally up along my left breast and almost all the way to my left armpit. The razor had cut across my nipple along the way, actually bisecting it. The cut was so deep there that, once I mopped some of the blood away, I could see that he had actually sliced a piece of my nipple clean off. Fat globules and pale white tissue beneath were visible before the thick blood welled up again in the wound.

I could feel a panic attack coming on, but I fought it back with every ounce of my being. I would not allow Augustin the pleasure. Never.

Elevate. Direct pressure. Then pack and bandage the wound.

I lay on the floor, my back sticky with my own blood, and pressed a wet washcloth against the wound with both palms. It throbbed with my heartbeat. Every time I got up to see if I had stopped the bleeding, it started again.

In a weak moment, I thought of Cipriana. I imagined her holding me in her lap, smoothing my hair, and telling me everything would be all right. That is what finally drove me to ring downstairs. I tracked drops of blood to my foyer and pulled my bell cord, but, as before, it was ignored.

I was on my own. I lay on my back again and, wincing with the pain, pressed down on the horrible slash for fifteen straight minutes. With the bleeding finally stemmed, I cut several strips from a clean washcloth and packed the wound, using a white silk scarf as a makeshift pressure bandage to hold the dressing in place.

The immediate danger apparently over, I fell into a dark depression. I thought of my father's expression when he had found me, and I wished that I could just have the last two days back to do over.

Almost two hours later, I managed to motivate myself to get up and look at myself in the bathroom mirror. I washed Augustin's dried blood off my face. Though there was blood all over my bathroom floor, when I started to clean it up I saw that it was actually a thin layer. The contrast of the color red against the white marble floor had exaggerated the drama somewhat and it was easier to mop up than I expected. I did my best to hide the towels I ruined by wrapping them in a trash bag and stuffing them into the bottom of the bin.

Part of me knew that I was supposed to see a doctor, that no matter what Karl had said, such a deep cut was dangerous. But like a wounded animal that hides from others, I could not bring myself to reach out to anyone.

Augustin's words rang in my ears.

Do you want to be in even more trouble? I'm the heir. Mother will believe whatever I tell her.

Even if I had not been afraid of what Augustin might say to my mother (and might have been saying to her at that very moment), I could not bear showing weakness besides. Perhaps it had to do with what I had gleaned Augustin's intentions to be, but the thought of someone poking around my breast was abhorrent to me. I wouldn't let Augustin know he had caused a stranger's hands to fondle me.

Bernadette's words from our evening walk in the Italian Gardens came back to me.

"*What else is there to do but to go on?*" she had said.

What else indeed?

If it starts to bleed badly again I'll ring down for help again, I promised myself.

I need not have worried. Though the wound continued to throb as I crawled into bed, the bleeding had stopped, and so I was free to cry myself to sleep.

CHAPTER TWENTY-ONE

Malice of Absence

I WAS TOO AFRAID TO GO out the next morning. I was wounded, certainly, but in a strange sort of break with reality, that seemed a trivial matter. What loomed much larger was the prospect of anything that might hasten the arrival of my date with whatever punishment my mother had planned (and my imagination was eager to invent the most humiliating and hopefully absurd examples—forced to apologize in front of the entire domestic staff and stand in a corner for the rest of the day; spanked by Lucas; switched over my father's desk in front of Augustin and Bastien).

In retrospect, those humiliations were silly things to be afraid of. Despite what my mother had said, corporal punishment was essentially unheard of for us and should have seemed nearly irrelevant considering what violence Augustin had inflicted on me already. If, as I suspected, my eldest brother had mutilated Vim; had tangled her with barbed wire; had killed her, I had every reason to be terrified of him. But, because of the vault, it was Augustin's accusation that I was a traitor had sank in instead.

By dinnertime, what had started as an eagerness to be forgotten turned into a horrible sense of abandonment. Finally, when my clock struck eleven, I could stand it no longer.

I changed and, emulating Karl's example on the plane, unpacked the wound on my breast and dabbed at the oozing slash with a cotton ball saturated with rubbing alcohol. That produced blinding stabs of pain as the cold liquid lit up my exposed nerves and made my eyes water. I redid my makeshift field dressing, dressed in comfortable, dark clothes, and, relieved to find my doors had not been locked from the outside, crept out into the unlit hallway.

I am not entirely sure that I had a plan beyond the vague goal of finding my grandfather, who I hoped would offer me some measure of solace (perhaps even some hope that I might avoid being switched, caned, or worse, sent off to Academy Le Gudin).

I avoided the Grand Library the best I could and made my way toward the East Salon. I was just down the hall from my grandfather's door when I heard voices, but their tenor stopped me in my tracks.

I could not remember a time I had heard my grandfather really raise his voice, but he was nearly shouting at whoever was in the East Salon with him. I huddled in a corner in the hallway against the possibility that someone might find me listening. Then, in a tone I had never heard from her before—the pleading, mewing sound of a supplicant—my mother's voice.

"How can I know?" she was saying. "The old fool must have wandered upon the bloody scene upstairs. What he was doing up there is anyone's guess. Maybe he heard something? Why are you asking me? He was your friend, after all."

Inaudible murmurs from my grandfather, and I supposed those were better than shouting.

"Obviously, his heart gave out. Don't look at me like that, Phillip. You can't think I had anything to—"

More murmurs.

"Be serious," my mother said. "I had Hannah handle it. What choice did I have? We couldn't just leave him lying there, could we? Anyone might have happened along to see the rest of the scene, and where would we be then?" She began to sound more desperate. "Do you understand how serious a scandal this would be? Do you have any idea what it would do to this family? To Augustin? To Valentin? It is beyond lucky that he is not here. You must believe that. I beg you. Do nothing rash. This is the very last moment to fall prey to some misplaced sense of nobility. Your overdeveloped sentimentality will be the end of us all, don't you understand? It is not possible, even for you, to sacrifice this family for . . . one of them. Do you think they will thank you for it? Even in the thrall of your famous idealism you cannot possibly be that naïve."

I heard footsteps in the hallway behind me. My hiding place was awfully exposed to foot traffic from that direction and so I darted to the nearest doorway, eased open the latch, slipped inside, and closed the door behind me just before the footsteps rounded the far corner.

Safe for the moment, I turned to look inside the unused salon I had taken refuge in. The lights were on and that was strange. More alarming, I was not alone. Sitting on the floor, knees pulled up to his chest, rocking back and forth, eyes screwed shut, and emitting a low, keening whine, was Bastien.

SOMETHING WAS GRAVELY wrong with my younger brother. I knelt down next to him and tried to look into his eyes, but he refused to open them.

"Bastien," I whispered, trying to hold his shoulders gently to get him to stop rocking back and forth. But, if he even knew I was there, he gave no sign of it.

"Bastien, what's wrong with you?" I said, and tried to hold his face in my hands, but he only continued the repetitive and robotic motion, leaking out a low whine with every breath, a broken machine that could not reset itself. Then I saw something even worse: there was dried blood on the top of his shoes.

I started to cry. "Bastien, please tell me what happened."

I remember thinking that the estate was going insane, that everyone had lost all sense of reason. I felt like something alien; transplanted and rejected. Something that the estate's immune system was responding to; attacking. The feeling of being powerless to stop whatever was happening to me, to Bastien, to my grandfather, Augustin, my mother, the estate at large, began to slip toward panic.

There was a sound outside the door to the salon. I wanted to stay with my brother, to help him, to call someone's attention to the fact that something was seriously wrong with him. I had that opportunity. But I was too afraid. What if I was discovered with Bastien? Would I be blamed?

I looked around frantically and finally lit on the side door that led to the next room over.

"Bastien," I said, desperate to try once more. "Bastien, please open your eyes. I will take you out of here, but I can't carry you myself. You have to help me."

But there was nothing of my brother behind those clamped eyelids.

Someone started to open the salon door. I slipped through the side door, closed it behind me, crept out of the adjoining room into the hallway, and fled.

I left my brother Bastien behind that night, and I would regret it for the rest of my life.

IN RETROSPECT IT was obvious that I would make my way into the Grand Library and to Professor Lechner's office beyond. Whom else could I turn to for a sympathetic ear? I had betrayed my grandfather, reading private notes intended only for his son's eyes. I had no allies left except the Professor. We were inadvertent coconspirators, and I took a little cheer outside his door seeing the familiar brass plaque.

LECHNER HALL

PROFESSOR DR. DR. JÜRGEN SIEGFRIED LECHNER

There was a light on inside, and so I knocked softly, but there was no answer. I pushed the door, found it open, and Professor Lechner asleep with his head on his desk. Four neatly typewritten pages were set in front of him. I stood on my tiptoes to see them over his hunched form, careful to avoid waking him.

They were my letters of reference for the Academy Le Gudin, signed with his artful hand. I calmed myself, certain that he would admonish me for being overly excited. Then I put my hand on his shoulder.

"Professor Lechner?" I whispered, but Professor Lechner did not wake then, or thereafter.

Professor Lechner was dead.

I BARELY REMEMBER GOING back to my room. For the second time in as many days, I knew that the right thing to do would have been to tell someone what I had found. But something had broken in me. Whatever meager reserves I had left were exhausted and even Bernadette's inspiration was unable to stir in me any taste for courage.

I lay in my bed for a long time, unable to move, with my wounded breast throbbing. I must have finally changed into my nightgown and fallen asleep because I found myself dreaming. First of dark shadows lurking in the manor, mortal enemies, and then shades, afflicting the living, driving them mad. Mad like Augustin. Mad like my grandfather. Mad like Bastien. In my dream, if I stayed completely still, I thought that I might remain unnoticed as they floated through dark halls. The part of me that still communed with the conscious world registered my clock chiming two and then three.

There was a soft current in the air, drifting across the room and lightly disturbing the folds of the canopy around my bed. After it stopped, a dark figure loomed over me. I smelled my father's cologne, or something like it, sharpened just a little with a hint of spice. The figure was inside the canopy with me and touched my cheeks tenderly with the back of its hand, cool, but not cold.

When I woke, it was Karl looming above me. I must have made as if to scream because he clamped a hand over my mouth. Augustin had done the same and I was nearly seized with mortal terror. Had Karl been afflicted with the same insanity as my eldest brother?

But he softened, there in the dark. I could just make out his face. He was holding a finger up to his lips, the familiar admonition to silence. Only after I nodded my understanding did he take his hand from my mouth. I knew (or imagined I knew) he was there to protect me, though part of me wondered if I was still dreaming.

Refusing to let me change, Karl led me, barefoot, out of my apartments. The stone floor was so cold. There was urgency in his gait and it was all I could do to keep up as he led me on an obscure route out of the manor.

It was a gray night, overcast and chilly. Small twigs and stones hurt the bottoms of my feet. We made our way past the Italian Gardens and to the field beyond. There was a Land Rover parked behind some shrubbery on the far side of the field, as if it had been purposely concealed, and that made everything seem even more dreamlike.

Karl loaded me into the passenger seat and then drove the whole way to the helipad without turning the headlights on. When I saw the helicopter I couldn't hold my peace anymore.

"Where are we—"

"*Silence*," Karl demanded.

He stopped and pulled me from the Land Rover, lifted me not into the cockpit but the passenger compartment instead, and then climbed in after.

One of the jets was waiting for us at the airstrip, its red blinking beacon light the only color piercing the inky darkness, diligently warning anyone nearby that the engines were turning. After we boarded—Karl pulling me up the stairs, gently but insistently by my wounded wrist—he strapped me into the first passenger seat. A roller bag was under the seat on the other side. While I was looking at it, Karl did something very strange. He walked out of the cabin and down the stairs to the tarmac, pushed the stairs back up, closed the cabin door, and latched it from the outside. I was confused at first. I spun around to look over my shoulder. The cabin was empty. I was the lone passenger.

The plane's engines spooled up from idle. The jet started to taxi. I ripped off my seat belt, crossed the cabin, slammed into the opposite cabin wall (causing my left breast to throb again), and pressed my hands against the window to look out. Karl was alone on the side of the taxiway, fixed; watching me. A dark statue illuminated in bloodred spurts to the pulsing heartbeat of the jet's beacon light.

"Grandfather," I sobbed, blinded by tears, pleading with him somehow to hear me, wherever he was. "Please, no. I'm sorry. I promise I'll be good."

It was dark, but I could still see Karl standing near the taxiway as the jet lifted off and climbed. I watched right up until the last second, when the plane passed through the low ceiling and our lands below were swallowed up by a sea of dark gray cloud.

PART III

TRUSTS AND ESTATES

CHAPTER TWENTY-TWO

Exile

THREE HOURS INTO THE FLIGHT IT was obvious that I was not being taken to Academy Le Gudin, a destination that would have had us on the ground after barely an hour and a half. I should have chanced knocking on the cockpit door, but I was afraid the pilots would just ignore me and that the feeling of solitary confinement in the cabin would have been worse than if I had never knocked at all.

The wound Augustin had left me with throbbed every time I moved, but I was too full of nervous energy to sit still. An airborne captive with nothing to do, I decided to open the hard-sided, roller suitcase that had been left for me. Inside, atop a hastily packed bundle of wrinkled, casual clothes, I found a little, bright red covered book. There was a large white cross on the front where "Swiss Passport" was written in five languages. The document claimed to have been issued over a year earlier but smelled of freshly melted plastic. Though the picture inside the cover was the same as in my real passport, the name listed was unfamiliar and, according to the printed date of birth, the strange girl was fourteen, two years my senior. Someone, somewhere had erased me and filled the empty space with an older Swiss girl.

I thought of the Sophias, one apparently scrubbed from records by persons unknown over three hundred years before, and one created from thin air by my brother. It struck me how easy it was to delete or invent people.

Tucked under the wrinkled clothes, I found a thick envelope. Inside were several bundles of US dollars. Next to the envelope was a small wooden box I recognized instantly: Professor Lechner's writing kit. Had my grandfather thought to include it? Had Karl? Why?

Just thinking about Professor Lechner caused a flurry of emotions that threatened to reduce me to a blubbering mess. I put the writing kit aside and dug through the bag expecting to come across a note of some kind, printed instructions, some words of encouragement; but there was nothing.

Dejected, I dug around in the overhead compartments until I found the plane's med kit. I stripped off the makeshift field dressing on my breast. The bloodied washcloth strips stuck to my skin painfully when I peeled them away and started the awful laceration to bleeding again. After disinfecting it and packing the wound properly with gauze, I wrapped an Ace bandage around my torso to hold it all in place. I took some extra gauze and elastic bandages and stowed them in the hard-sided case. I buried the bloody washcloth strips and the ruined silk scarf in the bottom of the trash container and hoped that whoever cleaned up wouldn't find the gore-covered cloth.

After that, there was nothing to do but wait.

~⚬~

I WAS JOLTED AWAKE when the plane landed. The sun was up, and as the jet taxied I caught a glimpse of a sign: JOHN F. KENNEDY INTERNATIONAL AIRPORT.

We rolled to the general aviation section of the airport, where a man in a suit stood waiting next to a black limousine with darkened windows. The cabin door was opened, my bag collected from me, and I was led down the stairs straight into the car's empty passenger compartment, sealed off from the driver by a raised partition. We drove off the tarmac and onto the highway without delay. It was in this way that, without ever having seen my pilots or having been so much as glanced at by an immigration or customs official, I first entered the United States.

More than two hours later, well into Connecticut, the car pulled through a gate that read "Curie Hall." Unable to believe the coincidence, at first I thought I was dreaming. A pang of homesickness and thoughts of my grandfather came to me.

The grounds were pretty in the late Thursday morning sun. The buildings looked neo-Gothic, though I suspected they were not remotely as old as they were meant to appear. The light flickered down through tall trees and uniformed girls milled here and there over the deep green lawns in front of ivy-covered buildings, or sat on a number of white stone benches set around koi ponds.

Boarding school.

The main building was at the end of the long drive through the campus that terminated in a circular driveway. My driver led me in, past the reception area, and into an office, which, judging by the sign on the door, contained one Dr. Emily P. Templeton-Wright, PhD, Headmistress.

Ignoring my escort, the Headmistress tilted her head and looked at me over a pair of silver, neck-chained reading glasses. Surprisingly, my normally automatic urge to curtsy in such a situation was not too powerful to resist, and though I'm not sure why it seemed so important at the time, I managed to stand completely still instead.

"Ah, the late arrival." Her manner was businesslike, but not in a mean way. That much at least gave me some hope. "We are well into the spring term already and you have missed tryout day for athletics. I will have a word with the director to see if we might make an exception in your case. I suppose I must also send to the school store for your uniforms. I do hope the stocks are not empty at this late date. It seems we have already made a number of exceptions for you. I hope this will not become a habit."

The pause in her delivery seemed designed to elicit a response from me, and my plan to pose as a non–English speaker melted quickly in the face of her expectant stare.

"No, ma'am," was all I could come up with but, given Dr. Templeton-Wright's nod, it was apparently the desired reply.

These formalities dispensed with, she picked up the phone and spoke to an unseen secretary.

"Kathleen, will you send one of the girls to join us please?" She hung up without waiting for a reply.

"Ah, here is Miss Winkelman." The Headmistress nodded to the uniformed girl who appeared outside her office door: a perfectly manicured blonde who, though she appeared to be destined for a more zaftig figure later in life, as a teen was possessed of a sort of effortless and flawless beauty.

"Don't let's lurk around there in the hallway," the Headmistress scolded. "Come in."

Dr. Templeton-Wright handed a card and a key to the girl.

"Kindly escort our newest student to her room, help her get orientated, and show her around the grounds," she ordered. "Then make sure to introduce her to the House Mother."

"She gets to stay in Corbin House?" the girl said with a huff after looking at the card.

"*Now*, Miss Winkelman," the Headmistress said.

I HAD SPOKEN EXACTLY two words and been greeted in such a routine way that it made me wonder how often dazed young women, looking for all the world as if they had recently (and only just) escaped a serious car accident, or some other sudden trauma, arrived at Curie Hall in the company of a silent driver who then vanished at the earliest opportunity.

The blonde, Miss Winkelman, was maybe sixteen years old and had no interest at all in being friendly. We barely exchanged a word as I struggled to keep up behind her.

Corbin House was pleasant enough, a white, three-story building surrounded by well-manicured shrubs. Having delivered me, my unwilling guide handed me the card and key.

"Have fun," she sneered, and then added a cryptic closing: "We'll see you later."

With that she turned and left me standing alone. My orientation tour and introductions had been neglected, so I went inside. In the little foyer I was greeted with crusty-looking portraits on the walls and a few well-worn wooden chairs and tables. I must have arrived at an odd hour, because aside from one girl I passed on the stairs on my way to the third floor, the house seemed empty. Though I knocked twice on the door to my room, no one answered, so I let myself in.

It was a tiny cell. There were two single beds crammed against opposite walls in the little room. Not only was I to be confined to a living space smaller than the closets in my apartments, but it seemed I would be sharing that meager space with a roommate.

The missing girl's things were littered everywhere. Obviously, she was not expecting company.

It wasn't even noon, but a wave of crushing fatigue crashed over me.

Looking up from the little bed, I took in the ceiling, which felt so close that I thought I might be able to reach up and touch it. When I closed my eyes, I felt sure it was inching toward my face while I wasn't looking.

Time did not improve matters. An hour later, I shivered with chills and my muscles ached. It felt an effort even to breathe. After another hour, I couldn't even get out of bed without a Herculean effort that left me drained and in great pain. At first I thought it might be an infection from my wound, but when I changed the dressing again it still looked clean. Still, whatever I had caught from the new environment, the symptoms were miserable.

As time wore on, somewhere from the inky dark, I had a fevered memory of disjointed voices.

"Some new firsty is sick," I heard one say.

"Why is a new firsty in our house?"

"How should I know?"

I kept expecting someone to notice and tell the "House Mother" or take me to the school nurse or whatever passed for a medical professional at Curie Hall, but I was left to my own devices. Had Miss Winkelman even told anyone about my arrival?

I slipped in and out of dark dreams. In one dispiriting nightmare I imagined some girl poking me on the forehead to see if I was still alive. When I woke someone had left a set of new uniforms at the foot of my bed, which made me wonder if the dream had been real.

BY THE TIME I recovered, it was morning and I was sticky from sweating through my fever. I had no concept of how much time had passed. I stripped off my bandages once more, stuffing them in the bottom of the only wastebasket in the room and noting that I only had enough supplies for one more dressing. Then I found my way to the showers. I had to keep the water only lukewarm to keep from lighting up the nerves in my left breast, but standing under the showerhead—little more than a partially clogged spigot on the end of a garden hose, and a far cry from the torrential streams that flowed from half a dozen nozzles in my bathroom back home—was the restorative I needed.

Back in my room, I put my last bandages on, tucked my day bag in the little armoire on what I assumed was my side, and set out my new school clothes. The uniform I tried on—a dark red plaid skirt and matching tie, white collared shirt, knee-high socks, and a blazer with the school's seal on an embroidered breast patch—fit well enough, though I was unused to wearing shorter skirts and it felt strange having my knees and thighs exposed to the open air. How anyone had come to know my sizes so well was a mystery.

Trying to settle in, I laid Professor Lechner's writing kit on my desk. The inkwells contained blue and black ink and I opened them to try out one of the nib pens. Was it included to encourage me to write home?

I caught myself gazing out the tiny window. My stomach growled and so I tried to summon the courage to venture out of my room. I had just about resolved to explore the campus when there was a knock at my door. The moment I opened it, Miss Winkelman and three other girls barged past me into the room. Being unfamiliar with the machinations of packs of other girls my age, I did not recognize any of the warning signs that were written on their faces.

"Sasha, Mrs. Peterson is right down the hall," one of the girls warned, in a low whisper.

Miss Winkelman was not remotely perturbed. "No, she's off grounds today. Besides, you know that all new girls get the treatment."

That's when Sasha produced the ruler—a yardstick broken in half—from behind her back. It was a wicked-looking implement worn with use, and though I had never seen one before, it was immediately obvious to me what they intended to do with it. My heart started to race.

"Mara, Tammy, take her wrists and bend her over the bed. Laura, get her skirt up and her panties down."

The moment they heard Sasha's orders, the other girls transformed from interested bystanders into feral participants. Together they advanced on me with evident relish.

The thought came to me unbidden and in a flash:

If his forces are united, separate them. Attack him where he is weak, appear where you are not expected.

"Sun Tzu," I whispered.

"What did you say?" the girl called Tammy said, but my mind was already elsewhere.

Even the most adroit men have a weakness. It was Professor Lechner's voice. *Some have half a dozen.*

It was Sasha's perfectly pressed uniform and flawlessly coifed hair that gave me the rest.

Vanity.

I glanced behind me and Professor Lechner's writing kit caught my eye. It is a long way from conceiving a tactic or stratagem to taking action. I might not have been able to summon the energy to put the plan that formed into effect, but for the way the one called Mara grinned at me. It reminded me of Augustin and the razor, and that was more than enough to trigger my "fight or flight" response.

Almost before I knew it, I had hurled the black inkwell at Sasha with all my strength. The motion toppled the writing kit onto the ground but the glass inkwell hit her right in the forehead and a thin sheet of carbon-black ink cut the air between us and splattered the torsos and faces of all four girls. Whether unused to resistance or simply shocked at being splashed, my assault stopped them in their tracks.

"Oh my fucking god," the one called Mara moaned. "You've fucking ruined my uniform. Mrs. Peterson is going to kill me. My parents are going to kill me."

She looked like she was about to cry. Her voice cracked and she let out a long moan before turning and bolting out of the room. Wordlessly, the girl called Tammy followed her.

Deprived of the full complement of her assault group, Sasha looked at the remaining girl and reassessed her position.

"We are going to make you regret that, firsty," she said.

I suppose I should have been afraid, but with ink dripping from her face it was hard to take Sasha seriously. While I was considering this, the resolve of the remaining girl, Laura, I supposed, melted away too. After rubbing her face and looking down at her hands to find them covered in ink, she also slipped out of my room.

"We don't need them," Sasha said to the empty room behind her. "It's two-on-one."

"Not anymore," I said. I kept my voice even and calm, trying to emulate the way I thought my father might speak.

Ink was running into Sasha Winkelman's eyes. She tried to blink it away and turned around. When she saw that she was alone, her voice took on a desperate tone.

"Where the hell did you cowards go?" she demanded of the hallway outside.

Then, rubbing her eyes (which only seemed to get more ink in them), she made to bolt out of the room. Instead, her vision impaired, she clipped the side of the doorjamb. Her left cheekbone connected with the unyielding frame and emitted a disconcertingly loud crack.

Sasha dropped to a knee and, before she recovered to standing, a pain-stricken wailing emanated from her, loud enough to echo down the hall. Once she regained her feet, she fled and I closed the door behind her.

⌒

AFTER THEY WERE gone, I sank into a sitting position on the floor and tried to keep from trembling. That's when I noticed something strange about Professor Lechner's writing kit: the bottom had come loose when it had impacted the ground, revealing a narrow space underneath.

A hidden compartment.

Tipped over when I had flung its counterpart at Sasha, the remaining inkwell had emptied into the bottom of the writing kit and flooded the hidden compartment with blue ink. I mopped up what I could and lifted out the false bottom. Underneath, I found a piece of folded paper and a chain necklace with a dingy, oval pendant the size of a small coin. It looked like it was made from dirty pewter. It, along with the folded paper, was thoroughly soaked with blue ink.

I took the pendant to the bathroom and did my best to wash it off in the sink, but the fine lace-like metalwork of the piece was difficult to clean and, even after almost fifteen minutes, the little corners and crevices still harbored bits of blue.

Was it a gift from Professor Lechner? My grandfather? Karl? Only then did it occur to me that the paper might explain if the necklace was intended for me, or if it was some unrelated heirloom kept hidden in the writing kit.

Back in my room, I unfolded the paper but found the ink-soaked document illegible. Desperate, I held it up next to the bulb in my roommate's desk lamp to see if the author had left detectable impressions in the paper, but either they had not existed in the first place, or the paper had expanded when it soaked up the blue ink. Eventually I even tried to wash the new ink away, hoping that might reveal what it had tainted. But the paper was thin and fragile and I ended up with nothing more than a wad of blue pulp for my efforts.

Defeated, I did my best to clean up the ink splatters I had left all over the room, but most of it had dried, leaving traces of my altercation on the walls near the door, and a large blue spot on the floor by the desk.

I held the pendant in my palm for a long time, searching for answers that never came. Eventually, I gave up. The chain was quite long so I looped it double around my neck, which let the pendant hang just above my sternum and away from my wounded breast.

~◦~

MY ROOMMATE MELANIE appeared soon enough. She was a shortish brunette with nervous hands that never seemed to stop fidgeting and what I would later recognize as a New York accent, a drawl she proceeded to lash me with in a small tantrum over the ink I had spilled.

"Did you shower this place with black paint the moment you arrived or did you at least wait an hour?"

I didn't bother to explain that it was ink, not paint.

"I'm telling Mrs. Peterson," she screeched, when she found one of her plaid uniform skirts had been ruined. "You're paying for this. And stay on your side of the room from now on."

My introduction to Mrs. Peterson, Corbin House's "House Mother," followed hard upon, in a cramped room at the end of the hall, scarcely bigger than the one I shared with my new roommate. It was the middle of the day and warm enough outside, and yet the steam radiator had been turned all the way up and the air was sweltering. Our House Mother looked nearly seventy years old, and though I didn't fully recognize them until later, early hints of senility littered her behavior. She listened to Melanie's complaints passively before dismissing her.

"It is important to get along with our roommates," Mrs. Peterson said to me, once we were alone. Then she was distracted by something and fell to absent searching. "Have you seen my reading glasses, dear?"

"No," I managed, though I was quite sure that she was referring to the pair she was already wearing.

"Off with you then," she said, shooing me. "Or you will be late for dinner."
It was barely one in the afternoon.

Eventually I learned that Corbin House was an abode much in demand
owing to the fact that Mrs. Peterson (who, in her spare time, spent hours
methodically collecting random bits of string and yarn) routinely retired for
the evening just after six thirty (and slept like the dead besides). As a result,
she made for an entirely ineffectual chaperone.

It wasn't long before my encounter with Sasha Winkelman and the other
girls bloomed into a flurry of rumors that, collectively, had an interesting
effect. My fraudulent identity hid the fact that I was nearly two years younger
than the rest of my class, but I was smaller than the other girls, a first year,
and a redhead to boot. These things should have conspired to make me the
object of routine bullying and hazing, but after the scrap with Sasha, and given
the fact that I wasn't immediately expelled after the incident, I had a bit of a
reputation. In fact, no one in the faculty or administration ever mentioned
the fight to me, making me suspect that Sasha and the other girls had never
admitted my involvement to any figure of authority.

The gossip was understandable. The Curie student body was distinctly
homogenized, and apparently prone to melodrama. I once heard Melanie call
it the "WASP nest" and, once I learned the acronym, I saw what she meant.
The class lists were saturated with Ashburys, Hancocks, Whitneys, and even
the odd Worthington now and again.

I had little desire to socialize with my schoolmates, so being thought
of as dangerous in such company had its advantages. Nevertheless, vaguely
alarmed by the violence of my encounter with Sasha and her little clique, and
afraid that snooping and even theft might be within the capacity of certain
members of the student body, late one night after Melanie fell asleep I taped
my passport to the underside of one of my desk drawers. After that, I took
several hundred-dollar bills from the cash-filled envelope that had been left
in my suitcase and wrapped the rest in two plastic rubbish bags. Then I crept
outside and buried them near one of the maple trees at the edge of the grounds.

CHAPTER TWENTY-THREE

All-Girls

I N RETROSPECT, IF I GREW UP too quickly in my years on the estate, I "grew down" at Curie; or at least I learned to act more like I supposed the girl in the passport was expected to.

I tried not to think about the vault, my grandfather, or the way I had betrayed him and my father. Still, I couldn't forget the look in Augustin's eyes when he tried to drag me up the stairs. Or the horrific sound Bastien had made; the blood on his shoes. Or Professor Lechner's stiffening dead body. So many horrible things had happened in such a short span that I had no time to properly mourn. Curie, being in comparison rather slow-paced, even a little dull, was good for that, at least.

Happy for the solitude, I took to sneaking out onto Corbin House's roof to stare at the sky as the sun set and the stars came out. It was of no compare to the views into the valley from the spires atop the manor, or the stars above the estate, bright and brilliant in inky skies devoid of light pollution, but it gave me some comfort to be under an open sky somewhere, even if the twinkling stars seemed pale and distant.

Some of the other houses must have had inattentive chaperones as well, as there were several packs of girls who crept outside after "lights-out." They gathered in little gaggles, gravitating toward the shadows behind the houses to take turns sipping from a forbidden flask or smoking together in the dark. Some nights you could see the glowing embers clustered in several far-off groups—orange spots arcing up slowly, pausing, pulsing bright as they were force-fed oxygen, obscured by smoke, and then slowly fading again before darting down to waist level and waiting for the cycle to be repeated.

Curie Hall was not actually named for Madam Curie, but rather the unrelated founder of the school. Going by the oversize, faded, and dust-covered portrait of her that hung in the main hall, Elizabeth Curie was the decrepit widow of some long-forgotten industrialist whose memory she had hastened to erase by reverting to her maiden name immediately after his death.

The artist of the depiction had to be given marks for bravery. It was brutally frank, and the imperious and dour scowl on Mrs. Curie's face looked as if it had been fixed there for each of the seventy-two years she had lived prior to her sitting for the portrait.

I wanted to hate Curie Hall.

I wanted to hate the "all-girls" policy, which I was told was oppressive.

I wanted to hate all the girls, too, since, with few exceptions, my peers were the worst kind of vapid and boring.

I wanted to hate our clichéd red and black plaid schoolgirl uniforms and the (as-yet-unmasked) pervert that I was sure secretly manipulated school policy to mandate them.

I wanted to hate the campus itself, along with the cramped, faux-old buildings that comprised it.

I wanted to hate the trite curriculum.

Most of all, I wanted to hate that I was a student there against my will.

But I didn't. Not really.

For as much as my peers complained about the all-girls policy, it was novel to be surrounded by girls my age, or nearly so, a circumstance I had never before experienced. The only pervasive feminine influence in my life had been my mother (excepting perhaps the occasional bursts of warmth that Cipriana had shown me in private). But my mother had always treated me more as an inconvenient ward than a daughter. At least at Curie Hall there were moments when it was not just permissible to be a teenage girl, but required.

Slowly, I grew used to the uniforms and even managed to make peace with the campus, which, though no competition for the beauty of the estate, still had its charms.

As for my contempt for the curriculum, in this at least I had cause. For, whatever else might have been said about Professor Lechner's unconventional approach, he left me far beyond even my fourth-year classmates in classical studies, history, literature, and philosophy. I missed him terribly, but I don't think I really knew how brightly my affection for him had once burned until I sat through an almost intolerably shallow European History module at Curie Hall.

I had little choice but to learn to cope with the deficient academics. Still, it took me some time to understand that many of the topics the Professor and I had explored together (especially topics that I had most looked forward to discussing) had the potential to terrify both my classmates and teachers.

Only a week into the soul crushing European History lectures, I unwittingly stumbled onto dangerous ground. Somehow I found myself describing to my teacher the successful counterinsurgency campaign of the British in postwar Malaya, a notoriously brutal fight against mostly communist guerrillas that was particularly hard on rural civilians. Once I had finished my comment, the horrified silence of my peers and instructor alike made it obvious that the open-ended and free-flowing discussions I had been used to were more than out of place at Curie Hall.

Some weeks later, I made the mistake of repeating, this time in my philosophy class, my grandfather's comments about the necessity of leaders to be entirely amoral or even immoral in order to grant their subjects or followers the luxury of morality. Dr. Fredericks was so mortified by my statement that he held me after class for more than an hour to endure a somewhat hysterical lecture on ethics. After that, I almost never participated in classroom discussions, or spoke my mind when any member of the faculty or staff was within earshot.

In tenebris, salus, I recited to myself now and again. *In the darkness, safety.*

AFTER MY BRUSHES with unwanted attention, I resolved to spend more time observing my peers. At first out of boredom, but eventually as a kind of defensive reflex, I found myself experimenting with ways to predict, and eventually to influence, their behavior. It wasn't particularly difficult. Most girls were anything but discreet, and even the dimmest ember of rumor seemed destined to catch dry social tinder and flash across the grounds like wildfire. Intrigued by these dynamics, I set out to map the lattice-like interconnections of these social neurons. What I found was an alarmingly efficient communication network—one that was quick to speed news, gossip, and rumors to every corner of the student body, and beyond.

When one of the first-year girls repeated the rumor, later proved false, that Mrs. Bennington, one of the math teachers at Curie, was about to be fired, I sensed an opportunity. I overheard her relay the gossip to an eager huddle of whispering first-years sitting at the table next to me. When I found the source later and asked her where she had learned the tidbit, she was more than happy to brag about her sub-source.

Remembering the works of the Swiss Major Hans von Dach pertaining to identifying leaks in resistance, military, and intelligence organizations, I repeated this process several times and managed to trace the information all the way to its origin. After a few more such efforts, and many days of observing who spoke with whom in the dining room and the outdoor clusters that formed after dark, the contours of the networks began to reveal themselves to me.

As it turned out, most of the information that flowed through the student body originated from a girl named Katie Park, a third-year who had been the last editor of the Curie Hall student newspaper, which, as I later learned, had been disbanded by the administration after an article had (quite accurately) predicted a faculty member's impending divorce. Katie's mother taught French at Curie, which explained Katie's seemingly prescient ability to predict the private and official actions of Curie's faculty and administration well in advance of any formal announcement.

Less than two weeks after the disbanding of the official school paper, a newly created, underground newsletter that Katie apparently founded was discovered and also quashed by the administration. In the wake of the death of a free Fourth Estate on campus, Katie apparently felt it her honor-bound duty to keep the student body informed by other, more clandestine means: the sophisticated gossip network that laced through campus.

Now and again I saw Katie in the company of another girl, a second-year, though she looked at least seventeen to me, named Phoebe. The two of them were prone to whispering in corners, or sitting alone at a table in the dining room, where Phoebe made a habit of fending off anyone who wandered too close with a hard glare from her brilliant, cornflower-blue eyes. She was intriguing for reasons I couldn't have articulated at the time. Her face was framed with tangled, dirty-blond hair that she wore long, well past her shoulders, and her lips were chapped, suggesting that she didn't care for them particularly well. The natural set of her expression had a sad aspect. A rather severe-looking scar—harsh cuts of white on even whiter skin—was shaped like two sides of an equilateral triangle pointed from her temple at her right eye. The collective effect made her look predisposed to melancholy.

Right away, I had the impression that, in addition to her other high-level sources, Katie routinely leaned on Phoebe for the juicier bits of gossip she trafficked in. How Phoebe came across these morsels, I did not know.

Whatever their primary source, waves of gossip always seemed to originate from the upperclass houses. These were clustered together on the edge of campus farthest from the administration and classroom buildings. As the first-year houses were on the other side, close in to the administration offices and the faculty residences, the first-years were usually last to learn anything useful. They had to wait until lunch the day after the rumor's genesis, when table conversation finally spread the delayed bulletins to them.

If rumors were to reach the faculty or administration at all it was through the self-important and officious Gabby Carter, an unfortunately plump, essentially friendless second-year who was all too happy to relay anything and everything she heard directly to her mother, the assistant bursar. Gabby was Katie's cousin, which explained why the uber-popular Katie would deign to converse with a socially outcast second-year.

As a population, my peers seemed unusually prone to sudden spasms of competitive (or even malicious) behavior that I took to be driven mostly by the insecurities of packs of sheltered and nervous girls. In interacting with them, I learned to be quick to listen, even to their most neurotic and pathetic complaints, and to make the expected sympathetic noises in response, but hesitant to offer much of my own views or opinions. Being friendly with girls outside your usual social circles presented hazards, as you might find another girl threatened by your emerging relationship with their "bestie."

Even well-meaning kindnesses could trigger dangerous efforts at sabotage from unseen rivals.

After almost wandering into such a trap by talking once too often to Katie Park, a quote from Sun Tzu came to me:

> *To secure ourselves against defeat lies in our own hands, but the opportunity of defeating the enemy is provided by the enemy himself.*

I vowed to avoid overt affection with any other Curie girl until I was certain I understood the nature of her existing social bonds. Cautious and cultivated neutrality, I found, allowed me to insulate myself from many of the scraps and disputes in which other girls found themselves entangled.

～◯

IT WAS A bit Machiavellian of me, perhaps, but I couldn't help but test my newfound knowledge of Curie's social networks. It was Mrs. Rupert's English Literature exam that provided the fuel for the conflagration I started that first term.

One afternoon during lunch, I was witness to a conflict of sorts among the field hockey players. Beth and Stacey, the team's two cocaptains, were berating their teammate Daphne, an awkward and skittish first-year who spent more time with the school nurse than anyone else I knew, while a fourth girl, Amy—fork frozen in the air, halfway raised to her open mouth—listened intently.

"Hasn't anyone told you that the team has to maintain a minimum GPA?" Stacey demanded of an increasingly brittle-looking Daphne. "Coach Righter will make us all run laps until we drop, or even cut you from the team if she thinks you are going to get probation."

"I didn't know," Daphne said, and seemed to shrink even further into her already diminutive frame.

"Everyone knows that," Beth snapped.

Stacey looked furious. "Mrs. Rupert's exams are no joke. You fucking better hit the books tonight, *Daffy*."

"Hey," Amy protested, putting down her fork and looking around furtively. "Language."

Stacey and Beth rolled their eyes. When the three of them got up, Stacey made a point of bumping into Daphne's half-full glass of milk, dumping the contents right into her lap.

The rest of the field hockey team laughed, and Daphne managed to force a strained grin—good sport, that Daphne; nice to have first-years with a bit of salt for a change—but once the rest of the team started to filter away, I could see the beginnings of tears in her eyes.

THAT NIGHT, LONG after Melanie's breathing slowed, I lay awake thinking about what I had heard. Mrs. Rupert's exams were three-hour horrors that had never managed to reduce fewer than two girls to tears. They typically included four complex essay questions. One year's example included the soul-crushing demand:

> *Compare and contrast the themes of austerity, sacrifice, hope, and hopelessness in John Steinbeck's* The Grapes of Wrath *with the role of beauty, sensual fulfilment, and the redemptive function of art in Oscar Wilde's* The Picture of Dorian Gray. *In your analysis include your own view as to which view of redemption (or corruption) is more persuasive: that of Steinbeck's altruistic but murderous vigilante Tom Joad, or Wilde's hedonistic Lord Henry Wotton.*

Answers to Mrs. Rupert's tests had to be handwritten, and it was essentially impossible to pass without frantically filling in at least six "blue book" answer books. Even worse, Mrs. Rupert was prone to deduct points for poor penmanship. Her tests were frightful rites of passage and, as I lay in the dark, her upcoming exam seemed to me a singular opportunity.

A Sun Tzu passage surfaced again and again in my late-night thoughts:

> *A ground of inevitable contention is any natural barricade or strategic pass.*

The impending doom of Mrs. Rupert's exam had the dining hall buzzing, even among students who were not subject to the tyranny of her instruction. I started the rumor with five second-years huddled together at the table next to mine. I didn't know any of them particularly well, but they gave me the perfect opening.

"I hate her class," the brunette complained.

"Mrs. Rupert's?" one of the others, a girl with her hair up in a bun, offered.

The brunette was annoyed. "Duh. It's going to ruin my grades for the whole term."

"She grades on a curve, you know. Everyone, like, fails, so nobody does."

I turned around in my chair and whispered, "I heard that the curve is going to get wrecked."

As one, they froze and glared, trying to figure out who I was.

"You don't know anything," the bun girl insisted, once she recovered.

Laura . . . I struggled to remember her last name. *Williams? Willard?*

"No one blows the curve in Mrs. Rupert's class," Laura was saying.

"Someone has the test questions," I whispered.

"What?" the brunette hissed, alarmed.

Instantly, all five of them were fixated on me, hanging on every expression, looking for anything that would tend to confirm or deny this new and shocking piece of information.

"No way," Laura managed, but I could tell she believed me.

"That's not fair," the brunette said and, as it sank in, her expression shifted from skepticism to despair. "That's totally not fair."

"How do you know?" Laura said, hints of disbelief returning.

"That's what I heard."

"From who?"

"From whom," another corrected.

"Shut up, Jenny," Laura said, and turned back to me.

"I don't know." I shrugged. "Everyone is saying it."

The brunette's panic was growing. "Multiple people have the questions," she said.

I declined to point out that this was not, in fact, what I had said.

"Shhhh," Laura scolded, and glanced around. "Someone might hear you."

The brunette bit her lower lip. "Who has them?" she demanded of me.

"How should I know? I'm not even in that class."

She surveyed the dining hall, and I could see her sizing up her classmates. "This is so unfair."

"It's probably just a dumb rumor," I said.

"It's probably nothing, Kimmy," Laura said, and put her hand on the brunette's shoulder.

"Nothing?" Kimmy snapped, near tears. She jabbed a finger capped with bubble-gum-pink nail polish in my direction. "She's not even *in Mrs. Rupert's class* and she knows. I have to find out who has them."

"Isn't that an honor code violation?" the grammar expert asked.

"Shut up, Jenny," the girls moaned in unison.

⌒

I WAS READING IN our common room less than an hour later when I heard the rumor repeated between two third-year girls.

"I heard that, too," I volunteered.

They stared at me, annoyed that I had intervened in their private conversation.

"Mind your own business, firsty," one of them said.

"Who did you hear it from?" the other asked.

"I'm not supposed to tell," I said, looking down at the ground.

"I'm not going to tell anyone. I'm just curious. Come on," she cooed. "We're housemates."

"I heard it from Katie Park," I said.

"What? The third-year? Really? Wow."

The rumor confirmed, the two girls scampered upstairs.

⌒

BY THE NEXT morning it seemed there wasn't a single student who didn't know for certain that Mrs. Rupert's test questions had been stolen. In some quarters, the tale grew with the telling. The administration knew and was rapidly closing in on the perpetrator. The administration was clueless, and the thief had actually made off with the midterm and final exam questions for the next Rupert course, a rather unlikely claim. Mrs. Rupert planned to cancel the exam. Mrs. Rupert had planted the questions in an elaborate sting operation. Mrs. Rupert was so upset by the honor code violation that she was quitting forever.

Each new iteration seemed to breed with the existing corpus of gossip, mutate, and then emerge on the other side of the Curie information network in a different form. Even though I could not see any way that matters could be traced back to me, things were moving so fast that the entire situation was frightening, especially when speculation as to the identity of the perpetrator began to leak into the mix. Worse still, Mrs. Rupert's exam was scheduled for the end of the day.

Finally, in the dining hall for lunch, I made a point of sitting behind Gabby Carter, the assistant bursar's daughter. It took no time at all for the topic of conversation to turn to the pilfered exam questions. I waited until the right moment, turned my legs sideways to face my tablemate, a first-year named Becky, and cupped my hand as if to whisper in her ear, angling it so that, sitting with her back to me, Gabby would be sure to hear.

"It was Stacey from the field hockey team," I intoned in a loud whisper, remembering the taunting she and the other girls had given the hapless Daphne. "She was showing the questions around last night."

Out of the corner of my eye I could see Gabby's back stiffen. She even leaned back a little and cocked her ear in my direction.

"From Thorpe House?" my amazed neighbor gasped.

"Exactly," I said, taking a wild guess.

"Well, that figures," she said.

By then, Gabby was leaning back so far in her chair I wondered if she might not fall into our laps.

THE REACTION WAS swift. Not two hours later I was walking across the grounds when I spotted a cluster of students standing outside Thorpe House. My stomach lurched and I thought about running back to my room, but that would surely be noticed. Instead I steeled myself and walked up to the gathered crowd.

"What's happening?" I asked the closest girl.

"Stacey Lawrence got busted for stealing the questions to Mrs. Rupert's exam," she said.

"They found it in her roommate Beth's desk, not Stacey's," another girl corrected.

"That's not what I heard," the first girl said. "They only found a bottle of vodka."

"That part I know is true," the second girl said. "Dr. Templeton-Wright barged into their room and searched everything. They found the vodka right in her desk drawer and then Beth accused Stacey of planting it and Stacey called her a lying cunt."

A collective gasp from the assembled girls.

"That's not true," someone called.

"It's absolutely true. Katie Park said so."

"Really?" the naysayer gasped, cowed by the impeccable credentials of the source.

"I heard Mrs. Templeton-Wright slapped Stacey right in the mouth," said another girl.

"No, that's a false rumor."

"I heard the exam got canceled."

"Yeah," the tale-teller said, and smiled to herself. "That was pretty awesome."

I WAS SHAKEN BY the impact my scheme had, and more than a little intimidated that the power I had wielded had come to me so easily. My lessons with Professor Lechner, my grandfather's teachings, and the readings I had absorbed in those months had seemed so abstract back on the estate. Intellectually, I knew that the entire point of such knowledge was that it should eventually be used in practice, but actually seeing that power in action was something else. It frightened me. Moreover, I felt guilty for what I had done to Beth and Stacey. Had the tables been turned and had our room been searched for some reason, it was impossible to know what might have turned up in the bottom of Melanie's drawers.

To my alarm, a third girl, Jane, came under suspicion for a time, but she melted down into such a convincing (and pitiful) puddle of blubbering sobs and tears that no one believed she could be involved. Beth and Stacey seemed poised to bear the full brunt of the administration's lust for swift justice.

But Beth's father was an attorney and it was barely six hours after the vodka was found before he was sitting in the Headmistress's office. Between his intervention and the fact that Beth and Stacey's parents were large donors, what surely should have been an expellable violation was pled down to an admission of guilt, a one-term suspension, and a public apology by Beth and Stacey to the entire school, a penance they performed that very same night with admirably convincing humility.

I HAD SETTLED IN to Curie Hall the best I could but, even after the first two months and my apparent mastery of the social networks that drove my class-mates, the pull of the estate was never far from the surface of my thoughts. I had no particular evidence for the assumption that I could earn my grand-father's forgiveness (and the right to return to the estate) academically, but that didn't stop me from latching on to high grades with the hope that it was true. Unfortunately, it was hardly possible to indulge in the subjects I had found such a passion for back home. That kind of material simply didn't exist at Curie, and I was forced instead to digest a far different kind of academic fare.

The library at Curie Hall was a pale shadow of the estate's collection and Curie's repository had a number of more modern (and much triter) publications, particularly in the section where Curie students were invited to exchange their unwanted books with each other. Whatever the noble intentions of its founder, that corner of the library had become a dumping ground for pulp "young adult" novels, and trashy (and therefore well-worn) adult romance books carefully concealed behind the bottom shelves. The collection was capped off with a seemingly endless stack of time-yellowed teen fashion magazines.

I had never seen modern periodicals before, certainly not anything as frivolous as a fashion magazine. When I first found the pile of old *Seventeen* issues, I spent an entire evening alternately enthralled and horrified by them and then baffled that such topics—"Why I starved myself"; "The hottest guys in the country"; "Are you a psychic?"—seemed so popular. Eventually, however, the genre of "teen fashion" proved to be a critical tool in amassing the sort of pop-culture knowledge that underpinned almost all social interactions between Curie girls.

Having consumed several years of issues in a single sitting, I was taken by several observations. First, fashion was entirely and artificially mercurial. It was more or less impossible to keep up with the fads pushed by the periodicals. Obviously, the primary function of the chaos was to sell a new set of clothes and accessories every season (not to mention the magazines themselves). Second, a constant stream of profiles of new boy bands and teen idols served essentially the same function for the music and film industries.

My distaste for it notwithstanding, it wasn't long before the modern world found other ways to intrude. Curie's computer class loomed over the upcoming term and that put me in something of a panic. My grandfather hadn't believed in them and, though I had occasionally noticed my father with a boxy-looking IBM laptop (a device he refused to be seen with in the Grand Study), I had never so much as touched a computer and had no typing skills whatsoever.

Curie's computer lab housed nearly twenty new Apple Macintoshes and, desperate to conceal the degree to which I was ignorant of such things, I began to slip into the fluorescently illuminated room during off-hours first to use the typing instruction program, and then to practice basic programming. This, with great effort and many frustrations, I coaxed from a massive hardcover textbook on computer science meant for graduate students that I had pilfered from a professor's office.

But the modern world wasn't all sorrows for me. When our Humanities teacher wheeled in the video cart and played *Chinatown*, it was the first full motion picture I had ever seen. Captivated, I found myself near tears toward the end, not just because of the dramatic impact of the film itself, but because I was so taken with the novel experience of actually *watching* a piece of art. It was an emotion that was followed by a flash of resentful anger, directed primarily at my mother, that such a compelling medium, and one so rote to my classmates that they seemed bored by it, had been denied me for so many years. Eager to make up for lost time, I labored to consume cinema whenever and in whatever form I could.

All these novel experiences conspired to instill in me some measure of culture shock and, in its wake, a powerful bout of homesickness. I often longed for the anachronistic simplicity of the estate and, in so doing, began to develop a grudging sort of respect for my mother's more visceral horror of the modern. In difficult moments, I craved the familiarity of my old lessons, even my old tutors, but especially Professor Lechner; the smell of old paper in the Grand Library; my grandfather.

One particularly lonely night, I snuck away to the library and wrote the first of many letters to my grandfather. My early drafts were muddled, half-pleading screeds that made me sick to my stomach to reread. I threw many of them away. In later compositions, I struggled to broach the events that had occurred those last awful nights on the estate. Instead, I focused on topics of interest remembered from my studies with Professor Lechner. Toward the end of each letter I would try to pose an erudite question, hoping that I might prompt my grandfather to reply.

"Weitzmann's perversion of the term 'Renaissance' aside," I wrote in one, "I find works like *De cerimoniis aulae Byzantinae* emerging from this period more than worthy of the affront. Or have I become a Weitzmann apologist? I am certain I remember most of Weitzmann's works in the library. Unfortunately, the library here is of limited value when it comes to the Byzantine."

My missives were overwrought, trying much too hard. Though I wasn't sure how much overseas postage cost, nor entirely sure what address to use for the estate, I begged, borrowed, and stole stamps from the other girls, plastered a half dozen of them on my envelopes, and posted them anyway. Though I checked my box in the student mailroom every day, none were returned to me for "no such addressee" or "insufficient postage." This, at least, seemed promising.

As summer faded into fall and winter approached, I had written more than two dozen long letters to my grandfather. Despite this, I had not received a single note in return.

As winter break loomed, the girls on campus were abuzz with plans to go home. Melanie had taken to spouting seemingly endless monologues on her upcoming sailing trip to the British Virgin Islands, apparently a regular, monthlong pilgrimage for her family. Every day seemed to bring some new correspondence from her mother poring over the detailed preparations or reminding Melanie to bring books from her winter reading list, since there would be no chance to buy any in the islands.

I, on the other hand, had not had any contact whatsoever with anyone on the estate. Even if I'd had the courage to call someone, I had no idea what phone number I would have used or, having never used a telephone to call off the estate, how to dial internationally.

Finally, a few weeks before the end of the term, a letter addressed to me appeared in my student box. I opened the envelope to find a note from the Headmistress's office with the daunting heading: "Rules for Students Remaining on Grounds for the Winter Break."

Obviously, someone had decided that I would not be going home for the holidays.

EXAMS AND TERM paper deadlines fell on a Friday. Though I dreaded being left alone for the end of term, I was strangely content to find that, on returning from the dining hall after lunch that day, Melanie and the mass of packed suitcases that had somehow accumulated in our little room had vanished. Her last final had been that morning and she hadn't bothered to say goodbye.

Three hours later, virtually the entire campus had emptied, as if some wartime exodus had driven the Curie girls from their houses, fleeing before the advance of an unseen but terrible enemy. In its wake, a stark ghost town was all that remained and, minute by minute, the white houses grew ashen, their color abandoned to the pale dusk of fading light. Near as I could tell, no underclass students and only a few faculty members (including Mrs. Peterson) had stayed behind.

It had started to snow by then and, as evening fell, a cold silence descended over the campus and the entirety of the grounds was blanketed in white. As night came, I took to wandering, leaving behind lonely strings of footprints, solitary paths in the virgin snow.

When I walked past the darkened windows of Thorpe House, site of the Beth and Stacey vodka bottle drama, I caught my reflection in the featureless black pools of the glass: a pale ghost, shivering underneath an overly thin overcoat from the school store; white flesh devoid of the last hints of summer sun; red hair sprinkled with a dusting of snowflakes.

Difficult thoughts came to me then: that, in the end, exiles had no real impact on the world. One stopped looking for them; eventually one stopped believing in them, and then they were truly gone.

I remembered reading about the poet Ovid, whom, "for a poem and a mistake," Emperor Augustus exiled to Tomis, a port city on the Black Sea that had no libraries. Ovid wrote many letters to his friends and wife, pleading that they should effectuate his return, but he was destined to die in Tomis and never see the glory of Rome again.

I remembered my many letters to my grandfather and thought of the Northern Ruins and Andres, my seventh great-uncle whose family had been banished there, his children forbidden to marry. Did my grandfather intend the same for me? Was I to be condemned to the all-girls purgatory of Curie Hall until I too started to show the early signs of senility, like Mrs. Peterson?

Line extinguished, my grandfather's voice breathed at me from somewhere.

My hand went to the dingy and still ink-stained pendant I had worn around my neck ever since finding it in Professor Lechner's writing kit. It was a reminder of home and, in that moment, I hated it and entertained thoughts of tearing it from my neck and throwing it into the snow.

I looked away from the windows and tried to shake off those dark feelings instead. On the other side of the grounds, I could see the odd second-floor window of the upperclass houses illuminated with the dim yellow glow of a random desk lamp. Unsure exactly why, but drawn to the light, I made my way in that direction. When I rounded Poole House, I saw a curious thing. Ellis House was generally rumored to be the nicest student lodging on campus. The bow windows on the first floor were illuminated with the flickering oranges and yellows of the fireplace in the common room.

I crept closer, feet crunching in the snow, breath turning to white, until I was only a few yards away from the glass. Frost had collected such that, though I could make out a fireplace and a figure—a Curie girl, certainly—sitting in a high-backed armchair reading a book near the warmth of the hearth, there was enough distortion that I couldn't make out her face.

Owing to the administration's horror of fire, even a hot plate was strictly forbidden in the underclass houses. The fireplace in Ellis House was a rare luxury, and the entire scene brought back flashes of holidays past: my grandfather reading some old tome, smoking his pipe by the fire in the Grand Study in the days before my father had taken it over; the one year that my mother had spontaneously decided to have decorated with hundreds of lights (powered with their own generator) a single, towering Austrian pine, a beacon in the middle of the dark forests near the mausoleum; a young Bastien, complaining that the ascot my mother had forced him to wear was itchy, and anxious to know when his presents might be delivered.

I must have stood there gawking for some time because, after she had turned a few pages, the upperclass girl chanced to look up and out the windows. At first I had the urge to run, but she had already seen me, and her gaze fixed me in place. Still obscured by the frost and ice, she stood and made her way to the windows. Eager, suddenly, for company, for another lonely exile to talk to, I thought to call to her, or to wave. But as soon as she reached the translucent barrier of ice and glass that separated us, she yanked the curtains closed.

~⊙~

I TRACKED BACK TO Corbin House and, unable to cope with the claustrophobic solitude of my room, made my way up to the roof to watch the snow fall. I leaned back in the pilfered lawn chair I had snuck up the folding stairs and through the trapdoor in the roof, looked up at the darkened sky, and started to cry.

Hours passed that way and I nearly fell asleep in that chair. Snapping back to lucidity just as, beginning to feel that intoxicating warmth that presages the onset of hypothermia, I started drifting into the semblance of a dream. This was a very dangerous thing. I was partly covered in snow and, horrified, I sprang up, shook the figurative cobwebs from my eyes, and hurried back to my room.

I was stunned that I had done something so stupid, especially having lived so long on the estate and oft listened in wide-eyed horror to tales (not always apocryphal) of hapless members of the domestic staff who had become lost in the snows only to be found again after their corpses were revealed by the spring thaws.

Soaked to the skin by the melting snow, I took off my outer layer and made my way to the showers to try to warm myself. Alone in front of the mirror, I barely recognized the girl who looked back at me. She seemed much older than the frail and frightened young thing that had arrived at Curie Hall only the spring term before.

I peeled off my wet shirt and stood topless. The scar Augustin left had knitted itself into a dark red gash carved into the freckled porcelain of the too-pale skin on my chest. I had gone to some lengths to avoid scrutinizing my marred form too closely, but what felt like a real brush with danger, with death even—for the calm warmth that had begun to take me on the roof had that feel to it—somehow cut through my squeamishness. When I looked again and saw, really saw, what my brother had left behind of my left nipple—the pale pink of a faded pencil eraser hacked diagonally into a chisel point—it brought tears to my eyes. But my mutilation at his hands seemed insignificant compared to the label Augustin had given me: *traitor*. A traitor to the family; exiled far across the sea to be forgotten. A wretch unworthy of my grand-father's notice, much less a letter bearing words written in his elegant hand.

I shook my head to clear it, collected myself the best I could, took a hot shower, and put myself to bed.

CHAPTER TWENTY-FOUR

Huldufólk

I SETTLED INTO A KIND OF purgatory after that winter and, by the time the spring term was at an end and summer emerged, I was entirely unsurprised to find in my student mailbox a letter addressed to me with an all-too-familiar structure. "Rules for Students Remaining on Grounds for the Summer Break," the heading read. It was nearly a word-for-word rendition of the document that had been delivered to me for the holiday break.

Before that second letter, I used to play out a kind of rescue fantasy over and over in my head. As final exams approached, I would be called into the Headmistress's office. The man sitting with her would turn around, revealing himself to be my grandfather. He would raise his white bushy eyebrows at me and I would know that all was forgiven and it was time to go home. As the jet made its way back over the ocean he would explain it all to me: why the estate had gone insane those last nights; who had tried to have my father and me killed in South Africa (and how they had been dealt with); what had happened to Augustin and Bastien; what secrets Professor Lechner had wanted me to know before he died; but, most of all, why it had been necessary to leave me incommunicado for so long.

After that letter, however, I could feel the acid of time eating away at my hopes for deliverance until I was all but resigned to a lingering fate of indeterminate duration. Winter break had been bad enough, and that was barely a month long. Summer, however, was twelve interminable weeks.

Worse, students remaining on campus over the summer were required to complete the summer curriculum, a schedule of six classes that included two taught (for some definition of that word) by Mrs. Peterson.

Unlike winter break, I wasn't the only underclass girl staying the summer. The upperclass girls who were staying had their own program on their side of campus and would never dream of wandering over to our little complex. Instead I was stuck with summer classmates like Sadie Rogers (a campus orphan whose parents had been killed in a car accident and whose aunt lived in Oregon) or Lily Parker (whose mother was a B-list actress of some note and rarely left Los Angeles). Their company only rubbed salt in my psychic wounds.

Still, it wasn't long before the sting of that slight was eaten away too. In a way, with a student and faculty population just large enough to be socially self-sufficient, Curie Hall seemed almost designed to that purpose. A series of numbing routines and traditions administered in a tranquil campus (and one carefully walled away from the outside world) lulled students and faculty alike into complacency, until it seemed entirely reasonable to regard Curie as a holding pattern that was an end unto itself.

I continued writing letters to my grandfather, for a time faithfully posting them once or twice a month in the outgoing box in the student mail room, wondering now and again when (or if) I might be favored with a reply. But eventually even this discipline, this last connection with the outside world, broke down until two or even three months might go by before I composed another.

JUST BEFORE FINALS, in the summer of 1994, someone snuck a VHS tape of *Jurassic Park* onto campus. Watching unapproved movies on school audiovisual hardware was against the rules but I joined a nervous pack of seven Curie girls gathered in the common room of Poole House after dark to huddle around the illicitly borrowed VCR cart and watch the forbidden feature. It was a thrilling, if abstract, rite of passage.

About a week after final exams, with the campus emptied of students not staying the summer, I was called unexpectedly into Mrs. Templeton-Wright's office.

Certain that I had been named as a member of the subversive movie-viewing group, I dragged my feet as I walked across campus, dreading the thought of standing in front of the Headmistress's desk to endure a tongue-lashing. The reality was much different.

"Well," she intoned once I was in her office and, to my surprise, she gestured for me to sit in one of the high-backed chairs. "I must say that I'm very pleased with you, young lady. You have applied yourself ceaselessly since arriving here at Curie Hall, your marks put you at the very top of our class rankings, and your disciplinary record is spotless. You are, in fact, near the top of the running for valedictorian of your year."

I couldn't have been more stunned. In retrospect, earning the highest marks in my classes had seemed an almost trivial exercise. I could scarcely believe that my efforts would be worth any manner of accolade.

"But, I'm afraid that what I am about to suggest would mean sacrificing that honorific." She paused for effect. "You are scheduled to start your third year here with the fall term but, you see, the faculty and I believe that you should begin the fall as a fourth-year."

I just gawked at her and my mouth might have fallen open.

"With two summer terms completed, you have more than enough credits to graduate after next year's spring term. Though, because all four years are required for the valedictorian title, it would mean taking yourself out of the running. There would be some other changes as well. You would have to start applying for colleges or universities this coming year. And, while I see that you are scheduled to move into the third-year housing this summer, it only seems appropriate for you to skip up to the fourth-year houses instead."

I managed to keep my composure until I left Mrs. Templeton-Wright's office, but I am sure I had a silly grin on my face when I ran across campus back to my room.

HEARTENED BY THE prospect of an early departure from Curie Hall, and (for surely it would follow) my return to the estate after graduation, that summer term passed quickly. Sure enough, on a Thursday morning, the week before fall classes were to begin, I found my new housing assignment in my student box: a room in the highly prized Ellis House. I was so excited that I was in my room packing up my things not five minutes later. My personal effects were so meager that I could fit everything in my school backpack, a large canvas shopping bag, and the hard case I had come to Curie with. Had I reflected on that more, it might have made me sad, but Melanie hadn't come back from break yet, and I was rather enjoying picturing her reaction on finding my side of the room empty. I was so preoccupied with the image that I almost left without taking my passport from where I had taped it under my desk drawer.

I hiked across campus to Ellis House, climbed up to the third floor, and found my room at the end of the hall. The door was open and when I peered around the frame I could see that it was a corner room nearly twice the size of my little cell at Corbin House and with windows on two sides. Despite the size, the room looked like a single. Two study desks had been pushed together against one wall, and two single beds up to the other. On the makeshift twin lounged a girl with dirty-blond hair, her face buried in a book. She looked up when I knocked softly on the door frame.

"What?" she demanded, dropping her book to look at me.

"I think this is my room."

"No it isn't," she said, and just as she did I noticed her chapped lips and recognized her.

Phoebe.

"This is fourteen," I said, looking at the engraving on my key. "Right?"

"Look, firsty, you're lost." She had just a touch of an accent, but I couldn't quite place it. "Underclass houses are on the other side of the grounds."

"I'm not a first-year," I said.

Her eyes narrowed. "Wait, I know you. The redhead. The Peeping Tom."

"What?" I managed, but as soon as I got the word out it clicked: Phoebe had been the girl reading by the fireplace downstairs that first, lonely holiday break.

"What year are you?" she was asking me.

"What?"

"Well, you're not a fourth-year, so you aren't allowed in here."

"They gave me the key," I said, holding it aloft.

She made no move to get up.

"That's bullshit. If you are a fourth-year why weren't you at junior seminar last year?"

"They let me skip third year."

That made her blink, but she recovered quickly.

"I don't care. This house is fourth-years only and *you* are not a fourth-year."

"Mrs. Templeton-Wright said—"

"Oh, that's fucking perfect," she growled. And then her voice went flat. "Whatever."

With this she snapped her book closed and grabbed a small duffel bag from the foot of her bed.

"Don't touch my stuff," she said. Then she got up and stalked past me out of the room.

"What am I supposed to sleep on?" I called after her.

"Do I look like your private furniture-moving service?" she said, and was gone.

I MOVED ONE OF the beds over to the wall on the other side of the room, but when I tried to move the second armoire it was too heavy. I opened it to find it full of clothes. The first was just as packed. We were not allowed to wear anything but our uniforms on grounds, so why did Phoebe have so many outfits?

I puzzled over this for a while, not least because, given her order not to touch her things, I hesitated to move either desk. Trapped, I made as orderly a pile of my possessions as I could at the foot of my bed.

I spent the day exploring Ellis House, particularly the cozy common room and its lovely little fireplace, and then wandered the upperclass section of Curie's campus. In my wake, a number of whispers made it obvious that the story of my grade-skipping and promotion to the fourth-year houses had propagated through the gossip networks.

At lunch a pair of second-years, Dana and Marcia, sat at my table.

"Is it true you moved into Ellis House?" Dana asked, without so much as a hello.

"Yes," I said.

"Which room?"

"Fourteen," I said.

"You're roommates with that other foreign girl?"

Dana gave Marcia a look. "I told you," she crowed.

"That room is haunted," Marcia said.

"That's stupid," I said, but her blithely delivered quip ran a chill up my back.

"It's true," they sang in unison.

"That was Miss Elston's room," Marcia added. "She killed herself in there."

"After she got caught sleeping with a student," Dana said.

"Who told you that?" I demanded.

"I don't know," Dana said, shrugging.

"Then how do you know?" I asked.

"Everyone knows," Marcia insisted.

I changed the subject and, after lunch, tried to forget the whole thing. It was an absurd story but it was also a ghost story and so it bothered me. Halfheartedly and expecting nothing, I browsed the library's collection of yearbooks. Much to my alarm, Miss Elston was actually in one from several years before I had arrived at Curie. There was also a short dedication in the front inside cover:

IN MEMORIAM:
KATHERINE P. ELSTON

It was written above a small black-and-white candid of a slim and somewhat nervous-looking woman reading a smallish hardcover book. I recognized the setting: one of the white stone benches outside Ellis House. She had a sad sort of smile on her face, as if the passage she was reading at that exact moment had affected her in some way.

Suddenly my good fortune seemed tainted. I avoided going back to room 14 until sundown, but when I got there Phoebe was still gone.

That night, huddled in my tiny bed and bundled under the covers, I barely got any sleep. Strangely, Phoebe didn't come back that night. Or the next morning.

BY SUNDAY AFTERNOON there was still no sign of my new roommate. I had spent as much of that first weekend outside as I could. When finally forced to return to Ellis House for Curie's unofficial curfew, I found myself fighting through sleepless nights listening for the first hint that a ghost cohabited room 14 with me.

During the day, I did my best to learn as much as I could about Phoebe, but information was scant and questions about her often drew suspicious looks from my peers. After a bit of confusion, I found her picture in the most recent yearbook, only to discover that her name was not Phoebe at all, but "Pálhanna Aresdottir." Its mythic associations were charming to me (despite the mixed mythologies I found it amusing to be rooming with the "daughter of Ares") but I supposed that few people could pronounce her last name (or her first) and so everyone called her Phoebe.

She finally returned Sunday night, just before midnight. I was still awake lying in bed and gazing aimlessly out the window when I heard the key in our lock. She stumbled in and glared at me in the dim light from the hallway.

"So you weren't just a bad dream," she slurred. "Well, that's fantastic," she added, and collapsed into bed.

My last thought before I fell asleep was that she was drunk.

THE NEXT MORNING, I sat alone in the dining hall and lingered over some reading material as I ate.

Phoebe appeared about an hour later. Once she saw me she stalked over, took the chair across from me, and ate for about ten minutes before saying a single word.

"I heard you smashed Sasha Winkelman in the face with a yardstick your first year," she declared, without any effort at salutations.

"*What?*" I choked. "Where did you hear that from?"

"Everyone is saying it."

"Well, everyone is wrong."

"Someone else told me that you threatened her with a knife."

"That's not true."

"You roomed with Melanie Gray, right?"

"So?"

"She said she found a bundle of bloody rags in your garbage that same night."

The gauze from my bandage, I thought.

"Well?"

"That was my blood," I admitted, not wanting to be thought an attempted murderess.

"C'mon. I'm not stupid, you know. 'A bundle of bloody bandages,' Melanie said. That's rather a lot of blood for someone on the rag. Are you saying Winkelman cut you? Or what?"

"No, it was nothing like that."

"But you got in a fight with her, right?"

"Yes."

"Did they spank you?"

"They tried."

Phoebe blinked at me. "They . . . tried?"

"When they made to grab me, I threw ink at them."

"And then you smashed Sasha in the face with her own yardstick?"

I made a gesture I thought was sufficiently ambiguous, but Phoebe saw what she wanted in it.

"Really?" She sat up straighter. "I wish I had seen that. I couldn't sit for two days after I got 'the treatment.'" She looked out the window and it was a few moments before she spoke again. "Who are you?"

"What?"

"Well, your first year here you got in a fight with Winkelman and put her in the hospital."

"The hospital? I didn't—"

"And the Winkelmans are probably the biggest donors to Curie Hall. Sasha is a double legacy. Yet you are still here. So you must be someone."

I didn't know how to answer, so I said nothing. This seemed to confound her as she tried to decide what to say next.

"I'm Phoebe, by the way," she said after a minute. "Were you scared?"

"I guess," I said, puzzled why Phoebe knew so much about an incident from two years before. "Did someone report that whole thing or something?"

She laughed. "Report? To the police?"

It wasn't what I had meant at all, but I nodded.

"That would never, ever happen. How eager do you think the school is to have the publicity from a police report? It wouldn't do to have a student arrested. That's not the Curie way."

"What's the Curie way then?"

She affected a deep voice. "Self-sufficiency. Endure and press on, girls. Endure and press on."

I had heard our Headmistress intone that particular motto, and Phoebe's impression was spot-on. I couldn't suppress a laugh.

She smiled at me. "How bad was Sasha's face?"

"It didn't seem that bad," I said.

"Bullshit. Someone said she had a fracture and a concussion. She was gone for more than two weeks. How do you explain that if it wasn't bad?"

I was alarmed. Certainly, Sasha had disappeared for a time after her collision with the door frame, but I had assumed she was just avoiding me after losing the confrontation.

"I don't know," I said. "It was a long time ago."

"I heard they put her on suicide watch too."

"What?"

"She cuts herself. They found the marks when they examined her at the hospital."

I gave her a baffled look. I could see her calculating, trying to decide if the naïveté was affected or genuine.

"With razors," she volunteered, and I'm sure I looked like a deer in the headlights of an oncoming truck. "For the rush that the pain gives you. Don't you know what cutting is?"

I nodded, but I had never heard of such a thing, after my encounter with Augustin's straight razor, the concept horrified me.

"That's awful," I managed.

"You really don't know anything, do you?" She softened a little, leaned back, and scrutinized me. "Lots of girls do it. The administration doesn't understand it. They are terrified it is some precursor to suicide. Maybe that's part of the appeal. I guess they found fresh cuts on her arm."

"How do you know so much?"

"I have to head to the lecture halls," she said, deflecting my question. "I'm going to be late for class. Are you coming or what?"

~⌒~

AS ROOMMATES IT was impossible to avoid each other completely. For her part, Phoebe was polite enough when she had no choice, but she kept her distance otherwise. I would catch glimpses of her now and again: Phoebe crossing over from the administration building to the upperclass houses. Phoebe sitting on the stone benches by the koi ponds, reading in the sun, absently twirling her finger in a long lock of hair. Phoebe lounging in a far corner of the library, shoes off, ankles crossed on the sill, and stocking feet sticking out one of the open windows.

She seemed more than content to ignore me. On the other hand, the more I learned about her, the more intriguing I found her.

Katie Park, the only other girl I had seen Phoebe spend much time with, had graduated, and if Phoebe had other friends I was at a loss to identify them. Instead it seemed that Phoebe preferred solitude, and the rest of the student body seemed more than willing to let her have it.

In retrospect, it wasn't surprising that Phoebe wasn't more social. Curie was homogenized and populated almost exclusively by girls from the northeastern United States. Difference in anything from hairstyle to the way we knotted our school uniform ties was mercilessly persecuted. Phoebe, on the other hand, wasn't just "different." Phoebe was exotic. Phoebe had an accent. Phoebe was from Iceland.

Phoebe actually hated Iceland. Her name branded her as a foreigner, and though she hid her feelings about it well, her accent embarrassed her. I, on the other hand, found these details alluringly mysterious.

"Phoebe is my WASP nickname," she once told me by way of explanation, and delivered a warning besides: "With your hair and your accent you better be careful that they don't think you're Irish."

"My accent in English isn't Irish," I protested.

"Do you think they know that? Once they think you might be a Catholic it will be all over. You should act more English."

"What are you talking about?"

"Just stop trying to hide your accent. I don't know, spend some time talking about 'chips' and apologize repeatedly for nothing at all . . . just do something . . . natural."

I looked at her for signs she was kidding, but she didn't appear to be.

My elevation to the status of a graduating student spurred a flurry of letter writing on my part. Certain that the news of my early departure from Curie would prompt my grandfather to reach out, I found myself writing letters to him once or twice a week. When Phoebe came home early one Saturday, barging into our room after midnight, she caught me composing one. I was so surprised that, almost knocking over my ink jar, I reflexively swept the paper into my desk drawer and slammed it shut.

Phoebe cocked her head at the blank envelope still on my desk.

"Who are you writing?" she said, scrutinizing my writing instrument. "And who writes with a quill?"

"It's not a quill."

"What is this, the seventeenth century or something?" She rolled her eyes, but then, to my relief, let the matter drop.

While my late nights seemed transparent to her, Phoebe's nocturnal activities were difficult to shed light on. As midnight approached on Thursday nights, she would slip out of our room in silence. I didn't want to burst her bubble, so I took pains to feign sleep.

After some prowling of my own, it became apparent that she never deigned to join any of the after-dark clusters of girls that spawned behind the houses late at night. Often she was still gone when I woke the next day (and more than once until the following Monday morning). Obviously, she felt the social rituals of our peers beneath her, and that made me wonder if her absences took her off the grounds entirely.

One Thursday, just before midnight, I followed her as she crept out and across the grounds. I lost her in the dark by the tree line on the eastern edge of campus. I waited for nearly half an hour, but she did not return.

Whatever Phoebe was doing, it wasn't at Curie Hall.

THINGS CAME TO a head one Thursday at about eleven thirty at night. Phoebe was making more noise than usual getting ready for her midnight adventure. Feigning sleep was an ordeal I had to launch into an hour before her departure, time spent lying awake in the dark rather than studying or writing to my grandfather. I suppose I was finally tired of pretending for her sake.

"You might as well be able to see what you are doing," I said, leaning over to switch my desk lamp on after she banged into her chair a second time.

Phoebe blinked in the light and glared at me.

"Where do you go at night?" I asked her, trying to break her icy stare.

"None of your fucking business."

"What am I supposed to say when someone asks where you've been?"

"No one is going to ask."

"You don't know that. What do I tell them?"

"The truth. The truth is that you have no idea. See how well I've arranged that for you?"

"I know you sneak off campus and I doubt you have permission to go off grounds."

"You've been spying on me?"

"I'm always awake when you leave," I said. "The charade of it is stupid. Right after you leave I turn the lights on and sit at my desk anyhow."

"So then why don't you go back to writing your stupid letters and mind your own fucking business?" She finished putting a little black dress into her duffel bag, zipped it up, and headed for the door.

"No one is reading them, you know," she added on her way out.

"What are you talking about?"

She shook her head. "You don't know anything, do you?"

With that, she left. I was surprised she didn't slam the door.

THAT SATURDAY, A clearly tipsy Phoebe barged into our room well after two in the morning, a day early for her normal routine. To say she caught me off guard would be an understatement. Seized by a bout of insomnia, I had taken a shower barely an hour before and, somewhere amid the static sound of the water hitting the back of my skull, an inspiration came to me. I wrapped myself in my towel and padded down the hall and back to room 14. I was so focused on my little epiphany that I sat down at my desk without getting dressed and started writing a letter to my grandfather.

I was still writing when Phoebe came home. The ghost of Katherine P. Elston was still in the back of my head, and when my roommate burst through the door behind me, she scared the hell out of me. I yelped and whirled around so fast that my towel fell down.

"I told you no one reads these stupid things," she said, and hurled a bundle at me from across the room. It landed on my desk with a thump.

"What the hell, Phoebe?" I snapped. "Don't you knock?"

"Oh, relax," she said, as I desperately tried to cover myself. "It's not anything I haven't seen . . ." But then her gaze fell to my chest, and she trailed off. Even from across the room I could tell she was staring at the angry red scar and my mutilated breast. Her mouth dropped open.

"Turn around," I barked at her, snatching for the fallen towel, but she stood gawking until I repeated myself.

I changed into my pajamas and was about to yell at her when the bundle that she had thrown at me caught my eye. In it were dozens of envelopes tied up together. I recognized the handwriting immediately. It was mine. All the letters were mine. They were the letters I had written to my grandfather. There were no postmarks on the stamps. They had never even been sent.

I was so shocked I didn't even think to ask her how she had come by them. Instead, once it sank in, I took the bundle and ran out of our room in tears.

"Wait," Phoebe called after me. "Don't go."

Then she said something about being sorry, but I couldn't bear to listen to her. I ran downstairs and across the grounds.

Still in my pajamas, I sat in the dark on one of the stone benches for a long time. I thought about burning the letters, but smoke from a fire in the middle of the night would have attracted panicked attention. Instead I dug a hole with my bare hands near one of the koi ponds, buried the letters deep in the mud, and washed my hands off in the water. Muddy clouds of dirt spread to taint the clear pool, an evil fog from which the koi were panicked to escape.

I CREPT BACK INTO Ellis House and slept in the common room until the sun rose and then locked myself in one of the shower stalls until everyone had gone off to class. I had no intention of joining them and, instead, finding our room empty, crawled into bed and fell asleep.

I had meant to get up after a couple of hours and leave before Phoebe came back from class, perhaps stopping at the school nurse to fake some illness or another to excuse my absence, but I overslept and woke instead to Phoebe sitting in my desk chair apparently waiting for me to rouse.

When I saw her, I sat up in bed, intending to change into my uniform and leave.

"Don't go," she said, and her voice sounded almost sad. I stared at her. "I can be mean when I've been drinking," she added. "I'm sorry."

I didn't know what to say, and so I said nothing.

"What happened to your chest? Did Winkelman—"

"No," I said. "It was . . . before Curie Hall."

"It looks really bad."

"It's old," I said, suddenly close to tears.

Phoebe turned her head and pointed at the triangular scar next to her right eye.

"My father gave me this," she said.

I was horrified. When she saw that, she sat next to me on my bed.

"Actually, I sort of did it to myself."

"I don't understand."

"It was after my parents separated. There was lots of yelling, fighting over the house, that kind of thing. Finally, my mother intentionally ran into a door frame and gave herself an impressive black eye. She called the police, claimed my dad hit her, and got him arrested. There was a big custody battle. The thing is, they fought each other *not* to have me."

"Oh," I said, a little taken aback by how open she was suddenly being. I wondered if she had been drinking again, but I couldn't smell anything on her breath.

"Anyhow, the next time I was over at my dad's new place, I told him I had kept a diary of all the physical and sexual abuse I had suffered and that I would tell the social workers all about it at my next interview."

"Oh my god, Phoebe."

"No, no, don't look at me like that. I made it all up, but I really, really made it all up. I faked all the diary entries too. 'Dear Diary, he came to my room again after Mom went to sleep. It was worse even than when Mother took the trip to Finland.' Stuff like that. With a history of domestic violence on his record, that would have been bad news for him. Ironically, he was so angry he lost his cool and shoved me and I hit my eye against the corner of the coffee table."

"Ouch." My gaze cut to the scar next to her right eye. When I saw how well the shape mirrored the sharp corner of a table, I winced.

"I mean, I didn't try to block my fall or anything," she continued. "Actually, I kind of turned my face toward the table to see if I could get hurt.

"He cooled off and, when he got a good look at me, he got really quiet. I cut myself pretty bad actually."

"I can tell."

"There was a lot of blood. He figured out how much trouble he was in and started trying to bargain with me not to tell anyone. So I told him that he and Mom could fucking lick me and that if he wanted me to keep quiet he had to put money in a trust and send me to the boarding school of my choice."

"You had your choice and you came to Curie Hall?" I said. Phoebe ignored me.

"He figured he was getting off easy since the other possibility was jail and a lot more money. I even pointed out to him that the more he gave me, the less Mom would get. He loved that part. Anyway, she probably would have stolen half of the child support payments, or tuition, or whatever he wrote her checks for. I always wanted to live in the United States, so I came here. Another of the Huldufólk."

"Huldufólk?" I said.

"Hidden People. Elves. Elves and faeries are still a thing in Iceland. Hidden among the rocks, disrupting the normal activities of the real world. You have to be careful with construction projects because you might disturb the Huldufólk."

"You're kidding."

"Nope. These surveys come out saying twenty percent of the population believes in 'elves' and there's a mad rush to explain the results away. The government hates it. So here we are, hidden away at boarding school so we don't disrupt the activities of our parents."

"The Huldufólk."

"Exactly," she said. "Do you want to tell me what happened to you?"

I thought about it for a long time before answering. "My brother," I said. She looked like she was about to ask me something else, but I beat her to it. "Why did you have my letters?"

"Part luck, part lucky guess. I was looking for something else but I found them locked away in a drawer in Dr. Templeton-Wright's office. I saw your name on the return address and . . . I just took them."

"To flaunt? To show me how stupid I am?"

Phoebe flushed. "It was mean the way I did it. I know. I'm sorry. But I'm glad you know now."

"What were my letters doing in the Headmistress's office? What were *you* even doing there?"

"Where did you post them?"

"In the outgoing-mail slot in the administration building," I said. "Where else?"

"Do you think that's an official United States Postal Service mailbox?" I hesitated.

"It isn't," Phoebe answered for me. "The closest real post office is in New Haleyford, like almost seven miles north. The administration gives outgoing mail to the driver of the postal truck that comes here, but not all of it."

"I don't understand."

"They steal outgoing mail all the time."

"But . . . who would want to do that? Why?"

"Parents. Duh. Maybe they are getting divorced. There might be allegations of abuse, a custody battle, a court order not to contact the child, things like that."

"That's crazy, they can't—"

"Think so? Before you got here, Sasha Winkelman forged a note from her mother pulling her out of the summer term. This private investigator her father hired found her in the next state over in some hotel with this older guy and a lot of alcohol and drugs. Not just older, a lot older. Like, he was in graduate school or something.

"Her parents didn't want a scandal, so no one pressed charges. Anyhow, when she got back to Curie Hall they started seizing all her incoming and outgoing mail so they couldn't write to each other. She was none the wiser and thought the guy had just dumped her."

"This can't be true. It can't."

"It is. Haven't you noticed that not everyone has phone privileges here? A bunch of girls without them have to sneak off campus and walk all the way up the road to Phil's to use the public phone booth."

I hadn't known anything like this. I thought phone use was forbidden to all students.

"Who would order my mail stopped?" I said.

"I don't know."

I was quiet for a long time.

"Did you read them?"

"Of course not," Phoebe said, offended. "How could you even ask me that?"

I didn't want to, but I believed her.

"I mean, I was obviously curious. No one knows anything about where you come from. I couldn't help but see what was on the outside of the envelopes but . . ." Phoebe looked at her hands. "Look, I told you. Neither of my parents want me either. Curie Hall is a repository for inconvenient and abandoned children. It took me a long time to figure that out, and the sooner you accept it, the easier it is. Believe me."

"He was supposed to get them," I said. Tears started falling down my cheeks. "He was supposed to read them."

Phoebe wrapped her arms around me and held me tight.

"I know," she said. "But maybe he doesn't want to."

I buried my face in her chest and soaked the front of her shirt with tears. The intercepted letters raised more questions than they answered, but I could not believe my grandfather had actually abandoned me.

I cried harder and Phoebe pulled me into her lap, cradling my head under her chin. I managed to stop the tears after a few minutes, but she held me that way for nearly half an hour.

⁓

AT FIRST I was wary of Phoebe's sudden burst of affectionate loquaciousness, concerned that it might have been a mood swing or some by-product of her late-night drinking. She had intrigued me since I had first seen her, a mysterious and almost ephemeral figure I admired from afar. She was even more interesting close up and that she had let me through the many standoffish defense mechanisms she employed seemed too coincidental to believe. The entire experience left me feeling uncomfortably vulnerable.

Slowly, however, I began to sense that her tenderness and the protective way she was with me was not some artifice she planned to cruelly withdraw. Instead I came to realize that, though she put on a good front, Phoebe had been quite lonely when I moved in. She had been very close to Katie Park but did not often interact with other Curie girls. Katie had graduated and, whatever Phoebe might have said about enjoying living alone in room 14, without a roommate she had become quite isolated.

Her change of heart had come after she had seen the scar on my breast and I reasoned that, given her own brushes with domestic violence, something about that moment made her see me as a kindred spirit of sorts. Even back then, young as I was, the metaphor, that Phoebe had been horribly damaged in other ways I did not know about, was not lost on me. In time, I came to believe that the silent battles I was fighting that term only served to strengthen the bond between us.

I had convinced myself that my sentence at Curie Hall was a limited one; a year or two with time off for good academic behavior. My fantasy did not survive its inevitable collision with my new reality and for weeks I was devastated by the aftermath.

Eventually, I tried to just accept what Phoebe had been telling me: I had been discarded and would eventually be forgotten. But then, what would happen when I graduated? Didn't someone have to finally come to collect me? If no one was getting my letters, how would my grandfather know I was graduating early? Was he in touch with Curie's administration? Were my parents?

Surely, I thought, there must be some communication. After all, someone had been paying the tuition on time. At first I tried to discuss my hopes of a homecoming with Phoebe, but she was having none of it.

"Denial," she said, "is the most powerful intoxicant there is."

Not that I was all that disposed to it in the first place, and though it made me feel guilty to withhold things from her, after that I avoided talking about my family or home with Phoebe.

That's not to say I gave up on the idea of contacting my grandfather. Phoebe had said something about Curie girls trekking off campus to a pay phone next to some place called "Phil's." After a bit of research I learned that Phil's was a two-and-a-half-mile walk north on the county road just beyond the access drive that led to Curie Hall. It was an appealing notion in the abstract, though I had no idea who I would call if I were standing in front of a pay phone. Still, the exercise made me realize that, since arriving, I had never once set foot off the grounds of Curie Hall. It was the kind of thing one should notice but, given how I had grown up, being walled in on an isolated estate almost seemed routine.

I HADN'T WANTED TO buy into Phoebe's cynical views on parental abandonment, but my family seemed to be doing everything they could to prove my roommate right. Soon enough, their silence presented other problems. Week after week graduation seemed so very far off until, all of a sudden, it was fast approaching and my postgraduation life was a yawning void in an uncertain future that loomed before me. I had no idea what I was expected to do come summer, so I coped by pretending summer would never come.

For her part, Phoebe, who arguably knew the ins and outs of Curie better than any other student, transformed into some amalgam of a mother and big sister to me. It was a measure of how comfortable I had grown with her that, late one night with the wind up—creaking sounds as our windows sighed against the gusts—I worked up the nerve to ask her about something that had been bothering me since I moved in.

"Does anything . . . weird happen here late at night?" I said.

"What?" Phoebe said, annoyed. "Weird how?"

"I don't know, noises? Things like that?"

After a puzzled look, Phoebe started laughing at me, though not in an unkind way. "Someone told you the story, didn't they? About Ms. Elston?"

"Well, is it true?"

"So far as I can tell, yes, it is," she said.

I was stunned. "She killed herself in this room?"

"I think so. Look at the floorboards. They had to replace them because her blood soaked into them."

Sure enough, several of them were newer, even of a different wood perhaps, in a roughly oval shape near Phoebe's bed.

"Oh my god," I breathed. "How do you, I mean . . ."

"How do I sleep in here? Quite soundly, can't you tell?" She had a wry grin on her face. "It works out quite well. If they tried to room someone with me I would just create some signs of *ghostly hauntings*"—she wiggled her fingers in the air—"and they would cry and whine until eventually their parents would call and the administration would send my roomie to another house. I've gotten rid of two interlopers that way. The administration tricked you into this room because you didn't know the story yet."

"Did you ever try to get me to move out?" I ventured.

"Why bother? You're pleasant enough." I was charmed by her declaration, and I sensed that, with Phoebe anyhow, it was a high compliment. "You really believed the story?"

"No," I protested.

Phoebe came over to where I was sitting, took my face in her hands, and kissed me on the forehead.

⁓

PHOEBE'S PROTECTIVE STREAK took other forms as well. Once she learned that I had not taken even the first steps to apply to colleges, she was adamant that I submit to the same schools she planned to—Princeton, Cornell, New York University, the University of Pennsylvania, and Columbia. Four of which were in or relatively close to New York City, a metropolis that Phoebe had something of an obsession with. That made Columbia University, in upper Manhattan, the focus of her hopes and dreams. When I pointed out that NYU was in Manhattan as well, she winced.

"Greenwich Village?" she complained, wrinkling her nose and chewing her lower lip. "Ugh."

This species of urban snobbery was strange coming from Phoebe. Though I often spied her sneaking around with guides to New York City, or leafing through books with pictures of its skyscrapers, as far as I knew, she had never been.

"Plus," she hastened to add, "NYU is . . . well . . . NYU. It's just my safety school."

I was a little put off by her arrogance, but my own halfhearted research validated her standards. All of her choices were top schools (though I had to admit that the campus pictures in the Penn brochure always drew my eye and Phoebe's dismissive attitude toward NYU tainted that institution for me for years to follow). So, as with most things in that period, I followed her lead. I endured her editorial efforts on my essays, and filled out the same applications she had. After all, secretly I was beyond flattered that she wanted me as a schoolmate.

I ran into a stumbling block when I came to the financial aid sections. I could provide none of the information they demanded and so, after long hours of frustration, I simply threw them out and checked the "not applying for financial aid" boxes. I suppose I thought I would just pay the first-semester tuition and housing expenses in cash. Certainly, given the hoard of currency that had been left in my suitcase, I had enough on hand. Or, perhaps the entire endeavor still had an umbra of unreality around it, and planning to manage college bills seemed a distant and vague problem not worth bothering with.

Now I think that I went through the motions because it was expected of me, though I did so without much in the way of enthusiasm. Ironically, this lackadaisical attitude elicited deep suspicion (and not a little jealousy) from my peers. They would have been surprised to know that, in many small ways, I envied my classmates their stress, their desperate tales of panicked guardians, nervous admissions consultants, and overbearing parents.

Despite my pervasive disinterest, I scored exceptionally well on the SAT, well enough that I began to receive solicitations by the handful. Most were from elite colleges and universities, not to mention the United States Naval Academy (clearly unaware of my alias's citizenship status), but there were also a host of other offers by credit card companies and the like. After a couple of weeks of the postal deluge, I adopted the habit of searching the contents of my student mailbox to collect anything that was from my teachers or the administration, and, after a quick and hopeful scan on the off chance my grandfather had written to me, dumping the rest of the correspondence into the trash unopened.

CHAPTER TWENTY-FIVE

—

Vincenzo di Napoli

As SUMMER APPROACHED, AND WITH IT that dreadful period when acceptance (or rejection) letters would begin to pick off Curie students like some merciless meritocratic sniper, Phoebe deviated from her usual Thursday routine. We had retired early for a change but just before midnight, Phoebe woke me and I found her kneeling next to my bed.

"Get up," she whispered in my ear.

I rolled over to look up at her in the dark.

"Come on," she said, her voice still low.

"I don't understand."

"Put your uniform on."

I could see she was already wearing hers. "My uniform?" I said. "But—"

"If we get caught out of our rooms at this hour, do you want to be wearing your uniform or something else? I'll meet you in the hall," she said, grabbing her backpack. "Bring lots of money."

Then she was gone.

I pulled on my clothes and dug in my bottom drawer for the cash I hadn't buried. I had no idea what "lots" was in Phoebe's estimation. Keenly aware that she was waiting for me, I finally settled on $2,500 and ducked into the hallway. When I found her by the stairs, she took me by the hand and led me outside.

It was late April, but it had snowed only a couple of days before and the nights were still quite cold. I had goose bumps all over my legs as Phoebe pulled me across the darkened campus. The thrill of sneaking off grounds to some unknown mystery quickened my beating heart.

I followed her to a particular tree by the wall that enclosed the campus. Phoebe produced a large towel, draped it on the ground, and laid out clothes. After popping off her shoes, she stood on the towel and undressed.

"I'm pretty sure those are your size," she said, pointing to the outfit she had laid out near me.

Hesitantly, I turned my back and stripped off my clothes. Shivering in nothing but my underwear, I was in such a hurry to dress that I nearly left my cash in the skirt pocket of my uniform.

"Why do you wear that horrid thing?" Phoebe said, pointing at the ink-stained pendant around my neck.

Eager to change the subject, I held up the wad of bills I had brought. "Where am I supposed to put this?"

Phoebe handed me a clutch. I fumbled with the paper-clipped stack of bills and dropped them next to the towel, right in the mud. Phoebe snickered as I recovered the smeared money. I gave her a pretend dirty look.

She had brought me a long black skirt and a dark gray cashmere turtleneck along with a lovely gray scarf. The black kitten-heeled shoes were a little tight, and I did not look forward to walking in them.

I caught myself watching Phoebe as she changed. Though our school uniforms did her very little justice—thin and lanky lines, bony shoulders, pale skin, all angles and cheekbones—she looked quite lovely and elegant in designer clothes. With a little work (and some lip balm) she was the picture of the young model-to-be. Her outfit was far more elaborate than mine and she topped it off with a dark blazer that, though it was wrinkled from the backpack, fit her beautifully.

Phoebe packed our uniforms and the towel into her backpack and hung it from a tree branch, a gesture made quick and efficient by repeated practice.

"We'll get it when we come back," she said, and then motioned for me to follow.

I snagged myself on thorns more than once, but eventually we emerged from the woods and found ourselves standing by the main county road. There were no streetlights and Phoebe and I huddled together in the dark on the shoulder next to a reflective sign with a picture of a leaping deer.

Rendezvous at the leaping deer, I imagined a mysterious voice breathing on the other end of a mysterious phone line.

When I started to shiver, Phoebe unbuttoned the front of her blazer, put her hands in her front pockets, and enveloped me in a big coat-hug, wrapping her arms around me from behind. Next to me she was soft and warm.

We only had to wait a few minutes before headlights crested the far hill. The car slowed, as if the driver wasn't quite sure of us, before finally stopping right in front of the sign.

It was a black town car and Phoebe wasted no time getting into the back. I had no idea what to expect—teenage boys from one of the nearby boarding schools? a university student in a creepy, beat-up Toyota Camry?—but the car put me at ease.

"Hi, Brian," Phoebe said to our driver.

"Hello," he said. He was clean-cut, polite, and very safe-looking. "I see there are two of you this time. You are multiplying."

"Yes, this is my roommate," Phoebe said.

"Hello," I said.

"Off we go," Brian said.

Phoebe produced a little makeup kit from her purse. She made me up first, spending the most time combing the bed tangles out of my hair with a folding brush, and then concentrated on herself. Then we lapsed into a trancelike quiet, watching as the scenery turned first to well-lit highways and then back to the enveloping darkness of the rural Northeast. I was near bursting with anticipation but tried to emulate Phoebe's cool demeanor.

After an hour, we turned into a tree-lined driveway marked with a prominent but dated-looking sign hanging from a wooden spar. It was illuminated dimly from below by bulbs weakened and yellowed with age. It read:

VINCENZO DI NAPOLI

It was an older mini-mansion trying hard to look like a Tudor and just about run-down enough to pull it off.

Phoebe leaned forward and gave our driver a quick peck on the cheek. "Thanks, Brian," she said, already halfway out of the car.

"Sure thing."

I followed Phoebe up the stairs and through the door. Once inside, I realized that Vincenzo di Napoli was an Italian restaurant. The front room was completely empty as was the bar near the entrance, but a blast of wonderful heat, the smell of roasted lamb, muted sounds of conversation, and a snatch of laughter emanated from somewhere in the back.

A surly looking bartender stood idle behind the bar. He gave Phoebe an irritated look.

"Has she got ID?" he demanded. He meant me. I felt the beginnings of a knot clenching in my stomach.

"We are here to see Nicolo," Phoebe said.

Apparently this was the password, because the bartender mumbled inaudibly to himself before losing all interest in us, focused instead on polishing the bar for his nonexistent customers.

"Phoebe, no one is going to believe I'm of age," I whispered.

"Shush," she whispered back. "Have you looked at yourself in the mirror lately? You come off as one of those cute, twentyish, redheaded girls who look seventeen forever."

From behind me there was a slurred voice.

"Ah, bella."

I whirled around to see the lone occupant of the booth nearest the door. He was an anemic-looking man of perhaps seventy years, though as many as ten might have been added from drink alone. Other than suspiciously jet-black hair, his features were narrow and fair. It was a northern look with a character that was more Piedmont or Lombardy than Naples.

Phoebe smiled and walked over, grabbing me by the wrist as she passed.

"Nicolo, I want you to meet my very good friend."

"Ah," he managed, through a slowly lifting haze. "But she is so . . ." He closed his eyes, and for a moment I thought he might fall asleep, but then he blinked them open again. ". . . so young."

I elbowed Phoebe, but she ignored me.

Nicolo's expression darkened. Once we were closer, I could see that he was frowning at a short cocktail glass in front of him. It was conspicuously empty.

Phoebe sat down, dragging me into the booth with her.

"Nicolo, can we buy you a drink?" she said.

His reaction was slow, an overladen ship struggling to get up to speed and break through a thick bank of fog.

"Cristano," he bellowed toward the bartender, and then emitted a flurry of slurred Italian so accented that I could not begin to follow it.

"She is so lovely, your new friend," Nicolo said, once his attention had turned back to us. He leaned across the table and pinched one of my cheeks. "So lovely," he said again, before sinking back into the creaking leather of the booth.

Cristano was clearly in no hurry and I began to look around, mostly to avoid Nicolo's gaze. The walls were adorned with expensive-looking paintings, but everywhere a thin layer of dust prevailed. Vincenzo di Napoli had obviously been a chic venue in its day, but that day had long since passed.

A series of pictures of celebrities both major and minor adorned the walls in clusters. I thought at first that a snapshot of a familiar-looking, corpulent politician—cheeks and nose red, reeling slightly, left arm around the thin waist of a panicked-looking blonde, right arm around the thicker waist of a game-looking brunette—was just for show, but on closer examination I could pick out a booth and painting that placed the photo not fifty feet from where I sat (much later I would realize the picture was of Ted Kennedy).

Cristano arrived with a bottle of sambuca and three shot glasses.

And just like that, Phoebe and I were toasting something obscure with Nicolo and downing the sambuca. Following Nicolo and Phoebe's example, I slammed the drink. It was a huge mistake. It hit me like a slap and my eyes started to water. My desperate efforts to keep from coughing meant I almost vomited on the spot.

My vision was just starting to clear when I realized that Cristano was looming over me. It took me another moment before I noticed the little black plastic tray with the check on it. Both Nicolo and Phoebe were watching me carefully, so I extracted the clutch Phoebe had lent me and, eyes still watery, pulled out the first bill that came to hand and laid it on the tray.

Nicolo held the banknote up to the light before Cristano could carry it away. He scrutinized the dirt and scraped some off with a poorly manicured thumbnail before laughing and dropping the bill back onto the tray.

Nicolo bellowed something to Cristano in Italian to the effect that "the redhead" had dug up the bills by robbing a grave. Cristano managed only a thin smile and excused himself, taking with him two of the shot glasses (but not Nicolo's, or the bottle of sambuca, at which Nicolo's greedy hands were already pawing).

Phoebe pulled me up and away from the booth.

"Phoebe," I said. "My change."

Phoebe didn't stop. "Come *on*," she said, breath hot in my ear. "Do you want to end up in that booth all night?"

I hadn't even considered that there was more to the evening than Nicolo.

Phoebe pulled me through double doors into a smaller dining room with about fifteen tables. The tables were all set, but there wasn't a single guest. We passed through another door and into a back room.

The hints of fine cuisine that so tantalized me in the main room clearly emanated from this smaller space, and the aroma mingled perfectly with a background of woodsmoke and red wine. A small feast of pasta, lamb, and the remnants of a half dozen antipasti dishes adorned the middle of the large round table that dominated the room. A fire burned fiercely on the far side, and one of the nearby windows was cracked open. Competing currents drifted through the air, alternating hot and cold, giving the entire setup a schizophrenic feel. For a moment, I was reminded of the East Salon; sitting with my grandfather; the way that the scents of woodsmoke and his pipe tobacco blended together.

Fifteen chairs, all but four of which were occupied, surrounded the table. If a dated picture of an intoxicated politician seemed out of place in the contemporary Vincenzo di Napoli, the collection of late-teen and early twentysomethings—five girls and six boys—were from some other entirely. Incongruously, in the far corner there was a tattered video cart with a television and VCR.

We had interrupted them in the middle of a discussion and the entire group was looking at us. One of their number, a preppy university type with a carefully crafted mess of blond hair, starched shirt, and hazel eyes, broke the silence.

"Ah. Phoebe . . ." he said expansively. His voice fell off into a disappointed tone. ". . . and some new girl."

"Pierce," Phoebe said, "this is my roommate."

"Oh?" he brightened, and made his way over to kiss Phoebe on the cheek. "She knows the rules for newcomers?"

"Yes, yes," Phoebe said, waving a dismissive hand, and then to the room: "Someone pour me a glass."

Alcohol obviously being a key part of the social rituals performed by the group, my status as a neophyte seemed forgotten and two big red wineglasses were produced.

"Rules for newcomers?" I whispered at Phoebe.

"I'll tell you later," she said.

Pierce had returned to his chair and was talking to a pretty blonde on his right. Phoebe sat next to him, and I next to her. I was near enough to the video cart that when I looked closer I could see a tattered inventory sticker that someone had tried in vain to scratch away. It read: SAWYER LIBRARY, WILLIAMS COLLEGE.

Before I could even begin to spark a bit of conversation, a rotund man with a graying mustache and dressed in chef's whites burst in carrying trays filled with even more food. He distributed this cornucopia about the table with great flourish and a flurry of rapid-fire Italian. He doted noticeably on the blond girl sitting next to Pierce, and then started carving meat on the other side of the table. I did my best to blunt my excitement with the entire scene by downing half of my wine. Some girl I hadn't even been introduced to refilled it in passing only moments later.

Phoebe had excused herself from the table as everyone began to dig into the main course and Pierce startled me when he leaned over and spoke into my ear, struggling to be heard over the escalating din.

"So what do you think?" he asked.

"It's . . . strange."

Pierce laughed. "It is, isn't it? This place used to be very popular ten, twenty, or I guess thirty years ago. The official story is that some rich asshole a few doors down bought it, converted it into a restaurant, and brought over his favorite chefs from Italy to cook and run the place.

"He used his political connections to get Vincenzo and his understudy green cards and everything. I suppose it explains why the place is in the middle of nowhere, but the story sounds like a lot of mythologizing bullshit to me. Everyone and everywhere needs an origin myth, I guess."

"Well, there are a lot of famous people on the wall," I said.

"There is that, but it's a ghost town now. The celebrity world's loss is our gain. It is sort of a depopulated wilderness all the way out here. As long as we don't set the place on fire or something they leave us alone. And Vincenzo's former understudy Carmine"—Pierce motioned to the chef who was flirting harmlessly with the blond girl—"is a fantastic cook."

I was about to ask more, but Phoebe returned and monopolized Pierce's attention. I concentrated on the food instead.

I was on my third glass of wine and the beginnings of a food coma when the conversation began to lull and I wondered if the evening was already winding down. Phoebe had moved to the other side of the table to join another conversation and Pierce shifted to the chair next to me.

"So, you're at Amherst too?" he said.

I gave him a vague hum of assent, assuming it was Phoebe's faux origin story. To my surprise he accepted my answer without dispute. It was thrilling to be so easily taken for a college student.

"Enjoying the evening?" he asked.

"It's hard to be an outsider."

"Oh, don't mind that," he said, smiling. "The inner circle has known each other for a long time, but they will warm up to you."

"What . . . what is all this, exactly?" I said.

"Phoebe didn't tell you? The legend is that it started off as a comparative literature study group that managed to scam away a department VCR twice a week to 'study.' Eventually they had twenty people packed into this little library study room watching *Citizen Kane* and *Apocalypse Now*. Some completely bitchy anthropology major complained and shut the entire thing down. Tragic, really. So they moved the tradition here."

"That explains the video cart."

Pierce laughed at my question. "Yes, that was liberated for the cause." He made a fist in the air. "Power to the people. It's mostly totemistic now. No one seems to watch movies on it anymore."

Just then the fire popped loudly and a hot coal jumped out and landed on the rug where it began to smolder and smoke. Alarmed, I was about to stand up and call attention to the imminent hazard but, with great nonchalance, Pierce lifted his nearby red wineglass and tilted it, pouring wine directly on the ember. It was neatly extinguished with a soft hiss. When I looked closer, I could see that particular section of the rug had another half-dozen small burn marks surrounded by red wine stains.

I was about to try to revive my conversation with Pierce, but Carmine, in what was becoming a habit, burst through the door. With great enthusiasm he proceeded to distribute dessert menus to all present before clearing the wreckage of dishes, glasses, and empty wine bottles strewn about the table.

The fire was fading, but no one made any effort to feed it. I watched the glowing embers absently for a while. Coffee followed, and it was a good thing, too, as I doubted whether many of the guests could have made it out on their own power without some sort of stimulant.

Carmine returned and, standing at the head of the table, cleared his throat. An expectant hush fell over the room and all eyes were upon him. In a volume that startled me, the Italian chef began to sing and, with the art of a practiced tenor, delivered a rendition of Tamino's aria "Dies Bildnis ist bezaubernd schön," from Mozart's *The Magic Flute*.

As Carmine sang the piece, in which Tamino fawns over the picture of Pamina, the daughter of the Queen of the Night and the girl with whom he has instantly fallen in love, he performed for the room, playing out the part with great relish. His voice was so unexpectedly emotive and powerful, especially in the closeness of that back room, that it was impossible not to get caught up in the performance, particularly for the blond girl sitting next to Pierce. As the piece progressed, Carmine slowly worked his way over to her until, as he reached the grand climax of the piece, he knelt in front of her to take her hand.

As the last note faded, the room burst into applause and a very pleased-with-himself Carmine stood to take the ovation and bow to his public.

"Wow," I managed, trying to catch my breath.

"Incredible, isn't he?" Pierce said.

"Where did he learn to sing?"

"Carmine is a bit mysterious. I guess he's from some place called Varese in northern Italy."

I had to bite my tongue to keep from chiming in and telling Pierce that Varese was less than an hour away from La Scala, the famous opera house in Milan, and had also been the home of the tenor Francesco Tamagno. It was the kind of trivia that might have caused Bastien to call me a "smart aleck" had I volunteered it.

As the applause faded, and just as I indulged a flight of fancy picturing Carmine performing at La Scala, he worked his way in our direction. A subdued exchange passed between Carmine and Pierce before Pierce pointed at me. I was midswallow and almost choked on my sorbet when they both looked at me. Carmine smiled, glided over to my place, and laid a familiar-looking black tray in front of me. On top of it was the bill, face down. Aware that the eyes of the entire room were on me, I turned it over and looked at it. It was well over a thousand dollars.

"Newcomer pays," Pierce said to me.

PAYING THE BILL did not by any means end the evening. Instead, the odd pair or trio would spin off somewhere, perhaps to a corner of the nearly empty dining room beyond, to engage in a private conversation, or abscond to the porch outside to smoke. Eventually they would return to the back room and mix with the main body of the group again. Then a different pair would slip away and eventually return. There was a strange vibe to it, as if dinner was a ritual that presaged something else entirely.

It was nearly three in the morning when I went looking for Phoebe. She had drifted off about twenty minutes before and I was starting to think about going home. I came out of the back room to find most of the lights in the main hall extinguished, but here and there some were only dimmed.

I almost missed Phoebe in the dark. She was sitting at a table nestled in an alcove created by a set of bow windows in a far corner of the restaurant.

The blond girl, who I would later learn was named Cindy, was sitting on her lap with her arms around Phoebe's neck. Pierce was in the chair next to them, legs kicked up on the table, leaning back on Phoebe's shoulder. As I watched, Phoebe produced a pill, held it between her fingers, and put it on the blond girl's tongue. Then Phoebe kissed her, long and hard. She repeated the act with Pierce as he tilted his head back, and then took her own pill. Both sure and unsure of what I was seeing, and despite wanting to keep watching, I slipped away.

Phoebe's purse was hanging off the first chair she had sat in earlier and I rifled it until I found what I was looking for: the card for Brian's car service. I called him from the pay phone in the front and, twenty minutes later, I was on my way back to Curie Hall.

PERHAPS I SHOULD have been upset by what I had seen, but I wasn't. I left without Phoebe because I was surprised, and perhaps afraid that I was more attracted to the scene than I wanted to be. There was an appeal, rather a deep appeal, to giving in to and indulging the cult of hedonism that I began to believe lurked somewhere beyond the back room at Vincenzo di Napoli. After that first visit, I had many dark imaginings about what might go on after Carmine's last act of the evening. But the danger that seemed concealed there was both alluring and somehow far less threatening than the sort of intrigues that I had been embroiled in on the estate. It was a distraction that came along at exactly the right time. Now I often wonder how accidental that had actually been.

There was even a deeper allure that came to me later: I thought I recognized in the Vincenzo di Napoli group the signs of two entities (the overt and the covert). There was the "supper club" of Vincenzo di Napoli, and the more secret and illicit group concealed behind the facade. Was there design there? Did it mirror the classic public-secret pairing that concealed many secret societies? And if so, what were the goals and purposes of this new example I had stumbled across (or, perhaps, been led into)?

Even with the extra two years granted me by my faux passport, I was awfully young for the goings-on at Vincenzo di Napoli. Had Phoebe meant for me to see what I saw, or had she just been thoughtless, or carried away by the intoxicated moment of it all?

As I lay in bed that night, I pictured Phoebe as Paculla Annia, the high priestess who had transformed the rituals of Bacchus's mystery cult into nocturnal rites characterized by alcohol-driven orgiastic frenzies. Under her, the cult gathered to itself great power and influence. I suppose it wasn't surprising that fantasizing about such a thing was appealing; that belonging to something (even, or particularly, something so illicit) was seductive. I brushed off another memory the moment it came to me: when the Roman Senate got wind of the practices of the cult Paculla had bent to her own purposes, and of the influence it was wielding, they viciously suppressed it and executed thousands of its adherents.

Despite the demise of her followers, Paculla's fate, I noted, was lost to history.

CHAPTER TWENTY-SIX

Lost and Found

TODAY IT SEEMS THAT THOSE LAST terms at Curie Hall flew by, but at the time, enduring them was a seemingly interminable sentence of quasi-incarceration. True, in the abstract, Phoebe's antics and our clandestine weekly visits to Vincenzo di Napoli should have been unusual and illicit. But they still seemed tame compared to those weeks before I left the estate.

Perhaps the ease with which Phoebe slid into the big-sister or motherly role with me should have raised alarm bells, but it had the effect of making things more or less effortless. I was happy enough to allow myself to be led; to follow in her shadow.

The sole exception was after hours at Vincenzo di Napoli. Early on during my tenure at Ellis House, Phoebe was quick to tease me about any number of topics, sex included. When we had both settled down for the night, turned the lights off in our cramped room, and crawled under the covers, Phoebe liked to tell me "bedtime stories." Being older and much more experienced than I was, she was sometimes prone to demonstrate her worldliness by weaving these tales through with descriptions of sexual acts and gynecological details that would make me shudder and squirm.

I don't think she realized at first how sensitive I was to the topic. After one particular weekend, Phoebe started wearing turtlenecks despite a bout of warm weather. After the third day, when I worked up the courage to ask her about them, she looked around and, seeing no one, pulled her collar down for me to see. A cluster of ugly bruises, purple fading into dark yellow around the edges, circled her neck like a choker.

"Phoebe," I gasped. "What . . . ?"

"Pierce and I were in bed," she said, and gave me a glance, "you know. And he started getting rough and put his hand around my throat and started choking me."

Right then, I had a flashback so vivid my knees almost buckled: Augustin looming over Cipriana, boxing her into a dark corner of the manor, his hand slowly slipping up to her throat, gripping it, and then pushing on it to pin the back of her head against the stone wall.

"Phoebe, you have to tell someone. You have to call the . . ."

Phoebe was looking at me with such a strange expression that I trailed off. She blinked at me for a few seconds and then some understanding seemed to come over her and her expression melted into a big smile.

"Oh. No, no. You don't understand." She lowered her voice conspiratorially. "It was hot as hell."

Her description left me red-faced and trying in vain to hold back tears. To my surprise, she seemed horrified by my reaction. Her smile melted away and she pulled me to her and silently hugged me until I eventually calmed down. After that, her sexual storytelling evolved into tamer fare.

In a similar vein, I had been bracing myself to be pressured into something I wasn't ready for at Vincenzo di Napoli. But, though I found myself unable to stay away from the regular Thursday events, somehow that moment never came.

For her part, as Thursday's midnights approached and then passed, Phoebe seemed content to drift off into the shadows of the restaurant's dimly lit corners and allow herself to succumb to the effects of the pills that seemed in limitless supply, but she did so without entangling me. Certainly, the subtle invitation was there on occasion—a coy look from her; a sidelong glance from across the room as midnight approached—but when I cut my eyes away shyly, or turned to pour myself another glass of wine, she never pressed the issue.

I cannot deny that I found the proceedings enticing; that the apparent and all-encompassing bliss that the forbidden tablets induced in their users tempted me more than once. But I was still quite afraid of sex, and petrified of any substance stronger than whisky; anything that might cause me to let my guard down.

I compensated, now and again, by watching the couples (and occasionally trios) that congregated in the dark corners until, before anything too profane occurred, the feeling of being an illicit voyeur welled up and I called Brian to come and pick me up.

Sometimes Phoebe—full of Vincenzo di Napoli's residual bliss—would wake me up with a kiss on the mouth when she came home—lingering and dark, with hints of red wine or whisky. Then she might crawl into bed with me and I would fall asleep in her arms.

During the day we really didn't talk much about Thursday nights. Thanks to Phoebe's deft manipulation of our course load, our schedules left almost all of Friday either open or occupied by classes we could easily miss without drawing much attention (my increasingly senile former House Mother, Mrs. Peterson, taught a class on English literature that was perfect for our purposes).

I loved Phoebe, of course, as close roommates at boarding school must do, but I sensed that the depths of the relationship were much more textured for Phoebe than for me. Still, at least while we were still at Curie Hall, she knew enough to be careful with me and, even in those cases where she pressed outward on the envelope I had established, she was quick to pull back if she sensed I was getting uncomfortable.

I still had bouts of loneliness, of course. Having come home before Phoebe at four in the morning one Friday, not a little tipsy, I penned a simple letter to my grandfather with the most basic salutations and the request that I be allowed to return home. I sealed up the letter but, afraid that the post office would somehow know to give it to Curie's administration rather than forward it on to its destination, I omitted the return address. My grandfather knew where I was, after all. No one else needed to.

As the sun rose, in the chill of the early morning, I snuck off campus alone. Following my best guess based on the details I had gleaned from Phoebe, I hiked north on the side of the road.

The phone booth I found was a ragged-looking thing hanging off a rough stack of crumbling bricks posing as a building that, through some gross perversion of administrative law, had obtained for itself a liquor license. Despite the early hour, I could hear a commotion within. I could only assume that this was the famous Phil's.

With little fanfare, I summoned a taxi, rode into town, posted my letter, and made my way back to Curie.

More than a month later I still had received no reply.

ACCEPTANCE LETTERS STARTED coming in late that spring, and the looming panic that hung over Curie was punctuated now and again by squeals from the mailroom as one student or another received a favorable letter.

Phoebe had been secretly raiding my inbox for weeks and delighted in delivering my acceptance letter to Columbia University alongside hers. Though she was over the moon to have gotten her first pick, I was less enthusiastic about moving to New York City. I tried to be happy for her and cheerful that, if I went with her, we would be together, but it was an uphill battle to picture myself in Manhattan or, in fact, any major urban center.

Almost everyone at Curie was accepted to one of their top three choices and, after that, fourth-year scholastic motivations slacked away to nothing. Some nights, Curie's campus seemed so empty one wondered if the entire fourth-year student body had snuck off grounds for the evening.

On the last Thursday of the season, Phoebe vanished early, leaving me to gut out the day and then make my way to Vincenzo di Napoli alone. It was a warm, balmy night and though I was there as early as eight thirty the back room was already packed.

Everyone knew it was the last big hurrah of the year. The next day many of the members of our little clique would fade into the background to attend to their last exams, satisfy family obligations, and prepare for their first postcollege jobs (or whichever of their own private affairs steered them away from the back room of a random restaurant languishing in the back roads of the Northeast). They had become a sort of extended family for me and, like the rest of them, I indulged in the rank euphoria to avoid facing reality.

Even Carmine had been taken up by the soaring mood that evening and was more flamboyant than usual. He was already in the middle of his second Mozart aria of the night ("Ah lo veggio quell'anima bella") when I came in. I sat down and started to pour a glass of red wine from one of the bottles, but Pierce was having none of it.

"What?" he said. "No. We're celebrating. Someone get her a Scotch."

I had just begun to nurse it when I managed to catch a snippet of conversation between Pierce and the prissy-looking college type sitting on the other side of him. He was a new addition and had been staring at me since I walked in.

"Who's that?" the prissy guy asked, nodding in my direction. It was louder than I think he intended.

"Careful, Romeo," Pierce said. "Fifteen will getcha twenty."

My stomach tied itself into knots but Pierce only smiled at me and lifted his glass when he saw that I had heard.

He leaned close to whisper at me. "What, you didn't think I knew? Lying about your age in here is about par for the course."

"I skipped a couple of grades," I said. It was a weak offering. Pierce only smiled.

Things seemed on a fairly direct route to an intoxicated evening of disturbing proportions. It was about ten thirty and I was talking to Pierce about business school and careers in finance. I remember being taken with the idea that there was a sequence that could be reliably followed to secure a career; that one simply navigated from the right college, to the right internship, to the right business school, and then into a lucrative career in banking. I thought there was a great appeal to that kind of a formulaic process, and to fixing oneself on a goal and eventually attaining it.

Cindy made her way over and leaned down to whisper in Pierce's ear. Pierce listened to her, smiled, nodded, and then fished from the inside pocket of his blazer a clear, square plastic baggie about the size of a matchbook. In it was a single red pill. He slipped the baggie into Cindy's hand, and she palmed it before darting away.

"Interruptions, interruptions," Pierce said to me, and then frowned. "Ah, sorry. Not your thing, is it? I didn't mean to be so flagrant about it."

"What do you mean?"

"Well, that's what your roommate said, anyhow."

"Phoebe?"

"Do you have another roommate?"

I turned away, but the idea of Phoebe, without my knowledge, telling people how to treat me rankled. Though I had eaten a healthy portion of Carmine's delicious pasta dish, I was already tipsy from the several glasses of wine that had accompanied it. The combination of the food, the drink, and the prospect that it would be my last night ever at Vincenzo di Napoli may have bolstered my courage.

"What's it like?" I asked.

My voice came out meeker than I had meant it to, and suddenly I felt very young. Pierce gave me a confused look.

"That," I said, pointing at the breast of his blazer. "What's it like?"

"MDMA?"

"Do you have another drug?"

Pierce cracked a crooked smile. "I see what you did there. Funny," he said, and then his expression grew more serious. "How long have you been coming here?"

"I don't know."

"Somehow, I feel like I barely know you."

Pierce had a point. I had enjoyed myself on Thursday evenings, like the rest of them. I had eaten with them, drunk with them, laughed at their jokes, reveled in their stories, but I had revealed little of myself in the interim. Perhaps it was some combination of reticence, the fact that I was living under an assumed name, carrying a fake passport, and, not least, that Phoebe had apparently made a habit of warning people away from me.

Pierce was looking at me, waiting for an answer, but I just shrugged.

"See?" he said, laughing. "Impenetrable. Even your roommate claims to know nothing about you."

I was about to ask him what he meant, but before I could say anything he patted his breast where the inside pocket of his blazer was. "Is that why you are interested? Time to come out of your shell?"

I began to worry I had painted myself into a corner I didn't particularly want to be in.

"Also, aren't you a bit young?"

I frowned at him.

"Ah, so you do have a soft spot under there after all." Pierce dug into his inside pocket and produced another baggie, identical to the one I had seen him pass to Cindy, and put it on the table in front of him. "This is what you are curious about?"

Terrified that someone would see, I craned my neck around, but no one seemed to notice or care. Sitting on the table there was a kind of presence to it, the cherry-red pill inside a small glassine baggie; a presence that would not have asserted itself if either object had been without the other. One little baggie for one pill. It hinted at the potency of a single dose, that it should be so packaged; a carefully designed prop that almost seemed to exude its own energy. When I looked closer I could see that a design had been stamped into the round shape: a bunch of grapes.

"What's the design mean?" I said, suddenly even more intrigued.

"Grapes? Intoxication?"

"Dionysus," I breathed, almost to myself. "Bacchus."

"What?"

"Nothing."

"Phoebe was right. You *are* a strange one," Pierce said, eyeing me again.

I blew off the Phoebe comment. "Is it like wine?"

Pierce laughed. "God no. It is so much better."

"What's in it?"

"I told you. Methylenedioxymethamphetamine. MDMA."

"But, I mean, does it just make you really drunk, or . . . ?"

Pierce leaned back in his chair and sighed to himself, as if he were reminiscing. "At first, maybe even the first half an hour, nothing. It's subtle. Then it creeps up on you and hits you. It starts with this warm, rocking sensation in your body. Colors become amazing to look at, particularly blues and reds. Really, you start to feel them. Really connect with them. There is no describing it. Then your sense of touch is heightened, but in a sensual, not a harsh way.

"I remember one of my first times I spent more than an hour just running my hands up and down my arms because the feeling was so incredible."

I thought of the many times I had watched couples caressing each other in the far rooms after hours. The overtly sexual aspect that sometimes overtook late nights in the restaurant began to make more sense.

"That warm, deep appreciation of the sensual extends to emotion." Pierce sighed again. "You feel so connected to people. Touching each other is just bliss."

Pierce leaned closer. It wasn't a sudden move but, probably because of the tenor of the conversation, and because I knew he was much older than me, it startled me. I shifted away from him in my chair.

"Hey, easy," he said, alarmed. "I didn't mean to scare you. I was just going to say 'it's amazing.'"

"Sorry," I said. "It sounds frightening. Like, out of control."

"It's not like that. Look, it's not like you have to fuck when you're on it or anything." Pierce smiled at me. "But it sure is amazing to."

I must have given him a look because he put his hands up and leaned back in his chair.

"Don't misunderstand me. I'm not talking about you. What I mean is that I'm really going to miss fucking your roommate on it. Well, and off it, actually."

I had no idea how to respond to that. I knew from Phoebe that their relationship was sexual, but having it put so directly stabbed at me. On reflection, I was utterly astonished to realize exactly what was getting to me in that moment: jealousy.

"Look, forget all that," Pierce was saying. "The best way to describe it is that it's bliss. Bliss on tap. It's up to you what you do with it."

He swept up the baggie with the pill and returned it to his inside pocket. I found myself staring at his blazer, imagining the pill next to his heart.

"How much is it for one of them?" I said, finally.

Pierce's expression turned angry. "How much? You know what? Fuck you. I'm not a dealer. These are for members. We don't *charge* for them."

Pierce got up to leave. Even before I knew what I was doing, I grabbed the sleeve of his blazer.

"I'm sorry," I said. "How was I supposed to know that?"

He regarded me for a few moments. "Fine," he said, and then sat down again.

"Look, I know you're underage. You're not even supposed to be drinking. Plus, your roommate . . ."

I must have had a particular expression on my face because Pierce stopped midsentence and knitted his brow at me. Then he adjusted his blazer and stood up.

"I'll be back later," he said.

The way he turned to go was awkward and stiff, with his hands by his sides. I was at pains to hide my disappointment (and then upset with myself for actually being disappointed).

Just as I was about to turn my attention back to my glass, right as Pierce started walking away, I caught a flutter of movement from Pierce's jacket out of the corner of my eye. I looked down and saw it on the rug: Pierce had dropped the glassine bag with the red pill in it.

When I was sure no one was looking, I leaned down and scooped it up.

⁓

I HELD THE BAGGIE in my palm for a long time, trying to decide what to do with it. I was tempted to try it right away, but, safe as it felt in that back room, I could not imagine being comfortable in a hypersensualized state in the company of the Vincenzo di Napoli crowd.

Isn't that the point of the drug? I thought. *To remove your inhibitions? Of course you can't imagine what it will be like. What good would the drug be if you could?*

A shiver went through me and I tried to shake off that particular line of inquiry.

Stay within yourself and your capabilities, my grandfather's voice said. *Don't be lured into interactions that others control.*

I smiled to myself at the absurdity of it. Voices in my head debating the wisdom of illegal drug use. But even Pierce seemed to have misgivings about my using the stuff. Why else would he have engineered the faux accident (or so I assumed) of dropping the baggie? Or had he been trying to assuage his conscience somehow?

I finally put the baggie in my clutch and had just returned my attention to my Scotch again when Phoebe burst in. She had a strange expression on her face as she scanned the back room. This continued until her gaze fell on me.

"Look who I found," she announced to the room with a distinct slur. Then she took a half-step out of the door and, stepping back in, pulled a man into view by the lapels of his suit jacket, presenting him like a game show prize.

At thirty-five or so, he spiked the average age of the room up by a number of years the moment Phoebe hauled him past the threshold. As if to highlight the contrast even more, he was wearing a business suit and carrying a black leather briefcase. For one crazy moment, I thought Phoebe was going to announce that the two of them had just been married.

Phoebe looked at me. "Your *cousin*," she proclaimed to the room.

The assembly went quiet. Everyone was looking either at Phoebe's escort or me. I had never seen the man before in my life. He wore a "long-past five o'clock" shadow, as if he had been working on something since early that morning, but was otherwise impeccably dressed. Once he saw me, he stiffened and brushed off the lapels on his suit, as if Phoebe's touch had tainted them.

Having recovered from the shock of the man's appearance, Pierce stood up.

"This is a private event," he said, having detected that I did not recognize the interloper. "Can we help you with something?"

"I have business with the young lady," the man said, nodding in my direction.

I was gripped by an awful, foreboding feeling. Stranger or not, everything about the man felt like the estate. The expensive business suit (smart but not ostentatious); the hint of a British accent; his regal bearing. There was no doubt about it. He may not have been familiar, but his demeanor was.

I should have been elated, seized by the notion that I might be taken home again and that my exile had come to an end, but, unaccountably, I felt nothing but dread.

"About what?" Pierce said, after a beat.

I was a little charmed by his protectiveness, but his hesitation telegraphed weakness. Even if no one else in the room saw this, the strange man and I perceived it almost as one. Even as it happened, recognition also passed between us silently and instantly; two predators on opposite sides of a herd quietly acknowledging each other. Any doubts I had about where he had come from were dashed away.

"It is a confidential legal matter," the man said.

"Not here it isn't. You can tell us or you can get the fuck out."

The man said nothing, only stood in the doorway, waiting.

I stood up and made my way to him. "What is it you want?" I said.

"Madam," he said, leaning down to whisper. "It is regarding your grandfather."

CHAPTER TWENTY-SEVEN

⁓

The Hand of the Dead

THE ROOM HAD GONE SILENT AND everybody was staring at us when the man threw me a lifeline.

"Perhaps we might find a quiet place to have a quiet word?" he said.

I led the way out, trying to sober up as much as possible as I went. A stern-faced Carmine was lurking about outside the back room, showing an immigrant's concern with the presence of what must have looked like officialdom to him.

Do Italian immigration officials wear expensive suits? I wondered. *Probably.*

I smiled for Carmine's benefit and asked him in my best Italian to find us a secluded spot. It was early yet for lovers to drift off to the darker corners of Vincenzo di Napoli and the remainder of the restaurant was empty, of course, but Carmine had the good sense to seat us in an out-of-the-way corner. My "cousin" took the aisle seat and placed his attaché case defensively on the chair next to the wall. I hated that I noticed that detail.

Carmine hovered. I lapsed into English. "Just a coffee, Carmine," I said.

"A double espresso," my tablemate said.

I started to speak, but my faux cousin's upraised hand stopped me. He was looking over my shoulder. I turned around. Pierce was standing about thirty feet behind me.

"It's okay," I called. Pierce looked unconvinced. "Really, it's fine."

Pierce nodded and slipped into the back room.

Carmine returned with our coffees. The man watched patiently with a polite smile. Once Carmine had faded back into the kitchen, the man handed me a card:

FRÉDÉRIC A. KUHLMANN III
ATTORNEY AT LAW
BURLING WOLFF & ROHR

"Let me begin by apologizing for interrupting your evening. We have had a very difficult time finding you."

I stared at him, stuck on two points: first, the fact that this man had managed to find me, and apparently without help from my family. Second, that this meant that he knew I was living under an alias. If my family had not sent him, who had? Suddenly, I was afraid.

"My firm represents the Fulvia Flacca Trust, an entity established by your grandfather."

I tried not to react, but the mention of the obscure Roman's name sent a chill through me. If my grandfather had wanted to create a secret recognition code between us, he could not have picked a better phrase.

Tesserae hospitales, Professor Lechner's voice seemed to whisper from somewhere. But if this man was from my grandfather, why did he have trouble finding me?

"Everything will be explained, but I am not privy to all the details myself. You will want to speak with Mr. Wolff. My task is simply to bring you to our offices in New York."

"What, you mean now?"

"As soon as possible. I would not have involved your roommate, but it was unavoidable. Once we learned you were attending school here in the United States, we sent several letters; correspondence with ambiguous purpose and meaning intended to be opaque to outsiders. But, apparently, these did not reach you, or catch your eye."

I remembered all the correspondence I had been throwing away after my high test scores. A random letter from an unfamiliar law firm would have gone right into the bin.

"I would not have imposed on you in person if there had been another way. A 'cousin' seemed the least threatening story to use."

"Why didn't you just ask my family where I was?"

Frédéric A. Kuhlmann III rocked back in his chair as if I had struck him. He sat blinking for a few seconds before replying.

"But why on earth would we do that?" he said.

HIS MESSAGE DELIVERED (and an appointment to pick me up scheduled), the lawyer excused himself.

I had to sit alone at the table for a time to collect myself before I could brave the back room again and the dozens of questions I expected to face. After a few minutes, Carmine poked his head in. Our eyes met and I nodded silent acknowledgment that I was unharmed. He crossed the floor and, after hovering (uncertain, I think, if it would be appropriate to intrude or dare to sit with a customer while still wearing his chef's whites), smiled with great pleasure when I gestured for him to take the chair across from me. His expression transformed into worry once he settled.

"*Va tutto bene con la signora?*" he whispered.

"I am all right, Carmine. Thank you."

He hesitated, as if he had to work himself up to the next hushed question. "*Non è una morte in famiglia, spero?*"

I was taken by his concern and I understood what it must have looked like. A young girl, clearly from a wealthy family, her dinner party interrupted by a well-dressed man with important news. I switched to Italian and assured him that, no, in fact, no one in my family had died, only that my family's affairs were complicated and that they threatened to entangle me.

Carmine gave me such a knowing look then that I imagined that he too had faced such complications. After a long, silent moment between us, he nodded.

Then he smiled and, catching me off guard, stood, rounded the table, and knelt in front of me. He took my hand and made a show of being shocked by the touch. I think I recoiled a bit, as if for a split second I expected him to propose marriage or profess his undying love, but these were silly notions, disabused when he began to sing and I saw his performance for the effort to cheer me up it actually was.

Carmine launched into "Che gelida manina," the poet Rodolfo's aria in *La Bohème* in which, after blowing out the candle and leaving the pair in a dark room together, he remarks how cold is the hand of Mimì, the woman he has fallen in love with.

> *Che gelida manina,*
> *se la lasci riscaldar.*
> *Cercar che giova?*
> *Al buio non si trova.*
> *Ma per fortuna*
> *é una notte di luna,*
> *e qui la luna*
> *labbiamo vicina.*

> *What a frozen little hand,*
> *let me warm it for you.*
> *What's the use of looking?*
> *We won't find it in the dark.*
> *But luckily*
> *it's a moonlit night,*
> *and the moon*
> *is near us here.*

Carmine performed the piece beautifully, and twice I had to turn away to avoid the intensity of his gaze while he sang, lest the emotions welling up in me bring me to tears. Timid or not, for those several minutes, at least, I forgot my cares and imagined myself far away and without concern. In the long silence that followed, overwhelmed by the gravity of it all, it was some effort for me to keep from sobbing.

Shedding the cloak of performance and becoming just "Carmine" once more, he let go of my hand and smiled at me.

"*Vis, consilii expers, mole ruit sua,*" he said, in perfect Latin.

Caught off guard, I struggled to translate it.

Force, unaided by judgment, collapses through its own weight.

"Marcus Aurelius?" I guessed, and had to pinch my eyes closed for a moment to fend off the flash of a homesick memory—pipe smoke drifting, the sound of Latin on his tongue—of my grandfather.

Carmine adopted a greatly exaggerated expression of horror. Then he sighed and exhaled through his teeth with a soft hiss.

"Quintus Horatius Flaccus," he insisted.

"Horace," I said, feeling sheepish and not a little taken with the depth of insight and intellect that apparently lurked beneath the performer's mask Carmine normally wore among us.

<hr />

I RETURNED TO THE back room, where things had picked up again, but Phoebe was gone. No one seemed inclined to ask me about my mystery visitor. Though I could see his curiosity burning, even Pierce obviously sensed that it would not be wise to try to explore the topic further.

I ended up calling Brian for a ride home after another half an hour, only to find Phoebe's bed empty when I returned to our room.

The entire evening had thrown me for a loop. Could the lawyer's visit have been some sort of ruse? If so, it was an inspired one. The use of the name Fulvia Flacca was obscure and telling. For someone falsely purporting to represent my grandfather to stumble across it by accident seemed unlikely. My thoughts raced on and, as I drifted off, a chorus of voices seemed to speak to me from far away.

. . . heirs are particularly attractive targets for intrigue, one familiar one whispered to me.

<hr />

I ALMOST SLEPT THROUGH the assigned pickup time, but when I woke, there was still no sign of Phoebe. I flew in and out of the showers, jumped into my clothes, and ran across the grounds. I almost forgot to bring my passport, a point on which Mr. Kuhlmann had been particular. Thankfully, he was waiting in the back of a black town car parked by the leaping deer sign just like I had asked.

Neatly folded copies of the *Wall Street Journal, Financial Times, International Business Times, Handelsblatt,* and *Investor's Business Daily* were laid out on the back seat. I couldn't tell if they had been selected specifically with me in mind or if these were, as a matter of course, provided to the distinguished clients of Burling Wolff & Rohr. I was too overwhelmed to read anything and so we drove into New York City in relative silence.

I never got the chance to see the lobby. Instead we took an elevator from the garage directly to the firm's offices. I barely had time to register the massive reception desk in front of the large, brushed stainless-steel letters that spelled out BURLING WOLFF & ROHR before Mr. Kuhlmann whisked me down a long hallway. Everywhere echoes of "Good morning" followed in our wake.

Two stern-looking receptionists guarded the entryway to the office we came to at last. The older of the two stood up once she saw us.

"Yes, Mr. Kuhlmann," she said. "Just a moment."

Her voice had a strong London accent and a distinctly apologetic tone, as if Mr. Kuhlmann might storm out at being made to wait even half a minute.

She ducked into the double doors but emerged seconds later. Behind her, six stone-faced Japanese businessmen (studiously avoiding eye contact) streamed out of the office and made their way out to the hallway beyond.

The office behind those double doors was cavernous. Two banks of floor-to-ceiling windows met in the corner, offering a spectacular view of the city's skyline. Off to the right, out of the way and surrounded by twenty or more chairs, an oval conference table seemed swallowed up by the room.

I was so fascinated by the scale of the place that I completely missed the comparatively small wooden credenza and the diminutive gray-haired man behind it. It was only when he stood and spoke that I realized that Mr. Kuhlmann and I were not alone.

"Thank you, Frédéric," the man said. He must have been seventy years old, and his voice had a wise timbre to it.

As Mr. Kuhlmann turned to go, my host, who was barely taller than I was, made his way around his desk with a slight limp.

"You were instructed to bring your passport?" he said.

"Yes," I said, making no move to retrieve it. Given that the name in it was an alias, I had hoped that I would not be asked.

"May I see it?" he added, dashing my hopes.

He scrutinized the document when I handed it to him, paging through the stamps, feeling the paper between his fingers, even holding it up to the light at one point. Bit by bit he started smiling as his examination of the document progressed, until, by the time he handed it back to me, a warm and pleased expression had spread across the man's face. I was surprised, as I had been half-expecting him to angrily announce it as the forgery it certainly was. Instead, he acted as if he appreciated the workmanship.

The pleased expression faded, however, and as he handed it back, a serious look came over him.

"Do you have something else to show me?" he said.

"I'm sorry?" I said, puzzled, but the man said nothing, only blinked at me and waited. "I didn't know I was supposed to bring anything else. I don't even have a driver's license."

"Nevertheless," the man said, "I will need you to show me something else."

"I don't know what you mean . . ."

Something about the way the man was standing seemed odd to me. It took me a moment to put it together. He was holding his left hand in front of his torso. With his left thumb under his fingers, I saw him fiddling with a small, intricately carved silver signet ring on his pinky. It may have only been a nervous habit, but it seemed such an odd and contrived sort of gesture. Moreover, though I was sure he saw me noticing it, he did not stop. My mind raced.

What purpose could drawing my attention to the ring serve? Am I supposed to comment on it? To recognize the insignia?

I was too far away and the ring too small for me to see the design, and though I was tempted to draw closer to look at it, I was hardly comfortable doing so.

What is the meaning of a signet ring?

Professor Lechner's lessons came back to me.

Some bearer instruments can be worn, he had said, referring to his own signet ring, *and thus always available to the bearer.*

I wasn't wearing a signet ring, of course. What else had Professor Lechner said?

What if a sigil, a bearer instrument, were disguised as something altogether more ordinary?

The pendant, I thought.

I pulled the chain out from under my shirt and, though it felt beyond silly, held the pendant out for the man to see. He brightened immediately.

"May I ask you to open it?"

It had never occurred to me before, but I knew what he meant immediately. Excited, I lifted the chain over my head, sat in one of the desk chairs, and, anxious not to look like I was doing it for the first time, laid the pendant on the table and scrutinized it carefully.

Gently, I pressed and pulled and twisted at the small oval until, almost by chance, my fingernail caught a groove in the side. When I pressed in and then up on the groove along the rim, a tiny latch shifted and the pendant swung open like a locket. Inside was a red stone: a round cut ruby no larger than a peppercorn. The stone was held, but not mounted, in a little bracket.

A bloodred heart.

Almost giddy, I turned the locket over, laid the ruby carefully in my palm, stood up, and showed it to the man.

"May I examine it?" he asked.

I nodded, and with the most delicate touch, he picked it up and then hurried off through a side door in his office, which he closed behind him.

A metal puzzle box, I thought, and I was sure that the intricate locket had come from my grandfather.

When the man returned, all smiles, he returned the stone to me. Carefully, I replaced the ruby in its bracket, squeezed the locket together, and used my fingernail to press the tiny latch back into place.

The man sighed deeply before speaking again.

"You will have to pardon me," he said, "but I really do not have the words to tell you how pleased I am to finally meet you. My name is Wolff." I shook his hand when he offered it. "Please, sit down," he said, gesturing with great formality to the desk chairs.

Trying not to squirm, I took my place and began to survey the shelves on the wall behind his desk. Once it caught my eye, I couldn't tear my gaze away from one of the dozen or so photos there. It was a grainy black-and-white shot of what must have been a much younger Wolff. He was wearing a leather jacket with a fur collar and standing in front of an airplane.

"I do hope you will forgive the precautions," he said, "but I don't much trust anyone anymore. Frédéric is my most valued employee but even he might have made a mistake. But, to business. As I am sure Frédéric told you, Burling Wolff & Rohr is legal counsel to the Fulvia Flacca Trust. I am a trustee. I don't know exactly how much you know about trusts."

I was about to volunteer that, in fact, I knew quite a lot about trusts. Professor Lechner and I had discussed them many times in the context of the Library Foundation and succession planning, but I was more than a little overwhelmed and it was easier to say nothing.

"Your grandfather was the founder, and you are a beneficiary. The trustees have a duty to effectuate the wishes of the founder, however confused those may be, to the best of their ability. This duty is paramount and I take it very seriously.

"As is common for trusts, the founder, your grandfather, left instructions on how the trust's assets should be administered and distributed. However, your grandfather died almost immediately after the trust was formed and before giving us what we needed to find you. As you were . . . excuse me . . . as you *are* living under an assumed name, it took us some time."

"What did you say?" I said, sure that I had misheard him.

"Your alias," Wolff answered. "It made finding you—"

"No," I blurted out. "About my grandfather."

"Well, because he passed away before . . ." Wolff saw the expression on my face and stopped midsentence. "Impossible," he breathed, almost to himself. True anguish seemed to seize him. "How can it be that you didn't know?"

IT WAS ALWAYS an awful experience for me to cry in front of people when I was a young girl. Before I had been sent to Curie Hall, I had spent so much time in the presence of adults, and so little time with other children, that appearing "beyond my years" or "mature" was something of an obsession (and one enthusiastically encouraged by the adults on the estate). It was much worse in front of adult strangers, and certainly the formality of a law firm, much less an office as opulent as Wolff's, did not make it any easier. But cry I did. I couldn't help myself.

I am sure I embarrassed Mr. Wolff. He came around his desk and sat in the chair next to me, offering me tissues and waiting silently for the initial shock of that horrible news to wear off, at least a little. For a long time it felt like someone had sucked all the oxygen out of that office; that I could not catch my breath.

Eventually, he chanced an attempt at conversation.

"My dear, I cannot tell you how sorry I am. I am absolutely devastated that you would find out this way, much less that I would be the cause of such a horrendous faux pas."

"How did he die? When did he die?"

"Maybe these would be topics better discussed later. Can I bring you a water? Or something to—"

"Please," I said, and looked into his eyes. "Please tell me."

He considered this. Then, rather than answer, he made his way to a wet bar at the far end of his office. When he returned he had two small glasses, into which he had splashed a light brown liquid.

"I find that, in the present circumstances, I cannot do without a brandy." He held one of the glasses out to me. "May I invite you to join me?"

The liquid burned as I swallowed it, but then warmed me from the inside. Wolff finished his own, and then took a deep breath.

"His car left the road in Tochigi Prefecture, Japan, and fell into a gorge. Both he and his driver would have been killed instantly."

"When?"

"It was, I believe, early October. Three years ago."

It was barely a month after I had arrived at Curie Hall.

"That's not possible," I said. "No one told me. No one wrote, or called."

I looked at Wolff again, and then wondered if he knew about the incident in South Africa, or that my grandfather believed our family's enemies—unseen rivals—were attacking us.

"Was it an accident?" I said.

"We have no reason to think otherwise," Wolff said. Though I couldn't quite put a finger on it, something in the way he answered seemed off. Perhaps it was the very legalistic nature of the reply. He could have said "yes," but he did not. Perhaps it was the hint of hesitation, or the barely perceptible shift in tone when he spoke. Still, I had never conversed with Wolff before and therefore was ill-equipped to be sure that I had heard anything out of the ordinary. Too upset to dwell on what might have been a red flag, I let instinct press on instead.

"Why was he in Japan?"

Wolff put his hand on mine and patted it gently.

"I apologize in advance for the timing of all this, but there is some other business that we must discuss. Yes?"

I didn't want to allow the subject to be changed at first, but after a moment, nodded my assent anyhow.

"Very well then. I do hereby formally notify you that you are a beneficiary of the Fulvia Flacca Trust. There are some relevant instructions from the founder of the trust. The first is that the trustee is to present the beneficiary with this letter."

Wolff pulled a white envelope from his desk drawer and slid it across the desk to me.

"The instructions relating to this letter are specific. You are to open it and read it alone. Once you have read the letter it may either be destroyed or resealed and stored. If you elect to have it stored, we will place it in our safe here. You may return to view it anytime you like, but no copies or reproductions of any kind are to be made and it is not to leave these offices under any circumstances. Do you have any questions?"

I stared at the letter, almost afraid of what it might contain.

"Young lady?" Wolff prompted me.

"No."

"Very well," he said, and slid it to me across the desk.

"When you have finished, please seal the letter in the fresh envelope. You can then instruct me if you would prefer it stored or destroyed.

"I must ask that you not, under any circumstances, leave the letter unattended. Should there be a fire or a tornado, or should the heavens suddenly open, make sure to bring it with you on your way out of the building." I thought he must be joking, but he did not smile. "If you need anything, or if you have finished, just open the door and tell the receptionist."

"Mr. Wolff?" I said, as he was heading for his office door.

"Yes?" he said, turning to face me again.

"Mr. Kuhlmann said you were looking for me for a long time. Why didn't you just ask my family where I was?"

"We could never do that. The provisions of the trust call for absolute confidentiality. An unexplained call from a law firm regarding their young daughter would not have led to assistance from your parents without details that we would not have been able to provide to anyone but you."

Wolff certainly had that part right. I could just picture my mother angrily demanding explanations of the party on the other side of a random overseas call.

With that, Wolff left me sitting alone at his desk, dwarfed by the high ceilings and yawning chasm of his office, and struggling to piece together all the ramifications of his news.

I SAT FOR A long time just looking at the letter before I could open it. When I did, little pieces of wax from my grandfather's seal flew everywhere. I brushed them into a pile and unfolded the paper.

The text was obviously in my grandfather's hand and dated only a few weeks before Karl had put me on the plane that first brought me to Curie Hall.

My Dearest Granddaughter:

It may be gauche of me to observe, but your interest in our family history and your awareness of its import certainly eclipses that displayed by your siblings. Then again, you have always been the more curious, more observant, and more introspective of your father's issue. Your father does not see that as clearly as I do, but a father's love of his first son can be blinding (and how obviously the irony of that double entendre stands out now that I have written those words).

I cannot bear to see anything precious wasted, particularly not an intellect as vast as yours has become, even at such a tender age. I do so wish that this was the only cause for this letter and the actions that surround it, but I fear my motivations stem from darker places than a grandfather's love of his granddaughter.

As they must, dynasties keep secrets, some trivial, some terrible, and some that are kept (right or wrong) even from the patriarch. Ours has its secrets, even terrible secrets, and it would be difficult to describe what I have learned in recent weeks and months as anything other. I may or may not have written you this letter in any event, but events have now forced my hand.

I digress.

My son, your father, may come to see past the dull and merely historical appeal of patrilineal primogeniture. He may eventually fear, as I do, to leave the future of our family to your brothers. But even if he does not, I must urge you not to resent them. They cannot help that they are products of this age but unfairly expected to behave in what must appear to them an arbitrarily traditional fashion. They have not yet formed a sense of the importance of legacy in the difficult effort to preserve and grow a dynasty.

You have already transcended this chasm. I implore you to continue to exercise and expand your intellect and the pursuit of truth but, given what has come to pass in recent weeks, I am no longer certain that you will always be able to do so on the estate, or even the Continent.

My influence must necessarily wane in the years to come while your father's and your brothers' will wax. It is my task to smooth the transition to your father's rule as much as I can, but also to insulate the dynasty from harm. I am, however, powerless to prevent the premature friction I know Augustin's growing impatience will create. It is my wish that you be spared the collateral damage of these struggles.

There are no limits to the resentment and rancor that disclosure of my interference might elicit and, while I cannot yet explain, you must heed my warning: there are dangerous dynamics at work.

Unless something has gone terribly wrong, you will find that I have taken steps to provide you with a means to escape our family, and to broaden your horizons in a way that would not be possible if you were to remain with us. You will also learn that I wish these arrangements kept secret, in some measure even from you.

To be seen exhibiting this sort of favoritism would be understood (and rightly so) as a direct challenge to your father's authority. I cannot acknowledge these arrangements in public, nor in private, even to you. If confronted with them prematurely I will deny any involvement and cause the structures I have put in place to be unwound. Our family's enemies would be greatly emboldened by the revelation that I had usurped the expected line of succession in this way and the conflict caused may occasion the exposure of other more damaging facts.

No one can promise to know the future. Your brothers may simply be late bloomers. Your father may endure as patriarch for another fifty years, but we would be remiss if we did not prepare for contingencies, and so I commit the terrible sin of entangling you in a conspiracy against them (though it is our conspiracy, yours and mine).

And should matters in our family resolve themselves without need of us any longer, then the structures I have put in place today will give you the resources you need to be free of us if you so choose.

You have by now met the bearer of this letter, one of my oldest and dearest friends. I cannot help but think how impossible it would be that any letter of introduction I might offer would do justice to the trust and regard I have for this man. In this I must simply urge you to put your faith in him unreservedly. I have no doubt that he will represent himself (and my wishes) with great aplomb.

Whatever challenges await us in the fullness of time, you must never again doubt that,

I Am Ever,
Your Loving Grandfather

Below my grandfather's signature was more writing. It was still clearly in his hand, but apparently a later addition scrawled in a rushed cursive. When I looked closer I could see that the blue ink was just perceptibly darker than the earlier writing.

*Unforgivable as it is, I must nevertheless beg your forgiveness for
the horrible acts I have been forced to inflict upon you and the cold
demeanor you must endure from me in the days that must follow.
First, let me disabuse you of the notion that anything in my behavior
is related to the events surrounding your discovery in the family vault.
Reading papers addressed to another, particularly those of such a
private nature, is not an act to be excused lightly, but, strange as it may
sound, I understand your curiosity and believe it is worthy of praise.*

*As for my behavior, I can offer only explanations, not excuses. If
what I believe has happened has actually come to pass, to acknowledge
you publicly, even in the coming years, would engender suspicion, or
worse. Given the betrayal I am now guilty of, this is a risk I think
neither of us, you and I, would want to assume.*

*I am out of time and you must trust me that, while they may be
painful for you, the terrible things I have set in motion are for the best.*

Under these rushed passages there was no signature, just my grandfather's
handwritten monogram.

I had to stand up, for fear I might stain the letter with tears. It took me
several minutes trying to compose myself before I could focus again. I dried
my eyes the best I could before I sealed the letter in the envelope Wolff had
provided me and poked my head into the hallway.

"I'm to ask for Mr. Wolff?" I said to the older of the two receptionists.

"Of course," they said in unison.

I went back into Wolff's office but I was too nervous to sit down. Instead,
I went to his shelf to look at the framed pictures.

My eye was drawn to what must have been a family photo, a faded black-
and-white shot where two stately looking parents posed with five daughters
and one son, apparently the youngest, who I assumed must be Mr. Wolff. I
had just begun to scrutinize the antique silver frame and the crest engraved
in the metal (a laughing wolf with dramatic teeth) when the picture of the
aircraft I had noticed earlier distracted me.

Closer up, I could see that there was damage to the tail. Wolff was grinning
like a fox for the camera and pointing to a series of vicious-looking holes that

ran from the rear section of the fuselage up to the vertical stabilizer above the tail. I was about to turn away when I noticed a Balkenkreuz on the airplane's fuselage. When I looked closer I saw another detail: hanging from Wolff's collar was an Iron Cross.

Wolff fought for the Germans, I thought and marveled that I had not detected even a trace of a German accent.

"I was too short, you know," Wolff said, from right behind me.

I had been so absorbed, and he so quiet, that I hadn't heard him come in.

"To fly," he said. "The height requirements were quite strict, but my father knew all the right people. I was about to turn twenty-two when that was taken."

When I turned to face him, his voice trailed off. My eyes must have been puffy and he undoubtedly figured out that I had been crying again. His entire demeanor softened.

"Would you like to see it?" he said.

I nodded that I would. He picked up the framed picture and handed it to me before sitting in his chair. He had handled the picture so delicately that I was almost afraid to touch it. I sat down and put it in front of me on his desk.

"My partners dislike that I display this photo. I was never a member of the party, but I suppose that today, to outsiders in particular, even a mere officer of the Luftwaffe, a pilot from that era, is suspect."

"They shot at you?" I asked.

Wolff laughed at me softly. "That was the point, you know. It is interesting to me that you would focus on that picture. In a way that's why I am here." Wolff gestured around the room. "And why you are here too.

"You may not appreciate how unprofessional it is of me to discuss this, but still. Your grandfather and I were friends as boys. When I was old enough, I accepted my commission and joined the Luftwaffe. The war did not end particularly well for me, but your grandfather arranged to have me smuggled back to the West and eventually to London. Had he not been so kind to me, I might well have died in a Russian prison camp."

"The collapse of the Eastern Front," I said.

Wolff looked surprised at first, and then very pleased. "Exactly, young lady. So you might understand what an honor it is for me to be afforded the opportunity to carry out his wishes now that he is gone."

For a moment, I wondered if Wolff too would succumb to tears.

"Back to the matters at hand," he said, after a moment. "Would you like me to have the letter destroyed?"

"No," I blurted out, much louder than intended. "I'm sorry. No, thank you."

"I understand perfectly. Now that you have read the first letter we can discuss some of the trust provisions."

The first letter?

"The trust provides for a substantial distribution once you are enrolled full-time and in good standing in an accredited undergraduate program in the United States, and *only* the United States. Of course, you must think about university."

"I have already accepted an offer from Columbia."

"*Already?* Well, if I had any doubt that you are of your grandfather's line . . ." Wolff said, and then smiled to himself.

"Normally, I would give a new beneficiary a long lecture about the life-style and psychological adjustments required after coming into new wealth. I would point out that many people in the beneficiary's life may expect some of these resources to be expended on them and resent the beneficiary if those expectations are frustrated. I always counsel beneficiaries to keep these matters confidential and to be cautious about sudden large expenditures that may attract attention. Attention is the enemy of the wealthy. But I think you might already understand."

I nodded, but then regretted it, since part of me wanted to hear the lecture.

"The nature of these arrangements puts me in something of a difficult position. For reasons probably better left unexplored, your grandfather wanted you to enjoy certain benefits irrespective of your parents' wishes. I am sure you can see that this establishes an *adversarial* relationship between you and the trust on the one hand and your surviving family on the other?"

I had not considered this and it began to make me nervous. My grand-father's machinations were a slap in the face even more dramatic than the one he had delivered to my mother over the Academy Le Gudin.

"How much money is in the trust?" I said.

It was the most obvious question of all, and I could scarcely believe I had not already asked it.

Wolff shifted in his chair. "I am not permitted to discuss that with the beneficiary or anyone else aside from the asset managers employed by the trust."

For a moment Wolff looked tired. A long sigh escaped him. He sagged, just perceptibly, in his chair before extracting his pocket square, attending to something in his right eye, and looking up again.

"I know we are meeting for the first time and, normally, I would not permit something as petty as sentiment to encroach on my fiduciary duties, but it is important for you to understand something. Your grandfather was my dearest and most trusted friend. Whatever I can or cannot disclose, the lengths your grandfather went to in setting up the Fulvia Flacca Trust and the secrecy with which he did so should tell you what you need to know. He was obviously quite concerned with your welfare and had very particular ideas about how to secure it."

"Are there other beneficiaries? My brothers?"

Wolff darkened for a moment.

"This is a dangerous time for you, young lady. And, in a way, I am caught between instructions, but it is important for me to say something. Until certain matters are resolved, and that may take quite some time, years even, you must avoid your eldest brother. There are shifting power structures at play. Such circumstances do not inspire moral behavior and it would not do at all for you to find yourself caught between great powers vying for control. Do you understand?"

Because they may know the family's darkest secrets and may split the loyalty of a dynasty if recruited into a coup, heirs are particularly attractive targets for intrigue.

I was desperate to ask for details, but instead just nodded my assent.

"But do not despair. That your grandfather enlisted me rather than the firm your family has been using for more than three generations was not an accident. Now that the trust has finally located you, I will ensconce myself here in the city and abandon my offices in London.

"Before your grandfather came to me to form the trust, I was almost retired. I spent most of my time in my London office. My partner has had his eye on that space"—Wolff twisted his left wrist and pointed the palm of his hand over his shoulder to indicate the view behind him—"and this one for years. I am happy to frustrate him just a little longer.

"If there is anything you need, no matter how trivial or how insurmount-able you think it might be, you must call me."

Wolff presented me with a business card. It was printed only with "E. P. W." and a number with a 212 area code.

"You are the only one with that number. You may call it any time you need. *Any time*. If for some reason you cannot reach me, you can call reception here and ask for my office. Terri will answer and you may tell her that you are looking for me. For the time being, I don't want you to discuss these matters with Frédéric or anyone else here at the firm. If you are ever challenged, you may tell anyone in these offices that you wish to solicit my legal advice with respect to 'a charitable donation.'"

Spent, Wolff leaned back in his chair.

"Mr. Wolff?" I said. "Are you okay?"

"Well," he said, straightening, "now that we have been through all that, I think you must call me E. P."

I smiled, sensing that this was no small honor. "I have already taken so much of your time, I wouldn't want to—"

"I fired the last of my other clients this morning just before you came in," he said. "The trust is . . . in effect, *you* are . . . my only client now."

CHAPTER TWENTY-EIGHT

Chrysalis

O N A LARK I ASKED MY driver to stop at a jewelry store before we had
gone four blocks into my return trip. He found a quaint little shop
downtown and circled the block while I went in. It was a quiet space and
the proprietor, an elderly man who insisted on speaking in whispers, seemed
entertained at the novelty of having a young woman in his establishment.

I handed him the necklace and he laid it on a felt blotter.

"Is it pewter?" I asked, as he inspected the piece with a loupe.

The man looked up at me in astonishment. "Young lady, I'm not sure you
know what you have here. Please excuse me for a moment."

He vanished into a back room. For an anxious moment, I feared he might
abscond with the piece, but he returned a few minutes later. Far from the dingy
item I had worn around my neck since the beginning of my exile, the locket
he laid down on the felt was a brilliant silver color. I barely recognized it.

"What is it?"

"The only metal suitable for royalty," the man whispered. "Or so Louis
XVI declared."

I blinked at him.

"Platinum, my dear girl, though I have never seen it so tarnished before,"
he said. "But it cleaned up quite easily. Can you tell me how old it is?"

"I don't really know."

"It is an incredible piece. How much will you take for it?"

"No, I couldn't part with it," I said. "I was only hoping you'd be able to tell me something about it."

The man smiled at me.

"Only that it is some hundreds of years old and this seems almost impossible. Because its melting point is so high, platinum was almost never used in jewelry until recently. It wasn't until the oxyhydrogen torch was invented that it became easier to work and therefore more popular as jewelry. In fact, I have never seen a piece made earlier than 1795. This example was made by someone very skilled indeed. In a way I am glad you did not accept my offer. I imagine this piece is quite beyond my means and I am not sure I would be able to sleep if you had sold it to me for anything I could actually afford."

Before I thanked him and took my leave, I considered showing him the secret latch and the way the piece opened, but caution prevailed. The ruby inside was apparently a bearer instrument, after all, and I had no idea what else it might unlock.

I WAS SO OCCUPIED with the locket that it was more than halfway into the drive back to Curie Hall that the import of the crest I'd seen in E. P. Wolff's office came to me: it closely resembled the laughing-wolf elements of the depiction I had seen in the Letters from the Dead. Had the Wolff family once been members of the Order of Nyx? Were they still?

My head spun the entire way back home. It was already getting dark when we left, and I watched through the passenger window as the gray of the city slowly melted into the greens and browns of the country. It was a long drive, but in light of everything, I was happy for the time alone with my thoughts.

Had I imagined Wolff's hesitation before answering my question about my grandfather's death? Was there some awful truth he was trying to protect me from? I remembered what my grandfather had once said about removing patriarchs in our family:

The head of the family also must recognize when it is time to start the process of stepping aside, so the next patriarch can begin to take his place.

You mean Father, I had replied, and my grandfather had nodded. *How do you know when it is time, Grandfather?*

A good leader always knows.

What if he doesn't?

In that case, the decision is . . . made for him. Perhaps even by his own heirs.

I shuddered and wrapped my arms around myself, unsettled by the topics my inner monologue seemed determined to explore.

But why wouldn't Grandfather have stepped aside? I wondered. And I remembered something else he had once said:

My dear, the future: it is for the young. They alone are suited to bring a dynasty safely into their epoch.

Had he changed his mind when the time came? Had he ignored his own advice? Because of me? Because of his notorious streak of sentimentality?

My mother had even commented on it my last night on the estate when she and my grandfather had been fighting.

This is the very last moment to fall prey to some misplaced sense of nobility, she had said. *Your overdeveloped sentimentality will be the end of us all, don't you understand? It is not possible, even for you, to sacrifice this family for . . . one of them? Do you think they will thank you for it? Even in the thrall of your famous idealism you cannot possibly be that naïve.*

These thoughts swirled together in my head until, answers having eluded me entirely, they blended together into an incomprehensible morass.

I closed my eyes and curled up in the back seat for the rest of the trip.

BACK AT ELLIS House, and seeing no light under our door, I opened it as gingerly as I could. From the dark shape in Phoebe's bed I assumed she was asleep. I had just started undressing when her light came on.

"Where the hell have you been?" she said. I hated the bossy tone she was taking.

"Out, quite obviously. It's Friday night. I'm surprised you are even here."

"Well, I am."

"Look," I said, exasperated, and exhausted from the emotional ordeal I had endured. "I'm going to bed."

"No you're not," she snapped.

"Excuse me?"

Phoebe got out of bed and yanked open the top drawer of her desk. She held something up in front of her desk lamp.

"Want to explain this to me?"

She was holding the glassine baggie with the red pill in it.

"Where did you get that?" I demanded.

"The question is where did *you* get it."

"What the hell were you doing in my clutch, Phoebe?"

She ignored my question. "Tell me where you got it. I mean, right now."

I remembered what Pierce had told me about Phoebe's protectiveness and thought I understood what she was worked up about.

"I found it under the table on the floor at Vincenzo di Napoli." I sighed, and rolled my eyes for effect.

Phoebe gave me a hard look. I returned it with what I hoped was a vaguely irritated one.

If I was hooked up to a lie detector, I thought, *Pierce's little gambit might actually let me pass.*

Phoebe frowned and then seemed to accept my answer. She flipped the baggie into her top drawer and then slammed it shut.

"Hey," I protested. "Give it back."

"It's not for you," Phoebe said.

I'm not sure why it upset me so much. Perhaps I was tired of Phoebe's big-sister act, or still wound up by the horrible news. More likely her maternal stance toward me reminded me of my mother. Maybe that was what triggered something in me; something angry; more aggressive.

Phoebe turned away, maybe to crawl back into bed. Anger welling up, I stalked over to her side of the room, ripped open her top desk drawer, and started hunting for the baggie.

Phoebe whirled around and, once she saw what I was doing, grabbed my wrist and pulled it away.

"What the fuck do you think you are doing?" she said.

"Give it back."

"No. Go to bed."

It might have been the worst thing she could have said in that moment. I had to work hard to keep from exploding. Then she pushed me. It wasn't hard, exactly, but firm enough that I had to take a few steps back and ended up sitting on my bed when the backs of my knees hit the mattress.

"Don't think for a minute that I don't see through the entire 'for your own good' act, Phoebe," I snapped, near tears.

Phoebe seemed stunned, astounded to hear something so assertive from me.

"You are happy to let me drink underage," I said, catching a verbal stride, "keep me out far past curfew, and leave me to find my own way home at three in the morning because you are busy making out in the shadows. But you are somehow the authority on what's best for me. Right?"

Phoebe blinked at me, still in shock, but then slowly began to find her words again.

"Where is all this coming from?" she said.

"Maybe a year of being treated like your baby sister is a bit much? Maybe I've had enough of being ditched whenever you want to fuck Pierce?"

"Watch your mouth," Phoebe barked.

"Sure, Mom," I sneered at her. "Whatever you say."

I hadn't even noticed I was crying, but big tears fell from my cheeks onto my hands. Even as I felt an ugly emotion welling up in me and knew it was making me act out, I tried to pretend it away; to deny its essential nature: jealousy.

Phoebe was stuck again, not quite sure what she was supposed to say.

"Okay, fine," she managed, and tore her desk drawer open so hard that a pair of highlighters bounced out and onto our floor.

It was Friday night, and many of the other girls would be on a roof somewhere, off campus, or huddled together in one of the more spacious rooms in Randolph House, but we were getting loud enough that I worried someone would hear.

She retrieved and then spun the baggie at me like a Frisbee. It sailed across our room, rather elegantly, I had to admit, and landed in my lap.

"There you go, hotshot," she said. "Have at it. Let's see."

I picked up the baggie and looked at the bright red pill inside. Then I looked at Phoebe. She had a defiant expression on her face, daring me to call her bluff.

I didn't even think about it. I just put the baggie in my mouth, tore the

Ziploc end of it off with my front teeth, spat that part on the floor, and then upended the torn plastic, turned my head up, and dumped the pill into my mouth.

"No," Phoebe shouted. "*Wait.*"

She was across the room in a flash and for a moment I was afraid she would grab me and try to force my mouth open or something, but instead she just sat next to me on my bed and put her hand on the back of my neck.

"Please," she said, trying desperately to be calm. "Please spit it out."

The pill was bitter, horribly bitter, and shot through that was a deeply metallic, artificial taste. It almost broke my resolve, that and the fact that the authoritarian in Phoebe melted away when she was really worried about me; that she didn't seem able to bear that she had been physically rough with me. But I was too angry to turn back. Was she also a convenient target for projection, a place for me to redirect my anger with my mother? Probably, but I had lost so much in just twenty-four hours that, even being somewhat aware that I was doing it, I kept on for spite's sake.

I looked Phoebe right in the eye, gave her a defiant and sardonic smile, and then loudly crunched down on the pill in my mouth with my front teeth. The strong twinge of industrial metal washed over every part of the inside of my mouth. It forced a swallowing reflex and I found I had ingested what must have been three-quarters of the pill without even meaning to. The rest was stuck on the front of my tongue.

"I wish you hadn't done that," Phoebe whispered, almost to herself.

Phoebe let go of my neck and sighed, slumping back on my bed, looking up at the ceiling. Then she did something that astounded me: she started to cry. It was rare for Phoebe to get flustered. I had certainly never seen her cry before.

"I wish . . ." she said, through tears. "I wish you hadn't . . ."

A string of impulsive behavior had been building up in me since last night at Vincenzo di Napoli. Even so, I'm not exactly sure what fueled what began to come over me. I think there was more to it than emotional pain. I also think that seeing Phoebe cry, and realizing how much she really did care, is what triggered what happened next.

It was far too quick for the pill to have had any effect. But some feeling of independence rose in me, bolstered perhaps by the news of the existence of the Fulvia Flacca Trust. I had been so sad about the death of my grandfather that I hadn't fully absorbed what he had written to me in his letter. I no longer had to suffer under the belief that he had been furious with me, that my exile was punishment. Whatever his motives had been, anger had not been among them.

I barely thought about it. I just did it: I leaned close over the prone Phoebe and planted a deep kiss on her mouth. She fought it at first. I think more than anything because I had surprised her. Then she let me. And then her arms came around me. And when I shared what was left of the pill with her, pressed it onto her tongue with mine, she took it without complaint and swallowed it.

PIERCE HAD BEEN right when he had said "bliss on tap." About thirty minutes later, as it came on, I remember thinking that "ecstasy" was the wrong name for the drug, that the classic definition implied a debilitating rapture of the sort that seizes religious zealots, afflicts them with visions, or throws them to the ground in mouth-foaming fits. Instead, what I felt began as a subtle warmth and grew into a halcyon state. Occasionally the pleasure threatened to become overwhelming, hovered at the edge of a much darker and seemingly bottomless chasm of euphoria. But whenever I started to become fearful of falling into those shadows, the feeling of total contentment and well-being returned. It was almost as if even the hint of fear was actually triggering resurgences of the most relaxing serenity.

I think Phoebe took pity on me. She easily could have gone much further. At one point I almost urged her to, but there seemed to be an invisible line she would not cross. Perhaps she knew that, whatever I had claimed before that first real kiss, I wasn't really ready for more. Still, what liberties she allowed herself were more than enough. Kissing her, being kissed by her, her obviously experienced caresses on my skin—tickling nuzzles against my ears, fingers run through my hair and down my neck, lips brushed over my navel—each sent new shivers across my whole body and evoked from me soft murmurs and little moans my innate shyness was unable, no matter how hard I tried, to contain.

When it was apparent that the repeated crests and troughs she led me through threatened to exhaust me utterly, she held me close and we lay together, wearing next to nothing. First, facing her, I spent nearly an hour fascinated with how beautiful the brilliant blue of her eyes was to me. Then, spooned together, the warm skin of her midriff radiated an intoxicating heat into my back and I felt her heartbeat pulsing against my shoulder blade.

Pierce had been right about the sensuality extending to sight too. Phoebe had thrown a red T-shirt over her desk lamp, casting our room in a dim, burgundy light. Sleep was impossible and, for what must have been hours, I took in the crimson-tinted colors of the comforter on her bed, the wood grain of her desk, and the coffee mug on her bookshelf.

It was bliss on tap.

When I finally fell asleep, I dreamed of my grandfather. It was the dead of night and we were walking together in silence, navigating through the forest's snowdrifts. I knew it was terribly cold outside, but the temperature did not seem to affect me at all; as if Phoebe's warmth in the real world insulated me from the cold of my dream. My grandfather and I arrived at a clearing and a cloud slipped away from the moon, bathing everything in silver-blue light that was unspeakably beautiful. I recognized where he had brought me: our family mausoleum. My grandfather made as if to speak, and I knew he was about to tell me something very important but, before he could get a word out, I woke up and he was gone.

IN THE WAKE of my intimacy with Phoebe, I found myself painfully confused. Somewhere deep down I was afraid of getting too close to her; to anyone. But she filled so many empty places in my psyche. She was at once the mother I never had, the big sister I had lost when Augustin's prank was revealed as fiction, and, after that night with her, my first lover. Even had I wanted to, or had I been perceptive enough at that age to appreciate the potential danger, to break with her was unthinkable.

CHAPTER TWENTY-NINE

~

The Penthouse

GRADUATION CAME AND WENT. PHOEBE AND I skipped commencement, but I doubt anyone really noticed. With a stipend from the Fulvia Flacca Trust at my disposal, money was no longer an issue and we fled campus bound for New York City at our earliest opportunity. I only realized afterward that, in our rush to leave Curie, I had forgotten the bundles of cash I had buried next to the maple tree on the edge of the grounds.

In a way the forgotten currency was a metaphor for me. Phoebe had an independent streak a mile long, and with her penchant for self-sufficiency, she had one foot out of the door at Curie Hall years before she graduated. For her our migration to Manhattan was a dream come true. For me, leaving Curie Hall, especially for somewhere as intense as I expected New York would be, was uncomfortably intimidating.

It was months until registration, so Phoebe rented us a quaint, if small, flat in a brownstone on West Ninety-Fourth Street. It was walking distance to campus, and that made it almost perfect. To this day I have no idea how she found the place or convinced the landlords to rent to her (though I assume they came to regret it quickly in light of the events that followed).

Phoebe being Phoebe, and nothing if not a nocturnal creature, she quickly identified the elements of the local nightlife that she favored. It wasn't long before she presented me with an unusual gift: an absurd fake ID that for some reason everyone accepted. That matter handled, she delighted in taking me with her on her urban wildlife safaris, excursions that, strangely, began to include late-night architecture tours as we made our way to (or, increasingly, from) the latest drinking establishment on her "to visit" list.

It was only a few days until class registration and freshman orientation day at Columbia when the source of her mysterious fascination with nighttime viewings of darkened buildings was finally illuminated. We were walking home after hours, coming from a dimly lit lounge called the Cloisters, where Phoebe had gotten into a deep conversation about the tension between idealism and realism with a philosophy student at Fordham University. Thanks to Professor Lechner, I knew the topic well and, listening to them, I remember thinking that something had blossomed in Phoebe just in the couple of months we had been in the city. Or that her capacity for intense discussion had always been there, but Curie Hall had been too shallow an intellectual pool for her to bother wading into.

The realization occasioned in me a twinge of guilt. I had actively hid my own thirst for that sort of interaction, not just from Phoebe, but from anyone and everyone at Curie Hall. It had been a defense mechanism but, sitting there in the booth at the Cloisters, I regretted that both Phoebe and I had been, in a sense, hiding from each other for all that time. Phoebe had known somehow that Manhattan was an environment she needed, and I was beyond happy that she had found it, but I couldn't help but wonder "what might have been" had I not been too terrified to unveil my own intellect as well.

We walked home arm in arm along a wandering route, though by that time I knew well enough that our diversion likely had purpose. Still tipsy from several martinis, we ended up standing on Amsterdam Avenue looking at a large, red brick building.

"Now what?" I said, tired and a little annoyed. If past experience held, Phoebe would start to talk about the design of the edifice in a tone that reminded me vaguely of Sir Nigel's droning monologues.

"Just look," Phoebe said, and gazed up at the squat little spires jutting up against the night sky.

"A youth hostel?" I said, seeing the bronze lettering over the entrance. "Very glamorous."

"It wasn't always," Phoebe countered. "It is quite old, actually. It was built in the 1880s to house widows of the Revolutionary War."

An 1880s construction didn't seem that old to me, but I held my tongue and waited for Phoebe to continue.

"It was designed by Richard Morris Hunt, one of the greatest American architects of all time. He studied in Rome, Geneva, and I think he was the first American admitted to the school of architecture of the École des Beaux-Arts. He was a mainstay of the Gilded Age and designed dozens of homes in Newport, Rhode Island, not to mention a series of Fifth Avenue mansions. Though most of those were demolished."

Phoebe's voice cracked a little and I looked at her, concerned.

She sighed before continuing. "You had only really arrived as a 'Captain of Industry' when you moved into a Hunt. This is one of his last surviving works in New York City. I've always wanted to see it."

She had struck me dumb, and a long silence developed as Phoebe gazed at the building.

"Phoebe," I managed at last. "How do you know all this?"

I had never bothered to ask before, and it was a long time before she answered. "My father is a noted architect, with the ego to match. When it came to architecture he just couldn't shut up. I hated him so much . . . *hate* him so much . . . that I swore I would never have anything to do with architecture. But, well, I guess it is in the blood or something."

So many pieces fell together for me then. Cornell, Princeton, Columbia, Penn, NYU—all were renowned for their architecture programs. Phoebe's fascination with New York guidebooks and coffee-table volumes with glossy pictures of skyscrapers back at Curie wasn't some aspiring tourist's idle fantasy; she had been admiring the city's aesthetics.

"Phoebe, why didn't you tell me you were interested in architecture?"

"I don't know," she said, and then cut off the conversation by pulling me toward home by the elbow.

IT WAS PAST one in the morning when we staggered through our front door, and I think the vodka martinis were catching up with both of us. Phoebe got very serious. She stood in front of me and without warning gave me a big, long hug. She leaned back and just looked at me, her arms still wrapped around my neck.

"Kiss me," she said, and started leaning in.

"Phoebe . . ." I started to pull away, but then she paused, distracted by something.

"Did you leave the light on?" she asked, looking toward the living room.

"Uh, no?" I said, though suddenly I wasn't sure.

I scoured my short-term memory. I was sure that I had turned the key in the dead bolt when we came in and that the door had been locked.

Clutching each other, we crept toward the living room door. It was a particularly stupid thing to do. We had made so much noise coming in that, if there was an intruder, he certainly knew we were there (and what kind of intruder leaves the living room light on anyway?).

Clinging to me, and with great drama, Phoebe motioned that I should chance the door handle.

"Oh, whatever," I said, annoyed with the fuss, and threw open the living room door.

Phoebe screamed.

Sitting on the living room couch, reading a book, prim, proper, and composed as you please, was my mother. Behind her a dark figure towered: Karl.

IT HAD BEEN three years since I had seen her, and it jarred me into this pervasive sense of unreality, a dissociative certainty that I had drifted off somewhere and was caught between dream and consciousness, watching events unfold from elsewhere, even as I participated in them.

My mother had not changed a bit; not aged a day. She was perfectly dressed and seated exactly where the light in our living room complimented her most favorably. Because I grew up with her, it took me until adulthood to fully understand the impact she could have on others. Even though she had not said a word, I could see that Phoebe, her defenses already dulled with alcohol, was instantly in her thrall.

Wordlessly, my mother stood and glided over, closing the distance between us. Before I realized it, I had curtsied to her. I hated doing it in front of Phoebe, but the force of the urge was so powerful that I couldn't stop myself.

She gave me a thin smile, kissed my cheeks three times in ritualistic greeting, and then, in a gesture so unfamiliar it made me stiffen, embraced me gently and kissed my forehead. I was instantly aware that I smelled of secondhand smoke and vodka and I had to clench my jaw to keep from flinching away.

"My clever, clever little girl," she said, though what she was referring to was a mystery to me.

When she released me, my mother had an expectant look on her face and it took me a few seconds to catch the hint.

"Oh," I stammered. "Please forgive me. May I present Phoebe Aresdottir, my roommate." My voice was much meeker than I intended. "Phoebe, this is my mother."

"Pálhanna," Phoebe said quickly.

"Sorry?" my mother said.

"My name is Pálhanna Aresdottir."

My face flushed. As long as I had known her, Phoebe had never used her real first name with others.

"Icelandic, I suppose," my mother said, and looked her over. "Yes, I can see it now."

I could feel the horror building in my abdomen. What Phoebe might say to my mother while drunk was terrifyingly unknowable.

"My grandfather had some small role in Icelandic independence, you know," my mother said. In fact, I had not known this. "I visited once when I was quite young. How ever did you find your way to this place?"

"My father," Phoebe said.

I cringed.

"I see," my mother said. "What employment brings your family here then?"

Tipsy or no, I immediately recognized the import of her question. There might have been several things my mother abhorred more than the type of upper-middle-class family that would move to follow the father's career opportunities, but I couldn't think of any at that moment.

"None, really," Phoebe said. I could detect a sway developing in her stance. I thought she might stumble, but she held on. "I used my trust to escape to the States."

I held my breath hoping Phoebe would stop there. To my relief, she did.

"Well, then, my dear," my mother said, "how do you find them?"

"Your daughter makes it all tolerable," Phoebe said.

My mother absorbed this. I could sense her deciding if she should unleash the full force of her social Gorgon gaze upon the hapless creatures in front of her, but for some reason she refrained and her expression softened instead. Phoebe, bless her heart, had no idea how close to ruin she had come.

"Miss Aresdottir, I do hope you will excuse us, but my daughter and I have much to discuss. Surely you can spare her?"

"Of course," Phoebe said, but her voice sounded almost hypnotized.

My mother gave Karl a glance over her shoulder. As I watched, Karl picked his blazer up off the sofa before leading us out. I saw it then: he had laid it down so my mother would not have to sit directly on our couch.

⟲

AFTER SEEING US deposited in the back seat of a black town car parked right outside our flat, Karl took the wheel and we were on our way.

"Out on the town, were we?" my mother said, breaking the silence. I thought it a surreal start to a conversation given the circumstances. "A bit underdressed, I think, no?" I could actually feel the chill of her gaze on my bare legs when I saw her looking at the miniskirt I was wearing. "Well, hopefully your evening was . . . what shall we say? Sufficiently distracting?"

This comment was, I felt sure, intended to throw me off balance. In that it was effective. I could only nod, and murmur in reply. Thankfully, it wasn't long before we reached our destination: a small restaurant on an out-of-the-way street. It was approaching two in the morning by that time, but when Karl knocked on the front door we were greeted by a skeleton staff who ushered us through the empty place and into a back room where a single table was waiting with two settings atop white linen.

Karl held my mother's chair as she sat and then posted himself outside.

"Well," my mother said, scrutinizing me as I took my seat, "you seem to have endured your ordeal well enough, and at least they fed you well. We have that to thank them for, I suppose."

There were no menus; no ordering. Instead the staff served a preselected soup course. It was my mother's signature touch: the social ambush.

"How are you for money, dear?" my mother asked, but something about the way she avoided eye contact put me on guard.

Given what E. P. Wolff had said about the Fulvia Flacca Trust, what I wanted most was to change the subject. But if I delayed in answering, I knew I would be telegraphing more than I wanted. I used the cover of sipping my soup to buy precious seconds to think.

"Well, I still have most of the cash Grandfather left in my suitcase the night I left," I lied. "There wasn't much to spend it on at school. And Phoebe has been helpful."

My mother was watching me carefully, and it took some effort to mask my nervous deception. Finally, after giving me an oddly puzzled look, she went back to her soup.

"Why didn't you let me come home for the summers?" I ventured, almost surprised I had the courage. My mother put down her spoon and looked at me. "The school stole all my mail. I couldn't even write home. You could have at least let me come to Grandfather's funeral."

"What on earth are you talking about?" my mother said.

"He was wonderful and kind to me when no one else cared for my presence. He and Professor Lechner were some of the only people on the entire estate who I truly loved. He was a patriarch of the family and I was his granddaughter, and yet I wasn't allowed to mourn him. No one even told me he died. Why?"

"You are young and ignorant in the ways of the world, and—"

"I know more about—"

"Be *silent*," my mother hissed.

Some part of me knew better than to ignore her command or interrupt her again. She seemed to be calculating something in the lull that intervened and, even as I watched, the answer came to her. She gave me a look of sympathy, as one forced to explain the realities of the world to a small child.

"I think I understand now," she said, softly; her voice was honey-laced and filled with condescension. "Your grandfather, this man you worship, violated the traditions of succession, traditions that have endured centuries and that he himself never hesitated to extol the virtues of. He then attempted to usurp your father's rightful authority, kidnapped you and your brother—"

"*Kidnapped?*"

"—sent you away in secret and in the dead of night and refused to disclose your location to your own flesh and blood. My god. He abducted his own son's children to use as leverage in a depraved fight for power. A fight with his own heir, no less. He violated the most fundamental principles of this family, and he used you, an innocent child, to further his scheme. Do you understand?"

"You are a liar," I said, choking the words out to get them past the growing lump in my throat.

The room had shrunk down to a confined center, a micro-universe that, in that moment, contained only my mother and me.

"My darling, you have become a victim of Stockholm syndrome. Don't you realize that, once he died, we had no way to discover where you were? If you hadn't been so clever and slipped that letter past the censors at that horrible place, who knows how long it might have been before we found you again. I cannot tell you what a horror it was to deal with the Headmistress. It took Karl's intervention to extract from her the name of the university you had absconded to."

I winced, suddenly worried for Dr. Emily P. Templeton-Wright, PhD.

"On that note, do you know how hard it has been to continue to explain your absence? Do you have any idea what that *man* has done to this family? We are still struggling to recover from the little coup he and Lechner brewed up.

"We will, of course, do what is necessary to preserve his image in public to avoid tarnishing this family's reputation, but your grandfather was not some noble savior. Far from it. He was a child abductor, an embezzler, and a hypocrite. I will not hear his name or title again, and I hope that's perfectly clear."

My mother paused for effect, her eyes boring into mine with an intensity that frightened me. Then she wiped her mouth delicately with her napkin and pushed her soup away. "I find I have lost my appetite," she said.

"I want to go home," I murmured through tears. It had just slipped out. "I want—"

"I'm not sure you should take the results of your last foray into family politics as encouragement to launch another," my mother snapped. "Matters of great moment are being decided on the estate just now. It is not an environment appropriate for children. Be that as it may, I assure you that we will find quite enough to occupy you without adding to your portfolio in that respect. In fact, I think it is high time we started preparing your formal presentation to society."

"You cannot be serious," I gasped.

"Quite serious. I realize that it is traditional to wait until sixteen to apply as a debutante to the Officer's Ball and the Vienna Opera Ball, but I am certain I could pull some strings for the winter after this coming, and that's barely a year and a half away. It will be here before you know it, and you have a lot of catching up to do. Some girls your age have been preparing for their interviews to be among the young women presented at the Officer's Ball since they were ten.

"It is time for you to start living up to the responsibilities you have to your family. Augustin has his part to play, of course, and I will see to it that you play yours."

Somehow I knew where the conversation was headed, and the images that came to me were dispiriting. I saw myself enduring dozens of trite social events where the primary expectation of the young women involved was that they be pretty, talented at following the lead of their dance partner, and able to conduct hours of conversation without saying anything at all of import or controversy. I knew well enough that the life my mother was proposing for me would be a full schedule of such performances designed to exhibit and certify me as a delightfully harmless trophy (and heir producer) to be.

"There is an exceptional finishing school near Vienna that takes boarders. It would be—"

"*No!*" I shouted, much louder than I intended.

My mother glared at me and I could see the anger welling up. I almost imagined the dark limbal rings in her eyes pulsating with rage.

"I do not want to go to another boarding school," I said, lowering my voice and trying to keep it from cracking. "I want to come home," I repeated, but I wasn't entirely sure that was even true.

"Of course, I am cognizant of what you have been forced to endure, and in view of that I expect some allowances might be made for the occasional behavioral lapse. But what I most certainly did *not* expect to find at the end of this long journey was an insolent, self-centered, and ill-mannered child. It is painfully obvious that you have no concept or appreciation whatsoever for the challenges faced, or the sacrifices made by your family in your absence. All you can think of is yourself. What you want. What you think you are owed. Well, that simply *will not do.*

"You are expected to make your contribution to this family. And, let me explain this to you very clearly once more, I will see to it that you meet your responsibilities."

"By being turned into some sort of mindless doll?" I snapped. "Made up to look pretty at the ball and taught to recite stupid platitudes so that I can be married off to whatever husband you choose?"

"To whomever your *family* believes will be most suitable—"

"You mean whomever *you* believe—"

"—and most likely to further your father's goals, among other things."

"Further his goals? What on earth does that mean?"

"My poor child, it means whatever your father says it means. He is the head of this family."

"I have no intention at all of 'furthering Father's goals' if it means being treated like some sort of chattel."

"Then what, precisely, my dear, do you hope to contribute to this family? And how?"

I opened my mouth, prepared to blurt out something. But I think I understood how ridiculous anything I might say would sound to my mother. She dragged the moment out, letting me look foolish for an uncomfortably long time. Then she shook her head before speaking again.

"I had hoped that you would behave as a daughter of the line is expected to. I shall not make that mistake again.

"Still, in a way you've done me quite a favor. Your conduct here has convinced me that it is quite impossible for us to deliver to the most prestigious finishing school on the Continent a child so spoiled and possessed of such vile habits of behavior. I count myself lucky for detecting it early. I have no intention of rewarding such ingratitude, not to mention the fact that I can only imagine how difficult it would be to repair the damage if we permitted your foul attitude while attending such a storied institution to taint this family's reputation.

"My dear, I would be remiss if I did not warn you that the window in which you are able to exercise some agency in these matters, to exert some influence on these decisions, is closing quite rapidly. Before you know it, you may find yourself in a situation where choices you might like to contribute to are made for you instead."

My mother stood up, brushed down her long skirts, and headed for the door.

"Come along, dear," she said, and then to Karl: "We're leaving."

"But madam," the maître d' protested on our way out, "was the food not to your liking?"

"Quite the contrary," my mother said, and shot me a glance. "It was the company I found off-putting."

WE DROVE BACK to the flat in silence, but once inside, my mother acted as if nothing had happened. Phoebe was still awake, and I sensed she had waited up to see what might happen next. My mother did not disappoint.

"Ladies," she announced, "though I'm sure I couldn't be happier for you that you've been able to play house here, I've made arrangements for you to move to more civilized accommodations." She turned to me. "Your father has several residential properties in the city he acquired for investment purposes. I've selected a lovely spot for you closer to campus. I am certain you will find it far more suitable."

"But our lease—" Phoebe protested.

"Now, now," my mother said, cutting her off. "That is the least of your concerns." She looked at Karl. "I'm sure the present landlord might be made to see reason, no?"

"He will," Karl said.

"Good. It is settled then. You will very much prefer your new abode, I assure you."

"What about whoever is living there now?" I asked, trying to find some flaw in her scheme. "I mean, you aren't going to just *evict them* on our account, are you?"

My mother looked shocked. "Tenants?" she said. The effect was so real I wasn't entirely sure that it wasn't genuine. "These are *investment* properties. Do you seriously think that I would allow the second-generation heirs to the Midwest's third-largest commodities broker to taint your father's assets?"

"I think that will be quite enough discussion on the matter," my mother said, calming herself and glancing at Karl. "We are departing for the estate now. I'm sure you must be desperate for cash," she said, mostly, I felt, for Phoebe's benefit.

On cue, Karl produced a large handbag and set it on our dining room table.

"Honestly, dear, I respect your desire to exert your independence, and I'm pleased you have managed to fend for yourself since our last meeting, but this is no way for you to live." She glanced at Phoebe. "Nor can we allow you to rely on the largesse of others. Just let Karl know if you need more from now on. A fatuous flirtation with Marxism in one's youth is only quaint in families with less history than our own.

"Thank you for looking after my daughter, Miss Aresdottir," my mother said. "I do hope you will choose to continue to live with her. She could use"— she paused before continuing—"a mature feminine influence. Don't worry. There will be plenty of room for the three of you. There are, I believe, nine bedrooms."

"The *three of us?*" I said.

"Oh, my dear. You didn't think I was going to leave you girls alone, did you? What kind of mother do you think I am? Karl will be staying with you."

And with that she was at the door waiting, with great formality, for me to kiss her farewell.

Phoebe and I were silent for a long time after they left.

Phoebe finally broke our reverie with a whisper. "Your mom is stunning."

She was, of course, but Phoebe's comment threw me into a silent fury.

THE KEYS TO the penthouse were in the bag Karl had left behind. The address was typed on a piece of paper wrapped around fifty thousand dollars in cash. Had I grown up in some other environment, against the background of some other family history, I should have been horrified by my mother's behavior. She had, after all, spent all of two hours with her only daughter, who she suggested had been the subject of a grandparental abduction and thereby lost to her for three years. I should have been horrified, but I was not.

In fact, my mother's behavior was entirely consistent with what I expected from her. It did not occur to me how neglectful it should have appeared. On the contrary, in the aftermath of our meeting, I was most stricken by the threat of finishing school, and surprised that my mother had been so indiscreet with money in front of Phoebe.

Eventually, I reasoned that my mother either had her own reasons for playing along, or had taken Phoebe for "one of us" (perhaps because of the comment about her trust). Of course, my mother could never permit such a thing: a child of hers supported by some outsider.

As to what she had said about my grandfather, that particular set of accusations was so traumatizing that it took me several days to appreciate their implications.

PHOEBE AND I first visited our new residence the next evening. I think I sensed the trap my mother had set before seeing it, but somehow I couldn't bring myself to say anything to Phoebe. Part of me screamed to run away, far away from my mother's "charity." I suspected that, once lured into a dependence on my family, it would be beyond difficult to extract ourselves from it. Resisting that sort of trap was the point of the Fulvia Flacca Trust, after all, wasn't it? Still, I couldn't help but be curious about what my mother had arranged.

The building was just off Central Park and the views of the skyline were incredible. I was afraid to guess if it was just the penthouse we owned, or the entire building. Either way, as would be expected of any real estate owned by my family, it was absolutely gorgeous. The elevator was key-operated and opened directly into the foyer on the first level. I knew the moment that we set foot inside that I had made a mistake; that my mother had fully expected that I would put up a fight about finishing school and that she had prepared her contingency plan well in advance.

Stay within yourself and your capabilities. Don't be lured into interactions that others control, I thought.

Too late.

It was well after sunset when we first walked in. Standing in front of the floor-to-ceiling windows around the perimeter, we took in the city beneath, bathed in the glow of streetlights and the occasional touch of neon. I expected something ostentatious but the views surprised even me. Phoebe was entirely unprepared for them.

On exploring, we found a temperature-controlled wine closet and a pristine Steinway concert grand piano that occupied a recital room (acoustic panels and all) that seemed almost built around the instrument. The living quarters were upstairs and the entire space was furnished in a style that was both traditional and excessive. My mother's fingerprints were all over it.

Returning to the windows on the first floor, Phoebe positioned one of the Roosevelt chairs in front of the glass and sat there gazing out into the night for more than an hour.

"Can I ask you a question?" she said, finally breaking the silence. "You never talk about them, you know. I mean, what does your family . . . do?"

"Real estate," I mumbled, after a panicked search for an authentic-sounding answer.

"Oh. Duh. That's obvious," Phoebe said, and then dropped the matter entirely.

After touring the rest of the space once more, I returned to find Phoebe asleep in the chair. That, at least, left me with first pick of the bedrooms.

～の

PHOEBE FOUND THE "Churchill Room" the next day. It was an elegant little lounge, walking distance from our front door, and full of dark woods, dim corners, and plastered in Winston Churchill photos and other wartime-era Anglo paraphernalia. It was quiet on weekdays, but on weekends it was well populated by older bankers who made a habit of ordering drinks for us from afar.

Only a few days later, getting ready to head out for cocktails, Phoebe barged into my room unannounced when I was changing. It was a habit of hers and her timing was annoyingly inconvenient. I had just been picking out something to wear and was standing topless in front of my mirror.

"Hey," I protested, wrapping my arms around my chest defensively. "I'm changing, Phoebe."

"Oh, whatever," she said, but her eyes lit on the dress I had hung up next to the mirror. "Hey, that's mine," she complained, pointing.

"You said I could borrow it."

"I'm wearing it tonight," she insisted, which was a bit absurd, as she had given it to me in the first place because the piece was too small for her. Then, in what I had to admit was an amazing display of dexterity, she darted over, snatched it up, and, ignoring my protests, bolted out my door, giggling madly all the way down the hall.

It was a typical Phoebe flirtation. I was expected to chase after her and so, annoyed and amused in equal measure, I did. Phoebe ducked into her room and closed the door behind her, leaving me pounding on it from the hallway.

"Come on, Phoebe," I pleaded. "Open up." But she ignored me.

I turned back toward my room only to find Karl standing in the corridor. He had obviously been attracted by the noise. It was the first time I had seen him since the encounter with my mother. Surprised by his silent appearance, I froze in my tracks, only half-dressed and standing under the full glare of the white halogens that illuminated the hallway outside our bedrooms.

I was too stunned to cover up, even when I saw Karl's gaze fall to my marred left breast and the dark scar there. I thought for a moment I could see concern register on his face. I was convinced that he would ask me about the old wound, but instead he remained silent. All I could do was stand up straight and, with whatever shred of dignity I could still muster, walk past him and back to my bedroom.

Later that night, I remembered something my grandfather had once said: *It is impolite to gossip about battle wounds, you know.*

IT WASN'T LONG before classes were set to begin. I remember watching hordes of nervous freshmen moving into Carman Hall, and I grew anxious that Phoebe and I would be flouting the requirement to live on campus our first year. Phoebe made quick work of my concern though.

"Just because we have rooms on campus doesn't mean we have to live in them," she pointed out.

"Aren't they going to find out?" I protested.

"Didn't you learn anything at Curie? Go meet your roommate and ask her if she wants the place to herself for the year. How eager do you think she is going to be to rat you out?"

Phoebe was right, of course.

The university was much larger and more impersonal than Curie Hall. We found we could bury ourselves somewhere in the last few rows during lectures and read unrelated finance books (in my case), architecture tomes, or *Cosmo's Guide to Sexual Wellness* (as Phoebe was occasionally fond of doing).

Everything about her seemed to inspire almost rabid devotion among a certain contingent of the overcompensating male freshmen in our classes, and she basked in the attention, even if she rarely returned it.

I think their obvious and intense interest piqued my (hopefully more subtle) desires. I can still picture Phoebe lounging at her favorite table in Butler Library's main reading room, where, at a certain time of day, the light from the towering windows would hit her just right and make her hair almost translucent; strands of pale winter wheat in the sun that she would, now and again, brush out of her eyes with an absent gesture.

I was not her only admirer by a long shot, and it was never long before, out of the corner of my eye, I could spot the two or three would-be suitors trying desperately not to be seen gawking at her.

Occasionally, when I should have been studying, I would catch myself watching her, very much in the same way, waiting for the moment when the sky outside faded and dimmed, setting her instead against shades of dusk, fought off only by the warm yellow of the incandescent desk lamp next to her. This would last until just before eleven at night, when closing time loomed and we had to pack up for the evening.

Even as I settled in to university life, I found myself isolated from the rest of the student body. Somehow it was easy to wall off the rest of the world living with Phoebe, but that had consequences as well. It was only much later when people spoke of the "college years" or their "university experience" that I began to realize that my own time at school was so rarefied that it bore no resemblance whatsoever to the common understanding of those terms. Uniqueness, I came to understand, is ultimately a deeply solitary experience.

⁓◯

I FIRST SAW KARL in the Churchill Room a couple of weeks after classes had begun. Though he had obviously moved in, Phoebe and I barely saw him in the penthouse. In the Churchill Room, he melted into the background so thoroughly (hovering over a neat glass of Scotch that never seemed to get any emptier) that I wondered if it was the first time he had been with us there.

He wasn't watching us exactly, but sitting near the entrance, he had us well within his peripheral vision. He was the faux form of just another well-dressed but depressed banker, senses numbed by long hours, a bitter domestic life, and the volatility of the markets. He adopted the disguise so readily that I was afraid to be seen looking at him, lest I somehow break the spell. It felt as if we had concluded some wordless agreement to ignore each other. If Phoebe saw him, she didn't let on.

Knowing he was lurking in the background after that night, I started looking for him elsewhere. Having started looking for him, I started seeing him everywhere. I could have resented the constant shadowing or the intrusion into what had felt like the beginnings of some kind of grander independence for me, but in another way it was reassuring. Still, when he did actually make his presence known, Phoebe took it poorly.

"He's creepy," Phoebe said one Saturday evening as we were, as usual, preparing to embark on some secret nightlife itinerary of hers.

"He's just quiet," I said.

"That's what I said. Creepy."

"You have never bothered to get to know him, that's all."

"Oh yeah?" she said, looking up from her mirror. "What is he supposed to be anyway? Some kind of bodyguard?"

"He's not a *bodyguard*, Phoebe."

"Fine. So, what is he then?" I hesitated. Sensing weakness, she pressed on. "Where's he from? Is he married? Where did he go to school? Are his parents alive?"

"What does that have to do with anything?"

"You just said that I have to get to know him, as if you know him already. So, fine. Tell me about him."

I had no reply to offer.

"I thought so," Phoebe concluded, pleased with herself.

Angry, I stood up, went to my room, and locked the door behind me.

About half an hour later, I heard her footsteps pause outside my door, but she did not knock. Shortly thereafter, I heard her take the elevator downstairs.

I had been sitting on the floor of my bedroom pouting for nearly an hour when I heard the faint sound of music. I thought I was imagining it at first, but when I opened my bedroom door, I could tell it was coming from the first floor.

I took off my shoes and slipped downstairs in my socks. It was piano music (one of Chopin's nocturnes) and, when the sound eventually led me to the recital room, I found Karl playing the Steinway, and playing it with such depth and such feeling that it fixed me in place, mouth open, framed by the door. Karl met my gaze and offered only the slightest of nods before returning his full attention to the keys.

A talented piano player can weave a certain feeling into pieces; to imbue part of him or herself into the music so that the combined expression is both familiar and unique. The very best performers transcend even this union and draw the audience into something even greater than themselves.

I staggered in and sat in one of the chairs behind the piano, nearly moved to tears in discovering such moment and gravity flowing from Karl, this man I had known only as a stiff and somewhat brusque functionary with a dangerous (but well-concealed) affinity for violence. The tops of his hands, straining to contain the thick tendons that betrayed the remarkable strength beneath, floated across the keys. By the time he finished a third nocturne, I had to swallow hard against the lump in my throat. He let the final note linger—a long sustain that seemed almost unwilling to fade away—with his eyes closed and his head bowed.

When he opened his eyes again he stood, straightened, and even as I watched, transformed back into the hard fixture of a man I had known before.

It took me a long time to speak.

"Where did you learn to play so beautifully?" I said.

It brought him back for just a moment, my question, and his expression softened for a beat. A half sigh escaped him, but then the moment was gone, the hard man returned, and I knew he would not answer.

"You know," I said, desperate for some conversation, "you can have one of the unused bedrooms upstairs. It would be a lot more room for you."

"I do not require much room," Karl said.

"I'm sure it would be more comfortable," I added. Karl said nothing. "Also, the views are much better."

"I do not require a view."

"Well, but maybe you want a view."

"It is of no importance."

"Is there something wrong with the second floor?"

"It is not the first floor," he said. I tried very hard to look mystified. It must have worked because Karl continued. "The second floor is too far from the entrance. These are not topics to discuss."

"Don't you get bored?"

"This is not relevant," he said.

"Well, then why don't you knock on my door? We could play Monopoly or something."

"It is not your job to entertain me."

"Well, then entertain *me*. You could play piano for me."

"It is not my job to entertain you."

"Well, what *is* your job then? Aren't you our chaperone? Spying on us for my mother?"

"That is incorrect."

"Well, what then?"

"My instructions include keeping you out of harm's way. I have no instructions with respect to Miss Aresdottir."

"No instructions? What does that mean? Phoebe is a member of the household, too, you know."

"The young woman is irrelevant other than as a source of unannounced guests to the residence."

I tried not to wince. Phoebe had been known to entertain the occasional gentleman caller overnight, but I had thought her dalliances rare and subtle enough to escape notice.

"Wait," I said, catching what I thought was an important nuance. "Is it safe for her?"

"If she does not interfere."

"What is that supposed to mean? Interfere with what?" I demanded, but Karl would not answer me. "What if she were 'in harm's way'?"

"The United States is a first-world country with a highly efficient emergency services infrastructure."

I waited for more but Karl held my gaze unflinchingly until I looked away and he made as if to leave.

"Wait. Is it safer here? In the United States? For me, I mean? Is that why my mother wouldn't take me back to the estate?"

Karl said nothing, but it brought me back to a subject I had pushed far down and tried to forget: my mother's allegations against my grandfather. Suddenly I was desperate that Karl should tell me something to disabuse them, to contradict her horrific slanders.

"Isn't that why you put me on the plane that night, why my grandfather sent me here? Because it was unsafe?"

"These are not topics to discuss."

"You said that already." I took several steps toward him and, involuntarily, my voice took on a pleading tone. "You must have been there. In the manor that night. Tell me what happened before you put me on the plane."

His expression was unyielding stone.

"Did you know I was hurt when you put me on the plane?" I said, trying a different track. "When you left me all alone?" I put my right hand over my marred left breast. "That's when I got this."

I thought I saw Karl narrow his eyes, just slightly.

"I dressed it the way you taught me, you know. After South Africa. Direct pressure. Packing the wound. A pressure bandage, but it was still bleeding a little on the plane. I changed the dressing, but there wasn't any skin adhesive in the plane's med kit. I guess that's why it scarred so horribly."

It was almost completely silent in the recital room, so quiet that I could hear Karl's measured breathing.

"It was Augustin who cut me," I said, my voice almost a whisper.

Karl shifted, just perceptibly, on his feet. For a moment, I thought I saw something register; a flash of anger, perhaps, that then melted into something much harder to read. But, whatever it was, it faded quickly and the hard man was back.

"It is not for us to question your exile," he said, and then turned, walked out of the recital room, and into the hall beyond.

—

CHAPTER THIRTY

Wane and Wax

I BEGAN TO PAY MORE ATTENTION to Karl after the piano incident. Because he always seemed to be lurking near me, it wasn't particularly difficult. I once even caught him picking a flower.

Feeling listless, and with Karl in tow, I had meandered into the nearby conservatory in the park and chanced a look behind me to see him kneeling down to snap the stem. It was a lily of some sort, white and beautiful.

My curiosity piqued, I went to him.

"Is it for someone?" I asked.

He started a little, but then smelled the flower, savoring the fragrance.

"My daughter enjoyed them," he said, with a thin, faraway smile that evaporated like a wisp of smoke. Then he tucked the stem gently into his breast pocket so that the bloom was displayed next to his lapel.

I had no idea Karl had family of any kind. There was only the mysterious picture—a framed black-and-white photo of a teenage girl—I had once seen in his room.

Could that be his daughter? I wondered.

"Does she live in Europe?"

It took him a long time to answer. "The price of freedom is solitude," he said, and I knew from the chill that fell over his expression that he would brook no future discussion.

Even if Phoebe couldn't see it, I knew there was much more to Karl than simple brawn. But that occasioned more questions than it answered. Why use such an able and respected man as a simple bodyguard? Merely to protect me? From outsiders? Our shadowy enemies? Augustin? Then darker thoughts: What if it wasn't protecting me that was the goal at all, but protecting something from me?

It is the paradox of family that a patriarch must face. They are both the only ones the patriarch can really trust, and also the most dangerous to him in betrayal. However loyal your vassals, so to speak, they are not blood. Often, blood is the only thing you can count on, but also the most daunting threat from within.

I found it hard to believe that my grandfather could really have been threatened by me. Could my father? Or my mother? Or Augustin?

. . . tri-polar systems tended to be less than stable because any two actors could be tempted to ally against the lone third, Professor Lechner had told me.

My siblings and I had been permanently separated that last night on the estate. Had someone in my family been afraid to leave us together? Afraid that, together, any two of us would present too attractive a target to an outside enemy?

. . . heirs are particularly attractive targets for intrigue.

Was it possible that someone was afraid I would align myself with Augustin? For a while I even wondered if Augustin and I had been intentionally set against one another to prevent such an alliance. If so, by whom?

On that note, it was a complete mystery from whom Karl was actually taking his orders. When I had first met him, he had been my grandfather's man, but with my grandfather dead, it seemed my father had inherited him (although perhaps that process had been started already with our South African trip).

Professor Lechner said that it was my grandfather's . . .

. . . particular gift that he sees in others more than what they see in themselves. That he inspires them to realize greater destinies than they imagined they might ever fulfill.

How had Karl come to be in my grandfather's service, and what had my grandfather seen in him? What greater destiny had he in mind for Karl? What had become of those plans after my grandfather's death?

Moreover, my grandfather and my father were such different men, it was hard to imagine that it would be easy to switch loyalties from one to the other. I wondered how Karl managed such things, though I could reason out no answer other than his habitual stoicism and what I sensed was a strongly Germanic (or even Prussian) sense of duty and loyalty. Still, this seemed only part of the puzzle. It had been my mother giving him orders when I saw her again. What was her role with respect to Karl?

⁓

AS I SPENT more time with him, Karl subtly took on a role as a tutor of sorts, and in topics far more practical than theoretical. Whether this was just incidental on his part (a harmless effort to liven our otherwise deeply bland interactions) or the result of designs that were part of some grander plan remained a mystery.

I don't remember exactly how the games of "urban tag" began. Though Karl displayed a cold exterior by habit, I began to sense a sort of playfulness beneath the surface. Perhaps he could not permit himself any overt affection with me, but I came to believe that there was, deep down, some latent sentiment.

Coming out of class, I would catch a glimpse of him lurking somewhere nearby. Something would pass between us when our eyes met and the silent dance would begin. He would take up a leisurely pace; just another pedestrian on a stroll to nowhere in particular. I would follow him, always from a distance, trying to keep him in sight as long as I could while he meandered aimlessly through downtown streets or seemed to peruse the windows in a shopping district. Inevitably he would vanish, leaving me befuddled until a low whistle from behind me, or a tap on the shoulder, would have me whirling around to find him standing there expressionless. More than once, I found him holding my little wallet or some other personal effect he had lifted from my person.

Exasperated, I could do nothing but shake my head and marvel at how someone of Karl's size could so easily vanish and reappear almost at will, and, despite my guard being up, even steal from me. Having lost the round, it would be my turn to evade him. I would lose sight of Karl within minutes. I might continue evading my invisible pursuer for half an hour, using every trick I could think of. Eventually, certain that I had shaken him long before, I would turn a corner and collide with him where he stood, waiting in ambush.

Defeated, I would concede the match. In whose service, other than my grandfather's, I wondered, did Karl have occasion to become adept in such skills? Admittedly, I enjoyed both the mystery and his company. The most likely reason was that it was one of my few remaining connections to my grandfather.

One night Karl produced a deck and we started playing card games. For a month we played sometimes three nights a week. In all that time, I hadn't won a game. Not a single one.

"I give up," I said after he had already bested me nearly a dozen times in a single evening.

"You find me exceptionally talented at cards?" he asked.

"You're a prodigy."

"Why do you not win even once?"

"I don't know."

"Find out," he said.

Then he shuffled the deck, pressed the cards into a flawless bridge, slipped the deck into his inside coat pocket, and left me with my thoughts.

I finally beat Karl at gin for the first time a couple of days later.

"You have learned something?" he said.

"The face cards are marked. You can tell the kings, queens, and jacks."

I had discovered that spots in the corner design on the cards had been removed in different places. It was difficult, but over time one could tell which face card was which.

"This is incorrect," he said.

"Incorrect?"

"All of the cards are marked."

"How?"

He did not answer, only left me with the deck.

Enthralled, and after a long study of magic books, I learned the names for card-marking methods, terms like *cuts*, *dandruff*, *blocks*, and *line work*.

When I was ready to play again, Karl had a surprise for me. He produced a deck with a solid black backing.

"A fair game at last then?" I said, but he won every hand we played.

"Leave me with the deck," I said, after I was down ten games.

"Never put your secret in the pocket of another," Karl said, slipping the cards into his jacket. Then he left me in the kitchen to my own frustrated devices.

OTHER THAN THE trip to South Africa and a brief foray into Zürich, I had taken my first, cautious tastes of the modern world at Curie Hall. But my early explorations into the city (at first with Phoebe as my guide to the city's architecture, and then, after we moved into the penthouse, with Karl neatly in tow) were something else entirely.

Phoebe had her own relationship with Manhattan and I think that I needed one that was my own. As a result, my excursions involved sneaking away and, given the degree of naïveté about the modern world it would have telegraphed, I went to great lengths to conceal my growing amazement from her.

I felt guilty abandoning her, even for a random evening once in a while. I compensated by buying an antique pair of powerful ship's glasses: huge, tripod-mounted binoculars with Carl Zeiss lenses, instruments that had once adorned a German destroyer during the Second World War.

"So that the skyline's secrets might be laid bare before you," I wrote on the card I addressed to Phoebe.

She was elated and, before spending hours panning the glasses about the horizon, showered me with kisses and nearly crushed my ribs in a big hug.

The pace and noise of the city couldn't have been more different than Curie Hall or the estate, environments characterized by a peaceful country-side and, everywhere one looked, curated green vegetation. In the city there seemed to be a nervous energy underlying everything, a barely suppressed urgency that drove the chaos and speed of every aspect of metropolitan life and left the many urban surfaces—acres of gray concrete—well dusted with soot and dirt, to which its residents seemed oblivious.

It took some getting used to before I could endure more than an hour in the thick of things without getting a headache, but eventually I found myself actually embracing it all as a welcome respite from the insulated environs of our penthouse.

During the day, refuges I grew to know and love included the beautiful Beaux-Arts–style building that housed the main branch of the public library (Phoebe had introduced it to me on one of her architectural tours, of course), the shopping district—dazzling swaths of color and light on display in every window—and a number of restaurants in the upper floors of skyscrapers. Even more so than our penthouse, I was bewitched by the height of them, and content to linger for hours, gazing down from window-side tables, imagining myself a dispassionate deity, pleased to watch (but not interfere with) the vulnerable mortals milling about below.

Fascinated by the novelty of the transit authority, for a three-week period I rode buses and trains to and fro, sometimes to the ends of their routes, just for the experience. More than once I inadvertently forced Karl to gently guide me away from neighborhoods that an obviously wealthy young woman would do well, even with a capable bodyguard, not to be found in after dark (or, in some cases, broad daylight).

Phoebe nearly had a stroke when she found a pile of half-spent Metro-Cards on my desk.

"Where in the world do you keep going?" she demanded, but I just shrugged and made a point of being more discreet with them thereafter.

If I wanted to be alone, I could easily duck off campus after class, but it was more difficult to get away from Phoebe later than that. The unwritten rule she had somehow established declared evenings to be "Phoebe time," a privilege that she guarded most jealously. Even so, I found occasional excuses to slip away as the sun began to set.

Having first gotten a taste for cinema at Curie Hall, I was overjoyed to frequent any number of movie theaters in the city. I am certain I tried Karl's patience when, having discovered a multiplex for the first time, I jumped from theater to theater for more than eight hours to watch four different movies in one stretch. That I did so after buying only one ticket just added to the thrill (though to this day I wonder if I actually evaded discovery by the local management, or if Karl fended off the ushers before they could confront me about my blatant theft of service).

Of all those new experiences, however, the most visceral and moving, my first professional baseball game, occurred near the end of my first year at Columbia, just after my sixteenth birthday. It was a nighttime contest witnessed by nearly sixty thousand fans whose dynamic range spanned from a trough of ambient boredom to peaks of unbridled madness, the sounds of which were indelibly printed into my auditory memories ever after. The echo of the public address system, the roar of the fans, the blue-white glare of the lights making brilliant the pearl-white of the ball against the deep green of the infield grass—nostalgic flashes of my mother's Italian Gardens, the grounds of Curie Hall—and the reddish brown of the dirt on otherwise pristine, pinstriped uniforms, all conspired to intoxicate me.

It being my first game, I had no concept at all of the rules or scorekeeping practices, but it hardly seemed to matter. When, in a moment of deafening and collective insanity occasioned by the home team's timely run scoring, the fans went wild, I joined in without restraint, not knowing exactly for whom or what I was cheering. And when I, along with the rest of my section, was showered with cheap beer from the manic celebrations, Karl, who somehow managed to absorb a substantial quantity of airborne beverages with unflagging dignity, took one look at me, registered the ecstatic smile on my face, and, thankfully, refrained from inflicting grievous bodily harm on the unwitting perpetrators.

When, among thousands of intoxicated and still-jubilant fans, I walked out of that stadium and into the balmy urban night, I was in a daze, filled with giddy energy and captivated by the experience, a halo that crowned me even well after I returned to the penthouse. Phoebe noticed immediately.

"You little slut, you," she said, and a sly grin followed. "Who have you been fucking?"

"What are you talking about?" I deadpanned.

I realized that I had been grinning like a madwoman and I was embarrassed that I had left my guard down to let her detect any "non-Phoebe"-generated bliss.

"Don't give me that," she teased with a wry grin. "I know what postcoital glow looks like. Who was it?"

"Nobody," I said.

Phoebe looked at me for a long time, but then let the matter drop.

That night I lay in bed thinking. Even with Phoebe as an anchor, the city was a very different world than I was used to. Part of me wondered at the fact that my mother, whose horror of "the modern" was deep and indelible, even permitted me to reside in what amounted to the pinnacle of modern, urban centers. The paradox invited speculation. Was it a test? A rite of passage? Part of some plan to expose me to the modern world so that, with such experiences behind me, I could serve some larger purpose?

Certainly my exposure to contemporary influences was limited. My education after Professor Lechner had arrived on the estate had been anything but "modern." But of what use were his "philosopher-warrior king" concepts in the face of the chaotic pace and faithless mores of the hypermodern, Western city?

I remembered the final three Cole paintings (*The Consummation of Empire*, *Destruction*, and *Desolation*) and thought I recognized in the first work many elements of the city. How could an old-world dynasty resist the raw emotion and unmanageable energy of the modern world? Even the crowd at a baseball game, small in the context of the urban center I lived in, might, should they become unruly instead of jubilant, lay waste to entire neighborhoods. What might such an assemblage do to an old-world estate if loosed upon it? Might even the most casual of modern forces, as my grandfather and my mother both seemed to fear, be a serious threat to our dynasty? The idea unnerved me.

I thought of the passage my grandfather had written in his volume of the Letters from the Dead:

> *Our own lands remained relatively, and mercifully, isolated from the many arteries and veins that carried the red and fevered blood of "the modern" through blue, oxygen-starved aristocratic tissue.*

Figuratively, was it even possible for the estate to resist the primal, ungoverned, and dangerously intoxicating ardor I had seen in the city? If not, would it be dragged into Destruction and Desolation as the Empire of the Postmodern crumbled? Another thread came to me: Was the baseball stadium, like the colosseum before it, a gambit to vent otherwise dangerous energies away from the regime in power?

Unable to answer my own questions, I lay awake until late that night. Thereafter, I drifted off to sleep amid images of once great cities overrun by mobs and, against a backdrop of dozens of smoldering examples, the horror of empires razed to the ground.

꧂

I MET ETHAN FOR the second time at the Splintered Oar, the local English pub and pizza joint near campus that, likely because of its name, seemed to attract a large contingent of the Columbia crew team. Phoebe enjoyed dragging me to "The Oar" because the student clientele of the place made Karl, with whom

Phoebe seemed to have developed a low-key rivalry, stand out like a sore thumb. I think Phoebe made a show of it because the low-intensity conflict with Karl amused her, rather than on the basis of any real animosity between them. Either way, I did my best to ignore her little passive aggressions, but she was creative about her little pranks and sometimes I had to work hard to conceal my amusement.

Ethan had first introduced himself to me in the library, but it took me a few moments to recognize him when he came up to me at the bar of the Oar and made small talk for however long it took for him to work up the courage to give me his number.

"Is that who you were fucking the other night?" Phoebe said when I came back to our table.

"What are you talking about?" I said, but I could feel my face going red. I figured she was referring to the night I had returned home late from the baseball game.

"He rows crew," she said, cocking her head to scrutinize him from afar. "I bet he's in great shape. Is he your first boyfriend?"

"He's not my first anything," I replied.

"What is it with the crew team?" Phoebe asked rhetorically. "They all have names like Spencer, Devin, Colin, Chad, or Keegan. If it wasn't for the occasional Bobby or Sean to remind you that they started letting the Irish into university, you'd think it was all WASPs."

I neglected to mention that Ethan's middle name actually was Spencer and that his family were major donors to the university.

Phoebe squinted in Ethan's direction. "I will bet you any amount of money that he gets his back waxed. Maybe more than his back. That Ken-doll thing he has going simply cannot be authentic."

I knew that Phoebe was only being testy because she was feeling some hint of jealousy. At the time, I figured it was best to just try to ignore it.

I NEVER CALLED ETHAN, but that wasn't the last I saw of him. We began to run into each other around campus frequently enough that I began to suspect the encounters to be more by design than accident, a suspicion that was later confirmed in a rather foreboding way.

I had already bumped into him half a dozen times when Ethan came up to me outside Havemeyer Hall after my Principles of Economics class.

"Well, hello there," he said. "What a coincidence."

Karl, who, as was his habit, had been waiting for me to come out of my lecture, drifted behind Ethan and casually took up station. Karl was surprisingly adept at being unobtrusive on campus and, so far as I could tell, Ethan had overlooked his more or less constant presence.

"You know," Ethan said, "I'm always seeing you before your morning class. Why don't we have coffee together sometime? There's a pretty chill place right down the block that's open early. We could meet there and walk to Havemeyer together."

My first instinct was to decline his offer, but in our encounters he had always been charming. I couldn't help but find myself smiling at the way his mouth turned up when he grinned, or the light ring of his laugh.

"Okay," I said, and failed to suppress a shy expression.

Ethan beamed. "Here's to happy coincidences," he said, then proffered his goodbyes and took his leave.

"This is not coincidence," Karl said, having returned to my side. "This is the result of surveillance."

"I don't think he means anything by it."

"I will intervene."

"No," I said, turning to plead with him. "Please don't. He's just shy; a student with a crush."

Karl looked at me for a long moment, but then turned away.

MORNING COFFEE WITH Ethan evolved from the occasional, sporadic engagement to a twice-weekly ritual. Phoebe was hardly an early bird, so I was not missed despite my early departures from the penthouse.

Ethan was an engaging conversationalist, happy to wax on varied topics ranging from his prolific skiing and mountain climbing, to long but quite lovely descriptions of the many tourist destinations he had visited with his family. He had a particular talent for drawing the listener into the vision of a place and a time. I was happy to indulge him, and even happier that he never pressed me when I evaded his polite, if persistent, questions. Why did

I have an accent? Where was I really from? What did my parents do? How come I was never in my dorm room?

Perhaps I should have been more concerned about the tenor of his curiosity, or that he was spying on me, as Karl seemed to fear, but nothing about his interest seemed malevolent.

"You're such a mystery," he would say, and then give me that crooked smile of his. "It's sexy." Then, when we parted, he would hug me close and kiss me on the cheek.

The entire thing was flattering, and that, I suppose, made it hard to feel threatened.

It was probably inevitable that we would eventually end up meeting at the Oar again, or some other campus bar. As closing time arrived one Friday night—glaring lights brought all the way up; music abruptly stopped; half-empty pitchers on tables; some postgame sports analysis show blaring from the ceiling-mounted television; and swaying patrons navigating toward the door—Ethan leaned close and whispered in my ear.

"Let's go back to my place," he said, and then, without waiting for an answer, planted the beginning of a soft but deep kiss—beer and hints of the licorice of Jägermeister shots—on my mouth.

Phoebe had left the Oar for parts unknown a little earlier that night, but I was suddenly panicked that she would somehow see us. I recoiled more violently than I meant to, and pushed Ethan away harder than I intended. He had surprised me more than anything else, but over his shoulder, I had seen Karl take two hard steps in our direction. To my relief, Karl stopped when I made eye contact, picking up on a pleading look from me that he should not react.

"What?" Ethan said, and I could tell he was upset by the abrupt rejection. "Did I do something wrong?"

It had been reflexive on my part. In fact, somewhere deep down, a part of me hoped he would kiss me again, but Karl's eyes were hard and cold.

"I just need . . . a little time, I guess."

"I didn't mean to upset you."

"No, you didn't, really."

Ethan gave me a little affected pout, and I couldn't suppress a giggle. That made him smile again.

"Listen, I have tickets to the Ministry concert at the Roseland this Sunday.

Why don't you come with me? We could meet here first and then head over for the show."

It was an olive branch, and I felt I had to take it. Plus I hadn't been to a concert before, and the idea was appealing.

"Okay," I said.

"Hey," one of the bouncers bellowed at us. "Lovebirds. You don't gotta go home but you gotta get up outta here."

We said our goodbyes on the sidewalk, and Ethan pecked me on the cheek before drifting off into the night.

I waited until Ethan rounded a corner, then I turned to look for Karl. I found him standing some distance away, watching me casually. But, for just a split second, I thought I caught a glimpse of someone else before they slipped away into a dissipating crowd: Phoebe.

I WAS DUE TO have dinner with Phoebe the next night. She had picked a restaurant on the other side of campus that was famous for brick-oven pizza. We took our seats, ordered, and, after twenty minutes of small talk, Phoebe got strangely quiet.

"What is it?" I asked, finally.

"I want to ask you something," she said, suddenly shy. "What would you think about being more serious?"

"Serious about what?"

"I mean us. Our relationship."

"Oh," I managed. "It is not something I've thought about. I mean, you see other people."

"Not that often," she said. "And I don't have to."

She reached across the table to take my hand. When her skin touched mine it gave me butterflies.

"It's just that no matter who I'm with, I'm always thinking about you. But you could see other people. I mean guys, anyway. If you want to."

"You know I don't really date anyone, Phoebe."

"What about Ethan? I mean, I can see it. He's really good-looking, an athlete—"

"We haven't even done anything, Phoebe."

"I mean, if you did. That kind of thing doesn't matter to me."

"Phoebe, he doesn't know the first thing about me."

Phoebe gave me a particular expression. She was about to say something but then caught herself.

"If you saw guys now and again," she managed after a few seconds. "That doesn't really matter to me."

She hadn't given it voice, but I had recognized what she had censored right away. She had been about to protest that she barely knew the first thing about me either. It hit me quite hard, not least because the reality was even worse than she understood. Even the few things Phoebe thought she knew about me were lies.

She squeezed my hand. "All that matters to me is spending time with you."

I struggled to say something, but I couldn't get any words out. I remember thinking how lovely she was, and trying very hard not to get lost in those brilliant blue eyes. The truth was that I loved her, had loved her for some time, and she had done nothing to deserve my many deceptions.

In that moment, I wanted to confess it all; to tell her everything. To tell her about my childhood on the estate, my parents, my brothers, my grandfather, Professor Lechner, their mysterious plans for me, the assassination attempt in South Africa, the Letters from the Dead, the Order of Nyx, that last awful night in the manor, my exile, the Fulvia Flacca Trust, the pendant, E. P. Wolff. Everything.

In a split second, I had composed the apology in my head, an admission that essentially everything I had ever told her about myself was untrue. I would explain that I had been afraid, that I didn't know how she would react. That I was petrified that she would be spooked; that she would leave. She would have to listen to me, wouldn't she? After all, it was the truth. Finally.

I would start at the beginning.

That's when I realized that there were tears in my eyes. More than anything, that convinced me to bare my soul.

But then Phoebe did something I did not expect. She got up, sat next to me on my side of the booth, wrapped her arms around me, and kissed me long and hard right there in the restaurant. It didn't startle me; I didn't push her away. Instead I found myself lost in the sensation of it, barely able to sit still.

"Let's go home," she said.

She might have said anything else at all and I would have told her everything that evening. Anything but that.

I was speechless after her kiss and, before I knew it, she was leading me outside. When we got home, she took me to her bedroom and undressed me and, even well after the sun had come up, we hadn't gotten a wink of sleep.

I am still struck by the irony of that moment in the restaurant. My tears had revealed a truth, and not least to me: that I was desperately in love with Phoebe. It was a secret that, had I even understood the full depth of my feelings, I would have had no intention of revealing. In the immediate aftermath of that evening, I tried to convince myself that this involuntary disclosure was, for the moment, penance enough. But my tears also scuttled the confession I was on the verge of making, and thereby perpetuated a much larger body of lies.

This, it turned out, would have far-reaching consequences.

⁓

IT WAS AFTER ten in the evening the next day when Phoebe urged me to clean up and get dressed.

"Why?" I asked.

"We're going out on a date."

"Where?"

"It's a surprise."

I was exhausted, but also sort of charmed with the romance of a formal "date night." Lethargically, I went to my room, took a shower, and put on some clothes.

"Oh no," Phoebe said when she saw me. "There is *no way* you are going out like that. First, come here," she said, and dragged me by the hand to her room like a small child. Then she sat down in front of her mirror and got to work.

I was expecting the kohl-rimmed eyes and thick black strokes of Phoebe's typical style, but instead Phoebe pulled my hair down out of the French twist I had spent far too long working on.

"Hey," I protested, reaching up to stop her.

"No, leave it down. Your hair is long and fantastic," she said, pulling my hands away.

I was usually very self-conscious of my hair, but bolstered by Phoebe's compliment, my copper-blond locks suddenly seemed just right. Phoebe took her time and what she produced was elegant and refined. I was struck by the face that looked back at me in Phoebe's mirror.

Phoebe gawked at me. "Wow," she whispered. "Just, wow." She planted a greedy kiss on my mouth.

"Where are we going?" I asked, once she came up for air.

"I told you, it's a surprise," she beamed, but she was so excited that she was chattering on about it only minutes later.

Our destination was called the Consulate, a club that was purportedly situated inside an old consulate building since abandoned by the government that commissioned it (a casualty of declining national fortunes and the foibles of the global economy).

"The building it is in was supposedly half-designed by Wallace Harrison, who did the United Nations building, but the rumor is that he abandoned the project and a junior architect had to finish it off. I've always wondered what it looks like inside. Apparently, they even kept the top-secret vault where all the communications gear and secret files used to be," Phoebe said. "They even use the antennas on the roof to broadcast the DJ sets live on a pirate radio transmitter."

"Isn't that illegal?" I asked. Phoebe ignored me.

"They also have real diplomatic couriers."

"Couriers?" I said, trying not to sound intrigued.

"They have message pads at the tables and the bars. You can write a note and they'll deliver it for you."

"So they've regressed to some combination of passing notes in class and eighteenth-century footmen?"

"Cute. It will be fun. Anyhow, go and change into that black dress with the lace," she said, and sent me back to my room.

I hadn't worn the piece she meant—all black with lace in strategic places—since buying it earlier that year, but it fit perfectly.

I had just finished changing when, with something like horror, I realized that it was Sunday night. I was supposed to have met Ethan at the Oar hours earlier to go to the Ministry concert. After spending all night and all morning in bed with Phoebe, and given the way she had woken me up, I had completely forgotten. I hadn't set an alarm or anything.

Panicked, I called him, but only got his voicemail. I left what must have been a pretty pathetic apology, explaining the best I could, but when I hung up the sinking feeling of guilt lingered with me.

I WAS STILL FEELING awful about the Ethan mix-up so I didn't want to admit it, but, as Karl drove us in the black town car, I was increasingly curious about our destination. The Consulate actually sounded pretty cool.

The facade lived up to its name. It was an old four-story stone building and the entrance was guarded by a pair of faux embassy guards scrutinizing the people waiting to get in. We parked and walked to the building, whereupon Karl faded into the background. I could hear the muffled sound of the beat from inside as we stood in line.

As we waited, Phoebe drifted into distraction, hunting for something or someone. Once she spotted what she was looking for, she grabbed me by the hand, pulled me out of line, and led me around the side of the building to where a tall man in a dark suit was smoking a cigarette and talking to a beautiful blonde. Phoebe slowed when we were about fifty feet from the pair.

"What are you doing?" I whispered.

"Shhh."

As we got closer they both stopped talking and the tall man turned his attention to Phoebe.

"Good evening," he said, with a healthy note of suspicion.

"Beautiful night, isn't it?" Phoebe said.

"Yes, yes it is. Are you looking for someone?"

"Actually, yes. A girl with a red backpack," Phoebe said.

The tall man nodded. "Perhaps inside. Cynthia will show you the way."

The blonde took us around the corner and knocked a pattern like a Morse code C on a metal door. The door creaked open and we were whisked inside.

"What the hell was that?" I asked.

"That's the VIP code," Phoebe said. "You have to find that guy, ask him if it's a 'beautiful night,' and then they will ask you if you are looking for someone. The answer is in Monday's missed connections section on Craigslist. Whoever was seen near the water, or the swimming pool, or the lake, or something like that."

"You're kidding," I said.

"Not at all. They put one in every Monday."

The Consulate was dark and wonderful. Phoebe led me deeper into the club and up a flight of stairs to the landing over the already full dance floor.

Phoebe leaned in to be heard over the music. "Have you noticed all the keypads?"

I looked around. There was a little silver numeric keypad with a red and green LED over it in front of almost every door.

"The VIP rooms have codes," she said.

"How do you figure them out?"

"Apparently 1900 and 1729 were really cool last week. Of course someone keeps using 6969 but I'm not trying that. We can split up and try 1900 and 1729. Whoever finds something good, come back here so we can meet and go together."

Before I could protest, Phoebe had darted off. I almost started after her, but then I caught sight of Karl, expertly ignoring me from afar, and knew I would feel stupid if he saw me pathetically dashing after her.

Annoyed at being left, I took the stairs to the second floor. Every time I reached a door I tried 1900 and 1729, getting only a red blinking light in response. I began to wonder if someone wasn't playing a joke on me and so out of frustration added 6969 to the list of codes to try at each door.

I nearly jumped out of my shoes when, in the midst of a dark hallway, someone tapped on my shoulder. Figuring it was Phoebe, I whirled around ready to yell at her for startling me, only to find a uniformed footman holding out a folded-up note. Once I had taken it, he vanished without a word.

The intrigue inside the Consulate was catching. I opened the note and found it scrawled with a single sentence:

You are a vision.

It was unsigned. I looked around, but there was no sign of my secret correspondent. I couldn't quite decide if I thought it flattering, creepy, or both.

I had almost given up when a door on the third floor responded when I stabbed 6969 into the keyboard. The green LED blinked and the latch clicked. Intimidated, but quite curious, I pulled it open and stepped into a huge, dimly lit room with about forty people in it. The music from the dance floor was being piped in from outside, but softer, making conversation a much easier proposition.

The crowd at the Consulate was already a well-heeled bunch, but the room I walked into was beyond all that. They were smartly dressed and, though a few turned to look at me, for the most part they were engaged in their own interactions, gathered in clusters around the low table and couch sets, or at the bar on the far side of the room.

A couple of the girls were dancing together with martini glasses in their hands as a group of guys watched appreciatively. A set of couches and tables on a dais against the far wall seemed to be the social nerve center of the room. The prettier girls were all there (as was the majority of the alcohol) and the axis of the room seemed to spin around a figure at its core.

I convinced myself that I was wandering closer because I was curious about this person, but really I was looking for Phoebe. Despite the vulgar door code, if there was a place Phoebe was likely to be in proximity to, it was the center of attention in one of the VIP lounges of the city's coolest new club.

Once I was close enough, I could see that the central figure appeared to be the room's de facto host. Strangely, he was lounging on the couch in a white-tie and tails ensemble complete with three miniature ribbons on his left lapel, a level of formal dress that was both alien and reminiscent. He looked perfectly in his element, holding court between a pair of beautiful girls who, from opposite sides, took turns whispering in either ear. His eyes panned around in a way I found vaguely familiar, pausing to light on one or another of the more comely, evening-wear-clad derrières on the far side of the room. Yet, somehow, he also seemed to be absorbing all the plots and subplots in play around him.

The shock of recognition came to me at first slowly, and then all at once, just before he locked eyes with me and stood up.

"Well, *fuck me*," he said.

The man at the center of the room was Yves.

CHAPTER THIRTY-ONE

The Consul General

"WHAT CAN YOU POSSIBLY BE DOING here?" Yves said.

Abruptly deprived of their headrest when he stood, the two girls fell into the emptied space and knocked heads. It was all I could do not to laugh, but that meant that a wry smile crept across my face. From his expression, it was obvious that Yves thought I was smiling at him.

Those days on the estate came back to me. Frolics in the white, windblown drifts. Yves bearing me on his shoulders. The agonizing crush I had on him. The snow jumping. The Bureau of Secrets. But then my awful last night in the manor came to me as well, and I had to suppress a shudder.

It dawned on me how much he had changed. Even when he was younger, it was obvious that Yves was going to grow up to be a very attractive man, but I wasn't prepared for the raw charisma he was so effortlessly projecting. The intervening years had favored him well. He was taller, more handsome, and devoid of the baby-faced look that he had back on the estate. He filled out his formal attire remarkably well. The hair gel was gone, eliminating the overly slick look he had once sported.

He closed the distance between us and embraced me. I was reeling, and all I could do was stand there while he hugged me (a little too intimately and for a little too long). He stepped back, held my shoulders at arm's length, and looked me over. His smile widened, and that made me even more uncomfortable for some reason. Once he let go, I retreated out of his immediate reach.

"What are *you* doing here?" I said.

"What do you mean? This is the place to be. Don't you love it?"

"No," I said, "I mean—"

"Oh, in the States? Well," he said, pinching the bridge of his nose, "I might have been responsible for just a touch of mother-daughter rivalry getting just a touch out of hand. One might even say there was a bit of a *dramatic scene*. One might also say that my father's legal team thought it might be a good time for me to take a break from the Continent for a little while, but that's almost five months ago. This week is my colonial going-away party. Also, it was totally worth it." Yves's expression softened. "Speaking of which," he said, "you have become a younger, hotter version of your mother."

"Yves," I said, shocked with his forwardness.

"Oh, don't pretend you haven't thought about your mother that way. I certainly have."

"What the hell is wrong with you?" I sputtered. Obviously, the endearing childhood playmate I had once known was gone. "You can't just—"

"Your mother is a dish," he continued, heedless of my outrage. "And now you are a dish too. Like mother like daughter. Speaking of which, how is it you are old enough to drink in here?"

Without waiting for an answer, Yves flagged down one of the hostesses and pointed to his now-empty martini glass with an offended look. "Can we get her one of these, and another for me . . . *obviously.*"

Yves's behavior tore my image of him in two. On the one hand, I couldn't believe that the onetime subject of my preadolescent crush had transformed into a crass and misogynistic hedonist. But part of me could also trace the path that might have led him there, a path laden and bracketed on all sides by the wealth and power of the Böhm family. Klaus Böhm was already quite advanced in age when he had begun fathering children. As with their other issue, the Böhms had made a point of sending Yves away to school when he was rather young. This meant Yves, as the heir apparent, had to navigate his way without much in the way of guidance from his family or, in particular, his aging father.

I had little time to reflect more than that. It was impossible not to notice that all the eyes in the room were on us as the group collectively reassessed their place in the pecking order. I could almost feel the heat coming off some of the glares that drilled into me.

"Are you listening to me?" Yves said, bringing my attention back. "Muffie has a bunch of my really good coke. She's around somewhere." He pushed one of the newly arrived martinis into my hand. I took it reflexively, too taken aback to offer much in the way of resistance. "I've been meaning to talk to her about sharing more."

"That's . . . that's very thoughtful of you, but I'm okay."

"Not half as okay as you will be."

"Yves—"

"No, really, you have to try this stuff. We bought half a brick. Straight from the plane. Untouched."

"Uh, thanks," I managed, hoping that something would distract him before I had to think about how to decline his offer again.

As we stood there Yves took a step back and looked me over top to bottom for a third time.

"Whoooo . . . wow," he exhaled in a near whistle. "You . . . are stunning. Turn around for me once," he insisted, pointing his finger to the ceiling and twirling it in a circle in the universal sign language gesture for: "Let me look at your ass."

"I don't think so, Yves," I said, and made to leave.

He caught me by the wrist and pulled me, gently but firmly, down to the couch and close to him.

"Oh, stop," he said. "We simply must catch up."

Even through his formal attire, I could feel the heat from his arm through the lace on my shoulder. I might have made good on my threat to leave but, having been away from the estate for so long, my political reflexes were dulled, particularly when faced with a social predator as crafty and nimble as Yves had obviously matured into.

"Now, you must tell me what you are doing here. I heard you moved to the colonies but why are you in the city?"

"I'm just visiting," I said.

"Really now? With whom?"

"No one you know."

"Oh, come now. First of all, how would you know who I know? As it happens, I know quite a number of people. Second of all, stop being so coy."

"I came with a couple of friends. I don't usually come to places like this."

"Places . . . *like this* . . . with people . . ." Yves gestured around. ". . . *like these*? Is that what you mean?"

Yves made everything I said sound so snobby. In two minutes flat he had quite expertly put me on the defensive.

"No, that's not what I meant at all," I said, and then tried to regain the initiative. "Aren't you just a little overdressed? Are you even supposed to be wearing decorations in a place like this?"

In fact, I was sure he was violating several unwritten (and perhaps a few written) rules about formal attire.

"I had a thing earlier," he said, shooing my question away with the back of his hand. "You know, speaking of things, it is nice to have you here, but you need to loosen up. Where the *fuck* is Muffie?"

Yves craned his neck around and finally waved over a gaunt-looking brunette.

"Muffie, where the fuck is all the coke I gave you?"

"You say fuck a lot," Muffie said, rolling her eyes and doing her best to look bored.

"Really, Yves," I said. "It's fine."

"It is most certainly *not* fine. Muffie?"

Muffie sighed but then dug something out of her clutch and held her closed hand out to Yves like a pouty six-year-old. Yves cupped his hand under hers and then lifted it to his lips and kissed it.

"Thank you, my dear. Now why don't you go busy yourself with whatever feminine affectations are most likely to keep you occupied. I have to talk with my oldest, dearest friend."

As she turned to go, Yves gave her a sharp little spank. She emitted a gleeful squeak and scurried away.

"Mmmm," Yves said, admiring Muffie from behind as she went. "I must say, I do so love the way you girls pour yourself into impossibly skintight dresses." And, just like that, his right hand was down my gown and on my right breast. "Here you go," he beamed.

Once I managed to close my mouth, which was hanging open in utter horror, I almost whirled around and slapped him as hard as I could, but when his hand came away there was something scratchy between my right breast and my gown.

"Yves, what the hell?"

"Why don't you go powder your nose, my lovely?"

It occurred to me that he would badger me until I appeared to partake of the drug, and that I didn't want to sit there arguing while I had an unknown quantity of illegal narcotics stuck in my décolletage, and so I stood up, spun away quickly against the possibility that Yves would try to deliver me the same swat he had landed on Muffie, and stalked off for the ladies' room.

I took the closest stall, worried that Yves's little gift might slip down and fall on the floor. I pulled out my neckline and almost lost whatever it was right down the front of my gown before I caught it in my hand. At first I thought Yves had given me a condom, as it was almost exactly that size, but the illusion lasted only a second. It was stuffed full and the sides of the bag were bulging. I looked closer, expecting a dull white powder. Instead I found a coarse, shimmering, crystalline dust with irregularly sized chunks throughout. It seemed a little like rock salt but very white and with just a tint of opalescent blue. It looked forbidden. And dangerous.

I was alone in the VIP bathroom and, driven mostly by curiosity, I held the baggie in my fingers and carefully worked the seal open. My hands were shaking and I almost dropped the entire thing. Even if I wanted to try some, I had no idea how to go about it. Instead, with my hands still trembling I took a very careful sniff of the empty air just above it. It was a bitter, sharp scent tainted with the lingering bite of ether. It scared me. As quickly as I could, I sealed it back up and buried the baggie in the palm of my hand.

As I walked back toward the couch, Yves was conversing with what I could only describe as an American Yves-wannabe. Tall, well dressed, young, full of himself, and perfectly groomed. I could hear them almost twenty paces away as I approached.

"I like my women like I like my Scotch," the American was saying. "Sixteen years old and with a little coke in them."

"Dear God," Yves said. "Who puts coke in sixteen-year-old Scotch?"

"Well, but the women—"

"You don't hear me complaining about that part of the joke, do you? And here comes two fingers neat with a splash of coke as we speak." Yves beamed at me.

"Everyone can hear you, you realize?" I said.

"I know, darling, but, you see, the thing is . . . I simply don't care." He smiled. "So, how is it?"

I knew what he meant but I didn't want to be caught out in a lie. Could he tell I hadn't done any? Was that possible somehow? Something with the eyes?

"Here," I said, holding my clenched hand out to Yves, but he made no move to take it.

"No, no. Where's Muffie? Let her hold it."

Muffie must have known what was coming because she scampered over immediately and, with a practiced gesture, swept the baggie from my fingers and into her hand as easily as if she had done it a hundred times before.

"Pretty amazing, isn't it?" she asked. I just nodded. "He always gets the best stuff. Hey, why don't you come to the after party with us?"

"The after party? I don't think—"

"It will be fun," she insisted. "We have plenty of party favors. Other things, too, if you have different tastes." Muffie was much chattier than earlier, perhaps the effect of her most recent dose of cocaine. "How do you know Yves anyhow?"

"We—"

"—grew up together," Yves said, back in the conversation like a relapse.

"What, really?"

Muffie was oddly fascinated by this detail, perhaps surprised that Yves actually had a childhood instead of, say, emerging fully formed from a pulsating, vein-covered cocoon.

It was obvious that Yves was going to continue to dominate the conversational offerings unless I did something to derail his efforts. It took me a moment or two, but I realized that I might be able to kill two birds with one stone.

"Have you been back to the estate since I saw you last?" I asked.

Yves beamed at me, thrilled that I was actually engaging with him.

"Once or twice," he cooed. "Your mother loves me, you know."

"I sort of doubt that."

"No, it's absolutely true. I had lunch with her on the estate right before I took my little . . . vacation."

I was taken aback. "My mother . . . had lunch with you?"

"I told you. She loves me."

"I'm not sure my mother actually loves anyone," I said, but then regretted making a comment about a member of my family to an outsider, even one from our inner circle.

"Tut-tut. When did you become such a cynic?"

I gave him a sharp look before changing the subject. "How is Augustin?"

"Why are you asking me? How would I even know?"

"You said that you were just on the estate. You are trying to tell me you didn't see Augustin? You two were best friends, and—"

"That . . . is rather an exaggeration."

"You cannot be serious. You two were thick as thieves."

"What, five years ago? Anyhow, you know what Augustin is like now."

"Yves, how would I know that? I haven't seen him even once since the year you and I were last together on the estate."

"Really? How can that be true? Anyhow, I didn't go to see Augustin. He wasn't even there so far as I know. I was there at your mother's invitation."

There was something I simply couldn't picture: Yves and my mother sitting in the Rose Salon together, passing a lazy afternoon on the estate with a gourmet meal, mimosas, and nothing but conversation for entertainment. Even after several seconds trying to reason out what the two of them would ever have to talk about, I drew a complete blank.

"I don't understand. What happened between you and Augustin?"

"Nothing *happened* exactly. It's just that . . ." Yves searched for the proper turn of phrase. "Your brother has changed in the last few years. He thinks that the normal rules don't apply to him." Yves gave me a pensive look. "Well, with your family they don't, of course, so on a basic level he's right, but he has gone well beyond that by now."

"What is that supposed to mean?"

Yves narrowed his eyes for a moment. I had the impression that he was suspicious of my motives for asking, as if I had laid some trap intended to snare him in a frank answer.

"Nothing. Forget it. Anyway, I'm bored of this conversation." Over my shoulder, Yves flagged down one of the waitresses. "Two vodka martinis. Up. Very dry. Dirty. Four olives. And do hurry. My lovely companion is already suffering from alcohol withdrawal."

Our waitress nodded and hurried off.

"Yves, tell me what you were going to say."

"Really, my dear, I don't actually want to entangle myself in your family's affairs. I'm fond of an injury-free physique so I steer clear of your brother nowadays. If you want my advice, you should too."

Yves's declaration contained enough of a hint of violence that a little shiver went up my neck.

Our waitress returned at the most inopportune moment and, after taking both glasses from her tray, Yves pressed one into my hands. In the process, however, something on the other side of the room had caught his eye.

"What did you mean by 'steer clear'?" I said, trying to recapture his attention. "Did something—"

"I must say," Yves said, cutting me off, looking over my shoulder, and obviously still intent on the distraction across the room. "The VIP room lure is attracting all sorts of interesting prey today."

I followed his gaze only to discover that he was staring at Phoebe.

PHOEBE HAD A strange look on her face when she saw me and, given what I had seen of him already, I was rather sure that Yves would smell her curiosity a mile off. True to form, he got up and made his way to the newcomer. Having intercepted Phoebe before she got to me, he reached for her hand and made a large production of bowing and kissing it.

"Hello," he said.

I smelled disaster. Phoebe's new commitment to be more "serious" with me or no, I just knew somehow that Yves would be an attractive poison to her. If he read her right, he'd have no trouble mimicking the archetype that

Phoebe preferred for her occasional male flings: handsome, erudite, and not afraid of a vigorous bit of verbal fencing.

"And just who are you?" Yves cooed.

I could see she was intrigued, but Phoebe was still on her guard. She looked at me with a slightly worried expression, the one that meant she was trying to tell me something without being heard.

"You are detaining my roommate," she declared.

"Your . . . roommate?" Yves looked at me, probably caught me wincing, and then turned back to Phoebe. "My poor dear. I've known . . . your *roommate*, is it? I've known her almost as long as she's been alive." He stepped closer to me and slipped his arm around my waist. "I am very sorry to tell you that, far from detaining her, there's a bond between us that would be impossible for you to understand."

It was a masterful gambit, impeccably delivered. Whatever urgent business Phoebe had with me was, in that moment, forgotten.

"Is that so?" Phoebe said.

"It is, actually. I still have some catching up to do with my old playmate," Yves said, squeezing my waist for effect. "Why don't you get a drink, and . . . whatever else suits your fancy."

What Yves might say about me or my family, and which of my many lies to Phoebe he might thereby inadvertently (or intentionally, for that matter) reveal, were unknowable. I was increasingly desperate to find a way to decouple the three of us.

I felt guilty the moment the idea came to me, but Yves's oblique offer of drugs to Phoebe, whose many hedonistic tendencies he could only have guessed at, presented me with the best opportunity.

"You *have* to try the coke, Phoebe," I said, in a hushed tone that I hoped came off as a tempting bit of conspiracy. "It is amazing."

Phoebe blinked at me, obviously stunned by my declaration. Careful to avoid letting Yves see, I gave her my most pleading look, the one that insisted: *Please don't ask any questions. Just go with the flow. I'll explain everything later.*

Slowly, Phoebe seemed to absorb my anguished, if silent, plea.

"Is it now?" she offered, cautiously.

"Yves only gets the very best," I added. "Of anything."

Yves seemed as surprised with me as Phoebe, an emotion that melted into a beaming smile.

"I missed you, you know," he said, and squeezed my waist again before turning to Phoebe.

"Tell the rather anxious-looking brunette over there"—Yves gestured toward Muffie, who was excitedly talking to a group of guys by the bar—"that I sent you."

Phoebe gave him a smile, looked at me, considered her options for a few seconds, and then headed over to Muffie.

Back on the couch with Yves, I looked for an excuse to break away so I could discreetly collect Phoebe and slip away with her.

"So, just visiting, is it?" Yves mocked, his eyes flashing.

"That's right," I said.

"Your . . . *roommate* doesn't sound like she is . . . 'just visiting.'" I said nothing. "You two would look lovely together. Particularly 'just visiting' my bedroom, come to think of it."

"Knock it off, Yves."

"You are such a prude, my dear. Even the best 'caine in the city doesn't get your juices flowing?"

"I have a high tolerance," I said.

It was a miscalculation, and Yves lit up immediately.

"Well now, full of surprises once we relax a bit, aren't we? I shall rather enjoy putting that claim to the test."

I ignored him.

Phoebe was on her way back before long, arm linked with Muffie's and looking unduly cheerful. Her expression darkened with the memory of some unfinished business when I caught her eye. She mouthed something to me but I couldn't quite lip-read whatever she was trying to say from across the room.

She had to mouth it twice more before I thought I understood: *Eat him.*

I couldn't believe it. It wasn't enough that Yves had morphed into a postadolescent playboy; his cocaine had also apparently intoxicated Phoebe to goad me into sex acts with him. After the shock wore off, the insult of Phoebe's suggestion sank in.

Fuck you, I lipped back, and turned away, furious.

Temporarily, at least, I tabled the idea of collecting her and slipping out. She was still talking to Muffie when I looked up again. As long as she wasn't lingering nearby, where Yves could engage her in conversation that threatened to be dangerous for me, I was better off doing nothing.

In the meantime, I wasn't supposed to notice that Yves was gradually creeping closer on the couch and growing physically more intimate—a hand around my shoulders, then on my arm, a pat on my leg to accentuate a point, a gently whispered phrase under my hair and in my ear—but I did. I endured these efforts with refusals; subtle and polite, perhaps, but refusals nevertheless.

Yves was going on about the relative benefits of brunettes when something else caught me eye. It was all I could do not to stand up and flee when the flash of recognition came to me. At some point in the few seconds that followed I understood that Phoebe hadn't been mouthing "eat him" at me. She had been mouthing "Ethan."

ETHAN'S PRESENCE WAS a puzzle, as was the identity of the brunette whose elbow he had been holding on to. At first I wasn't at all sure how he had known where I was, but as I replayed my panicked voicemail to him in my head I realized that I had told him the name of the Consulate. I certainly hadn't expected that to summon him. Ethan hated nightclubs ("snotty digs for snotty kids," he once told me). Worse, he was intoxicated, and then some. How he had gotten in, especially dressed the way he was (he had thrown on a tattered-looking blazer over a shirt and jeans), was another mystery. His entire ensemble was a disaster, but it was the tennis shoes that stood out, and it was these that Yves locked on to.

"You have got to be kidding me," Yves hissed through his teeth.

I tried to shrink down into the sofa, hoping not to be seen, particularly in such proximity to Yves, but some sixth sense seemed to lead Ethan right to me, as if a powerful psychic ability were fingering for him the perpetrator of some horrible crime.

He stopped short the moment his dull leer found me and stalked over to the sofa. I could not will my limbs to move and so I just sat there.

"This fucking figures," he said, far too loudly.

Conversation in the VIP room softened as attention fell on the four of us.

"Whoever you are, you're lost," Yves said.

"I'm not lost," Ethan slurred. "She is." He pointed at me with his arm fully extended. "Come on," he added. "We're leaving."

"Oh, no she's not," Yves said, but I had seen enough already.

I stood up and took a step toward Ethan.

"Fine, Ethan," I said, and nodded in Phoebe's direction. "Let's just go."

"You know," he slurred, "fuck you. I have my own date now."

I could only assume that Ethan had meant the random brunette he had arrived with, but she had melted into the background and was standing a good thirty feet away. Ethan flailed around, reaching behind to find her arm, or anything to clasp so he might keep his balance.

"Ethan, let's get a cab," I said. "Okay?"

"Fuck that," he snapped.

"Yeah, fuck that," Yves echoed, stepping between Ethan and me.

"Yves," I pled. "Don't."

I tried to pull him back by the wrist, and then glanced around the room, for once desperate to see Karl lurking somewhere, but I had been quick to slip into the VIP room, maybe too quick to be followed. There was no sign of him.

"I'll fuck you up, you fucking faggot," Ethan barked, drawing on whatever reserve of prep school jock posturing he could muster.

He was taller and better built than Yves, but Yves didn't back down an inch. Instead, Yves just smiled and, with a sideways flick of his left arm (in what I had to admit was a very casual and elegant gesture), threw his nearly full martini right into Ethan's face.

Ethan first went pale and then, his face dripping with vodka, redder than I had ever seen. What happened next happened very fast. Ethan lunged for Yves, but was so impaired that he caught his foot on the leg of a chair. Yves just took half a sidestep and leaned away and Ethan came crashing straight into me. I fell backward and hit the back of my head on something.

And then everything went black.

⁓◯

I WOKE UP LOOKING at the ceiling. The whole room was spinning.

I don't know where security hides in such clubs, but they flashed out of the woodwork and, after a couple of well-placed blows, hauled Ethan out like a sack of dirty laundry.

Then there was a blurred path to the door. I was dazed but vaguely aware of Phoebe telling me she was going to find a cab for us, and then Yves's arm around me, leading me outside and away from the club. I was pretty sure I saw a handcuffed Ethan surrounded by police officers and security guards. The entire scene was bathed in blue strobes, but—and though I still wonder sometimes if I imagined it—near the end I could have sworn that I saw Karl there, talking amicably with a police sergeant almost as if they knew each other and Karl was appealing on Ethan's behalf, Karl's gaze shifted from Ethan, to the police surrounding him, and back again.

"I'll take you home," Yves was saying.

Somehow we were in what must have been his car. My senses were finally returning to me and for a time I focused on the back of Yves's driver's head as a way to settle down.

"Do you want a drink?" Yves asked, producing a glass from the in-car bar and pouring something into it from a sterling silver flask.

"No," I said, but I drank some of it anyway when he put it in my hand. It was probably vodka and it made my eyes water.

"Where are we going?"

"Home," Yves said.

"Whose home?"

There was a pause.

"Yours."

"Where do I live?" I asked, getting wise.

"You haven't told us yet," Yves said. "We'll stop at my house first."

"Stop the car," I said.

I was scared. Yves wasn't listening to me, and though he could obviously hear us, his driver was not paying my requests any attention.

"I need you to stop the car now. I'm going to be sick," I said, appealing directly to the driver.

"Stop the car and you're fired," Yves said, with a terrifying calmness.

The driver twisted his head just a little, but he didn't stop.

"Yves, if you don't stop I will scream."

"I'm not driving, my dear," he said nonchalantly.

I started to take a breath to scream and that got some reaction at least. Our driver finally slowed to a stop, blocking another car behind us. To my relief the doors were not child-locked and I sprang out of the car even though it was still rolling a little. I had moved too quickly, and my head started spinning again.

Yves got out too and, for a minute, I was scared he was going to chase me. I took four or five steps back, retreating onto the sidewalk, and ended up with my back against a building, but Yves simply walked over to the driver's side of his car and opened the door.

"Get out," he ordered the driver, who offered no resistance and stepped out into the street.

Yves unceremoniously climbed into the driver's seat and pulled the door closed. He drove a little ways and then made a U-turn right in the middle of the street. He stopped with the driver's-side window, which he proceeded to roll down, facing his bewildered chauffeur.

"You're fired," he said simply, rolled the window back up, and then headed off into the night, back the way we had come.

"Fuck," the driver said, after a long pause.

Regaining my balance, I walked toward him, about to say something (I wasn't quite sure what), but, without so much as glancing in my direction, he stalked off into the dark, leaving me standing alone in the headlamps of the black car that had stopped behind us.

I was trying to decide what to do next when I realized that the black car hadn't moved. I shaded my eyes trying to look at whoever was inside but the glare from the headlights was too bright. I was about to walk toward the nearest intersection to hail a cab when the driver's door opened and I heard a voice.

"I will take you home."

Karl.

We drove in silence but, when we got to the penthouse, Karl gave me a quick concussion protocol and, apparently satisfied with my condition, dropped me at the front door. I closed the passenger door and started for the entrance but when I looked back over my shoulder, Karl was still sitting in the driver's seat. He produced a cell phone from the inside pocket of his blazer and, after what appeared to be a brief call—a greenish glow from the tiny screen casting one side of his face in a cold, pale light—pulled away from the curb. I watched as the familiar black Mercedes prowled down the block, past the entrance to the building's garage, and kept on into the city.

IT WAS ALMOST five in the evening the day after we had gone out when Phoebe finally returned home. I could hear her choking back sobs even through my bedroom door. I hauled myself out of bed and into the hallway.

She was a wreck. Her cheeks were streaked with mascara-tinted tears, her face was puffy, and her hair was sticking up all over.

"Phoebe, bloody hell. What happened?"

"Leave me alone," she sobbed.

"Phoebe, tell me what happened." She stopped and looked at me. Tears were still dropping from her cheeks.

"I lost the contest and so he kicked me out," she slurred through sobs.

"What in the world are you talking about? Who?"

"Just fuck off," she screamed.

She tore off the jacket that was draped over her shoulders and slung it to the ground, then fled to her bedroom.

When it hit the ground I heard the sound of metal from the jacket. I picked it up and noticed the unmistakable ribbon bar on the left breast.

Yves.

I SLEPT FOR A long time. Even after I woke, I stayed in my room with the door locked and the shades closed, ignoring Phoebe's knocking, or the ringing of the phone, other than to accept takeout deliveries. By Wednesday afternoon, remnants of a half dozen pizza and Chinese food orders had accumulated on my floor.

That evening there was a tentative knock on my door. I had been furious with Phoebe, but, finally resigned to talk to her once more, I got up, unlocked it, and opened the door. I wouldn't have thought it possible, but she looked even worse than she had on Sunday. She was pale and it was obvious from her puffy cheeks and bloodshot eyes that she had been crying for some time.

"Oh, Phoebe, come here," I said, intending to give her a hug and comfort her. Part of me hoped she at least felt guilty for sleeping with Yves (as I assumed she had) only the day after committing herself to me, but she didn't move. Instead she handed me a copy of the *Daily Spectator*, the university newspaper. It was folded to an article on the front page. The headline screamed out at me:

NO SUSPECTS YET IN CAMPUS SLAYING

My heart started to pound, my face got hot, and I heard a hum in my ears. I knew even before I saw his name in print that it was Ethan. I skimmed the details—found shot to death Monday morning at 5 a.m. less than one hundred feet from the front door of his dorm; murder weapon recovered at the scene; a $250,000 reward offered by the family.

I knew right away that the reward was hopeless. Ethan's murder would never be solved.

~

CHAPTER THIRTY-TWO

The Wages of Aristocracy

AFTER CURIE HALL MY SOCIAL LIFE had become deeply monolithic, composed of a constellation of smaller, ephemeral bodies that circled around Phoebe and were like as not to fade out or spin off and away should she grow bored of them. But, after Ethan's murder, I found myself pulled in even closer. I decided to forget her indiscretion with Yves and never brought it up with her, hopeful that, whatever had passed between them, he had not exposed my many lies to her.

I loved her, after all, and needed her. Having taken up the nurturing parental role that was otherwise absent in my life, Phoebe unwittingly suppressed the growing void in my psyche (a dark chasm fed by Ethan's death). It was a fragile plaster over a gaping emotional wound, but at the time, it was all that held me together.

I have only vague memories of my suspicions immediately after that horrible night, but my recollection of the way Karl had driven off after my encounter with Yves did not fade easily. Moreover, I had no one to talk to about what I thought I had seen. I didn't dare discuss the matter with Phoebe, and I suppose that, in part, this was a convenient excuse to avoid confronting the issue. What, I found myself asking, did I really know about where Karl had gone after dropping me off?

Still, in the weeks and months that followed, my relationship with Karl soured. And when it did, he dutifully receded into the background once more. Sometimes, however, I resented even that.

Our playful bouts of "urban tag" were but a memory, and we rarely spoke, sometimes going for weeks on end without exchanging a single word.

Phoebe was all too willing to take up the slack. Ethan's death clearly affected her, too, though she was initially much better at hiding it. I was too numb, too desensitized to form anything like attachments to anyone else, and as a result, I found myself more and more in her orbit, defined more and more by my function as her companion: an audience for her various architectural tours, of course, but, increasingly, her escort to this nightclub; her second at that underground party; pulled passively along and destined to follow the itineraries she had set for us.

Not long after Ethan's death I began to lean heavily on my family's resources, a circumstance my mother deigned to allow (perhaps even encourage) even as it began to get out of hand. Asking E. P. Wolff to release funds from the Fulvia Flacca Trust meant a long lecture on prudence. My family's money, on the other hand, poured unfettered from several open and unattended spigots.

By my junior year at university it wasn't uncommon for me to run up eye-popping bills on the unsolicited American Express black card that had one day arrived at the penthouse. It was addressed to the name on my faux passport, and that was obviously my mother's doing. Though the card came to the penthouse, the statements did not, and I could not help but picture an old accounting type with a green eyeshade in the basement of the manor punching in the invoices and simply ordering the payments without scrutiny.

Even before the credit card arrived, it hadn't been unusual for me to pull thousands of dollars at a time out of the essentially bottomless bank account that my mother had arranged. I wasn't totally oblivious to the corrupting influence of that sort of money, of course, but, even as E. P. Wolff's incomplete warnings about the potential effects of excessive wealth lingered in my memory, I found any number of excuses to rationalize them away.

I had been right about the intoxicating potential of my family's wealth as well. The first time Phoebe and I tried to book a commercial flight to Los Angeles, Karl intervened.

"All travel is to be arranged through the operations desk," he said, and handed me a business card with nothing but an international phone number printed on one side. Then he explained the verbal codes to authenticate myself to the duty officers who would answer. That gave us essentially unlimited access to my family's private planes day or night, a little fleet that had expanded to six aircraft. Idly, I wondered what other exotic operations a properly constructed call to the "operations desk" could set in motion.

Access to effectively boundless liquidity and worldwide travel at our very fingertips had its corrosive effects in the years that followed. Five academic years after arriving at university, neither Phoebe nor I had graduated, though it was only her senior thesis on the architecture of New York City that separated Phoebe from commencement ceremonies. In my case, school seemed like an end unto itself, not a means to the end of obtaining a degree. After all, while Phoebe had aspirations to join a graduate program in architecture, what use did I actually have for such credentials?

Looking back, it is easy to see why I lacked the credits to graduate that term. Even as the specter of Ethan's murder receded behind intervening years, I think the memory of it was the end of Phoebe's love affair with Manhattan. It wasn't long before, classes or no, Phoebe and I were in the habit of spending weeks at a time in Phoebe's preferred jurisdiction: the United Kingdom, parked with Karl in one of the Mayfair or Kensington flats my mother counted among our "investment properties."

Phoebe was quick to guide me around London to various marvels of design, and even made noises about changing the topic of her thesis to European architecture, but, so far as I know, she never took any material steps in that direction. At one point it occurred to me that she was dragging her feet because I was stuck in a holding pattern and she didn't want to be too far out ahead of me. Whatever our respective motivations, if anyone back on the estate was aware of my chronic school absenteeism they either declined to comment or simply didn't care.

Even abroad, my family's resources continued to be devoid of rules or limits. As a result, I rarely asked E. P. Wolff for money. It was a circumstance that pleased him insofar as it left him with the horrifically erroneous impression that I was possessed of some measure of fiscal restraint (even if I could not conceal my academic indolence from him). Still, he took his long-past promise to my grandfather seriously and so, as trustee of the Fulvia Flacca

Trust, insisted on regular meetings with his charge, going so far as to carve out a space for himself in the London offices of Burling Wolff & Rohr when it was apparent that I was spending so much time in the city.

I played along but, at the time, found his well-meaning lectures and advice hopelessly cliché.

~⌒~

IT WAS A lunch meeting with E. P. Wolff in London in the spring of 2001 that finally set in motion the events that began to disrupt the vapid equilibrium I had found. The restaurant I had insisted on—a popular destination for London bankers and finance types—was usually empty at that time of day. As was typical of me before meeting with E. P., I had spent some time switching back and forth on the Tube and doubling back while walking, making sure that Karl was not following.

I had no concrete reason to ditch Karl, only that I had come to view him as an adversary of some sort. Using what he had taught me during our urban tag games to slip away from his watchful sentinel duties had become habit.

Giving Karl the slip had taken only about twenty minutes that afternoon, but I had started off to the meeting with E. P. almost two hours late. I suppose my casual attitude toward appointments was a measure of how bitter I had become, and how little I regarded my grandfather's legacy by that time (and, by extension, the efforts of E. P. Wolff to effectuate it).

E. P. looked very cross when I arrived. The restaurant was nearly empty, excepting a group of five businessmen who surrounded a far table, speaking in hushed tones, exchanging the tidings of secrets once kept, and unannounced deals recently uncovered. I made a show of kissing E. P. on the cheeks when he stood. The waiter held the chair for me and I ordered a martini even before I took my seat. Once settled, I studiously ignored the clock on the opposite wall.

"You could indulge an old man his sense of duty," E. P. began, "permit him that last fragment of his vanity that he might look after the favorite granddaughter of a lifelong friend after his passing, no?"

"Only granddaughter," I said.

"Of course. Forgive me, but I do wish you would try to be punctual. Perhaps just once? I fear the waitstaff was beginning to think me not in possession of all my faculties after my fourth time insisting that I was, indeed, waiting for a young lady to join me."

E. P. nodded toward a collection of servers. They were watching us closely at some remove, tittering to each other in hushed tones. I winced.

"I came across an old friend," I lied.

"What, here?"

E. P.'s eyes began to scan the room and, as might happen now and again, the normally latent instincts of the fighter pilot—always wary of wandering into an unseen enemy's ambush—came to the surface and darkened his expression.

"No, at Claridge's," I said.

He relaxed a little, but his tone was stern. "I would really prefer we not meet in public, you know."

"You say that every time we meet. Your London office is rather stuffy, and one grows tired of shuffling in through the tradesman's entrance."

"Secrecy is a necessary precaution," he said with a weary smile. "But you know this already."

I waved down our waiter and ordered a second martini. E. P. spoke again only after our server had retreated out of earshot.

"I must also point out that I have another appointment today," he said. "I will be very lucky not to be late."

"I thought I was your only client."

To my surprise, he changed the subject.

"Have you given any more thought to your degree? To graduate school after? I feel duty-bound to remind you—"

"I know, I know."

He looked at me for a long time, and then, in a gesture quite unlike him, reached across my setting and took my right hand in both of his.

"You will at least complete your undergraduate education? Yes?"

"You know," I said, annoyed, "somehow I doubt Augustin has to endure these constant entreaties to 'apply yourself' or 'realize your full potential.' For as long as I can remember, old men have been telling me what I should learn, how I should think, what I should and shouldn't do, and how I should or shouldn't do it."

I wasn't entirely sure where the comment had come from until after I let it slip. Perhaps the "favorite granddaughter" remark had reminded me that I, the only girl, had been effectively banished to exile and it was sitting poorly with me.

"Young lady," E. P. barked back at me, and that startled me, since I had never heard him do it before. He softened his tone when he continued. "I am surprised by this attitude. I have only ever wished to advise you well. My advice may be unwelcome but it is my duty to render it nevertheless.

"You may not think this matter of consequence, but I assure you that it is most grave. Your eldest brother is in the midst of a very difficult period. He must transform himself in the years to come; must shed many of the sentiments that do not serve an heir to the patriarchy of your family. This is a dangerous time for him and those around him. It was your grandfather's wish that you be insulated from him. If you will not see the seriousness of the situation, you force me to see it on your behalf."

I was alarmed by his unexpected declaration, and suddenly wary of what form his implied intervention might take.

"You will leave your eldest brother be, do you understand me?"

Still stunned by his initial outburst, I could do nothing but nod.

His rebuke delivered, his eyes took on the most tender appearance, and I felt ashamed for having taken his many attentions and kindnesses for granted over the years.

"And you will work to complete your studies?"

"I will," I said. "I promise." But, of course, I didn't really mean it.

"Well, try to eat something at least. Young people take such poor care of themselves these days."

I ordered a chicken salad to keep him happy, but I just picked at it for the rest of our conversation, which, mostly due to my apathy, quickly meandered into a miasmic fog of irrelevancies.

E. P. had asked for the check already when I noticed one of the businessmen at the far table. He was looking at me with a stare so rude that, for a moment, I could not tear my eyes away. Something about him (the powerful whiff of self-assured arrogance, perhaps) was familiar, but, hard as I tried, recognition eluded me. I finally looked away, but every time I caught sight of him in my peripheral vision, the man was still staring at me.

As was our habit, E. P. made to leave the restaurant first, but once he was out of the door, I found myself curious about the other appointment he had mentioned. The bill was paid and so, in a sudden burst of (admittedly intoxicated) curiosity, I darted out of the restaurant and went after him.

I spotted E. P. down the street and fell in behind him. It had the feel of some dark intrigue and I found myself looking over my shoulder more often than usual, ironically wishing that I would feel hints of Karl's protective overwatch somewhere behind me.

My curiosity burned, but I think rather it was some combination of boredom and two-martini courage that propelled me onward. I was surprised when E. P. went into the nearest Tube station. I had always known him to be driven about London in a private car. At first I thought it a ruse, but E. P. proved an easy subject to follow. He exhibited none of the countermeasures I had learned from Karl, and by the time he got off at Regent's Park station, I had almost bored of the endeavor enough to break off my pursuit.

E. P. meandered west until he stopped in front of a red and white brick building: the Royal Academy of Music. I watched from across the street as he greeted a very British gentleman with silver hair who had been waiting by the sidewalk. He shook hands with the man and then handed him a thick envelope with a rubber band wrapped around it. This strange transaction complete, the two of them strolled down Marylebone Road. Increasingly intrigued (and even sobering up a bit), I settled in behind them before they turned north and headed into Regent's Park.

We were almost to Queen Mary's Rose Gardens, just inside the Inner Circle, when the silver-haired man stopped and pointed toward the Japanese Garden Island. The men shook hands and then parted. I let the silver-haired man go and fell in behind E. P. as he made his way north again.

I heard him before I saw him. Strings. A dark but even melody rising up over the landscape and carrying in the light, early evening air. As I rounded a bend in the path, I saw a young man standing in a clearing just short of the rose gardens themselves. He was in the middle of what must have been an impromptu crowd of more than two dozen people. He was playing with his

eyes closed, lost in the music he coaxed and caressed from the violin he held.
E. P. joined the crowd to listen, but no one paid him any notice. The young
man was playing so beautifully that many members of his audience looked
totally taken up by the performance.

I think I recognized the instrument first. The young man held, cradled
really, the Guarneri named "Castor." It was my brother Bastien's violin. He
was older, certainly, and very pale and thin. But, after a moment's shock, I
saw that it was my brother Bastien who played it.

I COULD BARELY MOVE at first, trying to decide how to interact with him
and still avoid E. P. I willed myself closer, nudging my way through the
circle around him until I was close enough behind E. P. that I could have
reached out and touched him. I watched Bastien's hands, entranced by his
skill and talent. He played for another twenty minutes straight and never
once opened his eyes. I must have closed my eyes at one point too because,
when I opened them again, E. P. had left the circle. I just managed to catch
a glimpse of him walking away before he rounded a bend and wandered out
of view. I remember being surprised that he had left before the end of the
performance, but by that time I was nearly as intoxicated by Bastien's music
as the others around me.

When my brother finished with a long, lingering note, the woman next
to me choked back a sob and blotted tears from her eyes.

Hesitantly, I stepped forward. I think I intended to greet him, but I
paused, both anxious and afraid after the vast gulf of time and circumstance
that had separated us. Before I could say anything or reach for his hand, his
expression stopped me cold. The moment he stopped playing and opened his
eyes, I saw how vacant they were. It was as if he were merely a vessel, that
he was channeling that intoxicating music from somewhere else, from some
other plane, and it was the only thread connecting him to our existence. With
the thread broken, the bridge to us was gone. Nothing was left behind those
eyes; hollow, the empty orbs of someone trapped in a waking coma.

He ignored the crowd's applause and his expression was so hauntingly
alien no one dared try to approach him. Some of the crowd began to take

their leave, but others lingered, murmuring to each other, waiting, I supposed, against the possibility he might start playing again.

I inched closer.

"Bastien," I whispered. Then louder, "Bastien. It's me."

Stiffly, he turned in my direction, more a response to the hushed sound, I thought, than anything else. At first I thought he had looked at me, but I quickly realized that he had looked right through me. He reached up with his right hand—an awkward gesture, three fingers curled around the frog of the bow he still clutched—and I thought that he would acknowledge me, but instead he just brushed away some itch below his eye. It seemed to me then that he recognized nothing.

Such a wave of emotion welled up that it threatened to reduce me to despair. In that moment, I felt in my heart that my brother, the only sibling I might still count as a friend, was truly gone. It was so horrible that I thought I might simply fall to my knees before him and start sobbing. But something intervened: a man wearing a dark coat was standing on the other side of the crowd, lingering just behind the ranks; a tall and pale ghost robed in dark cloth, watching me carefully, finally willing himself to be seen after lurking for some time just beyond the bounds of perception.

Robotically, Bastien closed his eyes and transformed into an artisan once more as he started again. An intoxicating portion of Stravinsky's *The Firebird* (a melody almost more haunting than the first) flowed from the Guarneri. It seemed like it was the music itself that revealed the rest of the pale figure on the other side of the crowd, allowing it to resolve into something recognizable through my tear-blurred vision.

Karl.

——

CHAPTER THIRTY-THREE

Vienna

I FLED THE MOMENT I SAW Karl. It was in some part instinct, as if I was afraid that something terrible would happen to Bastien if I did not lead Karl away. But that was both silly and pointless. Silly because it was impossible to believe he would do Bastien harm, pointless because he just fell in behind me as I hurried out of Regent's Park, and then lingered in my wake until it seemed childish to pretend he wasn't there. Eventually I let him lead me to the signature black Mercedes and drive me back to the flat. I was furious with him—slouched down, arms crossed in the back seat like a pouting child—or perhaps only with myself, but I am not sure I could have explained why.

Phoebe was not at home and, in some sense, that was a relief. I didn't want her to see me that rattled. My efforts to forget what I had seen did not endure long. Karl was in the kitchen preparing an espresso for himself, calm and nonchalant as ever. It set me off, that stoic act, and my long-building anger with him welled up to the surface until I could contain it no longer.

"How long has he been in London?" I demanded.

Karl put down his espresso and looked at me, but said nothing.

"You must have known. You never thought to tell me?"

Nothing.

"It wasn't within the brief of your orders, I suppose?" I was almost shouting. "Not within the strict letter of your instructions? Not part of keeping me 'out of harm's way'? You don't think conspiring to keep my own brother hidden from me is a harm?"

He remained silent, and that just upset me more.

"What happened with Ethan that night?" I said. It was a topic I never thought I wanted to revisit, but I couldn't help myself. "Where did you drive to after you dropped me off?"

Calm as could be, Karl picked up his espresso and sipped it, never taking his eyes from me.

"I saw you, you know. When I came out of the club." Even as I was speaking, the pieces I never wanted to scrutinize fell into place. "The police were going to arrest him, weren't they? But, somehow, you got them to let him go. Didn't you? Then there was no place for him to go but home. Just another drunk, staggering in the dark. At least until he was almost home, where someone was waiting for him, right?"

Karl's voice was calm, measured. "In this dangerous period, the members of the direct line must not only be protected by the threat of deadly force, but must also be seen by others to be so protected. One cannot permit an outsider to do a daughter of the line serious injury, and in public, without consequence."

I began to shake all over when I realized what he was saying. I thought of all the times Karl had snuck up behind me in broad daylight, even when I had been on my guard, so close he could tap me on the shoulder.

"Strike your enemy when he is weak and unaware," I snapped. "He never had a chance, did he? Did he even see it coming? Did you even bother to look him in the eye first?"

Karl's expression darkened.

"He didn't even mean to hurt me. He tripped. You killed him because of an accident? To *protect* me? You weren't even there. You didn't even see what happened. If you had been there you could have stopped it. Instead, you killed him to make a point?"

"To permit such an act to go unanswered would be understood as weakness. The cause of the incident is irrelevant. Intentionally slipping outside of the protective envelope, even briefly, can have dire consequences," he said.

"I can't believe this!" I shouted, and the tears started. "It is my fault that you killed him? Killed him so that you could protect me?"

"It was you that led him into harm's way."

"How could he have known that?"

"You knew it for him."

"Where did this rule come from? Does Augustin know it? Does Bastien?"

"I have no instructions with respect to your brothers."

"Bullshit," I said, but really I wasn't so sure. "And what about my grandfather? Where were you when he was killed? Were you 'protecting' him as well, or did he slip 'outside of the protective envelope' too?"

I had been trying to get a rise out of Karl, furious with his unflappable certainty and horrified that he seemed to be confirming my worst fears about him, but when I saw the flash of anger in his eyes, I regretted it immediately. It was dark, cold, and intense, a terrifying malevolence that I shrank away from. The predatory look he gave me then melted my knees out from under me and I actually stumbled as I started to backpedal out of the kitchen.

As quickly as it had come, the fury behind his eyes faded. Then, much to my surprise, it melted into the warmest and most sympathetic expression I had seen on Karl—hints of the virtuoso who played the piano with such feeling and warmth that it was impossible to think him guilty of the crimes he had all but confessed to.

He took a step toward me, extending his hand in what I took to be a conciliatory gesture. But that seductive offering only terrified me more. Trying not to cry out for help as I did so, I fled upstairs to my room and locked myself in.

IT WAS MERE chance that, some days later, I unearthed the story about the murder. I might have let the entire matter pass except for a strange occurrence. I had taken to locking my bedroom door but, the day after my confrontation with Karl, I found the deck of cards with the black backings on my bedside table.

Was it a peace offering? I didn't know (or care) at the time. In fact, I was so angry I threw the deck in the trash. Later, feeling sheepish, I fished them out of the bin and put them away. I would look at them now and again but could never figure out how they were marked. Or, in fact, if they were marked at all.

I think that Karl's act of sneaking in my room got me thinking about Bastien again. I had been beyond moved by my brother's performance and I could not get the second piece he had played out of my head. Eventually I went to look up the Stravinsky work, hoping my research would reveal which recorded version I should seek out for my own use. In the process, I uncovered the story in the public library's microfiche archives.

Many years earlier, a violinist, a young woman who had studied at Juilliard, had disappeared from the Metropolitan Opera House, where the orchestra had been playing accompaniment for the visiting Berlin Ballet. During the interlude, a mere forty-five minutes, the violinist vanished, leaving her seat empty aside from her abandoned instrument, which remained untouched for the remainder of the performance.

A search of the opera house turned up nothing at first, until the next morning, when her body was found "nude, and broken," stuffed into an old trunk hidden in a ventilation shaft.

Such a story connected to such a famous venue became a national and international sensation, the subject of scores of articles and features. In the investigation that followed, it emerged that, backstage during the break, a young man connected to the opera house had lured the violinist alone up to an isolated section on the fourth floor where he made romantic overtures. When his advances were spurned, he became angry and rough with the girl, threatening her with violence if she did not disrobe. Matters escalated until he finally killed her, perhaps even, as he claimed, by accident, when he shoved her backward onto a piece of prop furniture, breaking her neck.

Stravinsky's *The Firebird* had been the last piece she had ever played.

I might have forgotten all about the awful tale and packed up for home. Instead, something about how Bastien had behaved in Regent's Park came back to me.

Had the gesture I thought I had seen, the three fingers brought to his eye, actually been a warning? Could it have been an effort to flash the old signal from the Bureau of Secrets? The one that meant that we were being watched? Could it possibly be a coincidence that the piece he had played was also the last one performed by the murdered Juilliard girl?

The image that came to me next was so horrible that I squeezed my eyes shut and pressed it out of my mind as fast as I could: Augustin looming over Cipriana, cornering her.

Don't you think I know that you've been hiding from me? he had said. *Eventually, you're going to come upstairs with me again.* Then his hand slipping up to her throat. *Why be so coy about it?*

I LOCKED MYSELF IN my room when I got back to the London flat, plagued by horrific dreams that I do not much care to recollect. When I finally emerged, I found Phoebe downstairs in the foyer with our well-worn day bags set by the front door.

"Hey, sleepy head," she said, and then gave me a once-over. "You look a wreck and you aren't even dressed. We are supposed to be at the airport in just over two hours."

The airport? Today? I racked my brain for long seconds before it came to me. *Vienna.* I had promised Phoebe that we would go to Vienna so she could show me the Schönbrunn Palace and St. Stephen's Cathedral, the seat of the archbishop of Vienna.

Travel-related memory lapses like that were actually quite common for me that year, the result of exotic trips planned in the gleeful blur of a drunken Thursday night, and nearly forgotten in the miasma of a Friday morning hangover.

In fact, whatever I had thought when I made the plans with Phoebe, I had no desire to go to Vienna. Somewhere, an idea was forming: that what I really wanted to do, needed to do, was go back to Regent's Park, to find Bastien and find a way to talk to him; maybe even to take him out of there entirely and home with me.

Still, I knew I was in no state to argue, and that Phoebe would be crushed if I canceled. I glanced at Karl, who lurked in the kitchen, annoyingly neutral, waiting for a path to be chosen.

"Fine," I said, and headed back up to take a shower. "I'll be ready in fifteen minutes."

I drank too much on the plane, of course. But that was nothing new.

PHOEBE HAD EXQUISITE taste in hotels and those particular travel comforts were rather important to me in those days. She had booked a deluxe suite at the Grand Hotel Wien and insisted that we both dress to the nines before dinner, a short-lived affair that was a little more than a warm-up for a reception she had planned to hold in our suite. She had invited a slew of friends she had in the architecture program at Vienna's Academy of Fine Arts.

Between Phoebe's friends, their friends, and various hangers-on, the reception was quickly playing host to nearly two dozen people. The drinking was accelerating and that, along with the fact that I knew almost none of our guests, started to make me nervous. Though I thought that I could still feel his presence, Karl had vanished sometime after we checked into the hotel.

I tried to enjoy myself, but my mind kept going back to Regent's Park, the vacant look in Bastien's eyes, the possibility that he had been trying to tell me something with the old hand signal (which I still wasn't sure I hadn't simply imagined) and the Stravinsky piece.

It was the second time that I heard glass breaking—whatever it was, I would surely end up paying for it—that finally sent me over the edge. I took a deep breath, grabbed my clutch, and headed for the exit.

"Hey, get some more vodka while you're out, will you?" some random girl called after me.

I might have snapped at the hapless guest, might have demanded to know if she even knew who I was, or who was paying for her increasingly debauched entertainment, but some other random answered before I could.

"Just order a couple of bottles from room service," she said.

Phoebe gave me a concerned look when she saw me leaving, but made no move to stop me.

⟳

OUTSIDE THE HOTEL, the Vienna night was bracing and I stood for a moment on the sidewalk taking it all in. The doorman was looking at me, obviously wondering if he should preemptively hail a cab, but I avoided his gaze, closed my eyes, tilted my head back, and took in a few deep breaths of the crisp air.

More or less randomly, I turned left and started strolling down the street. I hadn't taken fifteen steps, and had just started looking to see if Karl had fallen in behind me, when a car pulled over on the access road. A door opened and a man stepped out in front of me.

I was too shocked to react, and so he had ample time to reach into his inside jacket pocket, produce a folded piece of paper, and hold it out to me. It was an involuntary reflex on my part to take it. Once the paper was in my hand, he was back in the passenger seat of the black car, which sped off toward Opernring.

I stood there in a daze before thinking to look at the paper he had given me. The page was blank except for a typewritten address:

PHILHARMONIKERSTRASSE 4

Perhaps it said something about my circumstances in those years that I did not react more viscerally to being approached by a strange man outside my hotel. It was not unlike E. P. to resort to such cloak-and-dagger tactics to meet, or arrange to pass documents or a sentimental gift to me without alerting Karl (or anyone else). However, on reflection, a mysterious note with only an address seemed not quite his style.

Vienna's first district was quiet at that hour, and the address was only a few blocks away. Once I turned off Kärntner Ring, the side streets were a wonderful sort of dark, interrupted by the occasional neon of a shop window and the strange shadows cast by the city's iconic center-hung streetlamps.

Philharmonikerstrasse 4 turned out to be the address of Hotel Sacher. I was about to walk into the lobby when I heard a sound behind me. I was across the street from the back of the State Opera House and I turned to see two men standing on either side of an open door. A warm light streamed into the street from inside. The taller man took a half-step to one side and made an inviting gesture toward the door with a sweep of his arm.

I hesitated, but curiosity, well mixed with liquid courage, got the best of me. I walked over to the door and then in. Two officers of the Vienna police, armed with submachine guns and easily recognized by their distinctive hats, flanked the inside of the entrance. For a moment I expected to be stopped, but they barely scrutinized me.

It was nearly empty inside. I heard singing, and my shoes echoed on the polished stone floor. Two more escorts, ushers perhaps, suits complete with pocket squares, flanked the stairs but smiled and gave way at my approach. I was led in this fashion, navigating between successive pairs of ushers as if they were channel markers, until I was upstairs and standing at the door to one of the boxes. Another usher (apparently the last gauntlet to run) opened it for me.

Sitting inside, as if unaware of my presence, was my father.

THE SEATS IN the opera house were empty and yet the orchestra and company—wearing helmets and clad in black leather—were in midperformance. The singing was in Italian and delivered from in front of a dark set dominated by towering gates. My father and I were the only spectators.

Recovering from the shock of seeing him, I curtsied to my father's back but my eyes were locked on the stage. I should have held the pose until he acknowledged me, but my father, also intent on the production, didn't turn around. There was only one other chair in the box, so, though it was rather presumptuous, I took my place next to him and folded my hands in my lap. My attention was torn between the anxiety triggered by his sudden presence, the fact that he hadn't aged in the ten years since I had seen him, that we were both apparently ignoring the wide gulf of time that had divided us, and my fascination with the performance in front of us.

"How was your flight?" my father said, during a lull.

"Uneventful," I said, but I was suddenly very aware of how close I was sitting to him, and it was a reflexive answer.

"You arrived from London?"

"Yes," I said.

"We have offices in London, you know. In Vienna too. I thought you might have visited them at least once by now."

I mumbled something noncommittal.

My father was silent for a long time before gesturing to the stage. "*Don Carlo*," he said. "Do you know it?"

"I don't think so."

"Verdi's longest. It has been cut in many different ways. There are scores of versions. Those that are not in Italian take *Don Carlos* as their title."

Another silence divided us and the performance began to take me along with it once more. Even with the house lights down, the interior of the opera house—golds and reds just perceptible in the dim light; in the air, hints of heavier scents; velvet, wood, and leather—was enthralling. I felt enveloped, not in an altogether unpleasant way, by the dark, and the darkness of the drama being played out in front of us.

"I've never been to a private opera before," I whispered, without really meaning to.

"It is merely a dress rehearsal."

"Oh." I shifted in my chair.

"It is important to indulge in distractions now and again. How did you find London?"

"Well enough."

"You were visiting someone in particular?"

He asked it without intonation or emphasis, but his question set off alarm bells.

"Some old friends," I said, and tried to put E. P. out of my mind, as if my father might perceive the image; might pluck it straight from my thoughts.

"Oh?"

My father turned to look at me for the first time since I had come into the box. I hadn't been prepared for such questions and I didn't want to sound as if I were inventing answers. I had to come up with something quickly.

"Some of my roommate's friends, actually," was the best I could do, and I was terrified that he knew it for the lie it was.

My father held my gaze. There was a long pause in our conversation and all I could see in the dark of the box were his gray eyes. I thought I could perceive hints of his distinctive cologne—cedar, and pepper—in the air between us.

From the stage the report of a gunshot rang out. It was loud, and I almost came out of my chair. My father did not flinch.

"Posa has been shot by the Inquisitor's assassin," he said, turning back to the stage. "As he dies, he tells Carlo that his true love will meet him on the morrow."

I tried to find words, but nothing came to me.

My father turned back to me. His gray eyes were unnerving. "You must choose," he said.

"I . . . I don't understand."

"There is much to absorb in Verdi's work. Don Carlo, son of Phillip II, is beset from all quarters with conflicts. Between freedom and loyalty. Between the bonds of friendship and of blood. In the end, it is indecision that dooms him, and his grandfather Charles V emerges from the grave to take him away. To heaven, hell, or elsewhere . . . we are left to wonder."

A dark figure intruded on our box, leaned down to my father, and whispered in his ear.

"Enjoy the rest of the performance," my father said, standing up. Surprised,

I came to my feet and curtsied to him. "Liam will see that you have everything you need."

The dark figure—Liam, I assumed—bowed in my direction, and with a soft whisper of drapes and fabric my father was gone, leaving me alone in the box with the rising song of the final act.

I STAYED TO THE very end, of course, and watched with some mix of amazement and horror as the final scene my father had described played itself out. In the midst of the tomb of Charles V, cloaked figures, dark shadows, agents of the Grand Inquisitor, emerged from everywhere to converge upon and then seize Don Carlo. Before he was hauled away to execution, a white-clad figure appeared, a monk. But, as he started to sing, it was clear that the monk was Charles V himself, returned somehow from the dead.

The Grand Inquisitor's men melted away and, as the monk guided Don Carlo farther into the tomb, tall gates of black bars spanning from floor to ceiling closed behind them, locking the rest of the performers away so that Charles V and Don Carlo alone occupied center stage. Then, as the orchestra's crescendo rose, crested, and fell, the curtain dropped.

I was so moved by the climax that, as the echoes of the orchestra's final notes faded, I nearly forgot myself and stood to applaud. I managed to hold back when the house lights stayed down, when I saw that there was no audience to rise to their feet and cheer, and when none of the performers emerged to take their bows. For the ten minutes it took me to recover and take my leave, I was left alone, in the dark, with only my racing thoughts for company.

LEAVING THE OPERA house was beyond eerie. Liam, the dark figure, hovered at some remove but made no effort to speak to me. Excepting a few dimmed lights marking the way out, the hallway and lobby lights had been extinguished and the ushers and police had vanished, leaving me to walk through the opera house's interiors alone, until I exited onto Philharmonikerstrasse, and into the lovely Vienna night.

CHAPTER THIRTY-FOUR

Edge of Darkness

EVEN A WEEK LATER, I WAS still shaken by the meeting with my father and easily upset. Eventually, aided by the many walking architectural tours of Vienna led by Phoebe, or meanderings which, increasingly, I took on my own, my unease faded. When our departure date came, I was almost sad to leave.

As we gathered in the lobby to check out, we were greeted by a very beautiful (and very blond) receptionist, who hurried around from behind the front desk to intercept us. She invited the group to enjoy some champagne in the lobby lounge while our checkout was arranged.

Phoebe chose that time to dig through her clutch and did a double take as if surprised by something she had found.

In the months prior, Phoebe had developed the habit of leaving her party favors in her personal effects before boarding the jet for home. I had never known her drug use to get out of hand and so mostly ignored her habits. Karl, clearly focused on the risks involved in transporting illicit substances, was another matter entirely.

After looking the other way more than once, he had finally pulled her aside before one of our return trips and, in the face of steadfast denials that she had anything illicit in her possession, unceremoniously dumped the entire contents of Phoebe's purse into the middle of the street. He then returned the bag to her empty and ushered her into the car. Phoebe was too shocked (and too afraid of Karl) to object.

I nearly laughed when, like a sad puppy, she pressed her hands against the rear passenger window glass and watched her sidewalk-strewn personal effects, including her ID, all her credit cards, makeup, cash, and two mysterious glassine baggies, recede into the distance as we started off for the airport.

"That was my favorite compact," Phoebe had complained on the flight home.

After that, Phoebe made a big show of opening her purse for Karl whenever we boarded the jet. For his part, Karl ignored the melodrama.

Given our pending departure, I thought I knew what she had in her clutch that had prompted her double take there in the lobby.

"I'm going to go . . . powder my nose," she said, and headed for the ladies' room, determined, I supposed, not to let her hard-won narcotics go to waste.

With Phoebe gone, the receptionist's expression turned more serious. She had a small, embarrassed frown on her face when she leaned to whisper in my ear.

"I am very sorry, madam, and I wouldn't dream of discussing this matter in the presence of other parties." She glanced in Phoebe's direction. "But we cannot get an authorization for the credit card we have on file. Do you perhaps have another?"

I was surprised. When the receptionist showed me the bill it was eye-wateringly large. But if my American Express even had a limit, I hadn't found it (and that wasn't for want of trying).

"May I use a telephone?" I said.

"Certainly, madam. If you'll follow me."

When I reached an American Express agent on the hotel's courtesy phone, she was polite but unhelpful.

"That account has been suspended," she said.

"Did I reach the credit limit?"

"No, ma'am. The account has been suspended."

"What does that mean exactly?"

"I'm sorry, ma'am, but I don't have any more information."

My card not working was a problem on several levels. Often in those days, I carried large sums in cash on my person, but that particular night, I had less than a thousand euro and change on hand. That barely covered a few hours of occupancy in our suite.

Phoebe had emerged from the ladies' room and parked herself in the lobby lounge by that time and, as I watched, the waiter delivered her a bottle of champagne. I found myself hoping that it was complimentary.

Annoyed, I sat in the little phone booth in the lobby wondering how much money Karl had on him. Perhaps, I thought, some emergency cash, but I doubted it was in amounts likely to solve the immediate problem at the hotel, nor did I relish asking him for money.

I hated the idea of it, but I dialed E. P. Wolff's number next. In an emergency, he could arrange a wire transfer in almost any size directly to the hotel. It sure felt like an emergency but when I called his private number, it only rang and rang.

Preoccupied with that crisis, I jumped when the receptionist knocked on the glass of the phone booth.

"There's a call for you at the front desk, ma'am," she said.

American Express calling back to correct their mistake, maybe? I thought. *That was fast.*

I made my way to the front desk and took the phone.

"Hello?" I ventured.

"Karl is with you?" the voice said.

"Who is this?"

"Wilem Jäger."

It took me quite a few seconds to recognize the name, a name I had last heard in my grandfather's East Salon years before, after returning from South Africa. *A mercenary*, my father had called him.

"I don't understand," I said. "Why are you calling?"

"Is he there?"

"You mean right here?"

"Yes," he said. He sounded irritated.

I put the receiver on the counter and spotted Karl in the foyer. Once I caught his eye, I had barely inclined my head toward the phone before he was on his way to me.

"For you," I said.

Karl picked up the phone and put his hand over the mouthpiece, waiting in silence. I finally took the hint and walked away, though with my curiosity burning, I made a point of staying within earshot. I might not have bothered.

Karl listened impassively for perhaps thirty seconds and then hung up without saying a word.

"Come with me," he said, after closing the distance between us.

I was about to ask for an explanation, but he had already taken four hard and purposeful strides toward the foyer and the entryway beyond.

Phoebe was still in the lobby lounge, standing behind one of the couches, leaning down to whisper in the ear of a seated German gentleman who must have been in his late fifties. I called out to her and motioned for her to follow.

"Ma'am?" the receptionist called from behind the desk as we headed for the door. "The matter we discussed . . . ?"

"Yes," I said in passing, as Phoebe scurried to join me. "We'll be right back."

Karl held the passenger door of the rental car open for me and I got in without a second thought. For a moment, I actually entertained the idea that he planned to skip out on the hotel bill, but he produced a thick wad of cash and handed it to the bellman.

"For the bill," Karl said, just as Phoebe jumped into the back.

"You'll never believe who I just met," Phoebe cooed, but once she picked up on the mood in the car her expression darkened. "What's going on? Why the rush?"

I had no answer for her. I looked to Karl, but he only started the car and drove out onto the street.

BEFORE LONG, WITH the pale hints of dawn just beginning to brush the sky, we were pulling into Vienna International Airport.

Karl parked the car outside one of the executive terminals and opened the door for me. After Phoebe got out, he locked the car and slipped the car keys into the tailpipe. I stood gawking, but Karl was already headed toward the terminal.

Security for us was even more nonexistent than usual. The woman in the office unlocked the double glass doors, then guided us through the mini-terminal, around the single metal detector, and straight to the tarmac.

There I saw something that worried me more than anything: the Citation X that Phoebe and I had arrived in was dark. Sunshades were in the cockpit windows, and it was still parked on the far side of the tarmac. Waiting for us not seventy feet away, lights off except for the pulsing red beacons, was another, newer Citation X painted in my family's familiar jet-black and silver livery. The engines were turning and door was open, though the cabin lights were off.

Rather than wait for the flight crew to collect themselves and return to the airport, another jet and crew entirely had been sent to retrieve us. Someone was in an awful hurry.

Karl ascended first. There was no flight attendant, and I couldn't make out the pilots' faces in the dim blue-white glow from the Citation's glass cockpit. I had been nervous, but it was in that moment that I first realized that I was scared. Everything was happening too fast. I wanted it all to just slow down, to pause for just a few seconds so I could catch up. I hesitated at the foot of the stairs.

"What's wrong?" Phoebe said, but I couldn't find any words.

"Do you want to keep your father waiting?" Karl said, from the top stair, a baritone's voice cutting through the sound of the jet's idling engines.

My father.

"Your exile is ended," he added.

I blinked at him, disbelieving, but then I understood: the jet was bound for the estate.

I turned my attention to Phoebe. She was very beautiful in that moment and I lost myself in those brilliant eyes of hers. A flash of our night together after we had taken Pierce's ecstasy came back to me. For a moment, I saw the intoxicating blue of her eyes that way again, and felt a hint of the warmth of the drug reach forward through time to touch me once more.

I realized that I could finally discard the girl in the Swiss passport, and what I wanted to say to Phoebe, had been wanting for years to say to her, began to take shape in my head. I would finally confess that I had been living under an alias since I first arrived at Curie, that I had been lying to her since we first met. I would tell her about my family, and the estate.

A flurry of images assaulted me: showing Phoebe my home, the architecture of the manor, walking the grounds of the estate with her, on horseback exploring the edges of our lands with her, climbing through the Northern Ruins together, sitting among the spires on the manor's roof, stargazing into one of the estate's brilliant night skies, taking afternoon tea in the Rose Salon.

I wanted to describe all of these images to her, desperate that she should forgive me the years of deception, and follow me up the stairs into the jet.

I closed my eyes and pulled her to me. I kissed her long and deep. Her arms came around me. There was a desperate and ecstatic urgency to it and for a moment my knees almost buckled under me.

"What?" she said, when we came up for air, bemused by my expression. "What is it?"

"The answers you seek," Karl called, before I could reply to her. "She cannot give them to you."

His words summoned a chaotic specter of dark mysteries: the fate of my brother Bastien; my grandfather's death; the shadowy enemies of my family; the Letters from the Dead; the Order of Nyx; Cipriana; and, most of all, that last night on the estate. They threatened to overtake me, these inscrutable enigmas, and I feared I was on the edge of being seduced by the pursuit of some horrible truth, one that I might be forever captive to, or even totally subsumed by.

As I struggled to abandon that path, to turn back to Phoebe, my father's cryptic words in the opera house came to me:

There is much to absorb in Verdi's work. Don Carlo, son of Phillip II, is beset from all quarters with conflicts. Between freedom and loyalty. Between the bonds of friendship and of blood. In the end, it is indecision that dooms him, and his grandfather Charles V emerges from the grave to take him away. To heaven, hell, or elsewhere . . . we are left to wonder.

What had he said before that? I could almost hear his voice.
You must choose.

The wind, starting to pick up and disturbed by the air currents around the turning engines, swirled and buffeted against all of us, tearing normal sounds asunder. The gusts pulled at my clothes. Karl hadn't moved. I concentrated on his figure in the dark rectangle of the doorway. He stood half-in and half-out of the cabin door, with his right hand extended toward me. The door beckoned behind him like a portal to some other, darker world beyond.

I turned away from the dark and back to Phoebe.

"You lead her into harm's way," Karl said.

I recognized the turn of phrase. It was the same he had used in reference to Ethan's murder, and that shook me to the core. A horrible notion revealed itself: the dynasty was laying claim to me once more, and would tolerate no rivals. I tried to picture my mother having tea with Phoebe in the Rose Salon, and that's when I knew my daydream of taking her with me for the absurd fantasy it was.

Reeling and desperate for something to anchor me, I sought that captivating blue in Phoebe's eyes once more. But I didn't see Phoebe's eyes then. Instead, my gaze lit upon the scar on her face. I felt the approach of a horrible pragmatism, and started to shift on my feet and shake my head to deny it, but that only unveiled the pulse of the jet's beacon behind me. The throbbing light bathed Phoebe's face, her fair skin, in dark, bloodred beats.

That evening in the pizza restaurant with Phoebe came back to me; my temptation to confess to her, to tell her everything, and I was chilled by the realization that Bernadette had warned me about against such confidences years before.

There is always temptation to confide in a lover, she had said. *To tell them something more than you ought. If you succumb to this temptation you make your lover a useful tool to your enemies, to the rivals of your family. It is thus that you endanger them. Had they found me again, they would have used me against Phillip, the Nazis. I would have lost far more than a few fingers. Phillip could not bring himself to send me away. But, knowing what I knew, it was not impossible that those around him, even his allies, might have taken matters into their own hands to deal with me. Fortunately, I came to my senses first. In the end it was love that compelled me to leave him.*

It had been chance that I had held my tongue at the pizza restaurant, and perhaps that had left a path open to us. Phoebe did not yet "know too much." There would be less reason for my family, or our rivals, to harm her. But, if I refused to go with Karl, if I stayed with Phoebe, I could not confide in her. Not there on the tarmac. Not when we got back to New York. Not ever. We would be living a lie. Forever. And even then, would she be safe?

Love does not conquer all, Bernadette had warned me. *On the contrary. Your foes will use love, and those you love, to harm you.*

In the face of the impossible dilemmas that I faced, I found myself crippled; paralyzed.

In the end, it is indecision that dooms him, my father had said.

I looked into Phoebe's eyes again for a long time before speaking.

"Phoebe, you cannot come where I am going," I said. "It is important that you do exactly as I say."

"What the hell are you talking about?"

"I don't have time to explain. You must believe me that your life is in danger. Go back to the flat in London. In the safe in my room you'll find about fifty thousand pounds in cash and my ATM card. There's close to half a million pounds in that account. The PIN is 1789." I hated how my voice sounded. Emotionless. Stiff. It brought to mind shades of the curt and efficient tone my grandfather had adopted in the wake of the assassination attempt in South Africa. "Repeat that back to me."

"This is insane," Phoebe protested.

"Listen," I insisted. "I want to hear you say the PIN number, and that you understand."

"But, I don't understand."

"Phoebe, I know who murdered Ethan." She looked shaken. "What's my PIN code?"

"One seven eight nine," she said, her voice trembling.

"Go directly to the flat. In the drawer in my bedside table there's a deck of cards with black backs. Hidden in between the cards is a piece of paper with the password to my online banking account. Take the cards, the cash, and the ATM card and get out. Don't pack. Don't go back to the penthouse, or any of my family's properties."

She started to cry. "You are really scaring me."

"You can use the ATM card to withdraw small amounts, but eventually you are going to have to open a new bank account and use my online banking account to transfer the rest to yourself."

"Please don't leave me," she begged, but I knew she was starting to feel me slipping away. "This isn't you," she insisted.

How could you know? I almost said, and it was another bitter reminder of my many lies.

I embraced her again, but it was different; sterile, and I hated that.

"I love you," she said, holding my head between her hands to look at me. "I know you won't leave me because I know you love me too."

I made as if to turn to the jet, but Phoebe wouldn't let go.

"Look at me," she said. "I know you do."

I tried to shake my head, but she was holding me tight.

"Look me in the eyes," she demanded. "Look me in the eyes and tell me you don't love me."

I was caught once more in those impossible pools of blue.

"I'm sorry, Phoebe," I whispered. "But, I didn't. I wanted to, but I didn't."

It was the worst lie I ever told.

Phoebe held me even more desperately. Slowly, I urged her hands away from my head, and held them in mine for a moment. Then, I turned to go. But Phoebe seized my wrist and forced me to face her once more.

"You said you knew who killed Ethan," she said. There was a desperate and pleading look in her eyes.

I glanced over my shoulder at Karl, still standing in the jet's door. His dark eyes were unmoved, hard as stone.

You lead her into harm's way.

I locked eyes with Phoebe again, gazing deep into what lay behind them.

"I killed him," I said.

It took a moment to sink in, but when the weight of it hit her Phoebe's grip on my wrist slackened.

I tore away from her and, afraid my resolve would crumble if I saw her again, fought off the urge to look back. I stalked up the stairs and the plane's engines began to wind up past idle to the taxi setting. Trancelike, I ascended and crossed the black threshold of the rectangular portal. The plane was already rolling, and I caught a glimpse of the lights of Vienna one last time before Karl pulled the cabin door up and closed it with a disconcerting thud.

In the moment those surfaces scissored together, the darkness of the unlit cabin consumed me.

Involuntarily, a whisper crossed my lips: "*In tenebris, salus.*"

In the darkness, safety.

Secrets and Lies

H E ESCORTED HIS YOUNG CHARGE OFF the Citation X, across the tarmac, and to the helipad. It had been years since she had been on the estate, of course, but he remembered that, as a girl, she had liked to sit in the cockpit next to the pilot. And so he opened the black craft's cockpit door for her, helped her up, and climbed into the passenger compartment behind her.

Having delivered the girl to the manor, he had completed his task. He had imagined attending to a particular piece of personal business after that, but, well aware that he might never see them again, he found himself instead wandering the forests around the manor well into the afternoon. It had been a habit of his in previous years, and one it contented him to revisit.

His contemplative tour completed, he returned to the family's seat, intending to assemble the things he would need for the journey ahead and quietly depart. But, before he could slip away, the mistress of the house summoned him to the Grand Study. To his surprise, when he presented himself she dismissed her attendants so that the two of them were alone.

She looked into his eyes as if to judge first what she saw behind them. Apparently satisfied, she spoke to him in a hushed tone.

"In the middle of the Rhine river, between Strasbourg on the French side and what is now the German town of Kehl, there is an island called, appropriately enough, 'Île aux Épis,' the 'Island of Thorns.' In the middle of this island was constructed a building with two identical rooms, one on the French side, and the other within what was then still the Holy Roman Empire. Between these rooms, exactly astride the border, was a single salon that housed a table clad in red velvet.

"It was into the Austrian side of this building on the thirteenth of May in 1770 that the Archduchess Marie Antoinette was led, and then stripped of her clothes before being conveyed into the salon and presented to the French to assume her role as the Dauphine and, eventually, the Queen of France.

"You see, it was not permitted that the bride should retain anything that was once of a foreign court."

She walked behind the desk that was the center of the Grand Study and placed her hand on the back of the empty chair there before addressing him again.

"Karl, my daughter's betrothed-to-be is expected here on the estate at any moment. I expect the negotiations over terms to take some time. This is absolutely confidential, of course. In the meantime, I do not want my daughter confused by any . . . distractions prior to the wedding announcement. There will be no surprises. No . . . influences from a foreign court. I cannot make that more clear." Her eyes narrowed. "No more student athlete suitors. No more incidents at nightclubs. To that end, and until further notice, my daughter is not to leave the estate at any time, and she is neither to make nor receive any calls, or callers. Is that clear?"

"It is," he said.

"As for the Icelandic girl, I'm sure you understand that we have to take measures to . . . *eliminate* any possibility of unannounced appearances."

She let that particular utterance, and the dark implication behind it, hang in the air until he gave a subtle nod.

Satisfied, her tone of voice lost the undercurrent of conspiracy and took on an almost cheerful timbre.

"Karl, I do feel I must thank you for your efforts these last several years. I expect my husband will have more rewarding projects for you to undertake once this one is behind you."

"I am pleased to be of service," he said, and was dismissed.

As he left the manor, bound for the helipad and then the airstrip, the domestic staff swarmed around a car that had pulled up to the main entrance. They were just beginning the elaborate greeting ritual for the newly arrived guest. Doors were opened, luggage was extracted, and the visitor, a tall man with a wine-stain birthmark on his cheek, was fussed over deferentially and then led inside.

The Archduke.

As he watched, a flutter of movement from the manor's roof caught his eye. It was instinct that made him reach inside his blazer and behind his right hip, fingers on the leather holster there, ready to draw his weapon to dispatch any would-be assassin lurking above the entryway. But he recognized the daughter of the line by her red hair, set nearly aglow by the light of the rising sun. She was only watching, taking in the goings-on below from among the spires. She saw him, and their eyes met, but neither felt it appropriate to wave.

HE HAD NOT missed the implication of the reference to the ill-fated Queen of France, but the sentiment was necessarily well beyond his purview. After he had instructed his subordinates with regard to enforcing his former charge's forced isolation on the estate, he made his way to the airstrip where the jet was waiting with a flight plan for New York. He was expected to make a visit to Columbia University, of course. Expected to tie up that particular loose end. But the Chairman's wife had been just vague enough with respect to the urgency of dealing with the Icelandic girl, and this was a gift of sorts. After all, the private task he had already set for himself, another much older obligation, beckoned to him.

It was a responsibility that he had been forced by other orders to defer for almost a decade. An old charge (and one he knew he might not return from). Even pursuing it was arguably a betrayal of his standing duties to the Chairman, not to mention rank insubordination with respect to the orders issued by the Chairman's wife, but the old promise would wait no longer.

He did not believe that the Icelandic girl knew the location of the estate, or even of its existence. In fact, she knew next to nothing of import and was therefore no immediate risk. Neither did she have any concept of tradecraft, nor any skill for countersurveillance. He would find her easily enough when he wished to and therefore that rather distasteful matter could be settled; it could be dealt with rather promptly (and rather directly) after his trip to Japan.

Reclined into his seat and alone in the cabin, he calmed his thoughts and remembered the phrase from his former master.

A man of action is always unprincipled; none but the contemplative has a conscience.

Then, as he had done a thousand times before, he closed his eyes and, silently and ritualistically, recited the litany that settled his mind into the cold, predatory intellect required for him to begin.

Awareness. Stealth. Violence of action.

He could feel the familiar chill of it fall over him; the mental quietude and calculating calm that sharpened his senses. He basked in the purity of it; devoid of judgment; of the corrosive conceit of morality, cleansed of all but intellect. The passive and merely environmental parts of the world fell away. Only those elements relevant to his new, dark tasks attracted his attention.

He opened his eyes, unveiling them to his environment once more. He produced from his day bag the Fairbairn-Sykes dagger—an old, blackened blade employed with great effect by British commandos during the Second World War and which he had carefully restored for his own use.

Then he unholstered, stripped, and reassembled his handgun—an ancient Makarov chambered in .380 caliber—before giving it a function check. He was comfortable with almost any firearm, and others would have regarded the old Soviet weapon as an antique, but it was familiar to him, one of the first he had been trained with. And, though it seemed impossibly small for his powerful hands, after he seated the magazine and chambered the first round, it settled into his palm like the old friend it essentially was.

After holding it for a moment, he slipped the Makarov and then the knife into the lead-lined pouch. This he tucked into the false bottom of his hard-sided suitcase. Put through an X-ray machine, etchings in the lead would give the appearance of a laptop to the casual screener. A more astute observer might catch the ruse, but such missions were never without risk and he had taken a number of precautions to make it unlikely that he would be scrutinized in the first place.

With the firearm and the knife properly stowed, he stood and knocked on the cockpit door.

"Ready for departure?" the pilot said, craning around in his seat to address his lone passenger.

"Tokyo," he said to the pilot.

"But we were scheduled for New York," the copilot protested, and that earned him a hard glare from the pilot, one that silenced the younger man instantly.

"Yes, sir," the pilot said, and turned to the copilot. "Work up a flight plan to Narita International Airport with a fuel stop in . . . Moscow, maybe?"

The pilots dealt with, he returned to his seat and settled in once more.

He chose the Dutch passport and gave it a quick once-over to make sure it had the appropriate stamps and visas to look worn and authentic.

He planned his arrival then, considering his options. The immigration officers at Tokyo's Narita International Airport would give him a double take if he used his near-perfect Japanese. As a choice it was a trade-off, a calculated risk. He could present as a seasoned traveler to Japan and draw attention by frustrating the biases of such officials that Occidentals, particularly Europeans like the Dutch, were too ignorant and lazy to perfect so ancient and refined a language as Japanese. Or he could act ignorant of the Japanese language entirely and risk the extra scrutiny occasionally dished out to *gaijin*, sometimes just for sport. This he would decide at the last moment—only when he saw the immigration official.

From there it would be to the Iroha-zaka—a pair of winding roads located in the mountains of Tochigi Prefecture where he could examine firsthand the scene of the accident that occasioned his long and unsanctioned journey. After that he would pay a surprise visit to the vacation home of one Dr. Yasuyuki Sato, whose signature adorned a certain death certificate. The house was in the city of Nikkō, which, he had noticed, was just below the winding mountain roads where the Patriarch was supposed to have met his end.

Dr. Sato, he felt sure, would have answers. Answers, he also felt sure, that he could persuade Dr. Sato to give him.

As the jet climbed, he closed his eyes.

Awareness. Stealth. Violence of action.

The chill fell over him, embraced him, and braced him. His breathing slowed. He opened his eyes, unveiling them to his environment once more.

And then, he was ready.

Acknowledgments

I N 20 BC, EMPEROR GAIUS JULIUS Caesar Augustus (born Gaius Octavius, the great-nephew and heir of Gaius Julius Caesar), in his capacity as *curator viarum* (the authority responsible for the wondrous roads and highways of ancient Rome), erected in the great Roman Forum, rather near the Temple of Saturn, the Milliarium Aureum, the "Golden Milestone," thought to be a monument of marble and gilded bronze. It served as the central "mile marker" of the Roman Empire. All distances were, after its commissioning, measured from this singular datum, perhaps giving rise to the eternal phrase: "All roads lead to Rome."

It is doubtful that any future historian should want to track the origins of the decade-and-a-half journey that eventually resulted in the creation of the book now in your hands. But, if so, they might wonder after the "Golden Milestone" of *Letters from the Dead*. But not for long, for that title clearly belongs to my long-suffering agent, Matthew Snyder of Creative Artists Agency. It *may* be true that "all roads lead to Rome," but it is *certainly* true that all roads to *Letters from the Dead* lead *from* Matthew Snyder.

Along the way an exotic cabal of remarkable creatures contributed to *Letters from the Dead* in ways great and small, including:

"Wilem," who, quite literally, saved my life a half dozen times, and without whom I should not have survived, and this book would not exist. Jamie Zawinski, whose claim to the noble title of "original fan" must surely have been affirmed by the Lords of the Golden Era of Blogging (and whose enduring friendship has kept me from the dark abyss of author's despondency many times besides). Mollie Glick, my fearless literary agent, and she who gave me permission to submit long manuscripts. Nancy Rawlinson, who taught me more about audience than I ever hoped to know. "DDOP," whose early advocacy for my prose I can never forget and who will ever be Sir Nigel in my inner monologue. David Leitch and Kelly McCormick, whose peerless hospitality in Surrey and wide-ranging production tours (especially of their "war room") were so compelling as to transform my creative process forever (and forever for the better). "Lummer" for his condition-less support above and beyond the call of adroit management of all things financial. Herr Dr. Iur. "Kuhlmann," for his enduring legal defense and structuring in the early years when legal risk was existential and ever-present. Finn "The Counselor" Morgan, attorney and consigliere. Herr Fabian Wigger, keeper of all things intangible. Phyllis Grann, whose early interest in my efforts still leaves me breathless. David Grace of Loeb & Loeb, my Hollywood protector. Michael Marshall Smith, whose expectationless and boundless engagement with a new author (me) must be singular in the business. Heinrich Rahm, who probably thought I would forget. "Kempie," whose involvement is best left lost to history. Dee Cook, who somehow found the lost Flight Risk Radio recordings. "Korrie," the rarest of individuals whose love of wine (particular old Bordeaux and Burgundy) rivals my own. And, Shy and Strow, the last survivors of the unduly lethal "Originals" campaign.

But among the "existentials" I could not but commend to the highest strata Emily Bestler, for I am certain that somewhere in the world there must be a depiction of Minerva, the Roman goddess of the arts (among other things), that has been crafted in her image.

Finally, to "Phoebe," after whom I still wonder so many years later.

Many hands touch a novel so long in the making. I hope those whom I have, out of ignorance, omitted will forgive me this transgression.

Gstaad, Summer 2024